THE SWEEP OF ROMANCE

Gwalchmai, a participant in much of Earth's development, lives in worlds both magical and real. Throughout he carries the ring of Merlin, which gives him certain arcane powers.

Throughout runs the thread of the very moving love story of Corenice and Gwalchmai—lovers separated poignantly time and again by the adventures that take Gwalchmai from Atlantis to the Norseland, from the elf-world to pre-history, from Arthur's Court to the Far East, from Cathay to the land of Irish mythology, from medieval Rome to the burning of the Maid of Orleans.

Seldom has such a huge canvas so successfully combined major historic events with the worlds of magic and wonder.

In this epic fantasy of extraordinary sweep and drama, the story of Gwalchmai, godson to Merlin, and Corenice, an immortal woman of Atlantis—and of a love that spanned centuries of high adventure—comes dramatically to life.

Merlin's Ring

H. Warner Munn

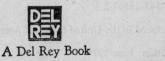

A Del Rey Book

BALLANTINE BOOKS • NEW YORK

A Del Rey Book
Published by Ballantine Books

ISBN 0-345-29667-2

Manufactured in the United States of America

First Edition: June 1974
Seventh Printing: August 1981

Cover art by Gervasio Gallardo

To your Corenice; your Gwalchmai;
By whatever other names you may know them;
In whatever Land of Dream.

About *Merlin's Ring* and
H. Warner Munn:

Through the Ages

The Ballantine Adult Fantasy Series has been in business for several years now, and among the many different varieties of the fantasy that have appeared under the Sign of the Unicorn's Head one surprising omission stands out. I refer, of course, to the Arthurian fantasy. This is due to mere chance, not to any antipathy for the subject. Most of the fine books centered on the Arthurian legend are in print—*The Once and Future King, The Crystal Cave, The Sword in the Stone* —to mention only a few.

Quite recently, however, an odd coincidence has occurred. Two different writers have written two very different books and submitted them to Ballantine Books; both happen to be Arthurian fantasies, and both happen to be superbly imaginative and thoroughly entertaining works of fantastic fiction. So at last we are able to complete the fantasy spectrum by including Arthuriana among all the other varieties of fantasy thus far published under this colophon.

The first of these books you will already have seen, if you are the sort of reader who haunts the paperback stands and regularly picks up the new releases in the Series. I refer, of course, to that spectacular romance, *Excalibur*, (August 1973) a new novel by a new writer named Sanders Anne Laubenthal. The second of these two books is the novel you are about to read, *Merlin's Ring*, by H. Warner Munn.

While Miss Laubenthal is new to the ranks of fantasy writers, Mr. Munn is an old hand at the craft. He was one of the original *Weird Tales* writers, and his first story, "The Werewolf of Ponkert," appeared in the issue for July 1925, during the second year of that magazine's existence. During the next fifteen years, Mr. Munn published about a dozen stories, including novels and serials, in that greatest of all pulp magazines, and his last tale appeared in 1940.

In those days *Weird Tales* was dominated by the circle of writers who centered on H. P. Lovecraft. Munn was one of this group and knew Lovecraft well. They exchanged not only letters, but visits as well; Lovecraft came up to Munn's home in Athol, Massachusetts, and Munn made the trip down to Lovecraft's home in Providence. Something in one of Lovecraft's letters started Munn off as a writer. In the letter column of *Weird Tales*, Lovecraft asked why no one had thought of writing a werewolf yarn from the werewolf's point of view. His remark intrigued Munn, whose thoughts led him eventually to write that first story, "The Werewolf of Ponkert."

Since he was, in a way, indebted to Lovecraft for a story idea, it must have pleased him to have been able to return the favor a while later. Munn had been mulling over ideas for a completion or a sequel to Poe's unfinished novel, *The Narrative of Arthur Gordon Pym*. Munn himself didn't get far with the notion, but his mention of it in their correspondence started Lovecraft thinking, and he was in time inspired to write one of his most memorable stories, *At the Mountains of Madness*, which remains the most celebrated novella of Antarctic horrors since the Poe fragment. Realizing that Lovecraft's story had turned out a lot better than his own try, Munn amiably abandoned the attempt.

A while later, having moved to New York, Munn was introduced to some of the writers of Lovecraft's set. "Through him I met Tallman, Kirk, Long, Loveman, Bodenheim, and some others of the junior literati . . . and corresponded with Seabury Quinn and other writers. It was a stimulating atmosphere," Munn recalls.

Writing for *Weird Tales* was an enthusiasm of his youth, and one he eventually put aside to face the serious problem of making a living. Munn says, "After I married, I drifted out of writing . . . under the stress of building a house and supporting a family during the Depression and the pre-war years, and gave it up, even as a hobby, during the war." Some years later he moved his family out to Tacoma, Washington, where he still resides.

Now in his early seventies, H. Warner Munn is one of the few living survivors of the early days of *Weird Tales*. Besides him, only E. Hoffman Price, Edmond Hamilton, Donald Wandrei, and a few others are still alive, and of these, only Munn is still writing steadily in the field.

For he returned to writing a decade ago, perhaps stimulated by the revival of interest in some of his early work. Don Grant, the Providence bookseller and publisher, reissued in 1958 in a limited, signed edition a book called *The Werewolf of Ponkert.* The book contained not only the title story but also its sequel, "The Werewolf's Daughter," which was a three-part serial in the magazine, beginning with the issue for October 1928. In a brief foreword, the publisher mentioned that Munn considered his finest story to be "King of the World's Edge." This novel, which ran as a four-part serial in *Weird Tales* beginning with the issue for September 1939, was revived in paperback by Ace Books in 1966, and was followed a year later by a new sequel called *The Ship from Atlantis.* Ever since then, H. Warner Munn has been working on a lengthy and intricate narrative about twice the size of an ordinary novel.

I mean *Merlin's Ring,* of course.

This new book is the culmination of a long and interesting career. In one way or another, H. Warner Munn has been involved with the figure of Gwalchmai for over thirty-five years, and with the mysterious and enigmatic girl from Atlantis, Corenice.

The strands of his plot are intricately woven. Three generations after the last of the Roman legions withdrew from the isle of Britain, Ventidius Varro, a centurion under the leadership of the man whom legend remembers as King Arthur, led a fleet from the doomed land, which lay helpless before the menace of the Saxons. Guided by Merlin, the sage and prophet, their ships ventured farther into the dim regions of the unknown west than any ships had gone before. They found an uninhabited realm there at the World's Edge, and, yet farther south, a strange and barbaric civilization called Miapan. There Varro became King—"King of the World's Edge"—and, anxious that this untouched new continent should provide a haven for a Rome beleaguered by its enemies, he dispatched his son, Gwalchmai, to cross the seas and bear news of the great discovery to whatever emperor then ruled beside the Tiber.

Thus the young Roman-British prince embarked on the

strangest journey ever undertaken by a human being upon
this globe, a journey that was to cover centuries of time
and would lead him into the most curious adventures known
to the annals of heroic deeds. In that mysterious region
known to explorers as the Sargasso Sea, the youth found a
weird metal ship surviving from the lost age of High Atlantis,
on which there still lived an Atlantean sorceress, an ageless
and beautiful creature called Corenice, who inhabits an eternal and deathless body of impervious metal. The love that
kindles between these strangers from the far corners of the
earth will transcend the ages and lead them through bizarre
and miraculous events, whose like the chronicles of marvel
have seldom recorded.

The story of *Merlin's Ring* is a colossal achievement of
sheer imagination. From the moment the wandering spirit of
the sorceress from Atlantis occupies the body of a Viking
maid and liberates Gwalchmai from his frozen tomb within
an iceberg, wherein he has lain in suspended animation for
centuries, the tale expands to include shamans and witches
and magical and supernatural forces. The vast canvas of this
novel pictures a panoply of figures from history and myth
and legend as background to a love story that survives the
ages and traverses entire continents. Joan of Arc is but the
most familiar of these, and the period of the Crusades form
but a segment of a much larger history.

Seldom have I encountered a more ambitious narrative in
my exploration of fantasy, and seldom has a gripping human
drama of such strength and vigor invested a story of such
sweep and scope and vaulting imaginative power. I am
amazed at the realistic detail, at the tremendous cast of
characters, and at the surge of centuries spanned by a single
tale. Prose epics of this magnitude are most often the work
of a writer in the first enthusiasm of his creative power.
But with the publication of *Merlin's Ring* a literary career
that began nearly half a century ago reaches its culmination;
and now it can be seen that the career of H. Warner Munn
is that of a writer slowly and meticulously developing and
testing his powers, in anticipation of a masterpiece.

For in all of fantasy few stories of this magnitude and
scope have been so vividly realized. The epic of the immortal adventurer who survives through the ages has given
us many classics—*Phra the Phoenician, Valdar the Oft-Born,*
and *My First Two Thousand Years* are examples that spring

first to mind. To these milestones of fantastic literature, it is our privilege to add one more masterpiece, *Merlin's Ring.*

—LIN CARTER
Editorial Consultant,
The Ballantine Adult Fantasy Series

Hollis, Long Island, New York

JOURNEYS OF GWALCHMAI
THROUGH A WORLD
AS HE AND
CORENICE KNEW I

INFORMATION GATHERED
BETWEEN THE YEARS
9564 B.C AND A.D. 1492

TO STROMSEY
AND
SNOWLAND

DWERGAR
COUNTR

THE
BLASTED HEATH

TO
KILSTALPHEEN
SKERD
TIR-HUDI

ELV

TO AVALON
LYONESSE

TO KR-IS

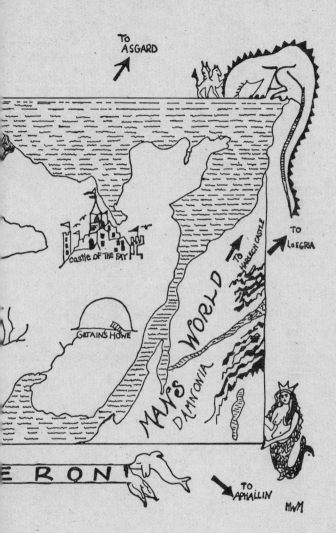

TO ASGARD

TO LOEGRIA

TO HARLECH CASTLE

Castle OF THE FAY

GETAIN'S HOWE

MAN'S WORLD

DAMNONIA

E RON

TO APHALLIN

MWM

Merlin's
Ring

PART I

Merlin's Ring

1

The Man in the Ice

Five days out from Streymoy, in the Faroes, having been borne far into unknown seas by a violent westerly, the little fishing boat came to a new land and a fair day.

When the wind and driving rain had stopped and the sun had come out to warm them, the crew of four were grateful to the gods. They had at no time experienced undue fear. They were all good sailors. Still, they had been glad to finger the small gold piece each Norse sailor carried, for it is an unlucky thing to go empty handed into Ran's Hall when one has been drowned.

Their greatest inconvenience had been the lack of warm food. Cheese and hard biscuit are nourishing but not tasty, and raw cod is a poor second. Now they were running out of water, though it had been nursed along sparingly and they had caught some rain.

There was floating ice, but it was new ice and still brackish, the salt not yet having leached out of it. In search of a better source they turned north where an ice-blink against the scattered clouds told them that land lay beneath it.

The owner of the knorr was Skeggi Harvadsson, whom men called Hairymouth, though not to his face. There was also Thyra, his daughter, and Biarki, to whom she was pledged.

Biarki was son of Orm, son of Ketil, the Strong. His ancestry was a curse to him, and Biarki took no pride in it, for he could not forget it and his means did not permit him to live as he would. Although he was Skeggi's partner and owned half the boat and enjoyed the promise, yet to come, that Thyra would be his, he resented his lot as a fisherman and longed to go a-Viking. Only in this manner, he thought, could he attain fortune and honor.

Besides these three, there was Flann, the thrall from Erin, who was wont to raise his eyes above his station. He also had a grievance. Although Skeggi and Thyra regarded him as a valued member of their family, he still wore the iron collar. It was his only mark of servitude. Although it was no thicker than a wire and scarcely marked by the others, upon Flann it lay as a yoke.

He had been taken as a boy, at the sacking of Lindisfarne, his parents unfortunately visiting that holy island at the time.

He had been traded from one master to another, suffering many a beating, but he still remained firm in the faith and was always willing to enter into argument with those he considered as heathen. He could read and write and one of his sorrows was the lack of books.

Because he had a fine voice and could chant to music he was liked by most people. Still, he was a contentious man and some felt that he spoke when he should remain silent. Biarki hated him for his quick tongue.

Now he sneered as Biarki looked down into the calm sea, stirred only by waves scarcely more than ripples and commented, "Ran's Bath runs deep, but Thor has quieted the winds for us and will guide us safely home."

Flann muttered, "The old gods are dead. Have you not heard?"

"Now, by Thor's hammer!" Biarki's moods turned easily into rage. He stood menacingly over the thrall. "How much shall a man take from this son of a black robe? Skeggi, I will pay the were-gild now and slay him! He is never quiet and I can stand no more. Here is his worth!"

He threw down a copper coin and seized his dagger.

Flann did not move or change his mocking expression, but Thyra stood up in the rocking boat and gripped Biarki's arm. Her face was pale.

Skeggi raised his hand from the tiller. "If he deserves death for an honest opinion, which I do not grant, then he shall have it on that day from me. He is my thrall, Biarki, not yours, and blood spilt from my household must be paid for with blood, not money. Put away your dagger, unless you are prepared to see mine."

Biarki glared. His face reddened almost to purple above his matted, salt-rimed beard. There had been times, men said, that his family had brought forth baresarks and Biarki was perilously near that uncaring mania at the moment. Still, the feeling of Thyra's small hands upon his arm was calming and his fury passed.

He grunted and sat down. Thyra remained standing, leaning against the short mast, looking out over the sea. Only occasionally now a gentle puff of air bellied out the drooping sail, but it always drove the boat in the same direction—in the way they wished to go.

At that moment, as though it were a good omen, a raven dropped out of the sky and circled the boat thrice, inspecting them wisely before landing upon the masthead to take rest. It cocked its head from side to side and opened its beak soundlessly, eyeing them as though it would speak.

Biarki took heart. "See, Odin's messenger! He comes to lead us to land. That is more than your god would do, thrall!"

Skeggi also turned sternly upon Flann. "This time you are wrong. The old gods still rule, for Ragnarok has not yet befallen. Your White Christ, of whom you continually prate, may be strong in the southland, but here he has no strength. If you pray for help, pray as we do to Odin, that we may be saved all together and not all lost to Aegir's net because of you. Nay"—when Flann would have spoken —"be silent! I shall hear no more. Now, by Odin, what ails the girl?"

Thyra, still leaning against the mast, had suddenly become rigid and with right arm raised was pointing toward the north.

Both Biarki and Flann, forgetting their differences, sprang up, but her body had stiffened like iron and she could not be moved from the hold she had upon the mast. Her eyes were glassy and fixed and her voice was no longer familiar to the three men who had known her through most of her life. It had a strange timbre and the words were accented in an unfamiliar way.

"Row!" she said. "Row hard! Row fast, if you would save a life! Row and do not stop and I will show you the way to go!"

Under the peremptory command, there was a softness,

but it was not Thyra's. It was an undercurrent of sound, like a scarcely perceptible second voice. It held within it a sensation, a breathing, of little golden bells very far away.

Biarki looked at her in horror. "She is possessed! What does she see?"

Flann passed his hand before her eyes. She did not blink.

"She is surely fey," he agreed. "Whatever she sees, she leads us to it. I do not feel that it is toward evil."

Skeggi nodded. "I have the same thought that a good thing will come out of this. Perhaps Thor's winds sent us to this purpose. Let us go as she guides."

So, like one who walks in her sleep, Thyra went aft, taking the tiller, and the three men unshipped the oars. The breeze strengthened, carrying them on a little toward the east.

The air was very clear and about midday they could see upon the horizon a plume of black smoke, high and huge, rising straight for a great distance before it streamed out in a fiercer wind that they could not feel.

Under this somber banner lay snow-covered peaks, and as they approached a low coastline became visible. Flocks of inquisitive birds came out to meet the voyagers—gulls, guillemots, and puffins rising from their breeding places on the small islands and coastal cliffs.

Preying upon them as they fed, eagles and falcons swooped down to steal their catch or to strike the fishers. In the water bobbed the round heads of seals, also feeding or playing, and Skeggi knew from unmistakable signs that here were great schools of cod and haddock. A whale spouted in the distance, and once a basking shark, awakened by the approaching boat, submerged hurriedly and the knorr tossed in the miniature maelstrom that it caused.

The men shared a biscuit apiece and drifted while resting, studying the coast. Thyra refused food and waited impatiently, holding the course for the land, toward which the breeze steadily wafted them.

As they approached closer, it was evident that here were no firths into which they might run for shelter against a sudden storm. The coast seemed uniformly even, with good beaches of black lava sand, cut frequently by streams of fresh water. Beyond, they could see grass and heather on the low parts of the hills, although so far north the perpetual snow line was seldom above twenty-five hundred feet.

Skeggi's keen eyes, never strained by reading, could pick out the forms of trees on the nearer slopes and the coastal plains. There were not many, although the grasses waved thick and tall wherever the lava had broken down into soil.

Over everything a light powder of black ash was falling, upon the land, the water, and the boat. This gritty substance was being precipitated from the cloud they had thought to be smoke, but which they could now see was rising from an active volcano far inland.

As the cloud came drifting toward them, the underside of it was lit by ruddy flashes, and the sound of the constant explosions came rolling out to sea like a distant cannonade. Beneath the cloud, and only slightly obscured by it under the full glare of the sun, they saw from whence the ice-blink came. It was a mighty field of ice stretching easterly along the coast and far inland, sending down its glaciers into the sea and calving its floes there as the ground shook to the repeated concussions of the eruption.

They could not know that it covered an area of over four thousand square miles, for as yet it had no name. Someday this land they had blunderingly found would be called Iceland because of this glacier, which would itself bear the name of the Vatnajokull.

Toward this menace Thyra unerringly steered, holding a course as steadily as though she sought a well-known destination.

To aid the fitful wind, the weary men took up their oars again with the thought of landing sooner at some inlet where they could fill the small keg with fresh water.

At the nearer edge of the vast ice field they could see a long gentle slope, interrupted by several small hills and intersected by considerable streams. Here they would have turned in to an excellent beach. Thyra refused it and continued coasting, until they reached a spot where the outliers of the field came close down to the water, hardly leaving room for passage between them and the sea.

Here, a tongue of ice ended in a cliff face, a hundred feet in height, where a firth had once run deeply into the land. The lava edges of the walls that formed this inlet could still be seen, once jagged but rounded by time and the action of the slowly moving glacier. Thyra scanned them keenly, as though the seared scars were well-known landmarks. When she was satisfied, she steered directly for the dangerous ice front. The boat grounded upon a tiny scrap of beach.

A stream met them, flowing out of a cavern melted into the glacier. It was murky with glacial flour, ground and reground from the rocks crumbled beneath the tremendous moving weight. The water was plainly unfit to drink. The men looked at Thyra in surprise that she should seek such a landing.

Her father said, "After Ragnarok, and when Asgard is no more, surely the gods will come to dwell in this land. They may imprison Loki in those fires, forever. How pleasant would be those flowering meadows to the tread of Freya's soft feet! I believe Balder, the beautiful, has smiled upon this place in spring. But, where we stand now, daughter, is fit only for the frost-giants. That rumble in the sky is not the chariot of Thor, coming to welcome us. It is doom to men! We shall be buried beneath the ice. Let us leave at once."

Thyra cast him one glance as though he were a stranger. There was an imperiousness and a disdain in it he had never seen. She struck aside the hand with which he had sought to restrain her, turned without a word, and darted into the depths of the tunnel in the ice.

With a hoarse cry of anguish, Flann, first to realize what she had done, sprang from the boat and plunged out of sight behind her, splashing through the shallow but rapid stream.

The others, disregarding the danger, followed the reckless pair and the cavern re-echoed with their shouts to return.

Hampered by the current, Flann could not catch Thyra with the distance she had attained. As they went deeper beneath the glacier, the sunlight through the clear ice, striped with successive layers of ash from previous eruptions, fell upon them in deepening shades, from turquoise through amethyst into indigo.

Beneath their feet the ground trembled. A hand against the ice wall on either side detected the almost continuous vibration of the distant earth shocks. Large cracks appeared in the ice with a sound of thunder, but only tiny crumblings brought particles down upon them, harmless as yet.

It was almost in darkness that Flann came upon Thyra near the end of the tunnel, flattened against a smooth expanse with her body pressed against the ice and her arms outspread as though she would embrace it.

Her eyes were closed and her cheek lay hard against the wall.

As Flann reached her, he put out his hand. He did not touch her, for it was plain to see from her ecstatic expression that she was not aware of him or conscious of any danger.

She pressed harder against the ice as though she would melt her way into it. She was much beyond herself and anything which Flann had ever known. He sank to his knees beside her, bowed his head, and began to pray. Above him, he heard her soft whisper and wept because he knew it was not for him.

"Oh, my darling, my only one! I have come back as I promised I would!"

Facing the ice wall, he saw that it was almost parchment thin. Behind it, with eyes now accustomed to the dim light, he could see an egg-shaped chamber. Within it, encysted there for a length of time which he could not guess, there lay a man, clad in leather, with a short sword and a flint hatchet at his side.

His eyes were closed, his head rested upon his arm as though he were asleep and the expression on his face was one of peaceful waiting and pleasant dreams. He had not lain down in fear.

It was at this moment that the others came upon them. Biarki struck Flann aside, hurling him down in the icy water, and Skeggi leaped over him and seized his daughter to drag her away.

With a strength he had never known she possessed, she maintained her place against the wall. Flann rose dripping, his face contorted in fury, and he was about to leap upon Biarki, but at that moment a crack appeared above them and a torrent of water cascaded down.

The sheet of thin window ice fell in fragments and the strangely dressed man was visible to all of them. The egg-shaped chamber began to change its form to a flatter oval. Its inhabitant would have soon been crushed had not Thyra now crept into the ever-narrowing slit, taken a firm grip on his deerskin shirt, and tugged him out.

His rigid body slid easily over the wet ice and into the shallow stream. None too soon, for as he struck the water the chamber collapsed and disappeared as though it had never been.

More ice fell from the tunnel roof. The three men forgot their differences at the instant and obvious peril. As Thyra had her hands wound tightly into the stranger's garment and refused to let go, they perforce were obliged to carry him along if they would save her.

It was not a difficult return. The water supported the man's weight and the current of the stream aided them in their mad flight to safety. Above, beneath, and all around them, the ice river groaned and rumbled. Behind them, forcing them on, without an instant of pause, the tunnel walls narrowed and pinched together.

A wave of water struck and hurled them out, but not to safety, for although they lay struggling upon the beach, ice blocks fell from the face of the glacier and smashed nearby. Splinters struck and stung like hail, but miraculously no one was injured more than suffering bruises and small cuts.

Thyra still wore her strange, determined expression. She did not need to give an order. At her commanding look, Biarki and Flann picked up her find and not until then did she loose her bloodless hands from the death grip she had maintained.

They hurried him down the black beach into the boat. Thyra's eyes closed. The color and the strength drained out of her face. Her father caught her up as she staggered and would have fallen. He threw her into Flann's waiting arms and slammed his burly frame against the knorr's grounded prow. It slid out among the clashing ice cakes.

Ash and pumice lay as a crust upon the water and ankle deep inside the boat. The waves came in like oil, without breaking, although they were large and increasing in size. Through and over the rollers, into a safer distance from shore, the gasping men strained at the heavy oars. The glacier itself was all in motion, heaving and sinking with the violent disturbance of the tortured land.

"Loki must be here now!" panted Biarki. "Sigyn is late bringing back the bowl. See how he writhes!"

Flann cast him a disgusted look, which Biarki did not see. Flann did not believe for a moment that the bound god was suffering from snake venom that dripped upon his face when his wife did not catch it to protect him. He did not believe in Loki, either, but he knew that this was no time to say so. He continued rowing.

It was well that they had not lingered. Soon the whole front of the glacier fell away, burying the beach and closing in the tunnel completely. No great bergs were to be seen, but enough ice fell into the water so that the boat rocked dangerously when the waves struck out at them.

As the sea became littered with grinding floes, they did not continue on in their original direction, but turned back toward the western shore. It was late afternoon, but being summer the sun was yet high.

In this direction they coasted for about two hours, seeing only bare shores. They ran out from under the falling ash and as though the distant mountain knew they had escaped its greatest danger, the violence of its eruption diminished.

Thyra's eyelids fluttered and opened. She looked around in bewilderment and for a brief time she seemed herself again. But before anyone could speak and ask how she felt, the look came upon her again and made her face unrecognizable to them, though more beautiful than before.

She gave a happy wordless cry, crawled to the man they had rescued, clasped him tightly in her arms, and dropped her head upon his breast. Her eyes closed once more. This time she slept. The mystery daunted them and they did not dare to touch her.

So the two lay, until the knorr was beached—the living and he whom they thought dead, for if he breathed they could not see any sign of it and he gave no other indication of life.

They ran the boat up into an inlet and drew it up on the rough shore. The water was quiet there, only stirred by a swift stream that tumbled over a rocky height. A salmon leaped, feeding, and they marked its probable lurking place, but shelter was the first necessity.

Beyond lay hills and farther yet a mountain hid the volcano, which still rumbled fitfully directly north of the inlet. They could see its glow, but the ground was mostly quiet. The sun beat down between the cliffs on either side, but there was a wolf wind blowing and though they were sheltered from it, the warmth of rocks was no comfort to them. Their clothes were too wet.

Skeggi gently disengaged the clasp of his sleeping daughter and laid her down upon some grass, between two rocks,

and covered her with a robe. It was all that he could do.
They lifted out the strange man and now had time to examine him more closely.

He wore leggings of deerskin, from ankle to thigh. His
tunic, or shirt, had sleeves that were fringed with thrums,
as were the leggings. Over the shirt he wore a sleeveless
vest of heavy leather, beaded with dyed porcupine quills.
When the vest was joined together in front, by its leather
points, the two halves pictured an eagle with broad-spread
wings. Its beak was opened as though in challenge.

His lean waist was cinctured by a strong belt studded with
odd silver and bronze coins, which seemed very old and
worn. The dates were undecipherable. From this belt hung
his short, heavy sword, by his right hand, and another nar-
rower belt crossed above, from which, on his left hip, a
little flint-throwing ax was suspended in a loose loop.

He had a breech-clout of white fawnskin and a pendant-
beaded strip of the same material hung down to his knees
before and behind. This too was fringed and all seemed the
product of much loving labor. Plainly, this man had once
been held in great affection or highly respected.

On his feet were beaded moccasins, not much worn. He
had no headgear, nor did he need any. A beaded band
circled his forehead and his long brown hair hung down
behind, clubbed into a single braid, held together at the
end by a beaded ring.

His skin was a deep, reddish brown and seemed a natural color, darker than a sun in these latitudes would tinge
it. Biarki's eyes narrowed, noticing this.

"Doubtless, by his swart skin, he is a man of Surt. He
lay there waiting to ride out of Muspelheim, with his dark
Lord, and fling fire upon the world to destroy it. We were
fools to take him out of the ice. We would do well to cut
off his head before he comes to life and it is too late."

Skeggi laughed. "It is you who are simple. The man is
dead."

His partner grunted. "It may be so and it may not be so.
Look, his legs and arms are flexible. His head moves from
side to side." He stirred it roughly with his foot against the
man's cheek.

"His face is soft. It should be hard as stone! Let me kill
him, for he is not dead."

He took the sword from its scabbard. It was good steel

and still held a fine edge. At the hard looks that were cast at him by both Skeggi and Flann, he pretended to be in jest and tossed the sword idly from hand to hand.

"At least, when we are sure that he is dead, I will keep his sword. Look, there are runes upon it!"

Flann stepped forward quickly and took the sword as one well accustomed to its use. When Biarki reached for it, growling, Flann did not resist, but the point seemed always to be the only part the other could grasp. The thrall examined it closely.

"I am well aware that you hold me of no more account than to cut bait, Biarki. One day you may learn that I have other talents as well. If you could read books as I can and had talked to monks, instead of murdering them, you would be wiser.

"I studied at the Holy Island under the Blessed Aldwith and I tell you now that these marks are not runes—as you would know if you could cut runes yourself.

"This is an inscription writ by a Roman smith upon a Roman sword, for a Roman soldier. I say also, for your further education, Biarki, that against it your ax and buckler would avail you nothing. In its time, it was the most deadly hand weapon on earth! It reads 'SIXTH LEGION, VICTRIX.'

"I know no more than you how this man came to be here, but I should beware of taunting him as you do me, should you ever face him in battle. Your ignorance and stupidity may yet be your bane!

"If he was a legionary, the Sidhe must have protected him, for in this reign of Harald Fairhair, in dread of whom you fled Norway, we Christians number the year of our Lord to be that of 873.

"Now I know from my reading, at which you sneer, that mighty Rome came to nothing in the year of 516. No Roman soldiers ever went on foray after that, so unless he be of Methuselah's kin, which meseemeth not, then he has somehow lain frozen here for some three hundred years!"

There is no telling what might have gone awry in Biarki's unpredictable mood. His slow flush betokened a hideous fury. Although Flann was watching him narrowly, sword at guard, Biarki's strength would have surely brought the thrall great scathe.

Skeggi eyed them both. He obviously had no intention of interfering, whatever befell. The moment was long and tense. It was, therefore, the more startling to all of the men when a scornful, imperious voice suddenly spoke.

Thyra was standing, but it was not truly Thyra—not as they had known her before today. The strange voice that had directed them still had bell notes in it, but of clanging iron rather than tinkling gold.

"Will you let this girl's body freeze while you worthless creatures argue? If she dies, he dies with her and he shall not die, if it must mean the lives of all of you. I will warm the bodies of both in your blood before that shall be!

"At once! I require food for this girl. I need shelter for me and mine and a fire so that my man may live again. Bring wood, gather rocks, cut long poles, and dig a pit! I will tell then what else you shall do. See to it without delay!"

Skeggi puffed out his cheeks and jutted his beard at his daughter. Before he could speak, she snatched the sword from Flann's nerveless hand and took a menacing step toward him.

Skeggi went—the others with him—like a lamb.

Once they had climbed the slope of sharp lava detritus, following upward along the stream, they came out upon a grassy meadow. Here was growing a kind of wild oats and a flight of ptarmigan took the air before them, frightened out of their feeding ground. They saw the tracks of a fox.

Flann motioned the others to move slowly as they neared a quiet pool; he leaned down and passed his hand cautiously under a large trout, whose fins were gently moving only enough to maintain its position against the lazy current. With a quick flirt he threw it up on the bank, barely disturbing the surface. Altogether he caught three more by tickling before others that he could see took fright and darted away into deeper water. He strung his catch on a willow branch and went on, carrying the fish.

The meadow was full of wild flowers, small and delicate, with bright bloom. Wild crowberries and bilberries were plentiful. They picked some as they walked, but did not delay. The days were long, but there was still a night to come and it would be cold.

On the slope of the nearest hill, from whence came the stream winding down from the distant glacier into the meadow, there were more willows and juniper bushes. There was also a small grove of dwarf birches, none taller than twelve feet.

Crossing the meadow toward the trees, they raised more ptarmigan and Skeggi flung a stick into the thick of them and knocked down a brace. He tied them to his belt. They skirted a bog and saw that the water oozing into their deep footprints was brown with peat.

Biarki looked about. It seemed a good land and empty. He mentally estimated its riches. There was stone for walls and paddocks. Sheep would do well here. There was excellent pasturage for cows and horses. What with fish free for the taking, the flocks of wild fowl constantly wheeling overhead, meat and eggs would be no problem. Eider ducks were nesting. He had seen seal and liked seal meat well. Perhaps there would be deer in the highlands, though as yet he had seen no sign of any.

He would not build a house. Let the others do that! He pursed his lips, considering. His thoughts always moved slowly, not like that quick-witted, insulting thrall. After the house was finished, he would kill Flann. It would be easy to find an excuse. There was never any difficulty in becoming angry enough to want to kill him.

Skeggi would be harder to get out of the way. Perhaps there would be an accident. He might fall off a cliff— be lost out of the boat, somewhere that the girl could not see whatever happened.

Then all this land would be his! Thyra would be his too. He had never been quite sure of her, for it was not her promise that he held, but her father's.

Oh, Loki take the lot of them! The stranger! He had forgotten the stranger. Well, if he was not dead, he would be. Biarki's face reddened and his little pig eyes narrowed. The stranger would die as soon as it could be arranged. Perhaps even tonight he would clip off that head as he had proposed. He could say that it was not a man he slew, but a troll who sprang upon him and attacked him. They could never prove different, for he would throw the head into the sea.

"Biarki! Stir your clumsy feet! Are you stuck in the bog? Did you come to watch us work? Get your ugly carcass up here!"

That was Skeggi. Flann only laughed. Biarki, the land-

owner, came out of his reverie with a jolt. He climbed the
hill where the others already had a good pile of poles cut
and stacked.

He bent and picked up an armful. He straightened up
and faced down the slope again. It was then, to the far west,
beyond a headland where might lie a bay, that he saw the
low smokes and knew that the land was not as empty as he
had thought.

He cast down his eyes hastily and said nothing. He hoped
the others had not noticed. Apparently they had been too
busy to look so attentively at the scenery, for they did
not mention the smoke.

Down in the meadow, Biarki could not see the traces
of man and breathed easier. It was still possible to fulfill
his plan. It would only be necessary to complete it a little
quicker. He might also have to build his own house.

2

Merlin's Godson

Sheltered by the cliffs at the waterfall, Thyra was busy
with the stranger who seemed so much more than that to
her. She dragged him, with a strength the others would
have never believed, into a spot where the sunlight was
strong.

She made a bundle of flowering thyme and put it under
his head for a pillow. Although there were fur robes in
the knorr, she left them until later. There is strength and
heat and life in the sunlight and she wanted him to have
all those things.

She handled him tenderly, stroking his hair, laying a palm
against his cheek. It was resilient, but so cold. There was
frost on his eyelashes and as she looked a little flake was

loosened and fell away. She thought his eyelid twitched, but could not be sure.

"Oh, come! Come back to me!" she prayed, and sprang to her work.

The bitter wind wailed in the hills and over her head the birds were streaming back from the sea to their nesting grounds. At this time of year there would be no true night, but it would be colder. During that chill twilight, until morning came again, she would have it not merely warm for him, but as hot as a man could stand and live. Then he would live! Then she would be alive again—for him! For this, she yearned so passionately that she thought the heart of this girl would burst with longing and forced herself to become calm.

She gathered bark and little twigs and leaves. Calling upon the memories in this mind, she shredded them in her hands and made a little pile near a large flat expanse of lava sand. She sought above the high-tide mark for dry driftwood. There was plenty, for the Gulf Stream washed these northern shores and cast up flotsam from more exotic climes. She heaped up a great store of it and when she was done, she began to gather stones.

Jagged lava pieces, lumps of basalt, round bombs of rock hurled from some ancient roaring crater—all these treasures that had known earth's fires—now destined to know flame again. But how to attain that flame?

The old Thyra would have struck flint against steel into tinder and had fire in moments. The new Thyra knew of the method, but Skeggi carried the tinderbox and he was not there. She considered using the flint ax and the steel sword. Two little lines of concentration formed between her eyes. Her face cleared.

She took the stranger's right hand and slipped off his ring. His hand had been clenched and it had escaped the notice of the men. Now his hand was open and the ring came off easily. It was very hot in her palm and she rolled it around, remembering.

He had told her that if danger was near him, it would be warm. So he was in great danger now? Well, she would see to it that he would be protected as he had never been before!

She picked up some of the powdered bark and held it in her hand and placed the ring upon it. The sun shone through the stone in the ring and made a tiny bright spot in the dust, but the tinder was damp.

For an instant, the strength and imperiousness drained from her face. She seemed no more than a small girl—alone —without friends, and lost.

Flann, if he had seen her then, would not have thought she was other than the Thyra Skeggisdatter he had known so long.

She closed her eyes. "Oh, Master of the Winds, Quetzalcoatl! If you ever loved your godson, help him now!"

A breath of wind swept across her hand like a caress. The ring became a shining circle of light. Beneath it, the tinder began to glow and smoke. Carefully, she tipped the tiny coal into the crumbled bark and lightwood pieces and blew upon it.

A feeble flame sprang up. She fed it into strength and added scraps of kindling. It seized upon them voraciously. A spiral of smoke rose into the air.

She clapped her hands together and laughed, throwing her head back. She was beautiful in her happiness. The ring was cold now and she slipped it back upon the limp chill hand. Had danger passed then? It seemed so.

Suddenly a rainbow sprang into being in the spray at the foot of the fall, like a symbol of promise. She faced it, head bowed in reverence.

"Ahunu-i! Spirit of the Wave! Forgive me! I know you are with me. I will not doubt again!"

Once more, eager vitality swept through the tired body. She built the fire high and threw on great pieces of wood, until the heat drove her back. Then she packed the stones into the mass of flames. The fire roared. The sparks cascaded into the air and the coals gleamed around the reddening rocks, shimmering with heat and sea salt—crimson and green and blue.

At last she could force the body no further. She sank down to rest, gazing into the incandescence, half asleep. It was in this torpid state that the men found her when they came, bringing back the poles she had ordered them to bring, and carrying the food they had found.

She came back to life after the short rest, and although they were weary too, after the trials of the day, she made new demands upon them.

At her direction, they dug a wide, shallow pit in the sand. Around it, the poles were driven in firmly and slanted to meet in the center. They were fitted together and tied at the top.

The curious men wondered what this labor would create, but the spell seemed strong on her again and she was wearing her strange look. Only Flann dared to ask and it is possible that no one else would have received any answer. He had been the first to follow her into the glacial melt tunnel—she hardly noticed the others.

"A booth?" The word seemed unfamiliar to her. "No, not a booth—whatever is a booth? A sweat lodge of the Abenaki—the People of the Dawn! Make haste, men!"

Make haste they did. They covered the poles with the sail; they threw the sand they had dug out of the pit around the perimeter of the lodge they had constructed. They raked out the glowing stones into the pit, leveled them evenly and covered them with the hot sand dug from beneath the fire and spread soft heather over the whole. The canvas sail bellied out on all sides with the heat when the flap was down.

Robes were laid, fur side up, upon the heather. Then, and not until then, the man from the glacier was carried in and laid on the robes, in the middle of the lodge.

The girl went in and motioned the others away. The door flap fell. As she lay down at his back, Skeggi came in also. He eyed her keenly.

At first she seemed resentful, then she smiled and extended her hand. He took it and squatted down beside her, not speaking. They looked at each other.

Skeggi did not know what to think. Was she still his daughter? If not, what or whom could she be? Strange things happen in strange lands, so travelers tell. Strange things are expected to happen, but such a wonder as this? Such a happening had never been told before by any skald or saga man.

Only when she smiled did she seem like his own girl whom he loved. Yet he admired the fire and spirit she had shown today. She knew so well where to go and what to do in this strange empty land that was so new to all of them. It was as though she had been here many times before; almost as though she had been watching and waiting for the right time to bring the man beside her out of the ice.

How could it be possible? They had never been apart, not

in Norway, not in the Faroes, not ever, since she was born.
Yet now she used strange words and names, she spoke of unfamiliar places; she gave orders like a queen—or a goddess!

Skeggi was a simple man, but he was honest and good.
Whatever she had done before had always been right in his
eyes. What she was doing now must be right, because she
was his daughter when she smiled—and she was still smiling.

He kissed her and her lips returned the pressure. He relinquished her hand and lay down on the other side of the man.
He gave a long sigh. Presently, worn out from the labors of
the day, he slept.

None of them had eaten, except that Skeggi had plucked
some blueberries during his journey; yet the girl was not
hungry. Excitement had superseded the needs of the body.
Now, as she lay in the stupefying warmth and the importance of haste had passed, she could scarcely keep her eyes
open.

She heard, from a great distance, Biarki and Flann snapping at each other, outside in the cold. She knew that they
were cleaning the birds and fish. Perhaps they would eat.
Perhaps they would sleep under the overturned boat after
eating—it seemed a matter of little moment. She had what
she wanted and she had wanted this so hopelessly and so long.
Her arms were about him! He was hers, and she could hold
him at last!

With fingers that trembled, she rolled him limply this
way and that, until she could take off his sleeveless vest.
He seemed a little warmer. She slipped off his soft leather
shirt, pulling it over his head. She thought she felt a throb
in his temples, but there was no sign of any heartbeat.

She stroked his heavily muscled arms and ran her fingers
along well-remembered scars on his torso. Here, this long
one down his ribs—a lance had struck deep and raked on.

Those claw marks on his back—a cougar's signature put
upon him when they dwelt among the People of the Dawn,
called so because the sun rose upon them first of all among
the northern nations of red men, on the continent of Alata.

Ah, Ahuni-i! It might have been, except that his magic
was strong and her goddess merciful, that they would never
have met.

Thyra's body trembled at the thought. She placed her

arms around him. Was there a movement? A little one? Only one? She touched the back of his neck with her lips and her eyes were wet.

So this was how humans cry! She had almost forgotten. He was so cold—so cold.

She unfastened the collar of her woolen shirt and untied the points that held her garment closed. She threw it wide open, drew the robe over them both and fitted her warm bare body tightly to his naked back. Her open palms she flattened across his silent heart, her cheek was against his —they were as one.

Now there was nothing more that she could do. She had no other magic than her love—no sorcery but her prayers to a goddess revered only in a continent long sunken in the deeps and remembered by no one but herself. The cold of him sank into this body of Thyra's, which was no longer wholly Thyra's, chilling it to the very bone, and her heart beat slower as the body's temperature dropped and bodily processes almost ceased to function. At the end, when unconsciousness came, she did not know if she was falling into sleep, or merciful but lonely death.

At this moment, the true Thyra Skeggisdatter, who had until this eventful day shared that body with no other, awoke as it were from a dream, to the knowledge that she was imprisoned within it. It is an awesome thing to realize that a body which has been always taken for granted is, after all, but a means of transportation for an inner self.

It seemed that she was no more than a midge or a tiny moth, fluttering to escape, beating helplessly against impenetrable walls. She knew, without knowing how she knew, that this tremulous prisoner was her real self, that very essence of being, which men call for lack of a better name— the soul.

She had been captured and thrust aside. She was imprisoned in her own body as completely as though a Viking jarl had taken a castle and had placed its lord in the dungeon keep until the invader decided what to do with the original owner.

She was very frightened.

Somehow it came to her that the new tenant of her body sensed her fear and was amused. She felt that a calm and

soothing voice spoke to her soul. The little shivering thing
that was herself was held warmly. She experienced a sensation of peace and supporting courage.

She knew then that the interloper was also feminine, for
there was an intertwining between them and an understanding that could come no other way. Knowing this, she began
to feel a rapport and, instead of anger, a deep pity, almost
akin to a sudden affection.

Yet all the voice had said, or trilled, for it was like a
series of running bell notes, was, "Forgive me, little sister!"

There was a weariness in it and a despair that made her
wish to weep. Here was the utter desolation that comes to a
soul which feels that no end can come to torment until
Asgard falls and the Fimbul Winter comes to still all
things that move and have being, until the new earth is
built for the Aesir.

So many years of waiting had come and gone and now
there had been hope and it too had gone. Now for this
strange visitant, which had for this one day been Thyra,
there was nothing more, ever again.

She felt a need to offer comfort to her captor, but there
was no way. Yet, it seemed that the thought, the wish to do
so, was in itself enough. Perhaps it was the outpouring of the
compassion she offered that caused her to forget her own
misery and fear, in the face of the greater agony of spirit
and hopelessness that she sensed the other must somehow
combat or fail completely in her desire.

Thyra had drawn strength from that other self. Now she
returned that strength. There came about a union of spirits,
a combining, and although they were still separate entities
they were no longer captor and captive, but as the visitant
had called Thyra in her plea—it was as if they were indeed
sisters.

There was a buoyancy, an uplifting in the coming together that brought about a resurgence in the two souls
which so strangely felt themselves kin.

A little warmth came back into the exhausted body. The
heart beat a little stronger. Some vitality returned. Now
Thyra knew that the other had overcome her distress. They
had reassured each other. The body would live. They could
go on in it together while that should be necessary and
there would be no strife between them.

Again it was as though the little bells rang. Thyra listened while the other spoke to her mind. They were now so close that it did not seem as a new thing to her, but more as though she was remembering a dimly recalled, half-forgotten tale of long ago. As she listened, she also watched, for she was seeing what the other had seen.

"There was a land engirdled by the sea, far away in the southern waters, its name Atlantis—" the voice began, and so she saw it, as it were from above. A country under a curse of dark sorcery and war. It planned an evil doom toward all the world and this scheming brought it finally to the attention of those gods who had loved that land, but in mercy and justice must sink it beneath the waves.

One only escaped. Alive, yet not alive. A young girl whose soul was placed by magical union into a replica of herself made of the unusually propertied ruddy-golden metal, orichalcum, which only the Atlantideans knew and used.

Thus prisoned, unable to reactivate the mechanism of the image by herself, she must await release by another hand. She floated and waited through millenniums, in one of the damaged swan-ships of Atlantis, above that sunken land. The ship, also made of orichalcum, absorbed the energy of the sun, attained a degree of intelligence, and took on a semblance of independent life.

Then she was released, by a man whose wooden ship had been caught in the weed that held her own and together they swore a pact of mutual help in the completing of separate vows each had sworn.

Her mission, with his aid, came to a successful conclusion, but she was unable to fulfill her vow to him because of the decaying of the metal in the ship and in her metal body.

So they separated, knowing love for each other and anguish at their parting. He, to be imprisoned in the ice, but—she had thought—not truly dead, for he was godson to a great mage and had drunk of the elixir of life. She, by the arts of Atlantis, preserved her identity, for she had the power of thrusting aside for a time the energizing spirits of other living things and homing there for such time as she must leave or her host must die.

So she had lived on, sometimes temporarily housed in the bodies of fish and seals, or in the airy apartments of the mind known to falcons, kittiwakes, and gulls. Later she knew the joy and affinity with humans, sharing briefly the lives of the infrequent visitors to those shores. Always she was watching over her lost love until the slow movement of the ice should bring him forth once more.

The long, long years of waiting! The anxiety, the dread that in the end all should go for nothing. Perhaps there might be no people nearby when the moment came to act. People had come and gone. How narrow the chance that she could do anything but watch helplessly when he would be freed, only to tumble into the sea, still locked in the ice and so be lost forever!

For what could a soul, as human as hers still knew itself to be, do to help him if imprisoned in a body without hands? Then, before the time had really come—the volcano, the shaking earth—and no time to reach other humans! In desperation, she looked down upon the water from the eyes of a raven and saw the little boat coming in toward the spot where it was needed.

And the new possession—and the happiness—and the effort—and the despair.

No true darkness through the night as they lay there waiting. Sunset, a brief pale twilight, then sunrise tingeing the ice-capped mountains and soon the light struck the walls of the sweat lodge until, seeping through the covering canvas, it dimly lit the interior.

The buried rocks still held heat by the time full morning had come. The sand was warm and comfortable beneath the robes and the smell of the heather was sweet. Beneath them the ground still trembled and at first Thyra and her almost-sibling felt no more than that distant disturbance. Yet Thyra's body, still so tightly holding the rescued man, sensed another vibration against it.

Scarcely daring to hope, the girl released her hold and rolled him over upon his back. Against her seeking hand upon his heart, she felt a feeble throb—another and a stronger one—and once more, falteringly, gathering strength, until the heart took up its task again.

His body was warm, the gray pallor faded from the dark skin—he took a long breath as though it were a sigh—and she fell upon him and covered his face with kisses.

He did not wake.

Thyra had felt herself again repressed and thrust aside, no longer an equal, for the other was dominant. This time, being aware of what was happening, she was not afraid. It did not seem wrong that she should no longer have control of herself.

Somehow, she was glad to be able to help the other girl, who needed help so badly. She felt a great trust in the other's integrity and was certain her body would not be misused.

Before she passed into a peaceful limbo of forgetfulness, she felt also that new lines were forming in her face. She must be taking on the appearance of the other girl. Would he see a resemblance in her? Then, while still wondering, it was as though she slept.

Skeggi felt himself being shaken, but he scarcely recognized his daughter. He seemed to see her through a mist, then, as he became fully awake and his head cleared, he made out in the dim light that it was indeed Thyra, but subtly changed.

By this time she had refastened the front of her shirt and had put on her leather jacket. She was vigorously massaging the stranger's naked chest. His head rolled limply to and fro.

Skeggi called the others from where they had been sleeping under the boat and they were glad of the warmth inside the lodge. They squatted down beside the stranger.

He appeared to be sleeping. His chest rose rhythmically and his breathing was strong. His long incarceration in the ice had not wasted his muscles. They lay in great bands across his torso and his biceps and thighs were hard.

When the massage was stopped, he lay peacefully, but beneath his eyelids his eyes moved as though he was watching something.

"I have often thought," whispered Flann, "that a person sees things in the land of dream that he cannot remember when he wakes. I have watched sleepers and seen many whose eyes move."

Whether in dream country or visions of the mind, the stranger undoubtedly saw something he feared. His face suddenly contorted, he threw his arms wide as though to catch himself from falling, and tossed massive Skeggi to one side like a child.

His eyes opened and the first thing he saw before them was the face of Skeggi's daughter. He sat up, with a glad cry: "Corenice!" And instantly she was in his arms.

The sudden action astonished the three fishermen. They

reacted in different ways. Flann turned and bolted out of the lodge, his grief and shock writ clear in his face. The other two had no eyes for him. Biarki, slow of wit, did not grasp the situation and how its implications were bound to concern himself, for an instant—then his anger rose. By that time, Skeggi had seized the couple with his great hands and flung them apart.

Each of the three had seen only Thyra. When the girl turned upon them in blazing fury, it was plain to them that Thyra she was not, either in character or facial resemblance. This was a person they had never seen.

During the hours in the lodge a change had taken place. It had begun in the boat, continued as time went on, and was now complete. This face was far more beautiful than Thyra's and it held an imperiousness in it that quelled Biarki's temper.

This could only be another personality that faced them, and of it they were in awe.

This was Corenice, and Corenice they did not know!

Corenice–Thyra stared down Biarki and without a word he left the lodge. She reached out a hand to Skeggi and after a little hesitation he took it. Corenice rose to her feet.

"This is Gwalchmai, whom I love. His name means Eagle and he is the son of a king. I know you cannot understand the meaning of what has happened, Thyra's father. Only trust me and all will be made clear. No one will be harmed and naught but good will come of this to both you and your daughter. I swear it upon your gods and mine. But you must and shall obey me!"

There was no doubt in Skeggi's mind that this was an affair for the gods to cope with. It was far too perplexing for him to understand. He did not try.

"I will do what you wish, Lady Corenice, who was my daughter. However, I want my daughter returned to me, in no way changed at that time from what she was. Failing, I curse the gods who have taken her and defy them to slay me! Thor, you joker, have you done this thing? Loki, trickster, mischief maker, is it you?"

Corenice smiled upon him. There was something of his own sweet girl still remaining in that smile—there was another sweetness, too, and an ancient motherly wisdom in her gaze.

His heart went out to her. He fell on his knees, as it were

to a goddess newly come to earth, and bowed his head. If someone had told him she was Freya, or Thor's wife, Sif—she of the golden hair—he would have believed and likewise trusted.

She ran her hand lightly through his graying curls.

"Then help me with my love, for he is most ill."

Gwalchmai's eyes had closed again. He was not quite unconscious, but he could not feel the ground he lay upon. He seemed to be floating. His breathing had become shallow and uncertain.

Corenice sat beside him and pillowed his head gently upon her bosom. He could feel rather than hear the even, comforting throb that stirred against his temple and brought him peace.

As during the night, he again drew strength from the girl's young vitality. Her calming nearness brought about a change. His pulse became stronger, his breathing regular. He was aware of his surroundings, but he thought he was back among the People of the Dawn, recovering from an illness in a village of the Abenaki. He opened his eyes and knew that he was not.

He remembered how Corenice had said, "You shall know me by gold!" He recalled the promise she had given him: "We shall meet and live and love again—though it be two hundred year!"

His arms closed about the waist of this beautiful girl with the golden hair. She was no longer metal—she was soft and dear. She was Corenice, returned against all hope.

She loved his face with gentle hands. She reveled in his growing strength. She looked up quietly at the still kneeling Skeggi.

"Now you may bring us food. My lord will live!"

Coals of fire still lingered under the ashes, where Biarki and Flann had cooked and eaten the trout, before they slept.

When Skeggi came out, amazed with what had happened, Flann was moodily nursing the flame back to life. Never before had the thrall been so conscious of his status as a slave.

Biarki had cleaned the ptarmigan and cut them up into pieces. Their one small copper kettle was ready to begin a stew. There were no vegetables, but Biarki remembered seeing lupines in the meadow. He thought the little flat beans they bore might be ripe enough to eat. The season was early, but he found a great quantity of dandelion leaves and filled his pockets with the eider duck's pale green eggs.

The eggs went into the hot ashes to roast and the dandelion greens were stewed, together with the little birds. It was an unsavory-looking mess, but it was good to smell. A fox looked down from the top of the cliff and barked querulously.

When all was ready, Flann set out the wooden bowls and filled them with the hot mixture. He shared out to each person a half of one of the hard rye biscuits that had been their stay on the involuntary voyage. These tasted better now to the wayfarers, but to Gwalchmai the flinty bits were impossible to choke down.

He drank some of the broth and sank back weakly to rest. Corenice fed him with tender care, selecting the best pieces of the soft meat and placing them between his lips with the horn spoon. He ate a little of the greens and made a face at their bitterness—then suddenly craved them and managed to empty the bowl.

By the time he had finished, he was feeling much more like himself. He asked questions of Corenice and, watching her face as she explained how he had been rescued, saw that she was and was not the one he had loved and had fought beside. He knew what she had done to protect and save him and knew also what he now must do.

He staggered when he stood up, and when he came out of the lodge into the open air, the sound of the waterfall, the smoke from the fire, the brilliance of the sunlight made the world he could see blend into a rushing blur. The cold wind revived him. Then he saw clearly the faces of the staring men.

Biarki glowering. Hate and menace there! Flann, whose face held a look hard to describe; it was distant, reserved, almost impassive—but in it was more than a hint of renunciation.

Of course! Flann also loved this girl, but not the one Gwalchmai knew so well. Here was sorrow, buried deep.

Skeggi, the girl's natural father—this was easier. Here was a waiting for a promise to be fulfilled. How well Gwalchmai knew that look! With a pang, he realized that the promise he had once made had been delayed far beyond the lifetime of the one to whom he had made it. To explain that promise to these strangers was the opening of a wound.

"My name is Gwalchmai. It is a British name, given to me by my father who was likewise British, although he thought of himself as Roman. He had a mighty friend, whose name was Merlin. Men called him an enchanter, in Britain.

"These two, and others, came exploring from Britain in years far past and discovered a land, westward from here. There, my father made himself a king, and Merlin became hailed as a god.

"The Feathered Serpent they named him—Quetzalcoatl, the Lord of the Winds. I am his godson. This ring you see, and which, I am told, made you fire, I hold as his inheritor. Let no man of you touch it. I, only, can wear it with safety.

"There have been those who said that Merlin is not dead, although my father saw him buried. I only know that when his tomb was opened to satisfy the argument, no body was in it. This, I saw. Perchance he slept awhile and now but visits the Land of the Dead he sought, and will return. His desire, and my father's, was that the land of Alata be placed under the rule of the Emperor of Rome.

"For that reason, I was commissioned to be my father's messenger. I have lost the message, yet I mean to go to Rome's Emperor, as I gave my sacred vow on the cross hilt of my father's sword.

"It may be that Rome is in dire peril. Alata shall be the refuge of its people. It is my duty to provide that refuge for those who need such a haven. In their ships I shall return to my home.

"All I ask of you is that you help me on my way. I have a little magic, gleaned from my godfather's books. We can be of use to one another."

He looked at them all. No one spoke at first, but he could clearly read their thoughts. Corenice—Thyra glowed with love and pride.

No doubt of her, although he could now see that this golden-haired girl was different in many ways than as he had first known her. This was only to be expected. Still, Corenice dominated the body. Until she left it for another housing, she *was* Corenice.

There was hate in the hearts of the others. Flann's face was now open to Gwalchmai's scanning. He would have

made a good friend under other circumstances, but he did
not try to hide his feelings because of the apparent loss of
the girl. Hatred was not as strong as the relief that a
dangerous rival might soon be gone.

Biarki's reasons were not as plain. Gwalchmai read envy
and he suspected greed—perhaps jealousy there, also. Biarki
would bear watching.

He was more concerned with Skeggi. Although the fisherman dimly understood what had been done to his daughter,
did he realize the necessity of it? It might be that Skeggi
resented the liberty that had been taken and feared others
still more dreadful might follow. Obviously, he was a doting
father.

Gwalchmai tried to reassure all of them with a smile,
but none would directly meet his eyes. Yet each promised to
speed him on—each for a different reason.

The knorr had sprung a strake upon the floating ice.
They did not leave the inlet that morning. While Biarki
and Flann caulked the boat with moss and tar out of stores,
Gwalchmai and the girl went in search of eggs in the upper
meadow.

Skeggi went with them. He was loath to leave his daughter
out of sight for long. The three found a great supply of eider
duck's eggs, more than they needed, but it was easy to preserve them by boiling batch after batch, for a few seconds
each. This would effectively seal off the interior from the
air and leave the central contents still raw, but fresh for a
long time.

When the work was finished, the day was far advanced.
No game had been sighted, but they roasted a brace of
ducks and feasted nobly, despite the lack of red meat.
Biarki was not satisfied.

Now that he was safe and dry and warm, for all ate in
the lodge, out of the ever-present wind, he craved ale, which
was lacking. The more he thought about ale, the more he
desired it. He could shut his eyes and see jugs and casks,
leather bottles and drinking horns—all filled with delicious,
heady, foaming ale.

Food was good, warmth was good. Ale was both. In
addition, it brought dreams, luxurious visions that sharpened
his slow wits.

He licked his lips and frowned. Tomorrow, or the next
day, if they went on to the west, they would come to the

smoke he had seen from the heights. Wherever there were people, there would be ale.

Wherever there was ale, there were those who drank it and drinking companions made friends easily. They thought alike. They did favors for one another. It was quite possible that a good friend might help in the elimination of an enemy.

Biarki slept better that night than he had the night before.

3

The Celi Dei

When the pale darkness brightened, once more into morning, they rose early. Already they were accustomed to the sound of the waterfall, but they heard the squawking fowl going out to fish and knew that it was time to break camp.

They ate sparely, without building up the fire to do so. The boat was quickly run out on rollers of driftwood and discovered to be sound. The sea was most quiet, a rare thing for that coast if they had known, and although it was a gray day with threatening masses of dark clouds, there was no heavy wind to move them.

Such breezes as filled the sail blew westward, which pleased Biarki, and the others were well suited, for they had no desire to go back toward the glacier and the still falling ash that misted it.

They rowed out of the inlet and some distance out to sea before they caught a fair wind. Once they raised the sail, oars came inboard and they went on westerly, following the forbidding coast a mile or so out, for there were white streaks of foam that told of jagged concealed volcanic upthrusts of rock nearer the shore.

There was a good view, at this distance, of the black

snow-capped mountains, some of which were steaming in spurts and plumes of white vapor, and others were spouting smoke—all due to the inner fires bubbling under this tumbled land. Yet it was beautiful in its tortured grandeur.

Skeggi said, "This must be the place that Gardar, the Swede, found some ten years ago when he went a-Viking in the Hebrides. He was blown off course, as we were, and he landed somewhere on the coast of an uninhabited country he called Snowland. Perhaps it was near here."

"There was talk in the Orkneys, when I was last there," said Biarki, "of a man from Norway who heard of it and went out to settle. He was called Floki, the Raven, because he loosed three ravens from his ship to find him land. One went home to Norway, one returned to the ship, but the third went straight on westward. He followed it and found land.

"I would call him Floki, the Fool! They say he liked the country so well that he forgot to cut hay for his beasts and when the winter came the cattle starved and he was like to do so himself—he and all his folk.

"At last he came home a poor man and called the place Iceland, lest others go there and fare as he did. But from what we have seen, I would think it well to stay here and take land, for we could make ourselves wealthy."

"It might have been Floki's raven that visited us. He seemed used to men," said Flann. Gwalchmai and Corenice–Thyra only looked at each other and smiled and said nothing at all.

A little later the coast swung toward the north and became rougher. Inlets and firths widened into bays. Here they shared a biscuit all around and here Biarki gave up his hopes of ale.

What he had thought to be smoke, from the viewpoint of the mountain meadow, could now be seen as steaming fumaroles. Ever and again a fountain of boiling water rose and fell among these, coughed, bubbled, and hissed and rose again.

All around there were good green fields that would make fine pastures. The land was not forested, but it was wooded.

Once a walrus broached the surface, a ton of excellent meat, as all were aware. Some miles farther on, a pod of whales hastened by toward the Arctic Ocean to enjoy the short summer season.

They set out hand lines and caught cod to cook later. On a black strand they saw where a careless whale had found its end, for broad ribcages upthrust out of the crumbled lava beach, like the bones of a wrecked dragon-ship.

The sight of so much food made Gwalchmai ravenously hungry. He could not eat much at a time, but he was munching steadily—a mouthful of biscuit, seasoned with a scrap of kelp or seaweed; a slice of raw fish; a little crab picked off a floating log.

Never satisfied, always nibbling; gaining strength while Corenice gazed upon him fondly, watching him eat.

Before them loomed a headland, bold, fantastically contorted and torn. It looked stern and menacing, but it shielded a bay that was broad and calm. This steamed with hot spring overflows and there were more smokes back from the broad beach.

These smokes came from low houses of stone, shaped like beehives and rounded over with turf. Near them were people, and not far in from the point of the headland, just in front of the explorer's oncoming boat, was a man fishing from a walrus-skin kayak.

He raised his head and peered at the knorr standing in to harbor, under sail. The sun was in his eyes and at first he could not make out clearly what he was seeing. When he was sure, he quickly wound in his line and hailed the shore.

The alarm had already been given. A man was beating with a mallet upon a long bone hung between two posts. At the not unmusical sound, which carried clearly to the visitors across the water, other folk came out of the houses and thronged the beach.

They did not appear to be armed. Men and women alike wore long robes. A few of these were cloth, but most were made of fox skins. Here and there could be seen a person of more commanding presence than the others, though all were mainly a rather short, dark people. Many of the men had white beards.

One, carrying a long staff, came down close to the water's edge and called out to them, "If ye be friendly disposed, brothers, come without fear. If not, then depart in peace."

Skeggi had already taken in the sail and the knorr was holding its distance, under oars. He looked at the man, narrowly. He was not sure if the shout had been to welcome them in or to warn them away, but when it was repeated in Norse, his face cleared.

He had already made out that the staff had a crook in the upper end and could be nothing but a bishop's crozier.

Flann was already satisfied of this, for the language first used had been Erse, and he recognized the phrasing.

"Celi Dei! The Children of God! We are among friends."

Skeggi smiled. He had known many such in the Faroes and found them all to be good men—harmless, devout, though somewhat narrow and rigid in their principles. They were definitely a strong-minded group, acknowledging no other master than the Christian God.

Secretly, Skeggi had some leanings in that direction, having observed the effect of their teachings upon other men, but old beliefs die hard and his loyalty was to his old gods.

Flann understood them even better. The Celi Dei, or Culdees as they were commonly called, lived a life of austerity, disciplining their bodies to increase the glory of the soul. To know the will of God was their joy, to do it was their life. They lived apart from large groups of mankind, not to win their own personal salvation, for they were already convinced of that; their motive was to testify by their own example the blessedness of a simple way of living.

However, the roistering, blustering, fighting Norse had another way of life. Although the Culdees possessed no treasure, the Viking raiders could never believe it. Time and again the Culdees' settlements were sacked and their people killed or taken into slavery, as Flann had been. So the Culdees fought in the only way they could and still remain God's Men: they left every place that the Norsemen penetrated and sought another safer home.

They had been pushed out of Ireland and Scotland, north into the Orkneys, the Shetlands, and the Faroes. For three quarters of a century this little group had dwelt peacefully, as far away as they thought man could go—in the land that they supposed was the most distant on earth and that the Greeks knew as Thule.

No wonder that, recognizing the lines of the knorr as Norse, they stood in dread upon this black strand, their backs against the ocean, which stretched westward to limitless expanse, offering no other haven. They had been discovered. This might mean invasion, slavery, and further persecution.

Yet so kind of heart they were that their Bishop now invited the wayfarers to land in good cheer, offering them rest, comfort, and peace—providing only that they came in good will.

Biarki grunted in contempt. "Good will toward the West-men?* Good will toward thralls? Sooner would I take what we need with our axes than anything they would give with open hands!"

Flann shot him a look of hate, but Skeggi said, "You will keep this peace they offer, hothead, or you will answer to me! We are in their land, not ours, and you will do well to remember it!"

Raising his voice, he called out, "We accept your hospitality, Gaffer. We come only in peace." Then the oars struck the water and in a few strokes the keel grated on the shingle.

The sides of the boat were seized by willing hands and it was dragged high upon the beach. Now that their dismay was over, the Culdees surrounded the strangers with smiling faces. As Skeggi had first thought, their appearance marked many as of a distant Pictish descent, although some were tall and fair and a few had red hair and blue eyes.

All looked on Gwalchmai with curiosity, admiring his strength and stature, but wondering at his strange clothing and reddish-brown skin. They did not know his mother had been a girl of Aztlan. The information would have meant nothing to them, but they recognized him as something beyond their ken.

The Culdees crowded in, clapping the newcomers on the shoulders and shaking hands. The Bishop came forward and bestowed the kiss of peace upon Skeggi's hairy cheeks. Women and children timidly gathered around Gwalchmai and Corenice, fingering the fabric of Thyra's gown and admiring his flamboyant beadwork embroidery.

It was plain to see that they had long been separated from knowledge of what women were wearing in Europe.

No one offered to kiss Biarki. His frown caused the men to keep their distance. The burning glances he directed upon the prettiest of the girls made it plain what was in his dark thoughts.

Flann bent down and picked up a small child who had

---

*The Norse term for Irishmen.

fallen and was crying because of a hurt knee. He nuzzled his
nose into the boy's soft neck and crooned to him, blowing
warmly down his collar, which tickled and made the child
laugh. He hugged and kissed Flann, who set him gently down
and gave him into the hands of his smiling mother. Children
always liked Flann.

Corenice glanced tenderly at the man from Erin. She
knew that, deep down, where Thyra lay in dream, this
action had not gone unnoticed by her.

The little group was now urged toward the beehive huts,
which were quite low, being partly dug into the ground for
warmth, made of stone, chinked with moss and well roofed
with turf. Most of them had long entrances, roofed over
against the prevailing winter winds, and the rooms were
quite comfortable, surprisingly large and commodious.

The Bishop's house, to which they were invited, consisted
of two buildings connected by a narrow passageway. In
the larger of the two, Maire Ethne, his wife, a buxom little
woman, made them welcome.

She was a busy, cheerful person, who bustled about preparing a stew that bubbled over a central fire. There was
no chimney, the smoke finding its way out by itself through
a hole in the conical peak of the roof. The glowing peat
beneath the kettle cast off a pleasant warmth and the dim
light it gave was increased by several open grease lamps.

These were carved from soapstone in a design unchanged
since Roman times and still in use among the Esquimos. The
Culdees burned seal or whale oil and used wicks made of
white-headed cotton grass, which grew profusely everywhere.
The single lamp that was different was a small brass one,
evidently an article of pride and value, for it was kept
burnished and gave a brighter light.

Upon enquiry, the Bishop explained that it was a family
heirloom and was fed with a finer oil, pressed from the
breasts of the great auk—that unfortunate effort of Nature
to create a penguin out of a puffin.

Altogether, these various burning fuels combined with the
fragrant stew to create an aroma that made the visitors
feel faint with hunger.

Flann was sent to bring in the remaining biscuit and
cheese as their contribution. This was a great treat to their
hosts, since no cereals could grow in the short summers and
they had not tasted bread of any kind for years.

The low table of driftwood planks was hastily set with wooden bowls and spoons, intricately carved with loving care during the long dark winters. The voyagers were about to fall too when they noticed that the Bishop and his wife had bowed their heads in prayer. They watched, in uneasy embarrassment, not quite knowing what to do.

When the short blessing had been asked upon the meat, Flann, Bishop Malachi, and Maire Ethne made the sign of the cross over their bowls and began to eat. Biarki defiantly made the sign of the hammer over his and after a moment's hesitation Skeggi did the same, in deference to Thor. Corenice spilled a little water on the floor in honor of the Spirit of the Wave.

It was not evident that the Bishop had noticed the actions of the others, but he beamed when Gwalchmai likewise made the sign of the cross, for he supposed the Aztlanian was also a Christian. He could not know that whatever leanings he had in that direction, Gwalchmai had absorbed them from the questionable books of Merlin Ambrosius, the Druid Mage.

There was little talk during the meal. Biarki hinted for strong drink, then for ale or beer, but this austere community had neither. There was no cereal or fruit for its manufacture. After eating, the cups were filled with a light but unfermented wine made of crowberries, and with that Biarki, to his disgust, was obliged to make do.

He made a mental reservation that if plans he was vaguely formulating should turn out successfully, many changes would take place.

When the company was replete, a further blessing was said and another prayer and then Bishop Malachi settled back comfortably for talk, while the table was being cleared. When his wife came back, she sat down with them and began sewing upon a foxskin cap.

Neither pressed their guests with questions, but when they were told of the Norse fishers' journey before the storm, it confirmed their suspicion that this was indeed Iceland. The wonderful rescue of Gwalchmai was not mentioned, nor his identity.

Skeggi, as spokesman for the party, said nothing of that which had befallen his daughter, for he did not understand it himself. Neither could he make himself yet fully believe in this strange changeling whom he had fathered.

The bishop was too polite to probe into mysteries he could sense, for he was a good judge of men, and instead brought the conversation around to himself and his flock.

Thus the Norse learned that this happy, contented people had lived upon the island for seventy-five years, having established a community and an economy that suited them well. They had come there in curraghs of oak-tanned hides, made of three layers in such a way that air chambers were sealed in. Such boats were still in use. The curraghs carried a mast, with a triangular lug-sail also made of hides, and were fitted for oars as well. Even when loaded, the craft drew but a few inches and when empty was easily carried up on the land and stowed away.

The original colony had been increased by several other shiploads of the Children of God during that time. They had sought a peaceful refuge and found it here, some in curraghs and others in ships of wood large enough to hold sixty people.

Some had brought sheep and a carefully tended flock was now increasing, though somewhat harassed by foxes. Wool was as yet in short supply. They had no cattle and no horses —and they had thrown away such weapons they had come with, for they trusted in the protection of God.

Biarki grunted, thinking his own black thoughts, but said nothing of such folly.

The Bishop went on, undisturbed.

As other visitors came, less kindly minded, the Culdees had withdrawn before them to the little islands, hidden their skin boats in places made ready for them, and kept their larger ships upon the other side of Iceland proper. So it was that neither Gardar, the Swede, nor the Viking Floki had ever been aware of the people and had thought the land to be uninhabited.

However, the Celts knew that this isolation could not continue and it must come about one day that they would be discovered by those who had driven them for so many weary years and hundreds of sea miles. Now there was no other place to go, unless they submitted to slavery or death by returning to their southern homelands.

At this, Gwalchmai started, remembering his own warm homeland of Alata. It would seem a paradise to these people, who lacked so many things and who were in such dread-

ful danger. But at this time he said nothing and, catching
the eye of Corenice, he saw that she concurred with his
opinion.

The heat and the warm food began to take its toll among
the weary wayfarers. Soon one, then another, began to yawn.
The Bishop, noticing this, broke off his discourse.

"Enough, brothers," he said. "Let us pray and sleep. There
will be time for talk tomorrow. Woman of the house, will
you put away your sewing now, for I see you have done little upon it in all this time. Our guests would rest now."

The robes were brought in from the boat and spread
down upon heaps of heather in the farther chamber. It was
not large, but there was room for everyone. After all necessary things were done, the Bishop took down one of his
holy books from a short shelf and prayers were said. Flann,
as thrall, was delegated to smoor the fire.

Well accustomed to the task, he quickly covered the coals
with dry peat, damp peat, and ashes, following these layers
with a good coating of wet peat on top. The banking would
last through the short night.

Then, under the warm cloud of smoke and steam that
layered the upper part of the room, adding to the streamers
of soot that hung there, he lay down on his pallet near the
fire where he could tend it if he must. He blew out the
remaining grease lamp and was soon asleep, although
thoughts of Thyra disturbed him in his dreams.

In the following days, it was a marvel to the voyagers
to see how lightsome of spirit these people were. It was not
an occasional gaiety, but a steady outpouring of happiness
that extended to all. They were a hardworking folk, for to
prepare for the winter no time could be wasted. The men
fished every day; the women laid by the berries in great
store, drying them in the sun; the young boys danced and
played, but gathered eggs, cotton grass, and salt from the
evaporating pans. Birds were snared, their flesh likewise to
be dried and salted, and seal meat and oil were put away.

All the time, through the long days now perceptibly growing shorter, they laughed and sang.

Biarki laid their high spirits to the taking of strong drink
and at one time or another he visited all the houses, hinting
and peering about. He could never believe that their

laughter was due to sheer joy of life and the feeling of brotherhood that permeated the entire settlement. His temper grew uglier as his frustration increased.

He took to swaggering through the village with buckler on his arm and battle ax loose in his hand, swinging it to and fro as though he was instantly ready to strike out with it. His scowl brought soberness to all he met and nothing Skeggi could say deterred him in this growing habit.

He watched the women as they worked and one day followed one of the girls on her way to tend the sheep. When he found that they could not be seen from the village, he approached and drew her down into a hollow. As they struggled, a group of children seeking eggs came up, singing, and Biarki let her go with no worse to befall her than torn clothing.

She said nothing, for she was in fear of her life, but because of her manifest terror whenever she saw Biarki, Bishop Malachi suspected what had happened and afterwards no child watched the sheep alone.

The others took a hand with their hosts and shared the work. They were well liked and the Culdees considered them, except for their alien faith, as valuable members of the community and would have been glad to have them stay.

There came a day when Biarki was more restless than usual. He had disdained any kind of labor and he was bored. At the same time he was angry, for Flann had newly become a free man.

Skeggi had long considered making him so, for he felt that in all but name Flann was not a thrall. His willingness to obey orders, though his status irked him, was cause for admiration, and it seemed to Skeggi that Flann should be in a position to bear arms legally now that Biarki's temper had become so strained.

Also, it seemed to him that if the Irishman was able to mingle among them all as equals, this might in some way, which his own slow mind could not comprehend, bring back his girl to her senses. Skeggi had always known that the two of them looked upon each other kindly, until this stranger man had come between them and become responsible for this weird change in her. At times he had regretted pledging her to Biarki and never more than now.

So thinking, he called Flann to him and snapped the iron thrall collar in twain between his strong fingers.

"Never call any man master again," he said.

"Nay, master," said Flann, in deep gratitude. "No man but you!"

And so the matter ended.

Now, for some little while, it seemed that this action had brought about a change in Thyra. She smiled upon Flann and appeared to pay a little attention to him as for a few days he also went about the village with ax and buckler. He did not strut as did Biarki and no one shrank out of his way. When he found that Biarki avoided him or spoke to him politely as was fitting between equals, he gave over wearing his weapon and spent much of his spare time reading the Bishop's books.

But Biarki was biding his time and planning with his slow mind what he meant to do. In accordance with this plan, he invited Skeggi to go on a journey to see the interior of the island and view some of the wonders said to exist there. Skeggi was nothing loath, for work had palled upon him and he too had heard tales.

They started early, for the days were much shorter now. The first night they slept upon ground warmed by a nearby hot spring. The next day, moving north, they came upon a region of rising ground where meadows changed into a high lava plateau. Eider ducks had nested here in quantity and they saw foxes that had preyed upon the young and were still lurking about, hunting laggard strays. They took one of these foxes, kept the skin, and cooked and ate some of the rank meat without much relish.

Waterfalls abounded here, some of great size and turbulence, and a few of the streams ran warm from other hot springs, for much of this plateau had been laid down not too long before, as earth's clock counts time, and the fires beneath still flamed.

Here Skeggi ran down two of the auks, which, being wingless, were easy to capture. Mindful of the oil their bodies contained and which was so highly prized by their friend the Bishop, he wrung their necks, tied their feet together, and went on, carrying them slung about his neck.

Lichens and mosses covered this young lava like a carpet of greenish-gray dust. The low hills looked like slag heaps and between them lay pools that steamed in the chill air. Near one of these, a deep pond of clear water in a white silica basin all of fifty feet across, the two men sat down to eat and talk.

They looked out, from their height, across a beautiful valley, and Biarki said, "I have been thinking, partner, that all we see here could be ours, if you would but play the man."

Skeggi said then, "Speak clearly. What would you have me do?"

Biarki, thinking Skeggi could be easily persuaded, replied, "Look you, now. First, we shall kill that troll who came out of the ice and holds your daughter under his spell. Then, when she is free, we shall be three axes together against these little people"—for Biarki stood head and shoulders above all but a few, and so looked down upon them—"and I doubt not that Flann, of the quick tongue, will be gladder to give orders than he was to take them. So we may make them all thralls and we shall be as jarls and own the whole land."

But he did not go on to say that after this was done, Flann's life would be short and perhaps Skeggi's as well.

Yet this thought came to Skeggi, and he said, "And if I will not, what then? For I am inclined toward these people."

Then it was as though a red mist rose before Biarki's eyes and the sky and earth came together as a melting flame and the pool was filled with blood and his face was as the face of a troll.

Skeggi saw his anger. He loosened his ax in his belt and moved a little way off, but he was hampered by the birds and he could not go far.

He was trying to rise when Biarki leapt to his feet in his fury, shouting, "Then, Skeggi Hairymouth, I call you niddering and no man!"

And with a single sweep of his ax he split open Skeggi's head and laid his partner dead at his feet.

His rage passed, and when Biarki knew what he had done, he was afraid. Even in this far land, he knew he was under Odin's eye, and he did not believe that the Norns had planned to cut the thread of Skeggi's life at this time. This was clearly a blood debt that would be held against him, and he did not wish to pay it, now or ever.

He walked over to the pool and looked into it. It was very deep. The water was boiling and bubbles rose and burst upon its surface, giving off little puffs of steam. Steam whistled and piped from little cracks around it in the rocky rim.

If a body would not stay hidden in the depths, surely the flesh would soon be boiled from the bones and dissipated into a scum, and the skeleton would sink of its own weight, never to be seen again.

Biarki laid hold of the body and dragged it to the water's edge. He did not like to lose the good ax, but it would help to weigh the body down. He rolled the body over and the water seethed about it.

There was not much blood on the rocks. A few cups of water were enough to wash it away. When he had finished, the body had already sunk out of sight in the clear depths.

He saw the auks and with a shudder of disgust at this reminder of the vanished man he threw them into the pool too.

They were large and heavy with fat and almost immediately a film of oil began to spread over its surface. It shimmered in the sunlight and the bubbles no longer burst through it. The steam was held within the water as the oil quickly covered the pool.

Then, as Biarki watched, he saw a strange and terrible thing that almost unhinged his mind. A moment longer the pool was quiet, then suddenly a round dome of water grew in its center, upon which Skeggi's body rode and tossed. It shot upward in a monstrous pillar of whitely boiling water and steam and as it rose it roared and hissed. As it rose, so with it rose Skeggi, up, up, and up—two hundred feet and more, into the air—and as he rose he beckoned to Biarki, with waving arms from which the flesh was already falling, as though he besought Biarki to follow him into the clouds.

For this pool, so placid in its seeming, was the monstrous Geysir—Gusher—from which all others in the world derive their names! Biarki fled screaming from this ghastly sight.

Now, as he ran, adding to his horror, a great gyrfalcon stooped down upon him out of the heavens, like a falling star, and fixed its talons in his shoulder, beating him heavily about the face with its wing elbows.

He tore it loose, strong as it was, and threw it to the ground, but it sprang into the air on its broad pinions, shrieked and rose, seeking altitude, and then Biarki again heard the whistle of air in its stiff feathers as it dived to strike and tear again.

This time, he was prepared. He flung up his buckler to protect his face, struck it sidelong down, cut a wing from its three-foot body and ran on, leaving it dying there. He was in too much fear to make certain that it was dead.

As it happened, the falcon was still living when a raven, always the hungry scavenger, dropped down to see. As the raven hopped closer, the falcon's eyes filmed over and its beak closed.

Curiously enough, the raven did not stop to feed. Instead, it seemed to forget that it was hungry. It flapped awkwardly up again and at a low altitude followed the staggering man as he ran on across the lava beds, heading back south toward the village of the Culdees.

During this time, Flann had been delighted to find that Gwalchmai had suddenly lost interest in Thyra. He could not understand it, but when Thyra sought his company, forsaking the stranger with whom she had become so close, he did not question her or his good fortune.

Thyra linked arms with him and they walked and talked as they had in gay moods before. That was enough for Flann. Once in a while she pressed his arm close against her body and they walked on without speaking. Occasionally she looked up at him as though she were seeing him newly, and was pleased at what she saw. It was almost as though she was comparing him mentally with Gwalchmai and had decided that she liked Flann the better of the two.

She raised her face up to him and Flann was sure that she wanted to be kissed. He was about to try when she looked up into the sky and the spell was broken.

The expression so familiar to him lately came again upon her face. She stiffened and pressed backward out of his arms. A raven had just flown overhead.

To Thyra, it was as though a beloved sister had come home and they had embraced in greeting. Corenice was back.

She had been worried, though dimly, when her father left with Biarki, for what Corenice knew, Thyra also knew, and Corenice had felt the other's anxiety. So, to relieve the minds of both, for pain one felt also hurt the other, Corenice had gone questing—in the body of the gyrfalcon.

Thyra instantly learned what Corenice had discovered.

She could not cry, for Corenice dominated her body, but there were tears just the same.

Corenice had learned to admire and respect Skeggi for his courage and integrity. Chiefly she felt anger, as she had at the geyser. This was a frightful deed, which called for justice and immediate punishment.

So it was that Gwalchmai and Flann were informed of the murder. Immediately arming themselves, although Flann could take the word he received only on trust, the little party moved north to meet Biarki—the two girls in the one body and the two men who loved them both.

Biarki meanwhile had covered much ground, being hag-ridden with fear. He was weary, but when he saw the three avengers coming from the village and marked with what determination they strode in his direction, he was aware that they knew what he had done.

He had planned a story that would explain Skeggi's absence, but he cast it out of his mind. Somehow he felt sure that it would be useless. The raven, Odin's messenger, had seen and told all. His doom was upon him and that it would befall and was not to be avoided seemed only just.

At this end to all his hopes and plans, he went mad. The tendency to go berserk, which had always cursed the men of his family, now descended upon him.

The familiar red tinge colored all his little world again. The yellow of lichen and the green of the grass became submerged in scarlet. He ripped away the shirt from his body. He felt suffocated from lack of air and must bare himself to the wind.

He bit the edge of his buckler until his teeth splintered and his mouth bled. He howled like a wolf and rushed, foaming, in great bounds and leaps, against his enemies under a bloody and setting sun.

He swung his battle ax first against Flann, for it was he who had been hated longest. Flann was less tired, but escaped only by sucking in his belly; the ax swung on in a figure eight and struck him a glancing blow in the back that laid him flat.

With scarcely a glance at him gasping on the ground, Biarki turned upon the others. Merlin's ring grew hot as fire upon Gwalchmai's finger and he knew he was in as great a danger as he had ever been.

His own buckler was up and he received Biarki's blow full upon it. The shock numbed his arm. His guard fell. He heard the girl scream. He did not know if it was Thyra or Corenice.

His drawn sword licked out beneath the drooping shield in the old legionary trick that his father had taught him. It drew blood, for he felt it strike upon bone, but Biarki seemed impervious to wounds. It was only with the utmost effort that Gwalchmai was able to protect himself against the rain of ax blows. Again and again the short Roman sword struck into Biarki, who roared with pain but did not appear to weaken. Then Gwalchmai's buckler fell.

The next blow took the sword from his grip and it slithered across the ground. As he also fell, Gwalchmai knew well that it was Corenice who threw herself upon him. Biarki swung up his ax in triumph. Gwalchmai's hand went up to push her aside or to fend off the blow. A gush of white brilliance shot from the stone in the ring, straight into Biarki's eyes, blinding him with its flare.

At that insant, Flann seized the sword.

"Biarki! Die!" he yelled and the giant turned upon him.

A little of Biarki's mania had worn away. He approached Flann, panting, swinging his ax in circles, his blood spattering the ground. Still, his strength was enormous and they could hear the whistling sound of the weapon through the air.

It was clear that Flann was no novice with the sword. He handled it well and despite its lack of length, he dealt Biarki two blows that would have dropped a lesser man— one in the biceps of the left arm, which caused Biarki to fling away his buckler, and another deep gash in the same side along the ox-like ribs.

Biarki bellowed and seized Flann in an iron grip. Flann could not reach him with the sword point, but drew the edge along his side until Biarki lurched back. Flann's face was dark with agony. He did not fall, but stood almost unconscious, struggling for breath, with the point of the sword touching the ground, balancing upon it.

Biarki reached for him again, bleeding profusely, but Gwalchmai had recovered now. He slipped between the two, carrying Biarki's discarded buckler, and brought it up under the madman's jaw with the sound of an ax blow. Like an echo there came a second crack as that stout neck broke.

Then Biarki fell like a tree that has faced its last storm

and the others collapsed, almost as far gone as he, while Thyra—Corenice hugged and kissed and prayed over both her valiant men—but in thankfulness to different gods.

4

Out Oars for Alata!

They stayed through the long dark winter with the Culdees rather than return south so late in the year. It was not so much through dread of the stormy seas that they so decided, although most of the electrical storms occurred at that time and the little boats remained in their housing. It was because there seemed no urgency to seek another sort of life.

Murder and bloody vengeance brought sorrow to the small self-sufficient community. The outside world had impinged upon them briefly enough, but these events caused long-buried memories to come to the surface and now the people went about soberly and with less laughter. They remembered persecutions and deaths and brutalities.

Maire Ethne took the fatherless girl to her heart, comforting and fussing over her, and both Thyra and Corenice felt her love and compassion. If these two had come to be as sisters, they now felt that a mother had swept them into her arms.

Once, in a moment when Thyra was dominant, she went to Maire and hugged her. "If ever I have a daughter, I shall name her after you," she said, and the bishop's wife kissed her, feeling honored and well repaid.

But Corenice knew sorrow, for she had longings too, and she knew well that this symbiosis, which gave her a semblance of mortal life, could be nothing but temporary and she did not know when the end of it might come.

So Gwalchmai and Flann and the girl dwelt in the village longer than they had expected to stay, hoping to show by their actions that they were of good will. By mingling thus and working with the folk they became accepted and when the sun came back the spirits of all were lifted.

During the winter, the communion of the three, who were four, became deeper. Flann's puzzlement was complete, but he learned to accept a way of life he did not like or understand.

Sometimes when Corenice was gone, roaming the undersea in the body of a seal, rushing through the water in play, his own Thyra emerged and smiled upon him sweetly and it was as though summer came into his dark mood. Then he was happy.

They walked along the beach or up into the hills. They talked or were close in long understanding silences; they spent much time together over the bishop's books, Thyra's expressive face pensive as she listened, half convinced, to the expounding of Flann's Christian faith, satisfied that they were together.

These moments came more often as the winter wore on, and Flann noticed that whenever Thyra was thus kind, Gwalchmai was absent. In fact, Corenice and Gwalchmai swam together upon occasion, for he was being taught the trick the Atlantideans knew and had learned to cast his spirit forth and live the life of others, though not as yet for long.

So this was the courting Corenice had so long awaited and that had been so long postponed. They journeyed together in the world of water as mer-man and mer-maiden, although when Flann saw Gwalchmai lying upon his bed with eyes closed, he supposed that his friend was asleep.

Despite the natural jealousy, they *were* friends—the more so because Flann did not nurture illusions and false hopes.

He had been a thrall. He did not expect Thyra to forget. He would never be able to forget it himself.

Then the spring came and it was the time of pairing, when girl and boy find each other good to look upon in their youth and their elders smile upon them—remembering.

Flann was alone on the beach, mending a boat, for Gwalchmai and Corenice had strolled into the hills, hand in hand. His heart was lorn and his thoughts were bleak. He would finish his work, provision the boat, and row away, never to come back.

Possibly it would be better to go out to sea with the leak unpatched. What, after all, was there in life without Thyra? Not at all unusual thoughts in spring—but perhaps Flann's musings were darker than most, for his misunderstandings were deeper than those of other men.

The two who perplexed him were behaving quite sedately, sitting and watching, by the edge of a warm little pond where two stately trumpeter swans were circling. Corenice was silent, for she was remembering the swan-ships of Atlantis and all the beauty and pride and grandeur that was gone forever. Gwalchmai's thoughts were elsewhere.

The swans were coming to an understanding. They laid their bills together and dabbled at one another's feathers. They intertwined their long necks and murmured, deep in their throats. It was easy to believe that they spoke of love and shared dreams and plans as human lovers do.

Gwalchmai said, "Trumpeter swans mate for life. If one dies, then the other pines away."

"So it should be," agreed Corenice. "If you were to really die, I would not want to live. It was only because I did not know that I could wait so long for you."

"And yet, we have each other not, my dear one, nor ever will, it seems, while we live thus and you keep your promise to this other one you dwell with!"

"It is not my house," she reminded him, gently. "I am only a guest in it. I must not forget and you must help me to remember."

"I am not made of iron, Corenice, and I love you."

Then there was a long silence. The gulls swooped overhead, peering down with their bright eyes. The ducks were busily at work, marking out their territories, gathering materials for their nests. Every living creature in sight, it seemed to Gwalchmai, was with a mate.

Even the lordly pair in the pool were content with each other. Only the two humans were so far apart—though seeming to be so close.

"How long must we wait, Corenice? How long shall our lives last, seeing that I have drunk the elixir of life and you, it seems, are immortal in the spirit? Suppose you feel that you must always give such a promise to she whom you inhabit?"

"Does it matter so much if you must needs practice patience for a little while, my heart's darling?"

"Only if one of our lives should end, for I do think our love will not. Why cannot we be as happy as those swans, who need only each other to feel that they own the world? Why should we not be as they?"

"If we should become as they, it would mean that we would never part," said Corenice, with unaccustomed shyness for her.

"We knew that long ago! Are you not content?"

"Then let it be as you say!"

Gwalchmai closed his eyes and lay back upon the moss. The huge swan lifted his head and stared around at them, as Corenice bent over the apparently sleeping man and kissed him tenderly.

The swan gave forth a clarion call and beat the water into froth with his wings.

"I am coming! I am coming!" laughed Corenice.

A second later, the swan's mate spread her ten-foot pinions and leaped into the air, to be followed immediately into the heights. They swooped down and up again, in a mad race, hastening into the sky, then falling with furled wings until they almost touched the ground, scattering the gulls, buffeting away the sticks and grass the ducks had heaped together.

They called to each other with their glorious ringing voices, like silver trumpets challenging the angels who man the ramparts of the castles of the clouds.

Then they glided down, merging their reflections with their bodies and came to rest together in the little pond.

Now they were alone, for Thyra, knowing all that Corenice had known, radiantly blessed them as they flew and went down to the village to seek out Flann.

The pond was still and no ripples stirred upon it. The royal couple floated side by side upon its glassy surface without moving.

Finally, as though such happiness as they shared could no longer be borne quietly, they soared again into the blue.

They rose as one, in an ever-widening spiral, singing their joy—a full-toned bugling that drifted down to Flann and Thyra, lost in each other's eyes, the boat long forgotten.

Into the sky rose the regal pair, still circling, still growing smaller, until they could only be heard, calling and answering and ever rising higher until their great sweeping round brought them far out over the southern sea.

This, their wedding—this, their nuptial flight.

Then far, far along that distant edge of haze where ocean meets the sky—many miles away, even from their position of immense vision—both descried a serried, jagged edge of little dark points jutting up all along the southern horizon; and gliding down the long slope of air toward this mystery, they saw that the sea was full of ships.

Harald Harfager, to please a girl who would not have him for a husband, had sworn that he would never cut his hair until he had unified Norway and made himself King. Therefore, to his friends, he became known as Harald Fairhair, but his enemies called him Harald, the Lousy.

After the sea battle of Hafrs Fjord, he became King and married his girl and had his long locks trimmed. The defeated jarls took the remainder of their Viking dragon-ships and fled in many directions, for Christianity soon became the law of the land.

Ingolfur Arnason and his foster brother Hjorleifur Hrodmarsson, both fierce and ruthless men, gathered together their goods and gear, their followers, with their women and children, and sailed, in two hundred ships, for Iceland, still holding for Odin and Thor.

It was this fleet upon which the swans looked down and through their eyes Gwalchmai and Corenice examined the invaders.

As they circled above at a safe height, beyond arrow range, they saw it to be a well-planned venture. The decks had goods stowed in every available nook, so it must be that the holds were full. There were high-prowed warships, their sides lined with shields and men at the oars, with mail shirts and arms close at hand. These were proud ships, with gaudy sails that made a brave showing, but many of them still bore the scars of war.

There were wallowing roundships, squat and low, deeply laden but steadily forging northward. Here there rose to the spying birds the bellowing of cattle, yonder the bleating of sheep and goats, and now and again the shrill whinny of a horse.

A cock crowed bravely, somewhere below decks. The keen ears of the swans detected an answering chorus from his harem of hens.

Children called out to see the beautiful visitors above them. Babies cried, mothers scolded, men shouted orders or talked from ship to ship with battle horns or six-foot lurs meant to carry sound across fjords or far out to sea. All this blended together in one vast diapason of sound rolling on in the van of the fleet.

Under it all, like a whisper, the rush of water against the sides and under the keels, the hum of wind in the taut rigging, and the steady thump of the long oars in their holes.

Gwalchmai and Corenice looked at each other. This orderly gathering of ships had not been blown out of its way by any storm, nor were they fishermen. They were manned by fighting men, retainers of great lords, who stalked those stout decks wearing wadmal, heavy homespun tweed, meant for long use and severe weather. They were gay in long cloaks of bright reds and blues and rich in ornaments of heavy gold or cairngorms set in silver brooches.

This was a fleet that knew where it was going—and these people were coming to stay.

Corenice communed with Gwalchmai. There was only one possible destination for these ships if they held their course, and that was the Bay of Smokes—and only one possible end for the Culdees, the Children of God—thralldom to the Vikings!

If the wind held, they were less than a day's run away. The Celts must be warned.

The two swans beat the air with their broad wings, arching away from the fleet, seeking altitude; then, leveling off, again at an impressive height, they headed north.

The Vikings, taking this as a good sign, followed the direction the birds had taken. With them as their leaders, the dragon-ships plowed on.

Flann was unpleasantly surprised to see Thyra's expression change to the long familiar, but less affectionate look. She left without looking back or giving any reason to him and went back along the path into the hills.

It was not long before she returned and with her was Gwalchmai. They clung to each other fondly as they walked and Flann grunted in disgust and turned to his neglected

work. The couple went directly to the stand where the long
whale bone hung and Gwalchmai beat upon it heavily with
the mallet, calling out the people.

The Culdees came running to the sound. Men and wom-
en left their work and children forgot their play, for they
knew that from this ragged alarm beat no whale had been
sighted or any ordinary council called. This was an alarm and
an urgent one.

Bishop Malachi came hurrying up, his robe hiked high,
to learn what was toward and behind him his chubby little
wife, red-cheeked and panting, easing her tight kirtle. They
paled at the dreadful tidings, but soon recovered.

He cried, "Be of good cheer, brothers and sisters! We
have been in danger before and the pirates have stayed only
a little while and have gone away. We have time to gather
our belongings and seek our hiding places in the West Islands. They will go again and we can wait them out."

Corenice did not dare tell them how she knew, but she
said—and they supposed her to be fey, for they had heard
she had the gift of seeing—

"I see this fleet like a great city moving upon us. It will
settle upon these shores and never go away. If you try
to outwait it, you will all die in thralldom under the whips
of cruel masters. Your daughters will be their playthings
and if your sons resist, they will have the blood-eagle carved
on their backs to the glory of Odin!"

At this they marveled, for all took her to be a girl of
the Norse and were surprised that she spoke thus against
her own people. Only the Bishop sensed something unusual
about her, for he knew her better than most, so he spoke
to her kindly.

"Tell us then what it is in your mind that we must do,
for we have nowhere else to go, unless we steer for Erin
or the lands of the Scoti from whence we were driven.
Surely our lot there will be no better—and we are desperate."

Cornenice replied, "I will let this man describe to you this
land from whence he came and which has not yet been
seen by any Viking raider. Then you may decide whether
or no you will go there to dwell, but if you so decide,
know that agreement must be made quickly for your danger will be upon you by the next sunrise. If you go there
can be no turning back, for no one else shall know of this

land. It is held in reserve for another people. He is the son of a King and carries this knowledge to Rome, to deliver over the whole country into the hands of whomsoever rules the Romans now.

"Yet there is room for you too, for it is a broad holding with fine forests and much wild cattle of all sorts, and there you can live out your lives happy and undisturbed."

So Gwalchmai told them of the country of Alata, where he was born far to the westward, and of the continent of Atala to the south of it, which he knew from travelers' tales only. Being homesick and feeling himself an exile until his mission was accomplished, he painted his descriptions with such bright colors that they sounded as though he spoke of Heaven itself.

Then, when their faces were glowing again with hope and renewed courage, the Bishop returned from his house, where he had gone to fetch a book he treasured, for he had been early convinced that Gwalchmai spoke truth.

As Corenice came out of her pretended trance and Gwalchmai fell silent, for his part of the work was done, the Bishop began to read a passage from the *Voyage of Saint Brandon.*

Now the Bishop loved this book. It was full of marvels and talk of holy things and a little of it was truth. He had never known how to separate fancy from fact, but he believed Gwalchmai spoke truly and it came to him that one passage he loved dearly must be true. So he told the people how the Saint, of whom they had all heard, had sailed northwestward from Mayo, on Erin. He had met with icebergs on the way and monsters, which they too had seen and knew to be walrus, and had come after forty days to a new land, which must be this Alata.

The Saint and his people, in a curragh no better than their own, sailed coasting southerly until—he sought for this favorite passage with his finger and found it—

" 'Then they came out of the dark mist and they saw the loveliest country that anyone could see. Clear it was and lightsome, and there was enough in it of joy, and the trees were full of fruit on every bough—and the delight that they found there could never be told.' "

Bishop Malachi paused and his eyes were moist.

"This is the land our friend has been telling us about. This is the lovely country he wishes to give us for a home.

This is the safe refuge where our enemies may never come. It is far away, but I mean to spend my last days there. If I can reach it, I shall praise God every morning and every night for His mercy and his kindness in sending our saviors to us.

"Now those who would come with me and my wife—gather your gear, man your ships, and—out oars for Alata!"

There was no hanging back, for there were no laggards. The Bishop's enthusiasm was contagious. Children ran to clear the huts of goods, utensils, and food. Men and women worked together through the long evening and the short night, stopping only briefly to eat. Everything was carried down to the beach, just below the tidal mark, and piled there to be loaded.

By morning, it could be seen that the work would not be finished in time. The three wooden curraghs, able to carry sixty people each, had long been idle in the hidden harbors of the West Islands, and much needed to be done before they could sail upon a long voyage. The hide boats, having been in constant use, were in better condition, but most of these were too small.

Very distantly, those with the keener hearing could discern the sound far out to sea which brought them panic. It was the Viking lurs, bellowing from ship to ship, talking musically of the new land. Although the dragon-ships could not be seen from the beach, their crews must have been able to see the snow-capped peaks that were their landfall. Soon they would be racing in to be first at the best land-taking, and the wind was behind them.

The Culdees did not slacken their efforts. New cordage of stout walrus hide had already replaced what was beyond repair. Sails of thinly scraped sealskin were ready to be run up when the lading was finished. The sheep had been gathered for loading and some were already on board, when Corenice, with lips trembling for the first time since Gwalchmai had met her, said, "We are too late!"

The striped sails were lifting over the horizon.

Flann said, bitterly, gazing out to sea, "I would I were where I could buy a wind from a Finn. It should sink that fleet before it came an ell closer!"

A thought occurred to Gwalchmai. "You shall have your wind, friends. My godfather was Lord of the Winds!"

He went a little apart from the others and took off his ring.

In extremely tiny letters on the inner band, intertwined like braided hair, was an inscription cut into the red gold. Following it, like a signature, was stamped a minuscule constellation no man had ever seen from earth.

Gwalchmai, facing the sea, read out the spell in a low voice and pointed the longer part of the constellation like a spearhead at the hurrying ships. Some had already broken away from the greater mass and were far in advance of the others.

Nothing happened at first. Then a little bat appeared, fluttering erratically as though blinded by the rising sun. It circled the head of Gwalchmai and chirped at him, its fangs clashing.

Gwalchmai whispered to it, still reading the involved script. It took a straight course out to sea toward the ships and, aiding it, an offshore breeze began to blow, increasing to a heavy wind.

Now the distant sails were taken in and the waves took on a sluggish majesty, as the ships forged on over the rollers, under a slate-gray sky, hindered by being unable to tack, but not stopped.

Gwalchmai slipped the ring back on his finger.

"Now you have a little more time," he said to the Bishop.

Out of the quiet Bay of Smokes slipped the small flotilla, heading westward with hope and faith, toward an unknown haven.

Three little wooden ships, laden heavily. Twenty small hide curraghs seemingly fit for only ponds and lakes, but rising buoyantly, valiantly following the wake of the larger vessels. These too bore heavy loads of people and of gear, for there was no one left behind except Flann, Corenice–Thyra, and Gwalchmai, who stood upon the deck of their fishing boat, watching them go.

Gwachmai whispered again to the winds. A strong gust bellied out the sealskin sails and pushed the ships toward the unknown west. Now they were free and exposed, but the headland still hid them from the Viking colonists. They took a northward bearing to keep the high mass of Iceland between themselves and their enemies.

The three companions looked around reflectively. Rubbish

littered the beach—stove-in curraghs, a floating oar, broken staffs, a forgotten crozier, bells, a child's rattle, and a burst-open bale of fox furs. Because there had been no time to pick them up, a few priceless books had been discarded or left behind. They fluttered their torn leaves in the wind. There was a lost doll stretching out her wooden arms.

They embarked in their own boat and raised the lug-sail. The wind filled it roundly, but the knorr, being able to tack, sailed off upon a course that would keep them also out of sight, but would in the end bring them to Norway.

The Viking fleet was very close. Their horns echoed against the mountains by the time the Culdee squadron was hull down upon the horizon. Gwalchmai could no longer see them.

"I promised my father that I would return with a great army and a noble array of Roman sail to take and hold Alata," he said, in self-contempt. "I cannot yet go home and what have I sent?"

"Two hundred and seventy-nine of the Children of God!" said Flann.

5

The Spae-wife

There was debate as to the direction in which they should travel. Gwalchmai, who was commissioned to seek out the Emperor of Rome to deliver the message from his father, and who must now do so verbally, wished to reach Rome in the quickest and most direct way. He hoped to avoid hindrance or trouble on his journey.

He would have preferred to travel by land rather than risk further danger by sea.

Flann, on the other hand, liked well his new freedom

and although he had little expectation of convincing the
others, Erin now tugged at his heartstrings. There he could
forget Thyra and her unpredictable moods. He had little
doubt that she would cling, in the future, to this fascinating
and glamorous stranger. She had rescued him and in some
strange way she belonged to him.

Flann was resigned to the thought, but very unhappy. He
wanted to go home and the shortest way was by sea.

Thyra also voted for a voyage, but to the Faroes, her
birthplace. To her mind, when not influenced by Corenice, the islands were her native land. Norway she feared,
for there was still fighting going on. Because of her father's family ties in high places, she must inevitably be
forced to choose sides in the quarrel between the jarls and
the King. Either way she would be forced into a marriage
for political purposes and her mind had been made up
since the death of Biarki. But of that, she kept her own
counsel.

Corenice was the only one who did not need to make a
decision. Her point of view was very simple. Wherever
Gwalchmai went, she would go.

To settle the question, Gwalchmai, as the one chiefly
concerned, must decide.

While thinking, they had been running south on a long
tack. The Viking fleet was out of sight and presumably had
landed, but if they were to come about and make for the
Norwegian coast they might meet laggards and perhaps be
captured. Possibly it would be better to set a course for
the Faroes and tarry there until sure that the seas were
safe.

He turned the ring absently on his finger. He studied it,
considering the course. The stone, a magnificent fire-opal,
the size of a hazelnut, was cut cabochon and the convex
surface caught the sun, flashing rays of red and green into
his eyes.

This bezel, for it was engraved intaglio with Merlin Ambrosius' monogram, had an M and A intertwined so that
the bar of the A formed a Christian cross, with the central
V of the M. It was held in the thick gold hoop by a surrounding ring marked by the Druidic mistletoe and sickle.

He knew that the jewel could be used as a speculum
and although he had never tried to foresee the future or

had need to determine a course of action in that manner, he knew the principle of scrying and it was obvious he could obtain help in no other way. Had he known that the stone had been mined in the Faroes, the thought might have deterred him. Perhaps it too might like to go home! So indeed it seemed to prove.

Bidding all to silence, he concentrated his vision and his thoughts upon the gleaming opal. There was nothing to distract him but the wind in the rigging and the slap of waves against the sides of the boat.

The sounds grew fainter. The outside world receded from him. The bright colors of the stone became dim. A milky cloud swept over it.

The cloud eddied and swirled in the depths of the opal. It was a thickening fog—it took on shape as it hardened into form. It was a face, looking up at him as from a deep well, but it was not his own reflection. Merlin's face, as he remembered it as a little boy!

The bearded lips parted, smiling, and he heard a voice infinitely far and as tiny as the hum of a midge say: "Go to the Spae-wife at Brendansvik and you will be told what to do."

Then a piece of driftwood struck the side of the boat with a sullen thump. The sound interrupted his trance-like reverie. The face disappeared into cloud and the cloud became a tenuous wisp and vanished. He was back in the world again and the stone gleamed only red and green.

It seemed to him that he had been gone a long time, but he knew his experience had lasted the space of but a few breaths.

His thought came to Corenice, who communed with Thyra without words. "Yes, there was a harbor near Stromsey called Brendansvik, because Brendan, the Navigator, whom the Celts called Saint, was reputed to have touched there upon his first voyage."

Flann knew nothing of the mental conversation or any decision, but he was disappointed when Gwalchmai spoke to him at the tiller: "Hold your course south, steady as we go until we reach your islands. We must land at your starting place."

This was the end of hope for Flann. He felt that he was returning only to be a thrall.

With fair winds and under a pleasant summer sky, the knorr made good speed toward the Faroes, but time dragged for the voyagers.

Flann had brought along one of the damaged books on the beach and sometimes he read quietly to Gwalchmai and the girl, instructing them in his faith. Much of what he heard was familiar to the Aztlanian, for Merlin, his godfather, had been a Christianized Druid and had possessed books on many subjects, which Ventidius Varro, Gwalchmai's father, had taught his son to read.

What she heard was new to Thyra and it fascinated her. At such times Corenice withdrew from her mind, for she loved her Atlantidean goddess, Ahuni-i, the Spirit of the Wave, and would have no other allegiance. So it was that, with a sisterly consideration and delicate courtesy, she slept at that time and Flann's words fell mainly upon Thyra's ears alone.

As he read, he did not realize that he was courting Thyra by the selections he chose, but the girl understood the deeper meanings beneath the rolling and majestic phrases and thrilled to the timbre of his voice. She drew nearer to him at such times.

There were other hours when it was Thyra who slept and Corenice spoke with Gwalchmai inaudibly, for since the swan-flight they were spiritually as one.

So, when Flann stood his watch Thyra was with him always, and if he slept, the other two were together. Thus, there was small jealousy on Flann's part, for there was little he saw to feed jealousy. There was within him only that sad happiness known as love.

A stone tower stood high at Brendansvik and it was supposed to have been erected by Brendan and his fellow monks. It was somewhat in disrepair, but habitable, and in it lived a woman whose name was Fimmilene. She was reputed to be a spae-wife.

There was some mystery about her. People said that she was of noble birth and had fled Norway rather than pay homage to Harald Fairhair. Others believed that she had seen and told too much when she should have kept silent and thus had made powerful enemies who sought her life. There were also those who claimed that she was secretly inclined toward the new faith and was in hiding from Thor's wrath. In support of this, it was marked that she had no dislike of dwelling in a building that had been lived in by Christian men.

All agreed upon one thing—that she had the gift of seeing and that she saw true. Therefore she was much in demand, both as a soothsayer and a finder of lost articles, and she never lacked for food.

When she went abroad she wore a robe of black wolfskin and polished boots of calfhide, with dangling tassels that were little human skulls carved from narwhal ivory. She was never seen without, unless her narrow hands were covered by her long gloves of white catskin. Upon these the claws still showed and appeared at times to either be flexed or withdrawn.

Folk wondered if she were a turncoat and ran the woods at night as either wolf or cat. No one ever was curious enough to ask, for one glance from those piercing eyes below her black hood, lined with lambskin, was enough to deter the most inquisitive and people did not like to meet her eyes directly. They were never sure how deeply she could read the secrets they wished to keep hidden when she looked into their eyes.

When the knorr sailed into Brendansvik, the three had already eaten and so needed not pause in seeking out the weird woman. This was well, for what loiterers there were at the waterfront were mightily taken with the strangers. Some of these knew Flann and Thyra, although this was not their home port, but none had ever seen such a man as companioned them, who carried an antique short sword and a flint ax for weapons and who was so oddly appareled in brightly beaded leather. Here and there, one would fain have questioned the group upon the missing Skeggi and Biarki, but without pausing the three hurried away and found the stone tower of the spae-wife.

The upper edge of the tower was crumbled and ragged. The roof was still sound, and the stout door was thick and made of new wood. It swung open noiselessly at their approach and they went in.

There was no warder, but it seemed that they were expected. A pleasant contralto voice bade them enter. A short hallway led into a large room comprising the remainder of the lower floor. Polar bear skins served as rugs, and a cresset with flaming knots of Norway pine gave added light

to that which a large fireplace flung, for stone walls are
sometimes cold and damp, even in summer.

The room was furnished sparely. A refectory table of
the old monks stood in the center, flanked by benches. A
brown, cracked mammoth's tusk hung upon the curving wall
that faced them and beneath its arch stood a high platform, elevated several feet above the stone floor. Upon this
dais was an oaken chair, intricately carven, and in it sat
the spae-wife, Fimmilene, gazing into a crystal ball upon a
small stand, over which was draped a scarf of dark purple
Chinese silk embroidered with dragons in golden thread.

As they entered, a raven with a split tongue cried out,
"Here come the ghosts!" and flapped his wings wildly, dancing back and forth upon the perch to which he was fastened with a chain, eyeing them wickedly sidelong as he did
so.

The spae-wife did not raise her head, but continued looking into the ball. She said, "Peace, Mimir," in an absent
way as though it mattered little whether he obeyed or not.
He fell silent, watching the strangers in a malicious manner as though he was something more than bird and ever
and again chuckling low in his throat.

Fimmilene kept her position for a moment longer, then
sighed as though weary and stood up, beckoning them to
approach.

She was slim and beautiful and at first they took her to
be young. Her clinging silken gown was a smoky crimson
and covered with glittering stones that picked up the color
of the cloth like a myriad red watching eyes from which
the light from the flames was reflected as she moved, spar-
kling the walls and ceiling with tiny rainbows.

Then they perceived that such beauty as hers was ageless,
for her hair was as white as her catskin gloves and her
eyes and smile were old and very knowing. This was not
a woman whom it would be easy to deceive. It was perhaps fortunate that they came seeking information, instead
of trying to withhold it.

Flann she dismissed casually as being of little importance.
Corenice then being dominant, the girl was favored with
a sharp glance as of one equal to another, but Gwalchmai
she studied intently.

"So here you all are," she said finally and sat down
again, studying them with her chin in her hand and her el-

bows upon the stand. "I have been advised of the coming of you three. The Irishman who perhaps does not believe in magic; the Norse girl who houses magic—of a sort; and the man who has studied magic, but does not know yet how to use it well, or wisely.

"Ask then what you came to ask and leave me, but remember that the answers come from a greater one than I am, or you, Wanderer, who have thus far failed and are doomed to fail again, can ever hope to be."

Yet, as she spoke, she smiled upon Gwalchmai with good humor, and the smile transformed her face and took some of the sternness out of her words.

"Truly," she mused, "you are goodly to look upon, as I was told. You must have eaten of those apples of Hel, which keep the gods young."

Now, at this, she motioned him to come up and look into the crystal ball, and as he did so, Corenice, who had taken an instant dislike to Fimmilene, went up with him and stood beside him, for she was jealous of this aged woman's young and ageless beauty.

Flann also stood upon the girl's other side, although his heart was hammering, lest Thyra should think him more easily daunted than his rival.

The spae-wife chuckled, for she knew what each was thinking.

"Look then, into the ball, in the name of the Great Mother, and think of your question and not of me. Each of you shall see what you came to see, whether or no it may be what you would like to learn." And as she spoke, she passed her hand above the sphere and in it pictures began to form.

Now it seemed as these began that each was holding the spae-wife by the hand and with her was journeying alone, for the others disappeared from them. Thus the pictures became realities to them and they passed separately into a strange land as her spirit led the way.

There was a place of terrible cold and darkness through which they traveled and there were barriers of fire from which they shrank and cringed, but through these dangers they passed unharmed and came into another world.

Then, to each, it appeared as though many spirits thronged around them, although each saw and spoke with different ones.

Corenice felt herself held in the arms of her father, who
had died when Poseidonis sank and Atlantis disappeared.
They talked long and it was a happy time, but to her it
was as one who listens in a dream and can remember nothing when it was over.

Then came another who greeted her kindly and spoke of
things to come and this she did not forget, for she held
this knowledge to be a promise. These things she kept in
her heart, for they concerned herself and Gwalchmai only
and she told no one, not even he at that time.

Thyra looked into the future also and she did remember,
but when she was mistress of her own body again, she looked
upon Flann with an increased shyness and would not tell
him what she had seen.

Flann likewise was silent and went away from that place
mused and in doubt, but later he came to believe in the
spae-wife more than he did that day.

To Gwalchmai came spirits out of the old time. They
had ruddy skin and dark eyes; they wore feathers and had
painted faces and they passed him by to the thump of a
shaman's drum, but all smiled upon him, for all had loved
him long ago. Then came two who were unhappy, for they
were his father and mother, who had bid him godspeed
upon his mission, which had failed—and although he knew
it had been through no fault of his own, he felt their disappointment and was sad. They also passed into the stream
of spirits who crowded by and they disappeared from his
view.

Lastly to him appeared an aged man in the robes of a mage
and he knew that this was Merlin, to whom he must speak,
for this face he had seen in the bezel of the ring.

He placed himself in front of Merlin, or so he thought
in his vision, and would have tugged his hand loose from
the grasp of the spae-wife, so that he might embrace his
godfather, but she held it tightly and would not let go.

Gwalchmai said, "I have come where you told me to
come. What word have you for me?"

Merlin bent a stern gaze upon him, under heavy brows,
and Gwalchmai felt as though he were again a very small
child.

"Apprentice, I have work for you to do and in this you
must succeed. You shall go to Rome as was planned, but
it will avail you nothing to take your message there, con-

cerning Alata. Rome no longer has an Emperor, nor is that city more than a city now. It can send no fleet, nor does it need one.

"Therefore you must seek elsewhere to deliver your message to a ruler with power to accomplish the desire of your father that Alata shall be reached by, and belong to, men who need a refuge.

"As I have an equal interest in this accomplishment, it is my will that this must be a Christian monarch only, nor shall any other take and hold this land.

"However, as this deed may take you longer than you will at present believe, there is no immediate haste and I have an errand for you to perform as you go upon your way.

You must go to Elveron, the Land of Faery, which the Romans called Mona. Here was the last stand of the Druids, in their defense, and in gratitude Elveron holds Arthur's sword, Excalibur.

"Sir Bedwyr, Arthur's trusted knight, left it there when he knew himself close on death, to be guarded by the fay, until the last great battles of the world when Arthur shall rise and will lead the hosts, who possess British blood, against their foes. Then he will need his sword again.

"The little people are planning to leave Elveron for a kindlier planet. This beloved Earth will not much longer be a happy place for them to dwell. There will be clanking machines and polluted waters and flaming winds. There will be no sweet clean air for them to breathe in this coming Iron Age, which men are soon to create.

"You must obtain Excalibur from them, carry it to Arthur's tomb and place it beside him, that he may have it in safety until the day of his need. I think you are magician enough for that, neophyte!

"Now firstly, when you reach Mona, you must seek out the barrow of Getain, who was a Sea-King of that island some while after your sweetling's time. He was slain in battle against the Fomorians and was brought home and there laid in howe. His tomb is the secret entrance to Elveron.

"Your ring will give you entry, but not without fee. Thor holds the elvish torque which once lay in Fafnir's bed, and guarding it is sleepless Mimingus, the Satyr of the Wood, whom you must make your friend.

"When you have obtained the torque, it will be the price you pay to enter Elveron, but first you must appease the

Loathly Dogs. Likewise, there are Watchers set over Arthur's tomb who may or may not approve of you, but you have read how to protect yourself against them.

"Secondly, you must be on your guard in all your journeyings against Oduarpa, the Lord of the Dark Face. He is greatly powerful in the world and my most ancient enemy. Long ago, he came to earth, bent upon evil. Men confuse him with Satan and some worship him to their cost, but he is no fallen angel. No!

"He is kin to those who dwell in the underworld and below the surface of the ground you place yourself in his power. He is most patient. When he learns, as he undoubtedly will, that you seek to accomplish my desires, he will bide his time to do you both an injury. Should you fall into sin, you place yourself in his power—and there are many kinds of sin.

"Thirdly, I now set a geas upon you and these are the terms of it. If you break one clause, you break all, and you will know sorrow. Therefore, attend.

"You must enter Elveron alone, for the signet of the ring will open the door for only one.

"You must take nothing out of Elveron except the sword which was forged by the Lady of the Lake, but which belongs to men.

"She may try in some way to get it back. Anything you carry upon you from the Land of Faery will weaken your grasp upon the sword. You cannot be strong in both realms.

"For the same reason, you must not eat or drink anything you are offered, however you may be coaxed, or how delicious it appears, during all the time you are in Elveron. The fay are not wicked, but they are mischievous. They will trick you if they can, meaning you no harm.

"Now go, my godson of whom I am proud, and obey your geas!"

"Stay, Godfather! I have so much to ask you!" cried Gwalchmai as Merlin retreated into the crowd of moving spirits.

"One question, then." He paused an instant. "Be brief."

"Your own tomb was found empty when it was opened. Did you truly die as we know death? Did you find the Land of the Dead you were seeking in the West? Is this place I see, Mictlampa, from whence the Azteca say they came up from below?"

"You have asked three questions instead of one, apprentice. When you have learned more and if we meet again, instruct me in the meaning of life and I will expound to you the mystery of death. Until then, farewell!"

With that, he disappeared into the crowd.

Gwalchmai snatched his hand away from the spae-wife's clasp. In that instant the world he knew came rushing back upon him. The spirits disappeared and he stood dazed and bewildered before the crystal ball. The spae-wife had not moved from the chair.

She swept them with an infinitely weary glance and motioned them away.

"I have traveled farther with you than I have ever journeyed before. Do not return, for I wish never to see you again, nor do I think that it would be well for us to meet, lest upon another such wandering none of us find the way back. Also I think that we have been watched by one who is no friend to any here.

"Go then, as you have been commissioned, and stay not. Do not forget that to enter where you wish to go, you must first bribe the Warder and feed the Hounds of Hell. For myself, no payment is required. I need nothing that you have."

So they went out silently, each thinking his own thoughts.

Now Gwalchmai did not know where his mentor had intended him to secure the torque with which he must reward the folk of Elveron for their guardianship of Excalibur. When he asked Corenice she knew no more than he, but the two girls communed together and Thyra told her of the temple of Thor on Stromsey that had been erected there by Thorgeir, the Viking, when he brought his people and wealth there from Norway, to spite Harald Fairhair.

It had many precious things in it and should have needed no guard, for few men were bold enough to affront Thor, the Thunderer, in his own house, especially when they must risk the perils of the sea to escape from Stromsey, which is an island.

Yet, since Thor was busy about the world, a guard had been set and, knowing this, Gwalchmai prepared a gift to win his friendship.

It took a little time, but by night it was ready and Gwalchmai led the way, bearing a covered dish of rough earthenware that had never been touched by any metal or been glazed by salt.

The little group met no one when they entered Thor's grove by moonlight and came to his temple. Only Thyra was once affrighted when a night-jar flew up shrieking, for she was divided in her thoughts whether the old gods or the new were the more powerful and this bird might have been the shape-shifting Odin in one of his avatars.

The door posts of Thor's temple were richly carved with snakes that seemed to writhe as they passed between them. His chair, made from a witch oak grown near Blokula until smitten with the lightning of Thor's hammer, at first seemed empty.

As they came beneath the lintel of the door they saw that this was not so, for in it sat, intently staring at them, what they first thought to be a shaggy man, until he rose and it became apparent that, if he were at all human, it was from his waist up to his curly crown. Below that, he was beast. His legs bent the wrong way and hooves clacked on the flagstones. As he moved quickly toward them, tittering, his yellow eyes gloated upon the girl.

Gwalchmai lifted the lid of the dish and held it out to the clutching hands. The satyr's gaze dropped. He snatched and snuffed with flaring nostrils at the steaming contents. He plunged his face greedily into the depths of the dish.

Gwalchmai spoke in soothing tones. "See, Mimingus, we are friends. We bring food for poor, hungry Mimingus, whom everyone neglects. Everything good is for Thor—the baked meats, the boiled meats, the rich pastries! Who thinks of Mimingus, but we who are his friends?

"Eat, dear friend Mimingus. Here are hearts of beef and sheep, hearts of mouse and mole and toad—all tasty food to make you happy and strong. Here are hearts of flying things, seagull and thrush and peewit—all fit to lift your spirits—and hearts of snake and fish and eel. When you eat the delicious morsels, you will feel a kinship with all living things, for all living things, in this way, will become a part of you. Because we love you, we give you our best and you shall have it all. Eat, Mimingus!"

And eat the satyr did, hunkered down on the stones, stuffing himself avidly, cramming his mouth full with greasy hands, casting his goat eyes from side to side in quick glances, lest this generosity be regretted and it be taken from him.

Only once, he muttered, "Dear friends, when you come again, remember—man's heart is best of all!"

Gwalchmai stepped softly to Thor's chair. Hanging upon its high back, waiting ready should the Thunder-god desire to wear it, was the heavy golden torque the three had come to seek.

As he laid hand upon it, lightning flashed distantly from a cloudless sky. Thunder grumbled far away, but Gwalchmai seized the torque with boldness and twisted it in a spiral around the biceps of his left arm. Then, chuckling with impish humor, he scratched a long-armed cross upon the back of the chair with the point of his sword. Under it he traced the monogram of Merlin, as it was carved upon his ring.

The thunder did not peal again, but the three hastened away to their boat, leaving the satyr still feeding, back turned to them. By morning, they were far from the Faroes and on the way to Mona.

Skirting the Shetlands, the knorr put in briefly at the Orkneys, where Lavran Harvaddsson, Thyra's uncle, gave them good cheer and they stayed at Stromness a short week. After they were rested, they sailed on southward through the Minch, without seeing kelpies or water-bulls or those dangerous Blue Men who delight to sink ships in that narrow gut. They made landfall again on the island of Barra, in the Hebrides.

Skarphedinn, the aged brother of Lavran's wife, sheltered them for a day and night, and kept them up late with gossip, for he also thought well of Thyra Skeggisdatter. When they left this island, they also left the edge of Viking-controlled waters.

When they entered the North Channel, it was after dark and with trepidation, for neither the men of Erin nor the Scots would give anything but scant mercy to a single Norse boat. They made most of the journey by night, hid on a little island during the next day, and by the time it was morning again they had reached the isle of Eubonia.

By traveling thus rapidly, it seemed that although they had incurred the anger of Thor they had thus far avoided the consequences, but now a terrific storm burst upon them. They had no difficulty in finding Eubonia—they ran into it. Fortunately they grounded on a fine beach where they were able to pull up the boat without damage. The next morning they were offered shelter by patrolling sentries in Jarl Orry's service when they found that the travelers were not loyal to the King of Norway.

Jarl Orry had taken the island from the Welsh, but later set up an independent kingdom there. When he learned the strangers' errand and that Gwalchmai had a smattering of magic, he would have liked well to keep them with him. It would have pleased him much to hold the land under mist to hide it from Harald Fairhair, as Mannanan-Beg-Mac-y-Lheirr had done, before Arthur's nephew Maelgwyn expelled the Scoti. However, when he found that Thor bore ill will toward them, he no longer urged their staying, but provisioned their boat in all haste and set them on their way again.

They made southerly coasting until nightfall, then steering by the stars struck out straight south into the Hibernian Sea. Just before morning, they made a safe landing upon Mona, having seen no boats during this run of over fifty miles.

They poled the knorr into a shallow winding channel issuing from a marsh, lowered the mast, and covered all with reeds. Then they set out to find the barrow of Getain, where lay the entrance to Elveron.

Fortunately they were in friendly country, for Mona was under the rule of the Prince of North Wales. Because the Irish were presently at peace and wandered the country freely, Flann had no difficulty in obtaining directions from a pretty cowgirl he met. Most women admired his tall figure and he had never been tongue-tied with any except Thyra.

He traded a copper coin for a piggin of milk, having bought pitcher and all for it and could have had a kiss to boot had he pressed his good fortune. He went away whistling and found the others where they were hiding, for until then they were not sure of their welcome—Corenice, because of Thyra's golden hair, and Gwalchmai, by reason of his clothes. Still, the latter was again among a dark people and only his height set him apart.

"We are in great luck!" announced Flann. "Only an hour's fast walk from here there are two cromlechs called the Twins and passing between them, sighting toward the east, lies the Sea-King's barrow. Can you not tell us why you must go there? The girl said no one goes near it and it must be a dree place."

Now if Flann had known that this was a country of the Sidhe, as the Irish called the little people, had he any choice he would not have come this far. And this both Gwalchmai and Corenice knew. Corenice had kept this one fact from Thyra's mind, lest she tell him, though in all other matters those two had no secrets and were in sympathy with each other.

So Gwalchmai made answer only that there the spae-wife had bid him take Thor's torque and place it in Getain's tomb, from whence it had been stolen, his errand once accomplished, their mission would be at an end and he could go on alone.

With this Flann was satisfied. He had not liked being in company with the purloined necklace, for he felt that luck was not in it. Moreover, to be alone with Thyra and free to go anywhere at all was his greatest desire and much more than he had hoped. So he made no objections, but went back after more milk and likewise bought a black hen, for Gwalchmai had need of both.

When they came to the cromlech Twins, they saw that these were the only standing stones of what was originally a large circle. Gwalchmai knew at once, from his readings in Merlin's books, that this barrow was incredibly ancient. Getain might indeed have been laid there, but it was not a howe that had been built for him.

As night approached there were stealthy snuffling sounds without the circle and a padding of huge soft feet or paws, which continually trod heavily some round of their own, just beyond their limits of vision, though as it grew darker, the sounds came closer. Occasionally they heard the click of long nails upon bare stone and thus they knew it was no trick of fancy, but that some actual presence was there, guarding the entrance to Elveron. Yet they felt that they were in no danger, provided the entrance was left undisturbed.

Without coming closer to the high mound of the barrow in the center of the circle, Gwalchmai cut off the head of the black hen and let the blood flow into the pitcher of milk. When the wings had ceased flapping, he threw the carcass far outside the circle and instantly he heard running feet, a deep growl, and a crunching, as the hen was snapped up, bones and all, by the unseen guardian.

Flann whispered fearfully; "The Dogs! The Loathly Dogs of Annwn!" He made his ax ready and peered about, waiting for the attack, but none came.

Gwalchmai stirred the blood thoroughly into the milk and ran with it toward the barrow. As he did so, Flann and the girl felt a great sinewy body bound between them following after, hurling them to either side. It ran across the greensward without noise, and somehow this was more frightening than the sounds of stalking that had dismayed them while they waited for the proper hour of sunset.

There was a great rough stone upon the mound. On its upper face a sun wheel had been carved in ancient times and where its boss should have been a deep cup was instead hollowed out in the wheel's center. Into this, Gwalchmai poured the milk.

At that instant he felt himself seized by a pair of massive jaws, which closed about his chest and raised him from the ground, shaking him like a rat, while the thing snarled in fury.

He heard Corenice and Flann running in toward him. He cried out, in gasping desperation, "Back! Back! For your soul's lives!"

It did not stop them from coming to his rescue, but it halted them for a few steps, and in that time he brought up the arm holding Thor's torque and laid it against the creature's cold and scaly muzzle.

He heard it sniff at the gold; then the jaws released the terrible pressure, the giant head dipped and laid him gently down upon the ground.

Corenice and Flann came and lifted him. The thing whined and fawned upon them in apology, rubbing up against the group like a monstrous cat. They waited for what might befall. All this while they saw nothing, but soon they heard the sound of lapping, a long contented sigh, and the beast was gone.

The moon rose late that night, but when the rays fell cleanly upon the barrow the three rolled away the stone. Beneath it was an entrance framed in rock slabs and steps that led down.

Gwalchmai turned to the others in farewell.

"Here I must go on alone, but I shall return when I have done what I must do. Wait for me."

They nodded, without speaking, for their hearts were full.

Torches had already been prepared, for Gwalchmai knew what he was to find. Now one was lit. He and Corenice exchanged one lingering glance. They did not touch each other and there was no other farewell. Close as they were, no embrace could have meant more to them than that look of understanding and union.

Then he was gone—down into that midnight world of Getain's barrow.

They waited. Dawn came, but he did not return. The sun shone hot overhead at noon. They remained inside the stone circle but did not follow him down. Birds flew overhead, bees buzzed, and once a rabbit came and fed close by since they lay so quiet—waiting.

Through another night and another day they watched. They had nothing to eat or drink and the stars wheeled overhead and paled and it was the third morning. Then they knew, against all hoping, that some ill had befallen Gwalchmai and that he would not come.

Faint with hunger, they returned to the boat to find water and food for their bodies' need and as the two walked despondently on, Corenice and Thyra communed.

Corenice said (but Flann heard no words), "Little sister, who are so much a part of me, I have kept my promise that I made you. It was a harder thing to do than you can know, but you are as you were and you can go to your lover with no loss of pride."

It was as though Thyra whispered (but again Flann heard nothing), "I know what you have done and what you have not done, and I love you for it—but what you will do now, if I go, I do not know. I do not know and I fear for you, for you are also a part of me."

Then it seemed to each as though the two embraced, understanding each other in this sad moment of parting more than they ever had before, and Corenice said, "I shall wait, as I waited before—as he asked me to wait, forever if it need be. What else can anyone who loves do for her man? Yet, before you and I leave each other, I will make you both a gift so that you will know no more sorrow."

Then she spoke through Thyra's lips and said, "Flann!"

And when Flann paused and turned, for he was walking ahead of the girl, he felt her palms against his eyes and suddenly he forgot what he had seen since he first landed in Iceland.

She placed her palms against his ears and he forgot what he had heard and felt upon all that long journey since he had begun it in the Faroes and had come upon the shores of Mona.

Then she stroked his brow and breathed upon it and new memories came to him—how he had stolen Thyra away from Biarki, who had slain Skeggi, and whom he hated. He remembered that they had fled in a small boat and now were not far from Erin and his ancestral home—but still he was not sure she loved him, for that was not a false memory any magic could place in a man's mind. Not even the very ancient magic of Atlantis.

Thyra felt herself alone, and a little fieldmouse scurried away into the grass beside the path they trod, but as it went it stopped and looked back briefly. All at once she knew the same memories as Flann had. She turned away from the mouse, for it meant nothing to her and Flann was now all her world. So they went on together, back to the boat, not remembering where they had been or why they had left it—and as they walked they did so hand in hand. After they had eaten, they poled the boat down the channel into the sea and the question was—where should they go?

Flann was unsure of himself still. It seemed that just beyond the edges of his memory there was something he had not quite forgotten and it perplexed and worried him.

Finally he said, "Are you sorry that you came with me? Would you rather I set you ashore or took you back to Stromsey?"

Thyra looked demurely upon him and said, "What is your will that I should do? Does a stolen girl have any choice where she may go? What would you have me do?"

Flann said, "My land of Erin is a green, fair land and there are not many girls in it with long golden hair and a beauty such as yours. Surely there you would be as a princess and everyone would love and admire you and no one more than myself. Yet, if it is your wish, I will take you back to your home, for well I know that there is no such sickness as that longing."

To this Thyra made no direct answer, but she said, "Do

you still have the book from which you read me tales on our long trip?" (For this was one of the memories Corenice had left intact in her mind.)

When Flann had fetched the book she searched it for a picture she remembered and said, "Read here."

And he read: " 'Intreat me not to leave thee, or to return from following after thee: for whither thou goest, I will go; and where thou lodgest, I will lodge.' "

He looked up and said, "Oh, Thyra!" But she only said, "Read on." And he read: " 'Thy people shall be my people, and thy God my God: Where thou diest, will I die, and there will I be buried.' "

A sob came in his throat and he could not go on—so Thyra finished for him, as she had memory of the lovely words: " 'Not but death part thee and me.' "

He looked up and saw her as through a mist, but still he could not believe and he said, "Could you really love a man who has been a slave?"

She said, "Oh, Flann! There was never a time when I looked upon you that I ever saw a thrall!"

And after that, for a long time, the boat sailed on toward Erin, by itself.

6

The Land of the Little

When Gwalchmai reached the bottom of the steps, he found that he was at the entrance to a long passage. The slabs of rock forming the sides and roof were of megalithic proportions. The light of his torch did not reach the chamber he knew must lie at the end of the passageway.

He went forward with caution. He had some dread of this underground adventure, mindful of Merlin's warning that in such places Oduarpa, Lord of the Dark Face, held greater power than upon the surface. Remembering tomb mounds of Alata, in the valley of the Ohion, and the traps set there for robbers, he felt his way step by cautious step.

He was alone. No one could follow to help him. Merlin's books had told of the pyramids of Egypt and of tilting slabs that would drop the unwary to their death in pits of unguessable depths.

A passage such as this could lead to unknown horror, if Oduarpa was aware of his entry. Had a bat, or a mouse, gone ahead of him, Gwalchmai would have taken it for a psychopomp guiding his soul to the underworld, but nothing moved except shadows.

He was afraid, but he went on.

Suddenly he came into the chamber. The passage had been less than one hundred feet, but it had seemed much farther. He realized that he must be quite deep in the earth, for the mound above had not been of great size and it must be the domed roof of the chamber—a dome formed by overlapping the successive courses of the side walls, which here were formed of smaller slabs, untrimmed and un-ornamented.

The roof soared upward at least twenty feet above him and the room itself must have been thirty feet across. It looked, from inside, much like one of the beehive huts of the Culdees.

There was nothing in it but a stone burial kist. It was obvious that grave robbers had been busy, but long before Gwalchmai's arrival. The stone cover of the kist had been tilted aside and the bones within scattered irreverently about the floor of the chamber. There were no articles of value to be seen—no rings, no bracelets, no amber such as the seafarers loved. There was not even a scrap of armor. Gwalchmai wondered if this was indeed the tomb of Getain, pirate and King.

He had an innate respect for the dead. He did not want to search the room and splinter the desecrated skeleton beneath his feet. Yet he must seek out the entrance to the Kingdom of the Fay, which obviously lay still deeper. He picked up the bones and arranged them in the kist, in such order as he could.

An amused voice interrupted his labor. "Well! The old fellow looks better now than he has for many a year!"

Gwalchmai had not heard anyone enter. He looked up, startled.

A slender youth, clad all in green from pointed toes to his peaked cap set off with a long scarlet feather, stood opposite him against the far wall. He leaned there negligently, his shapely legs, in their long hose, crossed casually and one hand upon his hip. He wore a jerkin, slashed and purfled, through which a fine cambric shirt showed its folds, having been teased through these slits, and across his broad chest a leather strap supported the cithern slung upon his back.

At his side hung a poniard, seemingly not of metal, but of some hard wood.

He straightened his limbs and made a leg at Gwalchmai, bowing low and sweeping the floor with his cap.

"You may call me Huon, Sir Gwalchmai. I am to guide you to my Queen, in Elveron. Are you ready to come with me now?"

"You know who I am?"

Huon had a musical laugh. "Surely all in Elfdom know by now of the famed Sir Gwalchmai, Hawk of Battle, and his mission. We have been advised of your coming long ago and an entertainment has been arranged for you. Will you follow me?"

"Where are you taking me?" Gwalchmai was suspicious of this delicate-looking, languid fellow, for he had been warned against tricks and mischief. Not all ogres and woodwooses appeared, at first sight, in their proper form. Kobolds, gnomes, and trolls lived underground, but he had thought to find the fay in an airier, lighter place.

"Oh, wherever you wish to go." Huon waved a casual hand as though he had all the world at his fingertips. "Elveron. Aphallin. Lyonese. Kilstalpheen. Kir-Is. All districts of the same realm. Avalon, maybe—later. But Elveron first, surely. Is not that where you have been first ordered?"

Gwalchmai became angry at that. "Ordered? No one orders me!"

"I have heard differently. With all your magic, you have not so many days to waste as I have. No matter how long life is, it is too short to quarrel. You should live those days peacefully."

"Small chance of that—the way I have begun!"

"Ah, yes. You have been most active indeed. It is no lit-

tle feat to fight monsters, make an enemy of a friend,
wed a spirit, antagonize a god, disturb an enchanter at his
pursuits—and now plan to aid an ever-sleeping King! You
should feel proud. Come now, pay your fee to old Getain
and he will let you enter Elveron."

"My fee?"

"The torque you stole from the Sailor's Guide. You knew
it never really belonged to Thor, didn't you? Of course,
it was not Getain's either. He stole it from Bran Mak Morn,
who got it from Siegfried, who had it out of Fafnir's bed,
but nobody is going to give it back to the dragon now. He
has probably forgotten all about it long ago anyway.

"I'd say it belongs to Getain as much as anybody, unless
you count the three who came in here and got it, but they
came to a bad end and couldn't get any fun out of having
it now. Getain wants it, so just slip it on his arm and we will
be on our way."

Gwalchmai, bemused, unwound the torque from his arm
and wound it carefully around the upper right humerus of
the detached skeleton in the kist, so as not to damage it
further, but he need not have bothered.

At the instant the gold was tightly fastened, a great click-
ing and clattering began. The bones came rushing together,
each into its proper place. Finger joints raced around like
mice; teeth snapped back into their sockets; tiny scraps and
splinters, which Gwalchmai had overlooked, drifted about
the room like snow. They swept up and into the kist.

When all was assembled, the skeleton sat up and turned
its hollow gaze upon the pair.

"Who is this?" it said, its jaws clacking. "Who would
bring iron into Elveron without the Queen's warrant?"

"He wants your sword." Huon nudged Gwalchmai. "You
must leave it here until you come back."

"My father's sword? The sword he carried in a hundred
battles? The sword of the Sixth Legion? Never! I will go
from here!"

"And leave King Arthur's sword for someone to steal,
after Elfdom no longer encircles it to hold it secure? Is
that a knightly deed? Is Excalibur valued less now in Man's
World than your little piece of cold iron? Just lay it in the
kist beside our juiceless friend and let him hold it in trust. I'll
venture that any visitor who enters to take it will get a

surprise, now that Getain has his toy back and is as whole as he is ever apt to be!"

Gwalchmai looked glum. It seemed as though there was nothing else to do. He reluctantly unbuckled the scabbard from his belt and placed it in the skeleton's fleshless hand. It lay back and crossed its dry arms over the sword, which it had tucked within the ribcage.

"How contented the old fellow is! It takes so little to satisfy him nowadays and yet he was a person of strange wants and savage desires. You would scarcely believe what a plague he was to himself and others. See how he smiles!"

"He does? I cannot see any difference." Gwalchmai turned, with a slight shiver, away from that hard-featured grin.

"Ah! That is because you have not known him as long as I have. Believe me, he is very happy. Let us leave him and be on our way."

"How about my ax?"

"Oh, keep that," Huon said, indifferently. "The Folk of Peace have never had any quarrel with the People of the Flint. See! The portal has opened! You are welcome now to Elveron."

Against the wall where Gwalchmai had first seen Huon, a little speck of light, no larger than the pupil of a mouse's eye, gleamed like a bright fallen star where the wall met the floor.

"Follow me, Sir Hawk, and you shall see marvels!"

They began to walk across the chamber. As they did so, it appeared to Gwalchmai that the room grew larger and the portal higher. It was certainly much farther to the ceiling than before. He had a feeling that the surface of the floor was rushing away from him in all directions. Deep, wide cracks opened before them that Gwalchmai had not noticed earlier.

They ran and leaped across these, but before they reached the wall itself, the last fissure had widened and deepened into a chasm.

Huon looked disturbed for the first time.

"Quickly! Quickly now! Get a good start and jump as hard as you can!"

They ran back a few steps and then fairly flew toward the dangerous rift in the rock. Huon skimmed over it easily, but Gwalchmai landed upon his chest at the farther edge, his legs dangling into the abyss.

Huon braced his feet and grabbed Gwalchmai's arm, but found himself being pulled down by the other's weight. Suddenly there was a rush of light feet and a crowd was about them, jostling, laughing, seizing them both, dragging them up across the stone lip and into a bursting splendor of radiance as they passed through the portal.

"Welcome to Elveron, Sir Knight!" a sweet voice said, and dainty Queen Crede, the ever-beautiful, came forward to meet him, proffering both hands for him to kiss, and behind him, smiling also, came Prince Auberon to bring him safely in to view the wonders of Elfdom.

Gwalchmai found himself in a long tunnel leading gently upward, but it was not the same as the one he had used to enter the barrow. This one gleamed with the cold glow of foxfire, casting no shadows. Walls, roof, and floor all shone with a running, spangled light that came as much from below as above and cast an added glory upon the richly costumed assemblage.

They pressed upon him—men in armor like ebony-lacquered leather, clapping him upon the shoulders, laughing, shaking his hands; ladies in gauzy gowns, seemingly too lovely and frail to be real, touching his embroidered jacket, exclaiming on his narrow escape, patting him affectionately with a total lack of reserve.

All the time that they were vivaciously chattering they were gently urging him on, up the tunnel, away from the dark, dangerous entrance. It was plain that they had a dread of it, though they seemed so gay and carefree, for they kept looking backward as though they expected their visitor and his guide might have been followed.

The light in the tunnel did not now seem quite so bright to Gwalchmai's eyes. It was not that he had become accustomed to the shining walls. He noticed that the people kept glancing at them too, as though estimating the length of time the effulgence might endure.

There was an intangible air of relief when they finally came to a long line of tethered beasts. Gwalchmai had seen pictures of horses in Merlin's books and in Bishop Malachi's little library, but he had never before seen a living one. To him they seemed almost mythical animals.

Most of them were brown, but a few were jet black. All looked spirited and sleek. Their coats shone and were glossy with good health. Gwalchmai had not remembered that horses had more than four legs, but he noticed that these had six. They stood, already saddled and bridled, each attended by a young page who relinquished the reins as the lords and ladies mounted, beginning with the Queen.

When all were ready they set off up the tunnel at a canter. Gwalchmai found the gait surprisingly easy and in a few moments was quite accustomed to it. Before long he was able to allow his steed to pick its way with no attention from him and was no longer worried about falling off.

By now the shining walls were perceptibly duller.

The floor of the tunnel was strewn with small stones, but traveling was easy and swift. The pages who ran beside the horses, holding to a stirrup, had no difficulty in keeping up and seemed tireless. After about three miles, the cavalcade came out into the open air and, without pausing, entered a thick forest.

Even in Alata, Gwalchmai had never seen trees such as these. He had not thought to see anything like them on Mona. Some shot straight up without a branch for a hundred feet and then splayed out into a broad palmate top. Others were shorter and more diffuse. Many bore huge blossoms from which perfume poured down upon the travelers when they brushed against the trunks in passing.

Sometimes a gentle rain of pollen sifted down upon the ground, which seemed covered more by moss than grass. The horses moved silently across the sward, without any jingling sounds, for no metal was to be seen anywhere upon their accoutrements.

The bits, stirrups, and ornaments were all of carved wood. The saddles seemed molded to the horses' backs and contoured to the comfort of the rider without the use of tools —at least Gwalchmai could detect no such marks upon his.

Once in the forest, the gay chatting and repartee came to an end. The people seemed to be more alert as they rode along, not with an expectancy of something to fear, but more as though it was with a sense of wariness and a being ready for anything unusual. Gwalchmai felt that this troop was fully able to cope with whatever might occur, but when he saw several in the vanguard unslinging the long bows they wore slanting across their bodies, he loosened his ax in his belt.

Others took out short, heavy javelins from the boot attached to the right side of their saddles and rode with them held loosely in their hands, points down, as though ready for a pig-sticking.

Only once they heard a crashing in the undergrowth from some heavy creature disturbed by the oncoming column. Those nearest bunched up and faced the danger, but whatever it was turned and hastened away.

Gwalchmai raised a questioning eyebrow.

"Probably a mantichore or a baby dragon." Huon answered the unspoken query. After a moment, the line moved on.

As the black of lava had been the predominant color of the country in Iceland, wherever the ground was visible, here in Elveron a verdant green met the eye everywhere, in all its various hues. In among the giant trees, they followed the track—a dark river of life pouring along between the smooth green boles, over the mossy turf.

There was much life in the forest. A chorus of bellowing voices was constantly around them. A strident shrieking or whistling sound was the only one that caused the crowd any dismay. They had resumed their conversations, but these cries caused them to fall silent for an instant; the croaking or booming roars they ignored. They also paid little attention to the distant shapes Gwalchmai could not identify. When he saw them directly, however, they appeared to be some form of life with which he was familiar. And suddenly, out of the corner of his eye, he glimpsed another that he recognized from Merlin's book of heraldry, a wyvern as it flapped heavily overhead. After it had passed over and high above, he caught a fleeting sidelong glimpse of it again and thought it was a raven. He looked behind him quickly, but it was gone.

He had never been with such a restless group of people. They were always falling back or riding forward to talk with some friend, whenever there was room to do so. When the narrow track did not permit this, they maintained their places fairly well, but if it broadened into wide natural clearings and park-like meadows, as it often did, then there was a great shifting around.

It reminded Gwalchmai of nothing so much as a shim-

mering swarm of midges or mayflies, which always keeps a
rough group shape, inside of which each individual is always
aimlessly in motion.

There were a few exceptions. Huon rode on Gwalchmai's
left side, and on his right an armored cavalier kept place.
Huon introduced this rider to Gwalchmai as Sir Periton, his
best friend, and whispered behind his hand that he was
enamored of the widowed Queen, but she would have none
of his attentions.

Gwalchmai learned considerable Elfland gossip on this
ride. From Sir Periton, in his turn, when Huon was momentarily absent paying court to a bright-eyed damsel who rode
back to tease him, Gwalchmai found that his first acquaintance had quite a reputation as a gallant. He flitted casually
from one to another, but remained heart whole always,
forming transitory liaisons for a short time until he was sup-
planted by another, more serious-minded, elf.

Withal, he was so well liked, Sir Periton said, that no
father, brother, or husband ever took offense, but rather
took it as a compliment that this gay frivolous fellow admired and amused their ladies as a group and would not
be committed to any one of them.

Huon was constantly plaguing his friend for his faithful-
ness to the Queen and both remarked upon the obvious
adoration which Prince Auberon had for one of the loveliest
ladies of the court.

These two never separated, but rode close together at
all times, and there was no doubt in Gwalchmai's mind that
when Auberon became King, Lady Titania would become
the new Queen.

Huon had unslung his cithern and to its accompaniment
was favoring the troop with roguish couplets and rhymes of
his own composition.

They now moved on as though danger was behind them.
Laughing, sportive, the merry crew showed their light-
hearted appreciation of his verses, even when one or another
of them was pierced by the rapier of the debonair minstrel's wit.

"What were you afraid of, back there in the tunnel?"
Gwalchmai asked.

Huon shrugged. "Nothing very dangerous for us. It might
have been more so for you. We wanted to get you away
from the dwergar as soon as we could."

"What are the dwergar?"

"They are elves who abhor light as we love it. They run their tunnels through the earth as maggots move through cheese in your world. They have been strangely roused lately. We think it is because they had news of your coming from one who bears you malice.

"It was one of their tunnels we used. Getain's howe is one of their favorite haunts. In fact, it has been Oduarpa's only actual point of entry into Elveron, although above ground —at least in the past—he has not disturbed us overly much."

Huon's face became overcast. He shrugged, forcing a lighter note into his voice. "Well-a-day! Times change for everyone. We lined the tunnel with glow, directly we knew you were entering, but you delayed longer than we expected. Our protection had already begun to fade."

"It seemed most brilliant to me."

"Ah, yes! To you, of Man's World, it would appear bright and to the dwergar, daunting and dangerous, but it was diminishing. One crack from Thor's hammer would have put it dark entirely, if he had decided to help your enemy. Then we would have had to fight the dwergar underground, to bring you in to Elveron. Thor doesn't have much affection for you, remember?"

"I must bear it in mind. Does he have power in your country as he does among the Norse?"

"Not as much. He can drive over it in his goat-drawn chariot. It shakes the earth with its rumbling, but we have places deep down that are safe from him and the dwergar. We are friends with the fir trees and are never bothered under their sheltering roots. I do not know if you would be safe. I hear that you must beware of your enemy most, whenever you are underground."

The cavalcade spread its formless grouping into a broad meadow. The trees were low and Gwalchmai saw a turreted castle ahead, magnificent with fluttering pennons and showy flags, emblazoned with the fantastic emblems of Elfdom's knighthood, and ramping unicorn of Queen Crede's lineage high above all.

From the bailey, under the raised portcullis, and over the lowered drawbridge, a stately procession of armored riders came out with caroling bugle-horns to meet and escort them within.

Before the two columns could meld and while they were

still some distance apart, the ground between them suddenly heaved upward, casting huge clots of earth in all directions, down the sides of which heavy boulders rolled toward the riders.

The steeds reared and fought their bridles in fear. The knights and ladies first reined them in tightly, then gave them their heads and they raced away with a smooth speed that Gwalchmai had not dreamed possible. These Elveron horses were faster than any creatures he had ever seen before and they had need of all their swiftness.

Up from the torn turf, which sent out broad cracks with a harsh ripping sound, out of the mound of dirt it had punched before it, an immense tapered head thrust into the upper air.

It was pink and blind and it reared, swaying in menace, questing in circular sweeps fifty feet or more above the scattering of elves and fays—as though smelling them out.

Its annular rings stretched and contracted and the forepart of its ponderous body fell heavily on the ground as the monster continued to pour out of its hole. When it was entirely free, it came looping across the meadow in Gwalchmai's direction.

Although nothing else came out of the hole, all could hear an exultant guttural laughter that sounded somehow glutinous and heavy as it reverberated from deep within the ground.

"Yonder exults the dwergar!" cried Huon. "They have chased out the Worm!"

Since Worm, in Merlin's books, was almost a synonym for dragon, Gwalchmai understood that meaning first, in view of the creature's immense size.

He did not realize immediately that the term was even then in disuse and almost archaic, until a vast shadow covered them all and darkened the whole meadow. A flying creature, as broad-pinioned as the roc of Araby, dropped down from the mist-hidden sky and seized upon the monster that so endangered them with its heaving convulsions.

Then, as the serpent rose into the clouds, twisting and writhing in the beak that held it—even in its agony giving out no sound—Gwalchmai recognized that it actually was what it had been named. For, dwindled by distance into its proper dimensions, he saw it to indeed be a worm, firmly gripped by a robin on her way to feed her young.

Horror and dismay came to Gwalchmai. He realized for the first time his true and severe predicament, coming thus to a knowledge of his minute present size in Elveron. If this robin and its prey were as others of their kinds were, and he had no reason to doubt it, remembering the shrinking of himself to a height necessary to enter Elveron's portal —then he and the elves were tiny almost beyond belief.

He had ridden through a worm hole into Elveron. These were the tunnels the dwergar used! He had passed through a forest aboveground, which, to a mortal, was only grass. How now was he ever to complete his mission by accomplishing the task Merlin, through the spae-wife, had set him?

How could he hope to grasp the hilt of Excalibur, or lift and carry such a massive weapon as it was to him now, and place it in Arthur's tomb?

How could he even find it? For to him, in his present size, the relatively small island of Mona was larger than the entire continent of Europe!

7

The Blasted Heath

When the scattered assemblage merged, there was excited discussion and a babble of voices. The riders regrouped, falling into line in order of rank and precedence. Gwalchmai looked down into the moat, as they rode over the drawbridge.

Beneath it a swift current flowed, but it seemed to be more a luminescent gas than liquid, for it heaved up in large slow waves that were carried along for some distance before they subsided. Riding these rollers and plunging through them, sylphs and nereids swam and played in gay sporting.

courage him in his resolve to obey it: His companions were lovely, but he knew a lovelier. Beyond the environs of Elfland, she trusted and waited for him to return.

He ate and drank nothing, but smiled and nodded to those who spoke to him and wished him well and drank to his health and success to his mission—for that was as dear to their desire as his.

No one seemed to be offended. Nadara, the fay, offered him candied rose petals, but ate them herself without urging him.

As drinks were replaced, she described their qualities, their ingredients, and their flavors in superlatives that made him regret his forced abstinence.

Cyrene, the nixie, the most mischievous of the pair, tormented him more than once by touching his arm when he pretended to drink and caused him several times to spill a few drops upon his robe or on the table. Her own robes were faintly dewed as blossoms are, just before the first rays of the sun jewel them with limpid pearls, for she was a water sprite and could not long abide away from moisture.

This outing was obviously a great treat to her and she seemed intent upon making the most of the short time she could dwell upon dry land. She would clap her little hands and laugh when the wine drops fell, as though this was what she had meant to do all along, and those who were watching laughed with her.

Gwalchmai took the joking as it was intended. There was fun and good humor here and no malice. Life was all a game and he was among the merriest group of players he had ever chanced to meet. Fuzzily he was aware that the mixture of these many fumes was making him drunk, but he was obeying his geas to the letter. He had imbibed nothing. He had not tasted a single crumb.

He felt pride in himself. Merlin should be proud of him too. As for Corenice! He doubted that she would believe his tremendous powers of endurance in withstanding so many temptations in so many intriguing forms, in which he realized quite clearly that both Nadara and Cyrene were included. Their languishing glances told him that. He was very drunk.

Finally the feasting was over. The food was cleared away and a new set of goblets and decanters were brought. The musicians tuned up for dancing to begin.

At intervals there was entertainment. Jugglers performed and there were singers and story-telling. Much wine was drunk and the air was thick with its perfume, for this wine had no lees. Heather ale was served in huge tankards and with every round the merrymakers became more gleeful, clamoring for this one and that of the company to perform his or her specialty, for it seemed that each had something to offer.

Nadara danced, shedding layer upon layer of her gauzy garments. She refused to let the last flutter away, although enthusiastically coaxed to do so. Even so, her perfect form shone rosily through it, as clearly as Cyrene's, who certainly would have been unable to compete in like manner for any length of time.

Gwalchmai was called upon, after all had drunk to Nadara's health. He had already considered what he might do and was not unprepared. He selected one of the many bucklers hanging on the wall, emblazoned with the arms of their owners, and looked up and down the board until he caught the eye of the elfin knight who possessed it.

The knight nodded that Gwalchmai might do as he would with it. He hung it carefully upon one of the rhododendron logs that formed the roof pillars, took careful aim with his flint ax, which he had carried for a sidearm as the others wore their thorn poniards, and split it in equal halves at a distance of fifty feet.

All the knights carried axes when they rode to battle, but they were of hard wood or oyster shell, good for a chopping blow but lacking the weight necessary for throwing. The distance, the accuracy, and the power Gwalchmai displayed was a surprise to them.

The warriors pounded the table with their tankards and roared at the discomfiture of the buckler's owner, who fingered it ruefully, but then laughed with the rest of them and took it in good part.

Rich sweetmeats of bee balm were brought on and golden pollen bread, cut in little wafers to be eaten with the preserved tips of honeysuckle blooms, but Gwalchmai let them pass by with regret.

While Cyrene declaimed a long and involved tale concerning a pixy who pinned a diaper upon a sleeping bumble bee and the unfortunate events that followed, the goblets were refilled—this time with a ruby drink that smelled like ambrosia.

When she had finished and sat down to the laughter and applause of the company, Nadara nudged him and whispered, "Surely you will drink to her. This is the very rarest of all wines in Elveron! It is made from the berries of the Quicken tree and inspires one with cheerfulness. If one of Man's World were a centenarian and ate but three of these, he would return to the age of thirty. They taste like honey— but the wine! Do but try a single sip? For me?"

She raised the goblet to his closed lips, as the other drank deeply.

At that instant Cyrene turned and saw him. She paled to a pretty olive color instead of her natural emerald hue and reached for his arm as she had done before.

The liquid in the goblet spilled and although Gwalchmai had no intention of drinking any of it, a drop spattered on his lip and instinctively he licked it off with the tip of his tongue.

It *was* sweet, far sweeter than any liquid he had ever tasted. That single marvelous speck of elvish wine made his head swim. The room raced around him; the gay voices rang in his ears with musical clarity; all his senses seemed sharpened; in fact, everything he saw was bathed in a new glamour.

The exhilaration that swept over him he knew now to be the normal feeling held constantly by all in Elveron, enhanced only by the excitement of this particular event. He understood their febrile restlessness. He felt himself one with the merry crowd of feasters.

He understood the nixie's words, but they made no immediate impression upon him.

"Oh, Sir Hawk! What have you done? She has played a trick upon you! The Quicken and the Rowan tree are one and the same. The Rowan is called 'Thor's Helper,' because it bent of itself so Thor could catch hold of it and cross the flooded river Vimur. She must be Thor's friend. Now you have placed yourself in the hands of Thor!"

He would have answered in some way, but an interrupting clamor arose of stamping and clapping. Huon, whom everybody liked, had risen to accept his challenge to entertain and some were calling for one song of his own com-

posing and some for another, for he was famous for his
singing.

A page hurried in with Huon's cithern and he tuned it
by ear, then swept his hand across the strings and held it
up for silence.

"What shall I sing?" he asked.

One clear voice rose above the others. "The Song of the
Unseeing Human!" In a chorus of laughter, he began:

"I feel so bored," complained Louella-May,
"Nothing at all has happened today!"
And yet at that moment, in the walls of her house,
A fairy was trying to saddle a mouse,
And a battle was raging all over town
To see which would conquer—the black rat or brown!
And the earth had rolled millions of miles on its way.
"Wish something would happen!" pouted Louella-May.

She sat there unseeing and looked out forlorn
At her neighbor's scarecrow who stalked through the
    corn.
She took off her dress and made ready for bed
And a pixy tweaked out three hairs from her head
To weave for himself, while everyone slept,
A charm 'gainst the werewolf that nightly had crept
For a month 'neath her window—fearing no lead—
Since only by silver might his foul life be sped!

A bat flew by, but she never knew
'Twas really a witch a-gathering rue!
Nor that an elf was squashed when she dropped her
    shoe!
'Ou-whei!' wailed O'Keefe's banshee,
But she thought it the wind in the apple tree.
While under her feet, working night and day,
The termites were lugging the house away.
"Things don't happen to me!" muttered Louella-May.

It was after this song that the really heavy drinking began. There was other entertainment to watch, for it seemed
that each one of the banqueters had some specialty. Girls
in gorgeous colors imitated butterflies, and it seemed to
Gwalchmai's blurred vision that as their arms waved their

fluttering robes, they rose into the air and flew. There was a juggler who had no respect for the laws of gravity. A contortionist imitated a green lizard and slithered about the floor, and if he was not boneless, surely his bones were not like those of men. Two elves fought a duel, but it was a contest of skill only and no one was scratched.

All the while Sir Huon and Sir Periton were matching tankard for tankard across the table, satisfied with their complete comradeship, paying little attention to the ladies they had escorted.

Nadara, the fay, pouted prettily and rose to leave the table, for her elf was already snoring beneath it, having consoled himself copiously with heather ale because of her neglect of him.

Gwalchmai could hardly stand, but he chose to make his own excuses at this time, for many others, both knights and ladies, were pushing back their chairs.

He bowed in the direction of the Queen, who returned the courtesy, and turned to go. The fumes of the ale and wine struck him forcefully and he would have fallen had not the nixie, who appeared to consider herself his confidante for the evening, supported him on the one side and Nadara on the other.

Between the two, he was guided to his chambers. He tumbled into his down-soft bed, hardly knowing where he was. He felt little hands loosening his belt and ax, removing them, taking off his boots and outer robe. The mist that lighted the room went dim and, still fading, went dark. He heard a whispered quarrel. There was the sound of a slap.

Only one of the girls went out, crying, he was sure, for he knew when the coverlets were drawn tenderly over him. When the mist shone again, indicating that morning had come, he had a dim memory that he had not been alone during the night, but whether this was so, or who it had been, or what if anything had happened, he could not remember.

He had only a feeling that there were few bounds to Elveron's hospitality.

There was no difference in the appearance of the sky when he looked out of the window. Thinking that the color of it might indicate either sunrise or sunset, he found that what he supposed to be a crystal pane was instead a thin slice of rose quartz, set in gold instead of lead. He swung the window wide and the perfumed breeze of Elfland swept in upon him. It was as exhilarating as mountain air.

He had no feeling of hunger and his head was clear. He was well rested and had, apparently, slept a long time. It must be late afternoon, he thought.

He was not aware at that time that in Elveron it was always summer and always late afternoon. But night was coming for the fay and this he was soon to learn.

He had not been awake very long, although he had bathed and dressed, when Huon came to summon him to an audience with the Queen.

Gwalchmai studied him narrowly. His guide seemed no worse for the heavy imbibing. Elves had harder heads than men—that was certain!

He found Queen Crede in the throne room, alone except for Prince Auberon, who arose and greeted him. As unfamiliar as Gwalchmai was with protocol or European royal custom, it was easy for him to bow and wish the young prince good morrow, as from one equal to another.

The Queen did not rise, but sat studying him, her hands clasped in her lap. She smiled with a gracious sweetness that put Gwalchmai instantly at ease.

He forgot his doubts and fortunate lapse of memory concerning the events of the artificial night. This was another day in a far different world from that he was accustomed to. The sooner he accomplished Merlin's errand and returned to his own world, the better.

It seemed the Queen was of the same mind. She beckoned him forward to a seat a little lower than her own. Sir Huon and the Prince remained standing.

"May I inspect your ring, Sir Hawk?" she asked. Her tone was musical and golden, and reminiscent of another's. With a pang Gwalchmai suddenly recalled that Corenice was still waiting with Flann at the entrance to the barrow they could not enter.

He had already spent too much time in Elveron.

He placed his hand upon the arm of the throne and Queen Crede closely examined the ring. She sighed.

"Ah, yes. It is my dear friend's ring. He told me once that if ever I saw it upon another man's finger, it would be because he was no more. Did he really find the Land of the Dead, which so obsessed him?"

"Every human finds that land eventually, Your Highness, but whether it was what he sought or where he expected it to be, I cannot say. I only know that I think I have seen him not so long ago, and I fancy that he told me of things I must do. Some of these I have already done and I believe you know what those are as well as I. Is it not so?"

"It is so. And I know also what you have else to do and we will aid you as best we can, but there are certain difficulties in your way and of these you shall now be appraised. Pray attend me, my Lords of Elveron, and do you likewise come, Sir Hawk, for I would show you a thing."

There were no stairs in the castle. Ladies in fine gowns of costly worth cannot glide in stately manner when ascending or descending steps, however wide the treads or low the risers, even though such be made of fine marble or polished wood.

So to properly form the setting for his lady love, the dead King of Elfland had commissioned his architect to design a castle in which she and her ladies-in-waiting would be the principal jewels. Thus it was that all the many floors were joined by ramps along which, to the admiration of those who watched, these darlings grandly swept—fully conscious of the eyes upon them.

Up these ramps the four went, to the very end of all, and so came out upon the windy walk that led roundabout the crenelated parapets. Here always a watch was kept, looking out across broad Elfland's marches, the walls manned with elfin archers.

Gwalchmai had not seen such a brave array of alert bowmen since leaving his father's capital city of Miapan so long ago.

He admired their well-kept gear. They snapped to attention as their beloved Queen passed in review. The little party moved slowly on.

A fabulous land stretched out beyond the walls, beneath the dome of glowing mist. Now that Gwalchmai understood his own dimensions, he recognized from this eminence that the forest was composed of grass and flowers instead of trees. But such flowers—and such a bewilderment of fantastic life!

As broad as lakes, the pools from a recent rain shone sapphire in the clear air, reflecting iridescent wings that swooped above them. Dragons, or dragonflies? They could have been either. Gwalchmai saw them as both at once. Which to his eyes was truth? Which was illusion?

Strange animals grazed, feeding upon herbage that was grass to them, microscopically minute to us. Small deer, indeed! Cornutely horned and cusped, they swung their heads and browsed. Like impala, they leaped enormous distance as they ran and played. To Gwalchmai, looking upon them, it seemed a happy world.

But there were dreads there, as everywhere. Octopoid creatures—scaled, hairy, fanged—stalked the herbivores. Gwalchmai saw these also feed. Spiders—or mantichores? They were lion-bodied, human-headed. One of them might have been eight-legged Sleipnir—Odin's Death Horse—pasturing here in these green fields.

Yonder slid a glossy, furtive thing. Was it basilisk or cockatrice? Perhaps it was only an inchworm, measuring its distance with rhythmic humps? Then why did the herd go thundering away in fear if this was so?

Huon exclaimed and pointed. A beautiful creature stood near the water, snuffing the air with flared nostrils. It arched its graceful neck, dipped low and drank without fear. Gwalchmai had seen unicorns in pictures, but white ones only—never one so satin black.

"We will hunt him later," said the Queen. "Look farther, Sir Hawk, at your destined journey."

Immeasurably far away, the land took on a look of somber desolation. Here, miles to the north, the green of healthy growth had vanished. Gwalchmai thought he could see the continuing forest, but it was gray and not a healthy hue. It was the color of blight and decay. Near it he could detect no sign of life, neither within the edge of this desert, which swept away in a long curve, nor within the circle it enclosed.

"The Blasted Heath!" said the Queen. "In its center lies Arthur's sword, which you have come to take away. Right glad we are that you are here, for yonder you see the mischief it has done to Elveron and the price we have paid for our friendship to Merlin. This is what cold iron does when it touches the Land of Faery!"

8

The Hunt for the Unicorn

"When Sir Bedwyr, Imperator Arthur's most trusted knight, threw only Excalibur's scabbard into the mere, Merlin meant to lay the sword, which was thus preserved, with his King in the hidden place you have been told how to find. However, knowing that it would not be wielded for many long centuries, until it be time for the Hoped-For-One to rise and unite all peoples of British blood and so end the final war, the Enchanter changed his mind.

"Sir Bedwyr had begged him for the sword to keep, as a symbol he could show to the Cymry. He knew that they would fight to the death behind a leader who wielded it against the Saxons. Merlin granted his wish, upon condition that when Sir Bedwyr knew himself hard on death, he should bring it hither lest other men, less worthy, should carry it and it be lost before the time of need.

"All his life Sir Bedwyr fought the Saxons and those stoutly defended Cambrian hills were never conquered. But all men die, and when Sir Bedwyr felt that his time was upon him, he brought Excalibur to us, and for love of our friend we made a waste of half our land.

"Raise your eyes higher to the north, Sir Hawk. Do you see where beyond the Heath a sable blot smudges our sky? Beneath it lies the evil boundary of the dwergar folk. Here they need not tunnel, for all is darkness, which they love as does their Lord Oduarpa, who plots to extend his dominions against us. Although they too fear the Heath, they count it as part of their spreading empire.

"From it they raid by tunneling and we cannot reach them, because the light with which we line our tunnel walls

will not last to carry us into that great distance and bring
us back unharmed. Therefore, they are nearer to us than
we can be to them and though we ride to hunt and till our
fields and visit our pleasances and capture what joy we can—
as you see, we are embattled."

Gwalchmai said, "Have you not thought of seeking another home? A place where the dwergar do not dwell? A
country where the Lord of the Dark Face has no power?"

Queen Crede looked pensive. "Such a thought lies heavy
upon us. We love our home. In our way, we love mankind.
They crowd us and endanger us with their carelessness, but
they are such a bumbling, clumsy, unseeing people. Such an
awkward, amusing folk!

"We do not know how we can live away from them. Yet,
in the end, they will drive us away or kill us, for they leave
us no room. I fear when we are gone they will know too
late what they have lost forever.

"We have selected another planet where it will be safe for
us. We could leave at any time, yet we linger, for men
need us more than they realize and we shall miss them
sore. Huon, sing that song you wrote. Perhaps it will explain
how we feel."

Huon was nothing loath. He unslung his cithern and began:

> In this savage world of ours
> There soon will be no elves in flowers.
> Pixies, nixies, dryads, gnomes,
> All must leave for other homes
> On a cleaner planet—a brighter star.
> There is no iron on Astophar.
>
> Sylphs find no mirror in limpid springs,
> Just cast-off trash and dirty things.
> Smoke fouls the air for gauzy pinions
> In every one of Man's dominions.
> Aeolus chokes in fumes so strong
> And war disturbs the siren's song.
>
> Where Aphrodite rose from foam,
> Man's refuse fouls the mermaid's home.
> Naiad and Undine pine and sigh

> For pollution slew the Lorelei.
> No plain for centaurs, no copse for Pan!
> We must seek a better plan!
>
> Men—leave us a little room, I pray,
> You will need us so much more some day!

Gwalchmai echoed softly, "We will need you more some day. Yes, my Queen, for I shall be honored if I may call you so—and you will remain as Queen, in my heart, when my eyes are blinded to you again—we need you now. We will always need you. All men, however harsh and mad and cruelly unthinking, need something precious and lovely to prize and hold secret. Something to nurture the soul lest it die. You fay are our last sweet delicate thing on earth. If you go forever, you leave us to a world of drabness and horror.

"Can you not stay with us, somewhere? Just a little longer, so that more of us will have a memory that they might never know except in dream? Some, even now, think that all dreamers are a little mad."

Queen Crede laid her hand on Gwalchmai's arm. Her eyes were misted.

"Almost you make me reconsider. Sir Hawk, where can we go? There is no safe place for us. This is the last redoubt for a people so frail as we. Our principalities have fallen to the enemy or lie drowned under the sea. I will not deceive you. I have no suzerainty elsewhere. When this dome of light fails us we must flit or perish."

"Why do you not go to your cousins in Alata? There is no iron used there."

"No iron? Tell us of Alata! Where is that land? We have heard of no such cousins!"

Thus the chorus of voices so high, so hopeful that for a moment the grim bowmen forgot their duty and glanced around at the group whose rejoicing Gwalchmai had inspired.

Loudly enough, then, so that the nearest of the sentinels could hear and spread the joyful news down the line, he told them of Alata. He spoke of the little red men, no larger than they, who dwell in the canebrakes of the Catawba and hunt gnats with bow and arrow; of the puk-wud-jees of the

Ho-den-o-saunee, Merlin's own nation, who delight in playing tricks and so must be kin to elves, and whom the Noualli —the Aztec magicians—use as messengers.

"Oh, the Pooka! We know them!" exclaimed the Queen, clapping her hands delightedly.

"It may be that he speaks of Puck, my Lady Queen," suggested Huon. "He has been absent from the court for long."

"Yes, we have missed his pranks. We must call him back. Go on, Sir Hawk."

"We have dancing circles in our land, as you do here, Queen Crede, and in them the Mikamwes frolic in the moonlight. Our people have seen them dancing in their feathers and paint, to the tune of their nutshell drums. Except for color of skin, they might be your brothers and sisters.

"As for the fay, who are winged like you, we have them too. They live in the forests and are as mischievous and lovable to our folk as men here have found you to be. We call them the Mamagwasewug!"

"What heavy names!" said Prince Auberon. "I marvel that they dance or fly, carrying such a load."

"I am sure I should never have tried to learn," indolently remarked Huon. He gave a weary but elegant shudder at the thought.

"Ah, yes!" The Queen made a little moue, and laughed. "We all know what a lazy fellow you are, Sir Huon."

"It seems we do have cousins in your strange land," said the Prince. "It seems also that they are warlike. Do you think they would be friendly toward us?"

"I know of no red men who have not been friendly unless they have been mistreated and I think the little folk have the same ways. I do not believe that they would cause you any trouble. It comes to me that they would wish you well and welcome you home—if you will make Alata your home."

Huon laughed. "You make this land sound mightily attractive, Sir Hawk. I should like to see it, but this is my home and if all the rest flit, I shall stay here. I love to wander and I worship my Queen, but Sir Periton and I made a pact long ago. Whatever comes, even if the dwergar win and these castle walls go down in thunder, we mean to live out our lives in lands we know—and die there in our

"We shall regret leaving you both, Sir Huon," said the Queen. "We know you twain are inseparable, but you will be lonely if all the lesser people of the skies should go to our friend's country. Even so, that far place may not be safe for us long.

"There was a time when men did not use iron here. There will come a day when the red men will use it. Then there is no other haven for us but Astophar. You should come with us now and leave Man's World when we do. Prevail upon Sir Periton, I beg you."

"That will be a grand flitting if all go! No kobolds in their mines; no nixies or nymphs in their seas and streams; no sylphs or dryads playing together in their forests; none of us to tease them and tie their horses' manes in knots! Ah, no, my Queen! They will need someone to plague them. Men should get their minds off being men once in a while. Sir Periton and I will have much to do. We shall stay whatever befalls."

"So be it then. We shall consult the Council of Elves, but I think the matter is settled. I am weary of the dwergar and their ugly plotting. It is time we sought new pleasances."

Huon pointed outward over the battlements.

"Then let us have one last outing together before all is decided. Let us go to hunt the unicorn!"

The magnificent beast was now grazing near the pool where he had drunk. He was six-legged, as were the elvish steeds, but he was huge. His horn had a spiral twist and was the only thing about him that was white. It glistened like pearl in the warm light of the cloud dome and now and again he dug it into the ground, flinging clods of dirt over his shoulders, either in play or with the object of dislodging some stinging pest. After this he would fall to feeding again with zest, as though the exercise gave him added appetite.

He was still there when the hunting party rode out. A pack of large red hounds, six-legged also, held on leash by the whippers-in, strained to take the lead, tugging their attendants along in their wake. Next came the Master of the Hounds, carrying his trumpet, which he had not yet sounded. Then the ladies and gentlemen to the number of thirty-odd, mounted upon heavy, but swift, destriers and lighter palfreys. Following them came an equal number of mounted bowmen and lancers, on cobs, piebalds, and skewbalds—a motley group without order or style, but as hard-bitten

crowd of troopers as any Gwalchmai had ever seen, either
in Elfdom or Man's World. A dozen armored knights brought
up the rear and, viewing them, Gwalchmai thought, Let the
dwergar come!

He was riding well forward when the trumpet sounded.
Sir Periton was a little ahead, Sir Huon and Prince Auberon
almost side by side with their guest. Gwalchmai had looked
among the ladies, but neither the deceitful fay nor pretty
little Cyrene was among them. He knew that the nixie
could not stay long out of water, but he had hoped to see
her again.

He felt strangely attracted to her and wanted to learn a
little more about the occurrences after the banquet; he felt
that his conscience might chide him less when he returned to
Man's World.

Then the hunting horn sang out its silver notes; the boys
cast loose the dogs; and, chiming, their answering voices
belled.

Out of a thicket sprang the unicorn. On his hind legs he
pawed the air as though to give challenge and meet his
foes.

He saw their numbers. With a great leap he took the pool
in stride, thrashing it into foam, and into it—following him,
still giving tongue—the dogs raced, needing no sniff of that
wonderful scent, for their quarry was full in sight.

Coal black he was, superbly indignant at his harrying,
tall, strong, and quick to take alarm. He ran easily. It
would take long to wind him, for his chest was wide and
deep. His muscles bunched in massive thighs and now and
again he bounded high, looking back to catch a full view of
his pursuers. They came, in a straggling line, lances at
point, almost overrunning the dogs in their haste. "Hoy!
Hoy! Hoy!"

The hounds scattered before Sir Periton's furious charge.
He rode in at an angle, but misjudged his strike. The
unicorn turned and spear and horn clashed, in short, fierce
dueling, an engagement brief and harmless to each contestant.

A dog leaped for the gleaming ebony throat, his fangs
clashing. The unicorn turned from Sir Periton and struck
the hound down in its blood. He would have tossed the
beast, but Gwalchmai and Sir Huon were upon him.

His powerful haunches gathered under him for a mighty

effort. He leaped with all his strength and flew into the air.
Foam fell against Gwalchmai's cheek. He saw the heaving
belly of the unicorn and the flailing hoofs above him. He
crouched in the saddle, but the unicorn was already passed
over and gone, galloping away, stretched out like a cheetah,
having diverged from his original course—heading straight
for the Blasted Heath. Other gentlemen were now driving in
hard from the side to the head him away from this dubious
refuge.

The splendid creature, head still high, mane tossing
wildly, withers streaked with sweat, red nostrils flaring, his
breath sounding like bugle notes, ran parallel to the perimeter of the blighted ground. Evidently he was no more
eager to cross that menacing boundary than the elves and
fays.

He was being forced to a decision. Soon he must enter,
fight, or be taken, for the pursuit was pinching him in
upon one side and the edge of the gray desert formed the
other angle.

He saw his danger. He doubled back. The dogs slashed at
him, howled and scattered. He tore madly into a thick copse
of tangled vegetation and was lost to sight. He did not come
out.

Sir Periton was the nearest. He rose in the stirrups and
waved the hunters back. Gwalchmai and Sir Huon were
coming in fast, for the second time.

Sir Periton waved his lance at them joyously. "My
trophy! My horn!" He couched his lance and rode laughing
into the copse.

There was a brief, fierce commotion; a crashing of
heavy bodies; then the unicorn broke, staggering, from
his covert. He ran a few steps and fell, carrying Sir Periton's
lance in his side.

The dogs covered him—tugging, snarling, tearing. Sir
Periton did not follow.

One clear call rose out of the thicket as the others came
pouring into the shrubbery in a mass—"Iron! Ware
Iron!"—then no sound more.

Sir Huon gave one dreadful, wordless cry. He urged his
horse into the deepest tangle, widened the gap the others
had made, and slid to the ground.

Gwalchmai followed him. By virtue of Thor's bright
liquor, still coursing in his bloodstream, sharpening his vi-

sion to that of the denizens of Elveron, he saw the hideous metal as they beheld it.

Here, directly before him, lay Sir Periton in agony. His side lay against a piece of ice blue horror, ten times the size of an elvish knight. It sparkled and flamed coldly like a frozen fire and wherever he had touched it, there his flesh was withered, gray and dead.

There was still life in his smoking body—life that suffered and lingered on—and there was consciousness and sanity, for he knew Sir Huon and tried to wave him back lest he too know pain.

His friend rushed forward and tugged at him, but it was like approaching a furnace. Whatever iron radiated for elvish dooms, it crisped Sir Huon's clothing and drew the skin tight upon his hands and face.

Gwalchmai saw great blisters rising upon that exposed skin. He seized Sir Huon and swung him to one side. The tiny drop of Rowan wine, which made him briefly kin to the fay, made him also feel some of their torment now. He was not immune, though he was still man, but he was able to grasp Sir Periton and pull him away to a distance where Sir Huon could seize upon him too.

He straightened the poor twisted limbs and Sir Periton tried to smile up at his comrade. "My horn?" he whispered.

The Master of the Hounds had already cut it free. He brought it and stood it up upon its bloody base where Sir Periton could see it.

His face was contorted, but it was still a happy smile.

"The largest one I ever gained! Was any other hunter burned?"

Huon shook his head dumbly. He could not speak and there are no tears for elves, for they were never meant to weep.

Gwalchmai said, "There would have been many hurt had it not been for your warning. You have saved them by that cry, for the hunt was about to pour through behind you, Sir Knight. There has not been a more knightly deed in my knowing."

Prince Auberon came up then, his poniard drawn, but Sir Huon caught his eye and the prince remained where he was.

Sir Periton tried to nod. It was only a tiny movement, but his friend understood.

"Take mine." It was a feebler whisper than before and there was torture in it. "It was always sharper than yours! Quickly—and strike deep!"

Sir Huon drew the maimed elf's poniard from his belt. He laid his hand against the seared cheek in a loving caress. He covered the pain-filled eyes and closed them gently.

"Flit to the mists, dear comrade!" And Huon drove the thorn deep into the fluttering heart.

Gwalchmai was horrified. He was positive that such an action would have been impossible for himself. He stood and stared at the cold fire of the iron rather than look upon Huon in his grief. Suddenly it took on a familiar shape.

He had seen such a piece of metal before. Huge as it was, in his present size, it was only a rivet from a piece of armor, lost and forgotten, or cast aside carelessly—to bring blazing dolor to the bodies of the Folk of Peace.

He turned away blindly, feeling some of man's guilt. Whose world was it, in God's eyes? Could man in his vanity and pride ride roughshod through space and time forever, forcing his will on all other living creatures, giving them life or death according to his sufferance? Must there not sometime be a day of reckoning also for man—when he must make an accounting for his custodianship of his brothers, who likewise breathed his air and trod his soil and knew sorrow, joy, and love?

He felt a soft arm about his bent shoulders. It was the Queen.

"You must not grieve, Sir Hawk, or turn from Sir Huon. His friend wanted it so. He would have done the same for any of us. Now you see the danger we have everywhere and why we must go away.

"Half an elves lifetime ago, the Romans fought the Druids here on Mona and much iron was left scattered after the battle. It still works harm where it lies lost to all but us."

"Let me go to Huon, my Lady Queen, I would remind him that all friends meet in Heaven. It may comfort him in his misery."

"It would add to it now. He knows they will never meet again. We have none of those inconveniences men call souls. We were given, instead, lives far longer than other living things, even yours, so lengthened by Merlin's magic. Yet those lives can come to an end, by accident or in battle. We have had our wars and we have our enemies, as you know.

"Who would wish to live those long lives crippled, maimed, or ugly? Better far to pass into the foam of the sea as the mer-people do, or into the rosy clouds of the dome above where we find our peaceful forgetfulness.

"We have no fear of the gods of men. We have seen them come in their arrogance and stay while men believed in them and offered sacrifices—and we have seen them perish as beggars, when that belief no longer nourished them. We fear little, except the touch of iron—and that we cannot withstand.

"Now, Sir Hawk, it is time for you to leave us. You are close to your destination. Here, where you stand on the edge of the blight, if you look toward its center you will discern the sword you seek. You can see its metal blazing high if you look. Go to it bravely now. It will not harm you, for you are man—and man is master of the world, for yet a little while."

She kissed him and let him go and others came up, Lady Titania with her prince and many another lord and lady of Elveron, whose faces had even in this short while grown familiar to their guest.

Lastly came Huon, who gripped his hand tightly.

"I will not say farewell, for although all leave for your Alata, I shall stay and it may be that we shall meet another day. I shall always remember the words of comfort and praise with which you smoothed my comrade's passing. It may be, in some dark hour of yours, that I can be of service to you. If such there be, I shall surely know, and I will come to you wherever you may be, and stand at your side.

"Perchance there may be a time when we may dine and share a drink together and see pretty faces about us who will find us good to look upon. That will be the hour in which to speak of the Elveron that has passed and so for a moment cause it to live again in glory—as I saw it burgeon and you have seen it in its fading. Remember me, comrade, in those days of twilight that are to come."

"I shall not forget you. I have had friends in several places, but none I feel more drawn to than those I have made here in a single day and night."

Huon's smile was quizzical, but he said nothing. He took

off his green cap with its long scarlet feather and bowed
with the same ironical languidness as he had shown when
first they met.

He waved Gwalchmai on his journey, with a long sweep
of his arm.

Gwalchmai took a step over the border, into the gray
desolation. A chorus of voices followed him, bidding him
farewell. He turned to wave.

Now that he had come within the influence of the spell
Excalibur cast over Elveron, by the blight of its steel, he
had an eery sensation. It seemed that there was a wavering
before his eyes as there had been a few times before, but
this time it was strong and growing stronger.

The voices were thin and piping. He could understand
the words, but the sounds were farther away. He waved and
they waved back. They seemed in size no larger than children. The warhorses were like ponies to him.

He shook his head to clear it and walked on. Now he could
see the crisp, cold, blue outline of the sword ahead of him.
At first it was a monstrous thing, fit for a Titan's hand.
This must have been a trick of perspective, he thought, for
as he drew closer it dwindled, and although it was still
huge, a veil of dimness lay cast upon it, crinkled and veined
with seams and lines of dark shadow.

Behind it he could see another dark line, the boundary
of the amorphous blot that marked the country held by the
dwergar.

Above it hung the menacing black cloud that surrounded
it like filthy smoke. For an instant only, it swirled and
coalesced and hardened into a Shape. He thought he saw a
sneering, malignant Face—a dark gaze of hatred bent upon
him from burning eyes.

It was gone—it was again a cloud—and under it in his
direction, upon the ground, a horde was marching out toward him, or it might be toward the elven lands.

This time the dwergar were attacking in force.

As they came, the dome of light was dimming before the
spread of the unclean cloud.

He looked back. He could hardly see his friends they had
grown so small. It came to him, then, that it was he who
had grown hugely away from them. He was a man again and
the stature of a man had come upon him as he neared the
proximity of the sword. The steel had worked its magic up-

on him as well, and this change in size had brought about
a bitter parting.

The earth beneath his feet was of normal color again. The
forest of giant trees was once more grass and flowers, as it
had always been to men. The castle he had ridden from so
gaily to the hunt was gone, with all its pinnacles and stout
walls, its spires and pennons so defiant in the wind.

In its place was a cairn of rough fieldstone. Beyond it lay
the barrow of Getain, the Sea-King, grass-grown and lonely,
and desolately above it wheeled the mewing gulls. This is
what eyes saw when they were not the eyes of the fay.

He had come only a few short steps from the cairn, as
man—yet in Elveron he had ridden many miles.

He looked down and thought he saw a movement near
his feet. He knelt carefully and scrutinized the ground.

There a pack of red ants was worrying the dead body
of a giant stag beetle. Near it, a spatter of cockroaches,
black, spotted, and shiny brown, was scuttling into the grass
and above them wheeled and merged a little cloud of midges,
shifting and shimmering in the bright sun. The rosy dome
had disappeared.

Was that Sir Huon standing there alone, near the beetle—
so tiny? No! Only a slender-legged leaf hopper—and yet, in
its claw—what was it holding?

A scrap of mugwort leaf, upon which it munched, or
could it be a microscopic green cap that it waved up at him
in Godspeed, as Gwalchmai grew huger in size and their
paths of life diverged?

He did not know, but—man, insect, or fay—he felt that it
would be long before he would find again such a gay companion or so gallant a friend.

9

The Sword of Arthur

He looked once more toward the threatening dwergar, which at last sight he had seen drawn up in a closely massed battle formation.

The black blot in the sky had disappeared and the dark city was gone. He walked a few steps in that direction. Nothing lay in its place but a huge anthill swarming with insects.

He should now be standing directly in front of the precious sword.

Gwalchmai looked down, scanning the ground. Excalibur was no longer visible. In the exact spot where he had seen its alarming flame and its incandescent outline, there stood a large boulder.

He revisualized the stratified ghost shape that had surrounded the sword. To an inhabitant of Elfdom, that veil of dimness would hide nothing. It might appear as solid stone to a human being. Somewhere in its interior, ensorceled, lay Excalibur!

He felt the cold rock. He kicked. It was hard to his moccasined foot. It lay there, grass-fringed, as thought it had so lain since the world was first created.

The ant army was massed a short distance away from its nest. Gwalchmai knew they could not see his hugeness —no ant has ever *seen* a man—but he also knew that they were aware of him.

He felt other eyes upon him. He sensed a malevolence that was close, more wicked, more patient than the avid hunger of the ants. Their desire was only for his flesh.

They were waiting now, no longer advancing. He knew what had halted them.

The dwergar had been described to him as short, squat beings, almost blind from living in the night of their dark city. Thick-bodied they were said to be, with broad shoulders and gripping arms and stout talons to hold and tear—a danger to all living creatures.

Thus they were to the fay. To men? If the dwergar were really ants—but Gwalchmai had given up speculating upon realities and illusions—why, then, no wonder that they permeated the earth as maggots do cheese!

Ants dwell everywhere. To an ant, it must seem that in their numbers, it is they who own the world. The largest nation of humans is smaller than the ant population in a few acres of ground.

Now he understood. If the dwergar were favored by Oduarpa, then it must have been the malicious Lord of the Dark Face who had inspired the plan Gwalchmai feared would now be put into operation against the fay.

It could be that Thor was also involved, but he did not think so. It was true that he was in Thor's bad graces. This was a personal matter. He did not believe that Elveron would be persecuted by the Thunder God, because it had sheltered him for a single night. But Oduarpa!

From what Gwalchmai had been told of Merlin's enemy —now his as well—it was not only the entire race of man that was despised and hated, but all else that was lovely, delicate, and free. This certainly meant the fay. They represented everything for which Oduarpa was the antithesis.

Thor was an honest, blunt, straightforward hater. From him Elveron should expect no danger.

The dreadful fact was that when Gwalchmai removed Excalibur from the stone—if he could, and he must—the curse of iron, which had blighted this broad section of the elven realm, would be lifted.

In that moment, not needing tunnels or secrecy, if they could stand cloud-thinned sunlight for a little while, the dwergar hordes could pour across the Heath in their tens of thousands, overrunning all the land.

It might even befall that the hunting party, unaware of its peril and now transformed into a funeral cortege traveling at a slow pace, might be cut off before it reached the castle.

Yet Gwalchmai had to have the sword, even though it might expose them to that risk. Horrible as its aspect must still be to the fay and their enemy, the glaive was as invisible to him now as it had long been to other men.

He was not even certain that it was inside the boulder. The cracks and markings upon the surface corresponded to the veinings he thought he had seen within the foggy heap which had surrounded the sword. This had darkened and thickened to stone as his elvish vision departed him. Was the sword still within it?

He reached out his hand and touched the bezel of Merlin's ring to the rock.

There was a little puff of displaced air. The boulder vanished like a punctured bubble and before him Excalibur lay waiting, upon a polished slab.

The sword, to his eyes, was the burnished blue of finely tempered steel. It had not been damaged by time or weather, for it had been protected by whatever magic had displaced light around it.

Although that shield had vanished, Gwalchmai had no doubt that the metal was still visible to the dwergar and the fay, it all its glaring fury.

He took the sword in his hand. Instantly, now that it no longer touched the earth, those he saw as ants surged forward into the previously forbidden ground. Above them, moving against the wind, a little dark cloud floated at the height of a man's head, rippling, eddying, expanding—keeping them always in the shelter of its shadow. Beneath it the warlike myriads scurried on, without discipline or order, in the direction of the cairn that was the castle.

There was only one thing he could do to help his tiny friends.

He passed the hallowed blade through the formless cloud. It could feel pain or its equivalent, for it coiled, shrank in upon itself and spun madly with the hurt of the blow. He heard a hissing like that of a scotched viper. The cloud disappeared and the full rays of the sun poured down upon the night-loving dwergar.

He laid the edge of Excalibur down in front of the invaders and swept them back toward their anthill city. He could imagine the flaming besom from the sky that they saw descending, flaying and withering them, laying corpses as in windrows, and he shuddered.

"Another mark against me in the records of both Oduarpa and Thor!" he muttered.

The small meadow that had encompassed Elveron's broad marches was now empty. At least, he could see nothing moving.

"Farewell, little friends!"

He walked back toward the entrance to the barrow, being most careful where he set his feet. He made another torch and lit it by the power of the ring. The stone no longer covered the entrance. He did not think this strange, for he did not know that Flann and Thyra had rolled it in place before they left.

The barrow had been entered since with impunity. The Dogs of Annwn no longer stood guard over the entrance to Elveron, for now the howe was dwergar country and the portal had closed forever.

Gwalchmai saw no sign of any of the ugly dwarfs, for he carried Arthur's sword, which was a balefire in the dark chamber, but he sensed eyes upon him and a feeling of whispering all about.

Getain's skeleton had crumbled away to powder and he wondered how this could have happened in the short time he had spent in Elveron. Then, looking up, he saw a beam of sunlight upon him through a hole in the roof, blasted there possibly by a lightning stroke, and knew that the dampness of the leaking rains had destroyed the ancient bones.

His own sword still lay in the kist. When he picked it up the hilt came away in his hand. He tipped the bronze scabbard and shook it. Only a trickle of rust came out.

A distant gruff mutter of thunder echoed like a grumbling chuckle and he knew that he was still under the unfriendly eye of Thor.

The golden torque was gone. Perhaps Thor had it back; perhaps someone else now shared his displeasure. Gwalchmai hoped that it was not Corenice.

He wondered where she might be. Perhaps Thyra and Flann had gone looking for food, now that he had been away from them a full night and a day. He regretted his thoughtlessness, but it would have been discourteous to have behaved in any other way.

He came out of the barrow and looked around. No one was in sight. The sun was bright. The bees buzzed in the afternoon heat. There was nothing to do but wait until his companions came back.

There was a hill not far away where he could get a fine view, but if he left the barrow and missed them, they would not know where to look for him. He climbed upon the mound as the next highest lookout. Still nothing.

After a little, he lay down in the long grass that grew there closed his eyes, and slept.

"There was a farmer and his wife who felt that misfortune lay too heavily upon them and they wondered sometimes if it had been for the sin of pride.

They had known pride in their country and to keep that pride alive and not let old glories be forgotten, they still called it Cambria, though almost everyone else named it Wales. They were proud that the Romans had not conquered it; that the Saxons had been unable to take the north, where they lived, though King Harold had overrun most of the southern counties; they were proudest of all that the Norman usurper had not dared try. True, his son, William the Second, had in three invasions done so. In this year of Our Lord, 1097, his armies had been thrown back with great losses for the third time, and they were proudest of all of that.

Had they know that it would not be conquered for yet another two hundred years, their pride might still have been overweening though not as great—for in that year just named, their necks were bent by the chastising rod of the Creator and they learned the meaning of humility.

They had felt pride of family, for though hard-working people, they had been well born and had come upon evil days through no fault of their own, which is a thing war brings to many.

When they knew that after the years of disappointment and almost at the end of hope, they were at last to have a child, their joy and pride were almost too much to be borne.

William said to his wife, Gwyneth, 'We should speak of this only in whispers, for surely some witch will envy our happiness and do us some harm.'

His wife laughed, but secretly she took all possible precautions, knowing that the world we see is but a battlefield between devils and angels. She wore around her neck a stone with a hole through it, on a red yarn string. Witch balls were hung at each window. A knife was buried under the doorstep, pointing outward from the house, and a switch of mountain ash was placed across the horseshoe over the door.

Both of them wore, tucked in their shoes, a piece of parchment with the Lord's Prayer written on it.

They were greatly pleased when the baby, which was a girl child, was carried its full time and was born without mischance.

However, as she developed into the age when she should babble and then learn to speak, it was a sore trial for them to find that she neither seemingly could shape words or do aught but coo and smile and laugh at the sunlight through the latticed window.

It was then that they realized that there was no light of sense in her clear blue eyes and that because of their sin it was through her that their pride was to be broken.

Those were hard days and nights that followed. To watch her grow to be a fair child and see only a sweet little body with no mind within it seemed punishment far too great.

William inquired, 'Is there nothing we can do for her, at all, then?'

The leech shook his head and answered, 'Love her. There is nothing more that anyone can do. You must not chide yourselves. I have read in the writings of the ancients that there have been cases where some, though very few, have been born and lived long and have never owned a soul. Surely this girl of yours is such a one. It is God's will, and it is for His own reasons.'

But they would not be consoled and they went away weeping and they had no more pride in themselves or any other thing.

Now when the child was three and was still without any wisdom, though seeming always in health and happy, there came a turn for the better.

Until then, she had no real name. They had called her 'Baby' and 'Precious One' and 'Little Love,' but in accordance with an old family custom they had vowed to name her according to whatever word she would first speak and she had never spoken.

The window being open, a corbie crow came and lighted upon the sill, looked inside, and strutted to and fro, croaking and cocking its head wisely at those within the room.

Straightaway, the look of intelligence came into the little girl's eyes as she watched the crow. She sat up in her wicker basket, for she had never walked and her parents had to carry her if they went abroad. Her chin firmed and she lifted her head proudly, still watching. Then she turned and looked at her parents, lifting her hand and pointing at herself, and mimicked the bird, saying, 'Caw! Caw! Cor— one!' (Which latter means Crow.)

As she had said her first word, her parents were bound by their vow; yet this seemed no name at all, for either girl or boy, and they regretted their clinging to family tradition.

On the same day, perhaps understanding their distress, for suddenly she became a most knowing child, she spoke again and again pointed at herself, saying, 'Nikky! Nikky!'

So she had a name, which she had chosen for herself, for although her mother was not much more greatly pleased than she had been, her father said, 'Surely it is no little thing to have the only girl in all the hills who is named Nikky, it not being a Cambrian name at all!'

So she grew to be a beautiful young woman, dark of skin and hair, and she became much sought after, but she was not ready for courtship.

She always stayed very close to her parents and re- turned bountifully the affection they gave her. Because of that, it was the so much stranger, when in the night, nearly at the time of her seventeenth birthday, she left the house alone, taking with her only a cloak and a small basket of food.

She disappeared and none knew where she went.

They were poor people, without great resources for journeying, but they sought her up and down the land with- out avail.

In the end they returned without news of their daughter. Wherever she had gone, it was far away and in haste. Per- haps, like Kilmeny, who visited Fairyland, she might re- turn without knowing where she had been or how long she had been away.

They felt that it would be too late for them.

Her father grieved and would not be consoled, but her mother said, 'I feel in my heart that she is safe and happy,

William bach. There is nothing more that we can do. I have
had the strangest thought that she was never really ours.
She only came to live with us and let us love her for a
little while, because we were lonely. Now the time has come
for her to go to her own place.'

There the matter rested, for they never saw her more."

(From *Singular Happenings in Denbighshire—from the
Earliest Times to the Present Day*. Compiled and An-
notated by Parson Evan Jones, Luddley Press, 1747)

Humbert, Count of Monteran, Lord Paramount of twenty-
four manors, had lands in the west of England that ran beside the Welsh marches.

He had no wish to stir up trouble for himself and would
have been gladly willing to have dwelt in peace with such a
hornet's nest as was in Harlech, to the southwest of his holdings.

Because of this he had held back from the invasions, to
the best of his ability, sending only a token force at that time
to join the Marshal of England, his liege lord.

Some spoke against him, saying that if he had been more
loyal, he might have added to his lands and they would have
thrived far better themselves, having shared in his increased
wealth.

His seneschal, Odo, the Black Boar, whom all feared, was
such a one. He resented his slim purse, for his birth was as
good as his master, the Count, and he felt that with money
he might have lands and honors and at least the title of
Baron.

Having no doubt of his own courage and his generalship,
he rode out of Count Humbert's keep one day, at the head of
a dozen men, and embarked with his horses in a ship lying
in Dee Estuary.

Down this they sailed, looking for some place to sack
that would bring them wealth without danger, but beacons
told of their coming and curraghs put out to meet them,
filled with archers.

So they coasted on at a safe distance until they saw no
more smokes in the hills and, adding a few more miles for
good luck, they brought the little ship in to a hidden cove
and disembarked.

From thence, having passed Caer-yn-arfon and most of Anglesea, they felt themselves unsuspected.

They rode through the hills, searching for some monastery or abbey that might yield tribute rather than have the red cock crow on their rooftree, but there was not even a small church to rob or set alight. The only person they saw for a long time was an aged shepherd, tending his flock.

Rather than permit him to give warning of their presence, Odo cut him down, and because they had no use for the sheep, they rode in among them slashing with their swords, until they were tired and the survivors were far scattered.

Then they rode on, their spite and anger somewhat slaked.

After a little while and a long way ahead, they saw a young woman walking quickly. She had a light step and they took her to be fair, although even were she not, as the Black Boar said with a cruel laugh, "At night all cats are gray, and it is always night below decks."

So they rode in her direction.

She was carrying only a small basket, and when she heard the hoofbeats and saw the mounted men following, she dropped it, unclasped her cloak, letting it fall, strung up her kirtle above her knees, and began to run.

The laughing men, in no haste, raised the view halloo and cantered easily after her—in no hurry to finish the hunt that could have but one end.

She ran like a young doe, her white limbs flashing through the tall grass of a little meadow they had just entered, but she was becoming exhausted and staggered as she went on across it.

There was a hill beyond and she appeared to be making for it, so the men spread out to intercept her. When she saw that she was cut off from this doubtful refuge, she cried out pitifully in a language they did not understand and suddenly turned and ran with all her remaining strength toward a mound in the meadow.

She threw herself flat on the mound as though the grass could hide her.

The Normans dismounted then and surrounded the mound, coming toward it with swords sheathed, joking obscenely in loud voices, some already shedding their mail shirts and helmets and dropping their sword belts.

Black-bearded Odo was first upon the mound, his little piggish eyes fixed only upon the girl's disarray. He was therefore, the more astonished when a man such as he had never seen rose beside her with a naked blade in his hand.

He was a tall man, garbed in gaily decorated leather. He was not burly like those in the troop of raiders, but he had a look of wiry strength and his arms, bare to the shoulder in a sleeveless jacket, were bunched with muscle. Odo had a short moment in which to realize this.

He roared and reached for his sword hilt. The steel was not half out of the scabbard when his head flew one way and his body fell another. There was another man who saw it, upon the side of the mound. He stood, stupidly staring, slow to take in what he had seen, and this hesitation brought death to him also.

Gwalchmai, for of course it was he, struck him down and, picking up the strange girl whom he had found near him instead of Thyra, whom he had expected, ran lightly with her through this gap in the surrounding ring.

The nearby hill was the safest haven. As he began to climb it, the girl struggled and he put her down. She looked indignant, but exceedingly pretty—in a dark way. Not to compare with Thyra or Corenice, he thought, but extremely nice to look at. Too bad that she had the temper of a wasp and no gratitude at all!

"Keep your hands off me! I can manage by myself!"

"Do it then!" he grunted and they climbed the hill side by side, followed by the remaining Normans, burdened by their heavy metal and panting in the summer heat.

On the side of the hill they crossed a ruined revetment and when they reached the top found a still more ancient ringwall of stones and masonry that had at some far time been subjected to an intense heat, as in places the fortifications had actually been melted and were fused together in a glassy mass.

They had no time to look, or speculate, for the pursuers were upon them.

At the entrance to this old fort, fallen rock had narrowed the gateway to a postern. Here the two made their stand, protected on both sides by the crumbled walls, but with nothing to shield them in the rear.

Here Excalibur flashed and flamed and cleft skulls, with or without helmets, for Arthur's sword had not lost strength or keenness in its long waiting for a strong hand.

Here men fell and others cursed and came again and fell.

Here the girl, Nikky, fought also, for when a man came over the wall and ran around to take them from behind, she picked up a fallen Norman sword and met him with its point in his throat.

Thereafter they stood back to back, but for a long time no one approached the postern.

There were four remaining of the raiders. These retired to the lower ruins and there held conclave. The horses rambled freely, grazing in the meadow. A few strays began to drift away toward better pasture and this decided the course of action for the unhappy remnant of Odo's followers.

It was clear that only hard knocks and no riches lay here. The men captured four of the wandering steeds and rode away in the direction of their ship, leading a couple of the others. The rest of the scattered warhorses were left behind.

In the hills the Normans were ambushed and killed, near the spot where the murdered shepherd lay, and Count Humbert never did learn what became of his seneschal, his missing men, and a stolen ship.

Now that the two were left alone in the fort, they remained ready and alert for a long time, not being sure that they were yet safe. Gwalchmai was hungry, but there was nothing to eat.

He was thirsty also. And there was water, for in the center of the ancient ruin a dewpond had been constructed for its defenders.

This was a shallow basin that had been excavated and lined with clay. Then a layer of straw had been added and more clay firmly packed over it, tamped down, and smoothed. As no air is entirely dry, this cool surface caused it to deposit its moisture as dew, and, condensing into drops, the water runs down and eventually fills the pond.

This clever application of a simple fact of physics enabled many an ancient hill fort to withstand siege where there were no wells or other water sources available. Now it brought relief to this hard-pressed pair.

It seemed to be the only pleasure they were to share. The girl kept her face resolutely turned away from her rescuer. She held her chin high as though she was angry, although Gwalchmai could not guess why.

It would appear that she regretted being rescued. He wondered if she were afraid of him. Perhaps, like some women, she would have welcomed capture. Perhaps she ran away only to be pursued.

He had known girls in his own country who expected to be chased. The customs of this people might be the same. Yet she had killed at least one man!

He approached her somewhat diffidently. She turned her back on him and gazed out across the meadow.

"Shall we go down and get a horse for you? I must stay here and await friends."

She appeared indifferent. "If you choose. I have nowhere to go. It is all one to me."

"Have you no friends then? Where were you going?"

"I thought I had one, a long time ago, but he played me false and now I have none."

"Then stay here with me. You can go on with us, when my friends arrive. I will go down and see if there is any food among the dead."

"No!" she cried and put her hand out to stop him. Then, as though she recollected herself—"If you like, but be careful. Some may be alive or the others may come back."

He chuckled. "No man I struck is alive." He patted Excalibur. "This is a great killer. I wish it were mine."

He went through the pouches of the slain and took what they had. There was not very much. A little dried meat; some bread made of wheat, which he had never before tasted; a small pot of honey carried by a soldier with a sweet tooth.

They shared the food and relaxed. It was almost evening and Flann and Thyra had not come. Gwalchmai began to get worried. Where could they be? The sooner they arrived, the sooner he would be able to talk to someone besides this angry, quiet girl.

He was not loquacious himself, but this silent resentment she had for his presence beside her, bothered him. He had no great vanity either, but he did not like to be ignored.

"This friend of yours—was he your lover?"

She glared at him and at first he thought she was not going to answer. Thinking better of it, she looked distantly away over his head and said—in such a low voice he could hardly hear it, "First my friend, then my lover—finally my husband."

"Is he dead?"

"I told you he was faithless."

"Perhaps he was greatly tried and is sorry you have left him. Why do you not go back to him and be safe? Can you not forgive him?"

She bowed her head. He could not see her eyes, but he felt that he was being mocked.

"I never deserted him. It was he who left me and had pleasure with another."

"Are you going to him now?"

She shook her head. "If he wants me again, he must come to me."

That created a dead end. There seemed no way out of this dilemma He was saddled with her, it appeared. A long silence fell.

He cast about for some other subject of conversation. His eyes fell upon the strangely melted stones of the fortification. He pointed at them.

"I wonder what caused this? What could have created such a terrible—such an intense heat?"

Her thoughts seemed far away. She glanced at the slag heaps, absently. "Oh, that? This is one of the vitrified forts. There are many in this group of isles. A long time ago, the Corialci stole some of our dyro-blasts and shot down several of the swan-ships.

"When the whole nation rose in armed rebellion, Atlantis sent in a fleet of Vimanas and the rays of our ships destroyed their forts and melted their walls. They were very reckless—too brave for their own good!"

She suddenly realized what she was saying and clapped her hand to her mouth. Then she began to laugh. Her eyes were full of mischief.

Gwalchmai's mouth had fallen open. He grabbed her by the shoulders and shook her. "Corenice!"

"You great fool!" She covered his face with kisses. Then she pushed him away, pretending to be indignant still.

"I ought to make you suffer a little longer, you deceitful wanderer!"

"Wait now," he protested. "I have never played you false. Where were you last night? Where are Flann and Thyra? What are you doing in this body?"

"I will answer you in order, if you answer me one question. You say you have been faithful to me. How about

Cyrene, the nixie? Do you think I do not know what happened in Elveron?"

"I swear, Corenice, if anything happened that should not
have, it was not through my doing. I was drunk with the
fumes of the wine, but I did not eat or drink anything,
though the elves must have thought me churlish. As for the
nixie—she was always teasing me, the same as you were.
Just a minute—was that you, Corenice? Were you at that
banquet? You puk-wud-jee, Corenice! You were the nixie!"

Her shoulders quivered in his clutch. She was laughing so
hard that she could not at first speak.

"So you did not eat or drink anything? How about that
drop of Rowan wine you licked off your lip? When you did
that you broke the geas Merlin laid upon you. I will tell
you where I was during that *night* you spent in Elfland!
It is not for nothing that I am the only living worshipper
of the Spirit of the Wave. We do favors for each other!

"Through her good offices and influence with the fay, I
was *invited* to the banquet and so could come there without
harm. I spent most of that night in your—our bed! Are
you not my husband?

"Strange you did not recognize me. I told you long ago, if
it must be that I change, you were to know me by gold.
You must have seen the gold on my gown!"

"There was so little of it, I only saw you. Corenice, it was
not decent of you to wear such a dress."

"You seemed to like it," she said demurely. "No, wait!
Don't touch me. I am still provoked with you. Because you
took that drop of wine and even though I spent much time
with you, I had to leave before you could, because a nixie's
body will dry up and blow away if it is out of water too
long. So I came back to Man's World. While I have waited
for you, Flann and Thyra have lived long lifetimes and have
died, and their children and their grandchildren have done
the same.

"The Saxons you thought you would have to fight have
been conquered and another people rule Angle-land. To take
back your ancient king's sword you must go through Cambria, which is free, into Damnonia, which is not, and thence
to the borders of sunken Lyonesse—unless you want to go by
sea.

"Would you like to go alone, since you have managed to
leave me by myself for over a hundred years because you

stayed in Elveron after I was forced to leave and live in other bodies?"

Gwalchmai gritted his teeth.

"Wife—a man can stand only so much! Would you like to be beaten? I shall surely go and cut myself a willow rod if you say another word!"

She backed away a few steps. "Very well then, I shall say no more. Yet—I think you should know that if you had let me speak, I would have told you that this is my very own body and no one lives in it with me—and I can do with it whatever I will!"

He reached for her. "You are angry still? You think I should have known you? You, with your dark skin and your dark hair! You—you shape-changer!"

"Oh! You do not like this shape? You would prefer a rat perhaps? A spider, maybe? Wait—I will become a toad for you!"

"If you do, you will know pain! Terrible things will happen, I promise you. Where is the gold this time?"

She opened wide the front of her gown. Around her slim bare waist, just beneath her perfect breasts, was cinctured Thor's golden torque. She laughed. Again it was the chime of golden bells that always so enthralled his ears.

"If you want it, come and get it!"

She began to run, but it was almost dark and she did not run very fast—or very far.

10

King Once—and King To Be

They lay in each other's arms in a soft nest of bracken. It was a beautiful morning and the sun beat down into the old fort.

Small roseleaf clouds swam in an inverted bowl of blue and little breezes stirred the sweet-smelling grass. It was not a day for haste, or immediate decisions. They kissed and looked into each other's eyes and loved one another.

After a while, they slept a little, and after waking they lay and talked.

Gwalchmai thought it would take some time to get accustomed to this new appearance of his dear one. Yet, as he studied her face, he could see something in it of the old Corenice. The expression that her personality had stamped upon Thyra's features he saw here also.

She had dark hair; her skin was darker; and she was smaller than Thyra. He had seen only a three-dimensional picture of Corenice in the flesh, taken when she was a living girl, although she had said that the statue she had inhabited, when imprisoned upon the swan-ship of Atlantis, was an exact replica of her.

This statue, actually a sentient being, made of that wonderful star-metal, orichalcum, had been exquisite. Thyra had been beautiful in her own right and her loveliness enhanced when her body had housed the spirit of Corenice.

As a seal and as a swan, when Gwalchmai had likewise sojourned in similar forms, he had thought her other avatars were each the most perfect of their kind. At this moment, through his own eyes, again he looked upon a different person, who was now his wife, but she too was as much Corenice as all the others had been.

As she was now, he saw a different aspect of her character. He had known her as warrior maid, steadfast to her vows, gallant companion, sympathetic to those in sorrow, courageous and honorable. Now he knew her as a playful, mischievous, teasing girl.

He was by nature dour and taciturn, with a latent strain of savagery and harsh arrogance that he continually had to fight down.

She provided the counterpart his moods required as balance. This was perfection—this was bliss. He hoped it would never end.

She yawned and stretched like a sleepy cat and he gazed upon her fondly.

"I am hungry," she said. "Is there anything left to eat?"

"In a little while. We will catch a couple of horses and be on our way. It is a fine day for traveling."

"I brought a basket of food for us, with such nice things in it, but I dropped it when the knights came after me." ·

"Those men are far from being knights. No knight would harry a helpless woman as they did."

"Oh, I was not so helpless! I had already prayed to Ahuni-i. She would have protected me if you hadn't."

"Then I should have let her. I went to a lot of trouble for nothing, didn't I? All that killing was hard work. Very tiring. Especially when you really did not need me."

Her face turned serious. "Never say that again," she said softly and laid her cheek against his. "You know I shall always need you."

"And I you. Tell me, how did you know when to come to meet me?"

"Well—when I had to leave Elveron in the body of the nixie, whom you did not recognize; it will be a while before I forgive you for that, you blind one! I left the nixie on the bank of the inlet, where the boat had been, and she went into the water.

"A big dog was nearby and I inhabited him as the nearest body. I went over to the barrow to look around. The rock had been rolled away, which Flann and Thyra had put back, and the entrance was no longer guarded, for the portal is closed forever.

"Someone had gone in looking for treasure, but he got none. Getain had taken care of him and he never came out. There were more bones lying about. I had a terrible time keeping the dog away from them. He thought he had found a great treasure!

"Getain's bones were all crumbled away with age. They lay in the kist like powder and the torque and your sword was with them.

"I knew he would not want either again and I was very angry with Thor for the trick he had played on you through that deceitful fay. I had the dog pick up the torque in his mouth and carry it out. I was going to get your sword in the same way and keep it for you, but out of a clear sky lightning struck the barrow and made a hole in the roof.

"The dog was greatly frightened and I could scarcely control him. He ran and I could only see that he did not drop the torque. We came to a churchyard and I had him dig deep and bury it in holy ground, where Thor had no power.

"I lived in several bodies after I left the dog. When I found this body, which was alive but empty, I took it. When it was grown, I was told by the Spirit of the Wave that your time in Elveron was almost past. So, on my way here to you, I stopped at the churchyard, dug up the torque, and here it is and here am I. Are you sorry I did not save your sword?"

"It was a good sword, but it has served its purpose. This one—" he patted Excalibur "—is a better. There are others around here. I will find one and use it, when I give this to its owner. I think we had better be on our way."

"Your clothes have served their purpose too. Look at them!"

It was true. While Gwalchmai's leather garments had been in contact with his body, the elixir of life he had drunk so long ago had preserved them in the glacier. In Iceland and in Elveron they had remained whole, though showing increased wear.

Now they had crumbled away to dust. All he had left that he had brought from Alata was Merlin's ring, his belt of coins, and his flint hatchet.

He looked ruefully at the fragments of leather. "The last remembrance of my country. The gift of the People of the Dawn."

He stripped the armor off one of the caitiff knights. Linen underwear went on first, leather boots over cross-gartered hose. Next he donned, with Corenice's help, a loose hauberk of leather covered tightly with sewed metal rings. A sheath hung at his left side, by a baldric slung across his body over the right shoulder. In it he slipped a long Norman sword.

He drew the hood of the hauberk up over his head, which protected his neck and cheeks with fine meshed links, and upon his head, over this, he fitted a steel helmet with a nasal strip that could be lifted or snapped down.

Corenice did the same with Gwalchmai's aid. Soon, having captured mounts, two proud Norman knights cantered out of the meadow. Each carried a short lance and wore a round shield upon their backs.

With nasals down, no one would suspect that one rider was a woman.

Behind them followed two great destriers, loaded with the remaining armor and equipment of the dead men. Excalibur hung in a second sheath attached to Gwalchmai's saddle.

All four horses were magnificent Spanish stallions, of the breed brought over by William the Conqueror. Gwalchmai, with thoughts of obtaining a boat, had been convinced by Corenice that money was necessary. It was a new idea to him. He was completely unfamiliar with the use of money, never having needed to consider that medium of exchange before.

The suggestion proved wise. The animals and gear purchased a fine boat at the nearest fishing village, with no questions asked. It was provisioned for the two knights without much comment. They swaggered about with hands on sword hilts, glaring at the villagers as though defying them to ask questions.

A purse of coins was added to make up the score, and when they had put out of harbor the fishermen spat into the water behind them, but it was not till they were well away and not likely to put back that the men cursed and shook their fists at the Norman enemy.

Gwalchmai and Corenice only laughed. With a good breeze they soon lost sight of land and headed the boat south, well out, to pass by Caernavon Bay and skirt the cape of Braichy Pwll.

That night they slept on board, at anchor. They rose early. The winds favored them and the weather remained fine. If Thor, the Sailor's Guide, still bore a grudge, he was biding his time or had scorned to take advantage of such a little boat.

They passed Cardigan Bay, went down Saint George's Channel without mishap, but then met storm in the Bristol Channel. There they lost a day by riding it out in harbor, where they stayed on board comfortably, but seasick, rather than risk a landing.

In ten days of leisurely tripping, they found themselves among the Scilly Isles, the Cassiterides—or Tin Islands—of the Greeks.

This was Gwalchmai's destination, for here upon the mainland lay Arthur's secret tomb and beneath the boat's keel, as it made its way toward the coast of Damnonia, lay Arthur's homeland, drowned Avalon. Here also, sunken Lyonesse, from whence came noble Tristram to become Arthur's knight and to die for love.

"Here is the place, sweetling, that my father told me

about," said Gwalchmai, pensively. He gazed ahead at the distant headland, jagged and blue with haze. "Often and often I heard from him how he came here with a few survivors from that last battle against the Saxons, bearing the still-breathing body of his Dux Bellorum, Arthur, the great War-Chief of Britain.

"There they stood, appalled to see that while they had marched hither to bring the Imperator to his home, Avalon had been covered by the ocean and nothing showed where we now ride but a sea of mud.

"Ah, yes, love. Other countries have known the raging flood besides your stately Poseidonis! I remember Flann spoke once of such cities in his own Erin. Skerd and Tir Hudi, both drowned."

"I know you are right, but there is more remaining beneath us than there was where you found my ship floating, my husband."

Corenice was looking down into the water. Gwalchmai could see nothing.

"Place your head beneath the water and listen."

He leaned over the low side. At first he could hear nothing unusual. He held his breath and went a little deeper. Then, above the slap of the waves against the wood, he heard an unexpected sound.

There, deep down, stirred by the currents of the sea, the sunken bells of Lyonesse were ringing, sweetly faint and far, where sixty submerged villages with their sixty churches lay, peopled now by the mer-folk and the mackerel.

They sailed on toward the main, borne smoothly by a warm south wind. Around them the fog gathered, shielding them from view as they neared the coast. Through it an accompanying cloud of gulls screamed and dove, for the boat moved in the midst of an immense school of pilchards. The sound of the little fish surfacing was like the sound of rain upon the water.

Now the Cornubian hills were plain to see. Other boats were out, mostly taking pilchards and mullet, but the fishermen had no eyes for anything but their work.

The voyagers sailed on undisturbed. Although they still wore armor, they were not remarked for that reason. South Wales was under Norman domination and Cornwall had rendered lip service to the invaders, who were already working the tin mines. Normans were no strangers there, although it was not wise for them to wander alone after dark.

Gwalchmai had made a wide sweep to come up thus from the south, as though the boat had come across from Brittany, thinking to reach his destination under cover of darkness, but the wind had been stronger than he had estimated.

Now he was glad that he still had an hour or more of daylight. Near the fantastic pinnacles of the headland, where the Channel currents met the rushing waves of the Atlantic, were seething eddies and whirlpools. Once through the rip tide, he breathed easier.

There was calm water in the bay beyond. People waved to them in a friendly manner, looking up from hanging their nets or mending lobster pots. They waved back. The Norman armor seemed to be of no importance to the fishermen.

They came in on a falling tide, dropped anchor, and beached the boat upon a sandy shore. As it appeared that they were among a friendly folk, they changed into clothing from a sea chest in the little cabin and went ashore.

Now Gwalchmai seemed to be a tanned, ruddy sailor, for there were many whom the winds had leathered to his hue. Corenice looked like a dark Welsh boy, her rather short hair hidden under a stocking cap.

There was not much to see. It was a small fishing village, which had been left undisturbed by the Normans and which profitted by their trade. Norman coin was welcome in the single tavern and the food and ale were good.

After eating, the two went out and strolled the waterfront.

The boat was canted over on the sand, until the tide returned. They sat on the sloping deck and looked out to sea. About a third of a mile away lay an island with a high peak of granite.

Upon this, crowning its summit, was a small priory, a cell to the abbey of Mont Saint-Michel in Normandy. This too was a place of pilgrimage, like its more famous sister peak, but the priory was its only building.

On the side facing the shore, a causeway permitted access by foot, at low tide. Looking at this, in the dusk of evening, Gwalchmai had a sudden impulse to put off no longer that which he had come to do.

With a word to Corenice, they set the anchor far up the beach, on a long cable, then, from the cabin, he brought out Arthur's sword, wrapped in a cloth. Both he and Corenice had worn their own swords while they ate, not so much out of fear of the villagers as because in their role as outlanders it would have seemed unusual if they had not. Thus armed and carrying Excalibur, they walked across the narrowing causeway toward the island.

The tide was on the turn and rising against their path, but they crossed it dryshod and kept toward the lower peak across a flat expanse of pebbled shore and rocky slabs. Looking back, they could see stumps and gnarled roots in the shallow water.

Gwalchmai said, "In the time of my father, this mountain stood in a broad forest. He called it 'the white rock.' Merlin stayed upon it for three days, working a magic, alone with the body of Arthur, and all that time a black cloud, filled with mutterings, hung about it—while he labored on Arthur's tomb."

There was still a remnant of the forest between the shore and the peak. They passed almost through it and came to a spot where a cleft, which seemed natural, reached like an avenue into the living rock.

Now, all about them, they heard whisperings—in the trees, in the grass, on the rocks above them—and Gwalchmai remembered Merlin's words, that there were Watchers set to guard the tomb, which must be appeased.

There *was* a feeling of being watched. Both knew that many fierce eyes were upon them, but those who watched were wary, not inimical to the pair as yet.

Gwalchmai unwrapped Excalibur and went forward into the cleft. Corenice followed, pressing close behind. The rock walls pinched together after a few steps, until they could touch the cold granite on either side.

At this juncture there were sounds of little following footsteps behind them and a scratching as of claws upon the stone above their heads. There was still light to see by, and although they could discern no definite forms there was a misty gathering all about and they knew that they were surrounded.

Gwalchmai had been told of the invisible people of Cornwall—The Spriggans, the Piskies, and the Jacks-of-the-Lanterns. He knew also that giants had dwelt here in times long gone. Who it was that guarded the tomb he did not know— but the ring was growing hot and danger must be close.

He held up his hand and turned it about.

"We are come here on a mission for your Master, Merlin the Enchanter, who set you here as Watchers. View his ring, which I bear, and do it homage for his sake. Show me where lies the door that I may open it and enter to lay this blade in the hands of Arthur, the Undying!"

There was a chorus of little muted voices. Surprise was in the tones and pleasure and a feeling of adoration all about the pair.

The padding feet still circled them, but there was no scratching: the claws were sheathed. Then, just before them, at the height of a man's eyes against the rock where the two walls of the cleft met, a spot of light came into being.

A replica of the monogram upon the bezel of Merlin's ring!

Without hesitation, Gwalchmai at once fitted the engraved opal into the carving upon the granite. With a grinding, rushing sound the walls retreated on either side, disclosing a bronze door, above which was inscribed in deeply incised Roman lettering, in Latin:

HERE ARTHUR LIES
KING ONCE AND KING TO BE

The door opened to a touch and Gwalchmai and Corenice stepped into a hushed and softly lighted room.

It was a circular chamber, rich with subdued color. Around its circumference ran a mural divided into three sections by lines of shadow cast from three bars of gold which curved about a glowing ball of light. This hung from the domed ceiling on a long golden chain, set in the center of a flower with twelve petals. Each petal was named after a Roman month, the series beginning with April and ending with February, according to the Roman year.

As the two of them entered and stirred the air, the delicate petals trembled. There was a tiny soft click and the lines of shadow moved forward along the mural by an infinitesimal degree. Three lines of letters moved with them along the upper border of the mural.

Gwalchmai read: "THIS IS WHAT WAS." It stood above the first section. The pictures were not painted, but cast upon the wall by the light in the pendant globe. Here were displayed Saxon dragon-ships upon the sea, engaged in crashing battle against Romano–British galleys supported by one great

dromon that rode the invading enemy down beneath its fore-
foot. Another row of pictures below this series showed
Arthur's twelve defeats of the Saxon hordes, and the third
and last set forth, in vivid scenes, the long journey of
Merlin, which brought his wounded King to this safe place of
refuge.

Gwalchmai looked between the next two lines of shadow
dividing the mural. "THIS IS WHAT IS," he whispered into
Corenice's ear, as though by speaking he would disturb the
sleeper who lay upon a bier beneath the globe.

The man was heavily boned and heavily bearded. There
was no mistaking the look of majesty in his face; it would
have been recognized in any country or under any circum-
stance.

Here reposed one who was born to rule—one who was still
his nation's hope—one who slept, biding a time of great
need. Arthur, the Hoped-For! The Great Pendragon! Arthur,
the Undying!

"THIS IS WHAT IS," Gwalchmai repeated and looked at
the pictures before him on the wall.

Here lay the sad representation of a conquered island.
Saxons in submission, their stiff necks bowed. The fury was
gone from their faces, replaced by calm resignation. Their
hands held hoe and shovel instead of ax and buckler, for
their wars were past, and Norman knights lorded it over them
in pride and arrogance. Norman keeps and Norman banners
held the hills, the waterways, the forests, and the mountain
passes, and Norman ships encumbered the sea.

Yet there was one little spot that still was Britain—the
mountains of the west, where dwelt the remnants of the
people the Saxons had never conquered and who now alone
defied the new invader. Here dragon standards still streamed
above marching men and proudly marked the castles of
the free.

It was not yet time to wake from sleep and take up the
sword for final battles. There was the third section to view:

THIS IS WHAT IS TO COME

Again the three strips of pictures covering the remaining
wall from ceiling to floor. At the top, men warred against
machines. The murky skies were lit by burning cities,
through the smoke of which slipped sleek birds of death.

The ground was alive with clanking flame-spouting horrors, but men survived.

In the center strip, much time had passed. Here there were no more cities—seemingly no more people. Machines fought other machines. The landscape was littered with rusting, tortured metal, the hills and plains torn and blasted. The trees were gone and the stumps lay black and decayed like rotting teeth. Above the desolation drifted clouds of dreadful mist, glowing a hard and deadly blue, reflected in pools of luminous liquid in which nothing lived.

Was there nothing green left then in this scabrous land?

At the end of the sequence there was one tiny picture, not as large as a baby's hand. It was bright and beautiful and Gwalchmai and Corenice bent to examine it closer.

Like looking through the window of a doll house, they gazed out into a garden of flowers, tiny as a mosaic made of pin-point jewels. Bees hummed there and butterflies tasted honey in swooning ecstasy. It was a summer day and there was no hint of war. In the garden stood two figures—a young boy and a girl who gazed upon the flowers, or was it that they looked above them into each other's eyes? They were embracing and about to kiss.

Looking upon them and their dream of hope, Corenice's own eyes were misty.

The end had not yet come.

There was one picture only, at the beginning of the third strip. All the rest was blank. It showed the entrance to the tomb in which they stood. Framed within it, shown from the rear, was the figure of a man in full armor of shining steel. On his left arm he bore a shield, which carried the device of a bull. The ancient emblem of the Sixth Legion, Victrix! In that hand he carried a lance with a dragon pennon and in his right hand the unsheathed Excalibur was grasped.

He stood against a flame-red sky seen beyond through the open door and just there, in his white robes, was a familiar figure to Gwalchmai's eyes, waiting to welcome his King to be—Merlin, who had saved him for this day to lead the rejoicing armies that would end war forever.

It was not for nothing after all, Gwalchmai thought. The weary hopeless years, the sadness and the desolation, the forgotten joys unknown to slaves; all those miseries had come and gone to teach men what must never be again.

All was not lost. Arthur was not dead. His life had been

moved out of time for only a little while, or so it would
seem to him when he awoke again to the culmination
of his anciently planned destiny.

His time was being measured by a clock that ticked off
not hours and days but years and centuries. Upon the day
of his waking he would look at the murals. He would know
what had happened. He would know what he must do.

Gwalchmai could not know what that destiny was to be,
but he did know that he had done his own small part in
making it come to pass. He had brought Arthur's sword.

He crossed the floor and laid Excalibur at Arthur's side
and placed the sleeper's hand upon it. The fingers were
warm; they opened and as slowly as the movement of a snail
they closed upon the hilt.

A sigh stirred the beard at his lips; the eyelids opened a
hairsbreadth only. The lips parted and Arthur spoke: "Is
————————————it——time?"

Gwalchmai put his mouth close to Arthur's ear. "Sleep
well and long, my beloved King! It is not yet time to wake."

The eyes closed again. The sleeper drifted back into his
long, healing rest. Gwalchmai and Corenice tiptoed back
into their own world—their own time—and the bronze door
closed behind them.

They walked a few steps away and looked back. The granite cleft was as it had been before. Nothing of the mystery
was visible to them. All around were the small friendly
sounds of the forest. In the distance they could hear the
waves and the wind.

While they had been inside the mountain, the sun had set.
Sweetly now from above came down to them the chimes of
compline from the priory, as the bells called the monks to
prayer.

Gwalchmai fell upon his knees. He had never felt closer
to Merlin's God than at this evidence of the beneficent
wizardry that had been performed by his godfather. He felt
certain that this was magic of the very whitest.

Corenice looked at the sea. He knew to whom she revered-
ly gave praise. He longed to see her goddess. For a moment
he felt an unworthy jealousy of the affection those two
shared.

About them, the couple sensed a gratefulness at their continued presence. The Watchers were pleased. It was well that

the visitors had come. It would be well with Arthur and the world.

Later, Gwalchmai and Corenice went down into the forest before the dark of darkness. They found a dry hollow out of the wind. Soft leaves made them a bed. Here they lay in peace, watching the slow wheel of the stars. They talked of many things. After they had loved, it was here they waited for the tide to turn and uncover the causeway—and while they waited, they slept.

Now, as Gwalchmai slept, it seemed to him that he awoke. He looked about and saw that his darling was close at his side and that they both were cradled closely in the embrace of a giant woman.

The bare arms that held them were cool and soft. He knew that she was friendly and he knew no fear. Then he noticed that the arms bore no soft down of hair as human arms do, but were faintly scaled and smelled of salt. He looked up and saw hovering over him a huge, but lovable, smiling face.

In his dream, it seemed to Gwalchmai quite natural that the eyes were square instead of being oval. This motherly figure could be no other than Corenice's goddess—Ahuni-i, the Spirit of the Wave—whom the People of the Dawn knew as Squant.

He was not afraid. The Abenaki had none but pleasant legends of her doings in the sea. It was obvious that she was benign.

But there was another here, who was no friend. A red-bearded Titan who leaned upon a tremendous hammer and who spoke in the rumbling tones of distant, rolling thunder. These two were discussing the sleeping pair.

"The man is a thief!" growled the colossus. "Give him to me!"

She smiled tenderly down upon them. Her arms cradled them a little closer. "He is so small. Have pity upon him, Thor. It was not his thought to rob you. He was told what he must do."

"It was he who stole from me. It is he who must be punished."

"Then make his punishment light for my sake. He is loved by one who loves me. I do not wish that she shall be hurt.

You know he has a geas upon him already. It binds him and he will suffer by it. Let that be enough. I will see that he gives back the torque. Forgive him, Thor."

Then it seemed that Gwalchmai spoke in his dream, and he said, "I will indeed return the gold, now that it has fallen into my hands for a second time. But if I do this thing, which I am not obliged to do, and promise it only for the love of justice and not for fear, what then will Thor do for me? It comes to me that justice is a two-edged sword and cuts both ways. I have been plagued already, inasmuch as I too have been robbed of something I valued highly. Thunder-God—nothing for nothing!

"You stole my sword with your lightning and your rain, by rusting it away in Getain's howe! Give me another in exchange and you shall have your pretty toy."

Thor chuckled grimly. "You see how men bargain, Elder Cousin? How he puts me in the wrong? This scoundrel knows I cannot return his own sword, for it is gone forever, so he makes it seem that I owe him a sword and he owes me nothing! He wants to trade something that is not his for a thing he has lost! Where then is the punishment? Stand aside and I will flatten him with my hammer!"

Then Ahuni-i stroked back the hair of Corenice with one huge finger and bent over her fondly. She whispered and in her breath was the susurration of little waves that tenderly caress the shore without violence and with no anger.

"Quiet, thou great and clumsy Thunderer, or you will awake my sleeping one. She is only a wife for a little while. Would you so soon make her a widow?

"Now if I were to rouse my father, Poseidon, against you—who still lives as you know, under many another name —I think you would find him more powerful than yourself. That Ancient of Days will be feared and respected when you and I are long forgot!

"You should raise your hammer not to threaten these tiny people, but to consecrate their vows. It ill behooves one thief to criticize another thief!"

Then Gwalchmai unwound the torque from about Corenice's slim waist, where she still wore it for safekeeping and held it up—or so it appeared to him in his dream, and boldly said:

"It comes to me that this trinket has been so many times stolen that it can now belong only to the last pair of hands to hold it, for surely it could never pass back into those which held it first.

"Therefore, it should be truly mine or perhaps hers who was wearing it, for Getain did not hinder her in its taking. Yet, I will return it to you, if you promise me a blade of fine quality and of equal value to the one you filched from me."

Thor tugged at his beard and frowned, pretending to consider. He covertly eyed the torque. The corners of his lips twitched with mirth and it was obvious that he had already made up his mind.

"And if I do? Will you render me your homage?"

"Nay! That I cannot do, for my godfather baptized me and I walk his trail in the service of another Lord. Also, you ask more than the value of what I offer!"

The Spirit of the Wave laughed, a liquid purling lilt of music, and Thor chuckled in spite of himself.

"It is a stout little bargainer, this man of yours, Elder Cousin! You do well to feel pride in him. He shall have his sword, but he shall earn it. The one I have in mind for him is far from here and he must journey to it, but it is the only one of its kind in the world. The champion who held it had no equal in strength and honor and even he could not break or otherwise destroy it when it came time to lay it down.

"Say, you shrewd thief, will you trade me my torque if I tell you where the finest sword ever raised in your Lord's service now lies?"

Gwalchmai looked up at Ahuni-i for guidance.

She nodded. "You can trust him in this. He is a great trickster, but he will not go back on a bargain. If he swears his vow upon his hammer, he will keep it, for that is as binding to him as to his worshippers."

"Then upon your hammer swear that I shall have this sword and the torque is yours!" cried Gwalchmai.

"I so swear!" growled the giant, and distant thunder rolled in the dense gloom as he touched his hammer to his brow.

"There, the bargain is recorded in Asgard. It cannot be withdrawn. Give him his plaything, man of my beloved daughter."

Gwalchmai made a loop of the soft gold and Thor lifted it up on the tip of his little finger and dropped it into his pouch.

"I give you in return, Durandal, held by Roland, Karlus

Magnus' finest Paladin—long-hidden, long-sought, long-desired, never forgotten. To get it you must seek the Pass of Roncesvalles, which separates France from Spain. I have kept my bargain. Trouble me no more, clever thief, lest I repent me of you!

"Elder Cousin, upon this sword Roland, the Paladin, lay down to die. With all his strength he had first struck it against a stone to break or mar it, lest it fall intact into the hands of the Saracens, his enemies. Of such a mystical forging it was that nothing could destroy it.

"Ah! Thickly, thickly, the Valkyries hovered over that field of battle! If he had been one of Odin's men, gladly would they have carried him to Valhalla, but there was another place for him and it was not permitted. Brünnhilde put it into the heart of a looter to preserve the sword by hiding it in a hollow oak, then she slew him to keep it secret for another time of need. It has remained there ever since.

"Do you think if this man gets it, he will raise it in your service as it was used before in the honor of his upstart Lord?"

"Cousin Thor," Ahuni-i said, "that Lord will one day supplant us both, whether by sword or not. When men forget us and make us no more offerings, we shall neither of us exist. My time will be and yours is coming. I have one worshipper in her and one follower in him, although you have many for yet a little while. He does not worship me, but he knows I exist, therefore he believes in me."

"And because two people, in all of Earth's millions, believe in you—and one only prays to you—you exist? It seems that this existence of yours is a chancy thing!"

"As yours also grows daily to be of late, dear cousin."

"Not as long as men fear thunder, or need guidance on the sea," grumbled the giant.

"Hush now. You will not be convinced until it happens, as it is happening to me. My weary little one is awakening. Give them your blessing, Thor, for he has paid his debt and we must go."

Thor stretched out his mighty hammer and its shadow fell upon them.

"Be blessed then, wee people. Though you give me no allegiance, I will watch over you on land and sea, for I would that you were mine. With my hammer I consecrate your lives. May you think of me as you wander. If you need help, call upon me once only and I will leave my mansion, Bilskirnir, and come to your aid. Farewell, stout little fellow and your sweet lady. May you attain all your desires!"

Then, as awakening Corenice blinked and rubbed her eyes, Gwalchmai saw the two giant figures thin into mist and disappear. Through them shone the bright rays of the rising sun.

Thor was an immense oak, under whose projecting branches they had slept, and the shielding arms of the Spirit of the Wave were no more than two great roots forming the sides of the leaf-filled hollow.

Which was dream and which reality? Gwalchmai did not know. Had he actually defied a god and bargained with him? Had he received a promise and made a mighty friend? There was only one thing certain. The torque was gone and, search among the leaves as they might, it could not be found.

After some while, he told Corenice what he had dreamed. She gave over the searching then, nor did she seem surprised. Afterwards he often wondered if she had dreamed part of the same dream, but he did not ask and she did not say.

Everyone should have at least one secret. This one was better kept in silence, unless he wished to believe, to his loss of pride, that he was not master of his own fate, but accomplished what he did by the will of a goddess and, through her, by the will of his wife.

When they came down to the shore, they found that the causeway was bare. From the priory, matins had already rung and fishing boats were setting out from the harbor. It was a fine morning.

As they crossed to the mainland, they saw a little group of well-dressed men and women gathered around their boat, inspecting it with interest. When they came up, a spokesman doffed his hat and greeted them courteously, coming a few steps to meet them.

"Sir, I am told by the fishermen that you are pilgrims and that this is your boat. My master, King Brons, wishes to purchase it of you to return in it to his hold of Morfa Harlech. We are likewise pilgrims and having walked hither the length of Cymru to accomplish a vow of his, the feet of

all the company are now weary. May I inquire if you will
sell us your boat and, if so, what price you may place upon
it?"

Gwalchmai and Corenice looked at each other in some
dismay. It was a dangerous thing to refuse a King anything,
even if he were out of his own boundaries. Those of noble
blood were apt to see things differently from commoners and
tended to be clannish.

They needed the boat themselves for ease and safety of
travel. Gwalchmai wished to go south instead of north, in
order to seek out the sword that had been promised. In addition, now that he had accomplished Merlin's errand he was
free to be on his way to deliver his father's message to
the Emperor of Rome.

If this should prove impossible, it might take much time to
find and convince some unknown Christian monarch that it
would be profitable and a worthy deed to send a fleet to
possess the land of Alata.

He was anxious to be off and he was certain that there
was nothing in the north for him, yet he was in no position to refuse.

"Tell your master that the boat is not for sale. However,
since I am also the son of a King, I will favor him in the
respect that if he will outfit myself and my lady with maps,
charts, and a guide to lead us safely past these Norman
shores and land us in Spain, he may have the boat and
welcome."

The man returned to the group and there was much talk
and shaking of heads. It seemed that the women were
especially voluble in argument against the idea.

King Brons finally came to speak with them and Gwalchmai introduced himself.

The king bowed as to a compeer. "Gwalchmai is an
honored name among us. I saw in you a look of the Cymry,
yet there is something strange about you. I have never seen
a man with skin so ruddy as yours.

"My people are faint-hearted. The ladies fear to sail upon
such a journey as it would be to land you upon the coast
of Spain, though it is a fair offer. Neither does any man
wish to separate himself from my entourage to act as guide
in that foreign land.

"Instead, I must beg you, if you will not sell your boat,
to take us first to my castle, where I will gladly reward you

with what you ask and give you wintering or good cheer for as long as you wish to remain with us."

Gwalchmai was ready to demur, when Corenice nudged him. He could see that her eyes were dancing and he suspected that it would give her pleasure to dwell for a while in a castle after the manner of royalty.

"Very well. Your gentlemen then will be our sailors and I their captain. The ladies—I hope they can cook—will tend our wants and you shall ride without sore feet to your hold."

By the time the tide was full in and had raised the boat, added provisions and another water butt had been stowed away.

Bedding was placed in the small cabin for the ladies. The anchor hauled in, the sail was raised and made fast and they moved out of the bay. Once free to the winds they turned toward the north, retracing their route of the previous days. It seemed like returning on the trail, but Gwalchmai consoled himself with the thought that if shelter were at the end of them, all roads were alike to the wanderer.

Now that they had people on board to whom the coast was familiar, they were favored with local legends. Thus Gwalchmai and Corenice were told, as they rounded Land's End and saw Sennen Cove to their right, that here King Arthur had met the invading Norsemen. With the help of seven Cornish kings, at the battle of Vellan Drucher, not a man was left alive to carry the news of defeat back up the Irish Sea.

In celebration the assembled kings dined together, seated around a large rock for a table. Merlin prophesied that even more kings would meet at that rock to repel another threat from the men of the north and the mortal encounter would be followed by the end of the world.

As they went on they were pointed out the sites of holy wells and shown where a mermaid had been shot with a longbow shaft and the sands there cursed by her forever.

There were ruined forts that had no names, on headlands overlooking land and sea, and everywhere cairns of huge granite blocks fit to mark the graves of giants.

They were shown where giants had fought battles in the clouds, riding horses whose hoofbeats were like explosions and who made war by hurling red-hot stones at one another.

They learned of the dangerous fairies that inhabited the

mountains and the pretty ones who lived in foxgloves and
danced in the moonlight—and they thought upon Elveron
and wondered if Prince Auberon and Lady Titania were wed
and if Sir Huon was yet sad, but of these things they said
nothing to the Cymry.

Along this haunted coast they cruised till they came to
Morfa Harlech and landed in King Brons' dominions, where
a wide half-moon of beach swept for miles in a huge clean
curve. Here the waves rolled in to break in semicircles of
creaming foam and here Harlech Castle rose on a frowning
outcrop of rock, like a nest for eagles.

The keep looked out upon a green and fertile vale beyond
and farther yet lay the sublime and impressive eminence Y
Wyddfa Fawr, "the great burial place" men of today call
Snowdon, where giants and demons dwelt long ago.

King Brons indicated the mountain with respect. "Here
King Arthur lies buried." Gwalchmai and Corenice looked
at each other and smiled.

King Brons' harper struck a resounding chord and sang
the triad:

> A grave there is for Mark,
> A grave for Gwythur,
> A grave for Gwgawn of the Ruddy Sword;
> Not wise the thought—a grave for Arthur.

And the company bent their heads to do honor to that
long-gone King.

Now bugle-horns sounded from the battlements of Harlech
and a questing squadron rode forth to see what visitors came
and with loud rejoicing, for they had not expected their
King so soon nor that he would return by sea, they ushered
the wayfarers in with pomp and ceremony.

As King Brons had promised, Gwalchmai and Corenice
were treated in a style befitting his professed rank and given
a suite of fine chambers.

Corenice or, more strictly, Nikky, as the Welsh girl had
named herself, had been somewhat ill during the journey.
She was afflicted with a lassitude that lingered longer than
the arduousness of her journeying appeared to explain.

Tender care brought back her health during the winter,
but she was satisfied to remain indoors when, with the
Cymric knights, Gwalchmai rode out to the borders and met

the Norman raiders in infrequent clashes. Throughout the season the marches were held inviolate, while the women waited to see who would ride back and which others would be lamented.

In Gwalchmai's short experience with horses, he thought he liked best the six-legged steeds of Elveron. An animal with a leg only on each corner had an unpleasant and uneven motion.

He soon became accustomed to the odd gait, however, and to the weight of his armor, which was heavier than that of the Norman knights.

Sometimes they ushered in Saxon refugees and Gwalchmai was amazed to think that such pitiful folk were once the terror of Britain. Hungry and gaunt, dull of wit through long years of serfdom, marked with the scars of whips and manacles, they brought home to the Cymry, as nothing else could, how the wheel of fortune can turn and the oppressors become the oppressed.

At such times they swore again and again that Harlech should never become Norman. King Brons, dandling his son, Prince Owalin Gwynedd, upon his knee, vowed that he would hold every foot of the land his forefathers had called theirs.

Small indeed was the present holding of the Britons, but proud were they of their heritage, for they had resisted the Romans, the Saxons, and now a foe that had taken more of the isles than any other enemy—and still they were free!

Yet there was an undercurrent of feeling that proclaimed to Gwalchmai that they knew well that bravery alone was not enough against great numbers and eventually there must come a day of doom. He could see it when the dead knights were borne in after a border battle; when ladies did not appear at the tables because they were mourning; when new faces were seen manning the walls.

Sometimes the King himself looked haggard and withdrawn and Gwalchmai knew that he had been ridden by the nightmare and that his thoughts were that perhaps the little prince might never wear a crown.

Corenice begged Gwalchmai to tell the King of Alata, so that if the worst should come this tiny remnant of the people Merlin and King Arthur had striven so hard to protect might in the end be able to take ship and find a refuge across the sea.

For a long time Gwalchmai refused to do this, feeling that the secret should be given only to the one it had been meant for—the Emperor of Rome. In the end, he came about to her way of thinking, although he said, "It seems to be the destiny of Alata to become, not an addition to the Empire as my father wished, but a home for refugees!"

"What better destiny could it have?" asked Corenice.

To his surprise, King Brons shook his head at the offer.

"I could never desert my people. With such shipping as I can command, we could move only a small number of the Cymry. Even if we made many trips, as our strength diminished the Normans would encroach upon us. Loegria—England—would absorb those who remained. It would be the act of a traitor.

"I realize that the offer was made in good faith and I honor you for it and thank you, but we shall fight to keep this land free and we need every man and boy to do it. Our women would have it no other way nor would I ask it of them.

"However, I shall have all that you have told me written down and put away in a private place. If ever we should come to terms with the Normans and dwell in peace along the border marches, it might befall that my son or his son perhaps might some time wish to seek adventure there. It was a kind thought, Prince Gwalchmai, but I must refuse it."

In the springtime of the following year, the border was quiet. Farmers tilled their fields undisturbed and no knights rode out to war; women's tears were shed, not because of policies made by the highborn, but because of the small troubles of their own houses.

Apple blossoms fell gently upon the tombs of the brave, fishermen hauled in their nets, and trading vessels came and went from the harbor of Morfa Harlech.

One day Gwalchmai and Corenice sailed out on one of these, a wine-ship from Malaga, outfitted as King Brons had promised. They carried such maps as could be procured, guidance in their minds as to where their destination might lie, and the blessings of their hosts.

King Brons and the people lined the beach to see them off and his harper struck up a lay of lament at the parting. For a long time they waved goodbyes and when they were still far out at sea, and the Cymry could no longer be seen, they kept their eyes fixed upon the gay flutter of the bright dragon pennons, whipped by the winds which were sweeping over the heights of Castle Harlech.

"Godspeed! Farewell and good fortune to those who depart and return no more!"

Such it was indeed for those of the court who remembered the strangers who came and stayed a while to depart and be held tenderly in their thoughts. Sometimes they wondered how those two fared, the tall, red-skinned prince and his dark lady who loved him so deeply and who had a lilt of golden bells in her laughter.

A harper made a song in their honor and it was often sung as time passed and a generation of people came to age and another followed and passed away. Sometimes the grandson of that harper was asked for another song after he had sung that one and was applauded. He would stop and think a moment.

Then he would strike a resounding chord from his harp and declaim, as a chanting prelude to his song:

"These are the Three Vanished Losses of the Isle of Britain—

"First, Gavran, son of Aeddan, and his men, who went to sea in search of the Green Isles of Floods and never were heard of more;

"Second, Myrdhinn, the Bard of Aurelian Ambrosius, and his Nine Bards of Knowledge, who went to sea in the House of Glass and there has been no account whither they went;

"Third, Madoc, son of Owalin Gwynedd, who went to sea with his three hundred men in ten ships and it is not known to what place they went."

After the singing there would be subdued weeping, for many remembered Madoc and some had known his father, Owen, and there were a few old people who had heard tell at first hand of King Brons.

It was these few who sometimes wondered if there was any connection between the advent of those strangers from the sea and Prince Madoc's disappearance.

They wondered also to what land they might have sailed, but the prince had taken the record with him and by that time only Gwalchmai and Corenice could have told them— and they were no longer in Britain.

11

Arngrim and the Golden Girl

The world had been long in turmoil. While Gwalchmai lay in the glacier massive movements of restless peoples had taken place.

Rome had collapsed before the terrible Goths, had been rescued by the Greeks of Byzantium and fallen again to the tribes of the Lombards, or Long Knives, descending upon them out of the forests of her ancient enemy, Germania. Men then began to think of Italy as a nation, for Rome was dead and those who still could call themselves Romans were refugees in the swamps of Venice.

The lights still shone brightly in Byzantium, but the boundaries of the Eastern Empire expanded and shrank like those of an amoeba. Sometimes they were broad and irregular during times of uneasy peace; sometimes they were confined only to the walls which surrounded that often beleaguered city, still the pride of Europe.

Scholars looked toward Byzantium as they looked toward Heaven. The religious found in it their holiest treasures. Raiders longed to sack it for its wealth. Military men studied its campaigns and strategy, and diplomats learned their involved art of swaying the minds of men by observing the trickery practiced there.

There were no finer examples of architecture remaining anywhere else that had not yet been vandalized; no other arenas still in use to entertain the people comparable to Byzantium's Hippodrome; no other rulers more conscious of their divine destiny in any land of Christendom.

The Moors had stormed north out of Africa during that long encysting of Gwalchmai in the ice. In Spain Christianity met Mohammedanism and was hurled back and northward toward the sea.

At one time it was said that only one mountain peak in all Spain was free and upon it only twelve knights and their families held out to contest the paynim hordes.

Charles the Great had built another empire, Roman only in name, and it too had been dismembered and the grandeur become a dream.

While Gwalchmai spent his night in Elveron and time went on unheeded by him, other movements occurred.

More mountains became free in Spain, for Christian and Moor learned to live with one another almost as neighbors, although they often fought as neighbors do. The north became a crazy-quilt of tiny Christian kingdoms, consolidated by way of war and marriages of expedience.

The south was Islamic, divided by the Moors—stern, bearded, intolerant Berbers from North Africa and the milder Saracens—the cultured, sybaritic Arabs. They scorned each other's ideals, but were united by their faith. Here also was a collection of warring states, where a single battle or marriage could change the pattern of power.

Then a third element was infused into the witches' cauldron of conflicting faiths and politics.

Rurik, the Norseman, had led his savage conquerors into Muscovy, burning, slaying, establishing an empire of his own. His sucessors came down the Don, into the Sea of Ravens, to attack Byzantium like a storm, meaning only to sack it and destroy.

His Varangians remained in the end to work for those they had hoped to conquer and to become the most trusted guards of the Byzantine Emperors. They were Christian only in name when they made that bargain, and for a long time after they still swore by Thor's hammer.

It was inevitable that these powers should grind against each other.

During the winter Gwalchmai and Corenice spent in Harlech Castle, a new jihad was being preached by a Berber warrior who called himself Abu, the Dawn-Maker. Horrified by the lapses of his kinsmen in faith and their love of luxury, he swore to purge all Spain by the sword and to slay indiscriminately both infidel Christians and apostate sons of Islam. With this aim in view, his fleet crossed from Ceuta and soon held all of southern Spain and the western end of the Mediterranean under his despotic rule. From these points, his riders and his ships harried the north both by land and sea.

While the wine-ship from Malaga, upon which Gwalchmai and Corenice had taken passage, wallowed down the coast of France and across the Bay of Biscay, a galley manned by Abu's corsairs had passed through the Straits of Gebal Tarik, likewise coasting, and was looking for just such a prize.

On the way north, it had rounded Capes Finisterre and Ortegal, made several lightning raids to gain supplies and booty, and had arrived about opposite Santander.

Here, because of a failing wind, the galley slaves were ordered to run out their sweeps and the ship soon picked up speed.

One of these slaves was no stranger to war. His story was later told by the skalds, in the great Hall of the Mercenaries at Miklegarth, as Byzantium was known among the Norse, when the feasting was over and the drinking horns were raised. It was then that the sadness of wine lay upon men and they wished for mead; their minds dwelt upon the glories of Valhalla and were filled with doomful thoughts of Ragnarok. Then someone would cry, "Let us hear again the Saga of Arngrim!" and the saga-man would begin:

"First it must be told that there was a man named Arngrim. He was a Varangian captain of the Northern Guard in the service of the Emperor Alexius, the First, of Miklegarth. He took the Emperor's pay and carried the Emperor's sword in his hand and looked on the Emperor's face upon the coins in his pouch. His joy was to strike down the enemies of the Emperor.

"He was the son of Steinar, the son of Thorvald, the son of Jodd, the Dane. He was the master of a patrol ship. His hair was black.

"Now the story turns westward, for hither through the Gates of Hercules flees Augmund, the Unwashed, son of Thorberg Snorrison, the Evil, busked and bound for Tonsberg, by way of Hrossey, with many goods on board reaped

from spoiled and burned churches on Lesbos Island. Behind
sails Arngrim, with his sword Life-Biter, heading the sea-
rover off from the landward veering, and the sea-stags drive
on so for six days into the northern ocean.

"Now back turns Augmund and they run their ships
alongside and grapple and the steel-storm begins; fire-pots
fall into Arngrim's ship, setting it alight and they cast off to
fight on Augmund's deck.

"Up and down the waist rages the slaying till mid-even,
when none are left but Augmund and Arngrim, both grue-
some at the man-hewing and well matched.

" 'Yield ye!' cries Arngrim, but Augmund comes against
him to smite at once with his sword. Arngrim catches the
blow on his shield and twists the blade short off, then with
Life-Biter he hews the sea-rover's legs away and the war-
spoil is his.

"So no more of Augmund."

Thus, the saga-man—but there were some things that did
not appear in the account, for Arngrim did not mention
them when he came home to Miklegarth with a golden girl.
Because of his tight mouth, these matters did not enter into
his saga.

Rais Salih el Talib captained a galley of weary men. His
soldiers longed for the shore and the shade of green trees,
as the sore-footed camel longs to leave the burning sand for
the oasis. His rowers pulled without spirit, even under the
whip.

He surveyed the benches with no enthusiasm. They were
a scurvy lot to begin with. Time had not brought improvement. He felt little hope that they would last out the trip.

Salih was a landsman himself. He had been given the title
of *Rais al Bahr*—Captain of the Sea—more as an encouragement to do his best than in any hope of his Al-mir-al that
such an event was likely to occur.

His eyes strayed up and down the two long lines of slaves,
straining at the oars. The new man was shaping up well. His
wounds were minor and were almost healed. His head was
up. The corded muscles moved easily under the skin of his
unscarred back. It had been unnecessary to use the whip.
After he had realized the futility of an attempt to escape, he
had done more than his share.

Since he had been picked up from the drifting wreck, he had proved himself a good worker, if not a willing one. The Rais idly wondered why.

Their eyes met and held. Salih no longer wondered. There was a flame in those eyes that told him this piece of flotsam lived only to kill. He would never be broken. What he was planning the Rais knew well.

At one time, the black-haired slave's nose had been smashed and carelessly reset. He could never have been handsome, but this gave him a savage appearance that denied trust. He was too ugly to resell for personal service to any great house. He was too dangerous as a slave. It would be like having a tiger on board.

When this voyage was over it would be best to have him killed. At present his strength was needed. With a little feeling of chill, the Rais turned away.

When he was no longer under observation, Arngrim renewed the conversation with his partner at the oar. They spoke in the faintest of whispers, with no movement of the lips.

"You say this is the coast of your people?"

The other indicated direction with the tiniest glance forward at the mountains in the distance. He was hugely built, barrel-chested, bullet-headed, with a large nose and blue eyes. He had the short, thick, slightly bowed legs of a born mountaineer.

"Yonder lies the home of Jaun Magrurin. There are the mountains of Escual-Herria,*" he said in halting Latin, of which both understood a little. "There I was born. There I shall die."

"You seem very sure you will not die a slave."

"Ez! Ez! Never! We Eskualdunak make poor slaves. We are the oldest people in Europe and the freest. We have never been conquered. For me to die here would shame all of my family and disgrace my nation. Even before you came I had already racked my bench loose at all its joints. I wait my time."

"And I also!" breathed Arngrim.

Then they could no longer converse, for the overseer strode along the walkway, swinging his flail.

Suddenly the lookout hailed the bridge. "Sail ho!"

*The Country of the Basques.

"Whither away?"

"Six points to the north. Merchantman under full sail, bearing south-southeast by east—riding high!"

"Under what flag? Can you make her out?"

"The Red Lion, Captain! Fair prey!"

At this period in their conquests, almost anything upon the seas was prey for the corsairs, but they had learned a healthy respect for the Viking banners. It was possible yet to see the Raven flag farther south than along this coast. They had met, even in the Mediterranean, opposite the beaches of France, and only to the detriment of the Moors.

It would be many years yet before the crescent banners dared appear in the harbors of England, but no one, not even the novice seaman Salih el Talib, feared the various flags of Spain. Moreover, a merchant ship that had disposed of its cargo and was returning empty to port must be carrying rich and easily portable treasure for which it had traded.

"Pick up the beat! Whips!"

The prow swung to intercept the merchant vessel, as the drum set a quickened pace and the rowers, under the crack of the lash, bent their aching backs to the oars.

On board the wine-ship, Gwalchmai and Corenice were leaning idly upon the rail, admiring the snow-capped peaks in the distance.

The ship lay helplessly in the water as it had for some hours, drifting becalmed, but moving gently toward the land upon the now incoming tide. It was about midday. No clouds were in the sky and there was no hint of any wind. All sails were full set to catch the smallest breeze, but there was hardly a ripple upon the quiet ocean.

Then the merchantman's lookout sighted the corsair. It was coming up fast, in a thrash of white foam along its wake and there was no doubt that they were on a collision course.

The sun gleamed upon the wet oars and their rapid motion could be discerned, as could the sparkle of light upon the Moorish soldiers' weapons and their polished chain mail.

In less than half an hour they would obviously be ready to attack.

The merchantman was not fitted for war or speed. As quickly as possible, boarding nets were set up and arms were served out, but there was little time to melt pitch or heat oil. However, stones for ballast were brought and lined along the bulwarks to be dropped into the galley when it came alongside. A barrel of wine slung at the end of the bowsprit, hung free to fall and so add insult to injury if by some miracle it could be cut loose over those boarders to whom wine was forbidden by their Prophet.

Gwalchmai almost wondered if this were some deliberately sneaky trick of Thor's, to avoid keeping his promise, but he put aside the thought as unworthy. If the tricky god had intended such a deed, it would have been unnecessary to go to so much trouble, involving so many people, in order to cheat one man.

He clenched his fists upon the rail. He still carried his flint ax, almost ancient now. He had the sword he had taken from the dead Norman knight after the battle at Getain's howe, but Corenice carried nothing but a dagger that had just been issued to her.

It was meant not for killing Moors but for her own death upon capture—which now seemed certain.

Gwalchmai's knuckles turned white as he gripped the rail tighter at the thought. His ring gleamed upon his finger. It was not even slightly warm.

Could it be that they were in no danger? Had it finally lost its power?

He took off the ring and read the spell engraved upon the inner face of the hoop, as he had done before to slow the Viking fleet from reaching Iceland's shore. This time he pointed the long arm of the mysterious constellation almost at the zenith, for the corsair was perilously close.

A little black cloud no larger than a man's cap formed instantly, less than a hundred feet above the bare mast of the galley. It rushed toward the corsair, for hanging in this position it moved with the speed of the attacker, but it grew in size as it came. It was fifty, then a hundred feet across, and it grew, it grew, taking on the semblance of a monstrous raven with ink-black beating wings that smote down great buffets of air upon the long low vessel striding the waves beneath it with oars for legs.

Under these powerful gusts, the corsair reeled and spun around. Above, the sable bird shape circled even more madly. The water was lashed to fury and a whirlpool took form. Its sides were glassy and streaked with foam that outlined the racing ship as it whirled about the edges of an opening funnel now plunging deeper and deeper into the sea.

With it, the corsair descended. It sank below the level of the flattened waves, until only the tip of the wildly waving mast could be seen, circling in dizzy wobbling sweeps to every point of the compass.

As the two ships were less than half a mile apart, those aboard the wine-ship could plainly hear the screams of the doomed men, but they came as it were from far below.

Then the wind stopped. The black cloud was dissipated and the whirlpool disappeared, the waters rushing in from all sides in a fury of tossing choppy waves in which there was no direction and only a small amount of floating wreckage from the sunken warship of the Moors.

Drawn in that direction by the currents set up by the disturbance, the merchantman soon entered the spin-drift and there they came upon the only survivors—two slaves barely kept afloat upon the rowing bench, which with their united immense strength they had ripped loose as the corsair went down.

Still weighted by their attached chains they hung there, faces awash—Arngrim, son of Steinar, and Jaun, the Basque.

Not long after being picked up they went ashore as free men, upon the reaches of sand leading to the green stone-walled fields and rushing streams of Escual-Herria—and with them went Gwalchmai and Corenice, set there according to their own desire. Gwalchmai knew he was coming to the conclusion of Thor's promise, for he was sure now that the god meant to keep it.

As the captain of the wine-ship said, "There have been many sudden squalls that have sunk ships in the Bay of Biscay, but I never heard of one before that came out of a cloud in the shape of a raven!"

And Gwalchmai knew that this had sprung from no plan of his. Thor had proved himself a true and trustworthy friend.

They had been landed almost at the angle of the peninsula. France meets here with Spain, separated by the Pyrenees, which lie across the country like a fern frond carelessly flung down, stretching from east to west. On both sides of the stem, the pinnate fronds are tall ranges running north and south and between these are valleys, peopled and cultivated for millenniums.

Here the cave-bears dwelt in ages past; here the Cro-Magnon race mysteriously appeared for the first time, with a culture strangely similar to that of those in the Americas, as though they shared a kinship and a common origin. In those same deep caves these doughty fighters and hunts-men pitted their strength and arms against the beast-like men they found there and told the story of their wars and hunts in wondrous paintings.

Here now dwelt the Eskualdunak.

Along the southern front of this mountain range marched the four companions, bound in the same direction for dif-ferent reasons. Arngrim meant to return to Byzantium, where he held a position of honor and life was soft; Gwal-chmai and Corenice wished to find the proper pass into France among all these dead-end northerly valleys; Jaun, the Basque, had promised to lead them there.

After they left the coast, the mountains began rising high-er and more sheer. There were snowcaps and later there were glaciers and always brawling rivulets and larger streams to cross.

Occasionally they slept in villages, more often in caves. Although Gwalchmai felt a crawling along his spine when he was underground, for he remembered the Lord of the Dark Face had more power there than elsewhere, they were never troubled by any enemies, either spirit or mortal.

He felt that around him were remnants of very ancient magics, and indeed some of these caverns were holy places even before Oduarpa came to Earth from the Morning Star.

In the settled places they found the villagers hospitable and friendly once their Basque guide introduced his friends, for he seemed to have cousins or acquaintances everywhere. They always ate well in the stone black-roofed houses of Magrurin's relatives.

Although Gwalchmai, while he wore the ring, could un-derstand any language Merlin had known, this strange ag-glutinative tongue baffled him. Corenice cried out in joy when she heard it, for she said it was the language of her youth, spoken by all in Poseidonis, but in a purer form. She wondered if colonists from Atlantis had come much earlier than that last sinking and brought their speech with them. Had they found life too hard and become savages upon that savage coast and lost all else?

No legends remained, but Corenice thereafter spoke directly to Jaun and interpreted between the others and the mountain dwellers, although she could not always completely understand all that was said.

One night they lay out under the bright stars and drank wine from Jaun's chahakoa. They passed it from hand to hand and watched the slow wheeling of the constellations.

"There is the Plough," said Arngrim, pointing up at the Great Dipper and extending the wine pouch to Gwalchmai. He drank and said, "My father called it Arthur's Wain. It guides the sailor and the men on the empty grass moors who hunt the humped cattle. My Uncle Ha-yon-wa-tha said that the little star, just above the bright one almost at the end of the shaft, was called 'The Papoose on the Squaw's Back,' but I have forgotten the story about it."

Jaun asked Corenice what they had said. He laughed when she told him. He began to speak, and Corenice then translated the story.

"The first two stars," she said, "are two oxen stolen by two thieves from a farmer. The next two are the two thieves following the oxen. The first star in the handle is the son of the farmer sent to catch the thieves; the double stars are his sister and her little dog, who were sent to find her brother and bring him back. Then, following all, is the farmer. He swore so terribly when he lost his oxen that God condemned them all to this endless journey."

"That was very wrong," said Arngrim, seriously. "Perhaps the others shared some of the blame of the farmer—but the poor little dog! It was not his fault that he went along with the girl—it was his duty to do so. I feel sorry for him. He should not have been punished. Thor would never have done it."

Just then a streak of fire shot soundlessly across the sky and Jaun crossed himself. "May God guide the passing soul!"

"Amen," said Gwalchmai. "Do you know any more stories?"

So the Basque told them of El Guestia, the ancient host, who travels about at night dressed in white with lighted candles in her hands, ringing a bell and muttering prayers for the dead.

His voice fell to a whisper. "She attacks all she meets and says, 'Travel during the day, for the night belongs to me—e!'"

He shrieked the last words and grabbed Arngrim's arm in an
iron grip. Arngrim shouted and sent him rolling over the
ground. Everyone laughed.

Gwalchmai told them of the witch of Aztlan who runs
through the streets wearing a necklace of human hearts,
bringing death to those who see her on the five unlucky days
at the end of the cycle.

After this they all occasionally looked over their shoulders with some unease. Jaun noticed this, and said, "We
have the Laminak, too. They are little people who live underground in beautiful castles and who are kind to lost children. They lead them home with firefly lanterns."

Corenice looked pensively at Gwalchmai and he knew
that she was thinking of the banquet in Elveron. He wondered, as he did often of late, if he would ever see Huon
again.

No one wanted to go into a cave that night, so they slept
out under the stars. Gwalchmai's dreams troubled him and
once he woke with a start, breathing hard. No stranger was
visible, but he knew he had lain under unfriendly eyes and
he was not sure that they were human. For some days he
had felt such a cold stare upon him. Something, he was
certain, was biding its time.

The next day they went on into the mountains, along a
dusty road lined with sycamores and poplars. They ate from
provisions they had bought in the last village with the few
coins that yet remained from King Brons' bounty, and while
they dined beside a clear stream a group of children came
by, dancing as they went to the music of tambourine and a
three-holed flute.

They were driving a small flock of sheep. Jaun got up
from the grassy bank and stopped them. There was talk
back and forth in Basque and Corenice strained to listen,
but she could not catch the conversation.

She said, a little peevishly, "Jaun tells me that they have a
saying here, that your devil has no hold on the souls of
these people, because he has never been able to learn the
language! Sometimes I think I believe him. There are many
words he uses to these children that were not custom in my
time."

"I wish I could be as sure about my soul," Gwalchmai
muttered to himself. The day seemed suddenly to have lost a

little of its brighness, as though a tenuous shadow veiled the sun for a moment.

When the Basque came back, he gestured toward a gap in the mountains. "I will take you that far. Then I must return home. Yonder lies the road you seek. That is the Pass of Eboñeta. The French call it Roncesvaux."

Roncesvalles! Gwalchmai's heart leaped. Now he would find out if Thor had truly forgiven him or no! Now he would learn if he had dreamed what he thought he had seen and heard on the slope beneath Arthur's tomb! Now, if all were true, he would soon handle and possess the sword of a hero!

"Will you take us through the pass?"

Jaun shook his head. "The children say that a Xana has been seen. I already have a wife who would miss me if I did not come back."

"So have I," said Gwalchmai. Corenice beamed upon him. She held his hand tightly.

"Anyone who thinks we do not love each other because they do not see us talking very much should ask your heart and mine about it, should they not, my dear? What is a Xana, Jaun, and why should it matter if a man is married?"

"A Xana is a beautiful nymph with long and flowing hair, golden and heavy in the hand. They live in caves and fountains, and it is said that some are not really sprites, but are lovely women who have been enchanted. A Xana will wed an unmarried man if he disenchants her, but if a married man does it he will never be happy until he has put away his own wife and taken the nymph instead."

Corenice held on a little tighter. "I do not like this part of the mountains. Is there another way we can pass through?"

"There are eight passes in all, but this one is the best."

"I think it is the worst. Let us seek another. I remember a silly fay—"

"And I am thinking of a nixie and a certain thin and supple willow branch that has not yet been cut," grunted Gwalchmai. "This is the road I sought and this is the pass I shall take. Are you coming, wife, or do I face this terrible danger alone?"

"I wouldn't let you go into it one step without me!"

Arngrim laughed. "Have no fear. I will stand between you and the Xana, Jaun. Come with us. She shall have no power over you or the red man. Lady, it has been a long time since a beautiful woman frightened me. I promise you, if we meet a lovely nymph who wants to be disenchanted, I am just the one to help her! Believe me, many women have looked upon this ugly face of mine and have been disenchanted by it. Moreover, I have no wife! Step aside, fellows! I shall lead the way!"

Taking the fore, he set off at a good pace toward the mountain gap. Jaun followed, but with some hesitance.

"Be not so foolhardy! This is Saint John's day. She may not be protecting her fountain, but El Cuélebre—the winged serpent—will be!"

Corenice was full of her own thoughts and angry. She did not bother to translate and as Jaun had lately been speaking to her in Basque and had so continued, Arngrim did not understand the warning. The big Varangian went on in haste and was soon out of sight of the others.

The three laggards entered the pass looking about them with curiosity. There was nothing unusual to see. Broad at the entrance, the famous Pass of Roncesvalles narrowed rapidly, with high cliffs and steep wooded slopes on either side.

Gwalchmai could see that a host would have been rapidly compressed into a thin column at many points along its line of march. Boulders and fallen trees littered the trail and a heavy mist, which was lowering, hid the snow-covered peaks among which the way meandered along toward France.

Rivulets talked to one another in this mournful place and a small stream rippled by their path. It was obviously well traveled, but they met no one. Neither was there any sign of their companion.

Jaun called out for him—a long yodel-like cry—but there was no answer. Then all shouted with no better result.

"Perhaps he has met the Xana and it is safe for us to walk a little faster," Gwalchmai said to the Basque, with a sidelong glance at Corenice. She sniffed.

"Perhaps it would be better if we walked a little slower. Then he will be sure to meet her before you do!"

Jaun smiled, but he maintained his place, a little behind the others. This time, the guide was not leading, but being led.

Both Gwalchmai and Corenice noticed this. They began
to regard the situation a little more seriously and soon Jaun
had to hurry to keep up with them.

An unnatural darkness was descending upon the mountains, as though above the mist thick storm clouds were
gathering. Occasionally a peal of distant thunder rumbled
and echoes fled along the winding narrow valley.

"Near here," said Jaun, "long, long ago, my people destroyed an army that was retreating into France. Every man
was slain and a rich booty was gleaned."

"I thought it was the Moors who attacked them. The
French are Christian; your people are Christian. How did
that come to be?"

"Friend Gwalchmai, religion, faith, and friendship all
stand aside when money comes to the front. If you have not
learned that yet, then do so quickly—it may save your life.

"This French army came to attack the Moors in Zaragoza, but the Moors paid tribute, so the army started back
with a mighty treasure.

"Great Carlos was both its General and its King. He
thought himself out of danger when he reached Roncesvaux, for the pass was held by the Eskualdunak, with whom
he had made a peace.

"The first part of the army passed through the whole
defile to the other side. Then came the wagons, laden with
gold and jewels and fine weapons and armor. There were
tapestries and carvings, and holy pictures crusted with precious stones. There were ivories and spices of all kinds.

"The mountaineers were poor people. All this wealth was
too much for them. They ran along the tops of the cliffs
and waited at the narrowest place, which we have not yet
reached. Everybody helped. Men and women worked side
by side and when the wagons got there, they set loose a
landslide and stopped them. Then they rolled down rocks
and tree trunks upon the helpless soldiers, and cut them
down with sling-stones and arrows.

"The soldiers were too proud to call for help until it was
too late. When only a few knights were left, they were ringed
around by many of our guerrilleros. Then one knight—his
name was Ruotland and he was warden of the Marches of
Brittany, it is said—blew such a powerful blast on his oli-
phant that it was heard on the other side of the mountains.

"Great Carlos led back his troops for a rescue, but when

he got there every man was dead. He had lost half his army and all of his treasure. He grieved so that he never came this way again.

"I have heard though that some of the treasure was hidden by the soldiers before all were killed. People still hunt for it, but none has ever been found. Most of us are poor in these mountains. I wish I could find some of it. My wife will be glad to see me, but she would be happy to see a bag of gold too!"

Suddenly through the mists came a wailing, prolonged scream that neared them at tremendous speed. Out of the cloudy ceiling, almost above their heads, a heavy body plunged into a tree top. They caught a glimpse of a long snaky neck, writhing and lashing about, its head armed with a swordlike spike.

"El Cuélebre!" yelled the Basque. "It has killed our friend! I must go and tell the bees that a man is dead!"

He turned to run. Following down into the tree, an eagle now stooped and struck its talons deep into the struggling creature. Then it flapped heavily up and they could see clearly what the eagle's prey had been. A large stork, dead now and limply hanging.

"Winged serpent, indeed! You believe too many of your own stories!"

Jaun was about to retort, but before he could answer Gwalchmai, a second stork followed the first, darting in upon the eagle.

The predator had no chance to disengage. The stork's mate was at him like a living lance, his neck straight and rigid, his beak closed and accurately aimed. The three fell together, the eagle pierced through and through—and the two storks with him, one dead and the other, unable to withdraw, who would soon die if it received no help.

The little drama was over.

"Now, by Saint Michel of Peril!" swore the Basque. "You may not believe in the winged serpent, but there is one. Surely, by now, our foolish friend has met it and it has slain him. I will burn a candle for him the next time I go into the new cathedral at Pamplona. Let us say a prayer for him while there is time."

Corenice ran to the dazed male stork. Gently she separated him from the eagle. He staggered erect, eyed his slaughtered mate, and rubbed his head caressingly against her body. Then he heavily took to the air.

Gwalchmai, listening to Jaun, also feared the worst for Arngrim. He was surprised and pleased to hear his familiar voice as they watched the rising bird.

"Say rather that I have met the Xana and she belongs to me!"

They looked up. Arngrim had approached noiselessly on the soft leafmold beneath the tree. He was smiling.

"See what I have found!"

In his arms he bore lightly an unconscious girl. She was beautifully clothed in wispy garments embroidered in golden thread. Her hair was golden also and it hung down over Arngrim's arm to brush his knees. She held a jeweled comb in one hand and water dripped from her clinging garments and from her tresses.

Her face was that of a sleeping angel and strangely reminiscent to Gwalchmai of someone he had known.

"Behold the Xana!"

Jaun shrank back and made the sign of the horns at her. "Now El Cuélebre will surely come! We are all dead together; there is no use to run!"

When Corenice saw her, she stepped between the pair and Gwalchmai. She noticed his keen scrutiny and misunderstood it, but he had already looked closely and he did not like what he saw.

"Where did you meet her, Arngrim?"

"She was looking into a clear pool and combing her hair. When I came up behind her, she turned quickly and fell into the water. I almost did not get her out, she struggled so. She was much afraid of me and I was even more afraid that she would drown."

"Xanas do not drown. They live in the water. She probably jumped in. That pool was her home!"

"Jaun, I shall soon forget you were my oar mate. This is a human girl and when she opens her eyes I will have her tell you so. She is the most precious thing I have ever held in my arms. I think I am in love with her already!"

"There is an easy way to tell," said Gwalchmai. He would have stepped closer, but Corenice seemed to be in the way. "Under the bezel of my ring is a little chamber and in it is powdered moly. If she is a nymph, it will not harm or make

any change in her any more than it would if she were
human, but if she has been enchanted, as I think she has
been, for to my vision her outline is only a blur, then it will
bring her back as she should be. No sorcerer's spell can
stand against moly. I will scatter a pinch of it on her."

Arngrim and the Basque looked skeptical. "Moly?" said
the Varangian. "I never heard of it." He peered into the
opened ring.

The opal was lifted back on tiny hinges and beneath it lay
a pale-green powder.

Arngrim clasped the girl tighter and backed away. "Leave
her alone. I like her the way she is."

"I have heard of it," Corenice broke in unexpectedly.
"One of those barbarian Greeks mentions it in a poem I
heard him recite in Ithaca a long time ago. Let me see if I
remember it—

> Stranger, pluck a sprig of moly
> Ere you tread on Circe's Isle.
> Hermes' moly, growing solely
> To undo enchanter's wile.

"Well, Arngrim, and you others, both Circe and Hermes
are as dead now as—as Homer, but I know moly still grows.
But not for you to use on a Xana, my husband! Here,
Arngrim—!"

In a flash, she snatched the ring out of Gwalchmai's hand,
leapt at Arngrim with a pinch of the power between her
fingers, sprinkled it on his hand, and slapped that hand,
powder and all, upon the girl's face and rubbed it in well,
before anyone could move.

"There!" she panted. "Now she is yours, Norseman! Take
good care of your Xana!"

She snapped back the bezel upon the rest of the powder
and gave back the ring to Gwalchmai. He had hardly placed
it again upon his finger before the girl opened her eyes.

Now he could see her outlines sharp and plain. The blur
he had noticed was gone, but other than that there was no
change.

She was as beautiful as before and just as wet. She did
not seem to notice or to care. She was looking only at
Arngrim and there was a light in her eyes that made his
throat choke and his heart leap in his breast.

She raised her arms and put them around his neck and hugged him tightly. His ugly face was transfigured by delight.

"I am Mairtre and now I am human again! The enchantment is gone, but I am here. If you want me I will be yours, handsome giant, for I vowed when I was spelled that whoever saved me, him would I wed!"

"Handsome!" he groaned. "Damsel, you are still ensorceled!"

And Jaun crowed, "See! I was right! She was a Xana!"

These are the true facts of the saga, which Arngrim did not tell to the skalds in Byzantium—and this was how he won his golden girl.

12

For the Honor of Roland

What other adventures befell Arngrim and the wife he had so unexpectedly won, as they later made their way to Byzantium, form no part of the present tale, although they were recounted at length in the Hall of the Mercenaries.

Gwalchmai and Corenice were not with them then. Yet, as the group traveled on through the pass, certain other events took place that affected all and so should be mentioned.

The pass narrowed still more, then unexpectedly widened into a little green meadow. Here was the pool where Arngrin had found the girl, Mairtre, combing her hair. Near it was an ancient oak, decayed but not yet dead, and farther along the path were other such giants.

They entered this small enclave and suddenly a sense of trespassing came over them all. It was as though they trod upon tragic ground, where a doom had befallen and which

even now held something of its horror. They paused, as
with one assent, although no word had been spoken.

Jaun looked up and gestured, with a sweeping hand along
the edge of the heights on either side.

"There stood the men and women of Escual-Herria—
waiting. On the road we have followed, the Moorish army
was coming to avenge the attack upon Zaragoza. When they
arrived here they found none but the dead. Just at this spot,
the rearguard of the French army was slaughtered.

"There the Paladins stood back to back. There the finest
of the champions planted his gonfalon—there he defended
it in a ring of the slain. Yonder boulder still bears the mark
of the mighty blows he dealt it to destroy his sword. Upon
it he leaned in mortal extremity and blew upon his horn, not
to summon help as some traducers say, but to warn Great
Carlos to beware, for he knew the Moors were pressing
close.

"It was so that the Warden Ruotland died, defending the
retreat of the main army. It was a knightly deed. We
Eskualdunak are proud of him too. We have often wished
he had been one of ours.

"Yet before the Moors arrived, the treasure was gone,
and they got nothing but wounds, for the army returned and
the struggle was bitter. So, both to us and them, this small
meadow will remain forever French although all the hills
around it be Spanish."

"I was never a war-chief," said Gwalchmai, reflectively,
looking at the heights, almost hidden now by the stealthily
lowering ceiling of mist. "If I had been in command here, I
would have sent my Valiants ahead to first clear and hold
the ridges. Then I would have brought my columns through.
This Charles may have been a great king, but he was not a
wise general."

They had progressed a little farther while speaking. Suddenly a branched and blinding stream of lightning ripped
down through the eddying whorls above them, striking the
old oak, splitting it asunder along the line of decay that ran
down the center of its trunk.

Part of it remained upright, but seared and smoking. The
remainder fell into the pool and the water therein splashed
out of it in a double wave to either side, leaving the pebbled
bottom of the pool bare.

Jaun fell on his knees, his teeth chattering. He crossed himself fervently.

"Saint Michel, a fistful of candles! I promise them! Protect us now, Saint Jago of Compostella, from the Powers of Darkness and the perils of storm!"

Under other circumstances Gwalchmai might have laughed, but he also had seen what had frightened the Basque.

It was a giant laughing face, formed for a split second by the disturbed and tumbling mist, the beard colored red by the upward striking glow from the burning part of the oak that still stood. It hung there, hardly longer than the flash itself, but long enough for Gwalchmai to recognize the features and long enough to see the eyes survey them and then turn toward the oak.

At once the thunder pealed, shaking the very hills, and the face disappeared, but Gwalchmai followed the direction of that gaze and saw in the exposed hollow of the tree a bright gleam of metal.

A long straight sword, with a cruciform hilt, embedded there, where it had been placed so long ago!

He knew then that it had been no dream, when he thought he had listened to the colloquy of the gods. Thor had kept his promise. Here, at last, was Roland's sword!

He strode quickly across the greensward and lifted it from its hiding place. In all that time of concealment, since the Valkyrie had caused it to be removed from under the Paladin's body—before other looters could find it and before Charlemagne's host returned to drive them away and meet the pursuing Moors again in battle, the sword had gathered but little rust.

The edge was still keen, the hilt unmarred by time.

"Ah, beautiful, dangerous Durandal!" thought Gwalchmai. "You splendid blade, fit for a king's hand—never touched before by any but Christendom's champion; how shall I ever dare to hold or wield you? Thor, you have given me more than I asked—more than I should have had. You have given me too much!"

He stroked his palm down the long clean line of the double-edged blade. He caressed it from tang to point and a few flakes of rust fell away. Under his hand he felt a vibrancy, a responsive thrill in the metal as though it was glad to come into the light again.

Just under the crossguard, five little crosses were stamped into the blade. He raised the sword to his lips and kissed them.

"I swear to you, Paladin Roland, this queen of weapons shall never be used in an unworthy cause. I am not the one to carry it. I will place it in trust, in the first safe place I find, for whomsoever shall come that next, by God's will, shall be considered Champion of France, in whatever day another shall be needed."

He swung it through the air. It hummed and sang as though in answer. He looked around at the others. They had not been watching him. Instead, they were gathered in a little group around the pool, into which the water was now seeping back.

A rather large bronze chest had been uncovered when the pool was emptied and Jaun and Arngrim were struggling with it. They had tugged it almost up on the bank. Gwalchmai went over to help and soon the three had it out of the deepening water. It was locked, but the hinges were only a mass of verdigris and a few sharp blows opened it. They forced back the lid and it fell away.

The women cried out in wonder and the men drew a sharp intake of breath.

Before them lay a part of the tribute wrested from Zaragoza. Golden coins, jeweled scimitar hilts, necklaces, crucifixes, all intermixed at random, as people had thrown them in to fill the chests with treasure and buy the city's liberty from the besieging Franks.

"See!" cried Jaun. "I told you she was a Xana! Now you will believe me! Now you know! They always make gifts of gold and jewels to those who find them."

"It is true I guarded it in the pool," said Mairtre. "It is not true I am anything but a human girl. Under the spell that bound me I acted as its guardian, but I never did anyone harm."

"Yours is an odd name," said Corenice. "I have never heard it before and yet it seems that I have known someone who bore it."

"There have been three Mairtres in my family. If I had a harp I could sing you my lineage, for by music I was taught to remember it."

"You are from Erin, then?" Gwalchmai casually asked.

"Yes, my father was a horse-merchant. He brought over

stallions to sell to the Moors, to improve the Arabian breed. Our ship was wrecked on the Spanish coast, not far from here. All were lost except for myself, and while lying upon the beach, half-drowned, I fell into the hands of a sorcerer."

Gwalchmai looked narrowly at her. Again he thought he detected a resemblance to someone he had known extremely well. That golden hair! Could it be?

"Was your father's name Flann?"

Mairtre was astonished. "Yes, it was, and my grandfather's! That is an old name in our family, too. Did you know him?"

"I think I have heard of him before."

"He is well known in Erin," said Mairtre, proudly. She gestured at the chest. "He has no need of such as this to be respected. It has little value to me, now that I have found my treasure."

She looked fondly upon the big Varangian and he pressed her to him in the crook of his arm. "Perhaps not to you, my love, but it is the greatest treasure I have ever seen."

"Then you should go to Cibola, where the very streets are spangled with it, or have walked in Poseidonis, where I have mentioned before how rain poured from the roofs through golden downspouts. This little heap is nothing to those sights."

Corenice's tone was elaborately casual, but her eyes glistened as she looked upon the flashing jewels.

"If it were mine, I would give it to all of you," began Mairtre, "but it is not——"

"Indeed, it is not!" A grim voice interrupted them and they turned in alarm.

While their attention was fixed upon the chest, a strange transformation had occurred.

To the eyes of all but Gwalchmai, who saw everything as being oddly blurred, they now stood inside an impressive hall. The mist ceiling had curdled, had thickened, had become a vaulted canopy of huge dimensions. Around its perimeter, it was supported by ribbed columns that had previously appeared to be oaks, while other pillars, set with flambeaux, supported the center of the dome.

The walls of the hall agreed in place to what had been the mounting slopes of the surrounding peaks. Now they were seen to be of cut stone, carved, decorated, but not in beauty, and hung with tapestries that pictured scenes most frightening. Here ghouls gamboled and fed upon ghastly battlefields under a gibbous moon. Here Herne, the Hunter, led his demon horsemen in mad pursuit of his fleeing quarry —a tattered man, clawed and stricken, who ran for his life across a gray moor where there was no covert.

They stood upon a thick, rich green carpet, their backs, now that they had turned, to a marble-rimmed fountain where water musically plashed and a vacant pedestal stood for some missing statue. Here lay sections of a fallen roof pillar and the floor was wet.

Facing the heavy boulder, which had borne the savage dints of Roland's furious strokes, they saw instead a high-backed and ornate throne.

Seated there, leaning casually against a heavy design wherein men suffered at the teeth and talons of grinning monsters, a thin black man observed them. By his dress, he appeared to be a Moor. He was wirily bearded. His left hand held a Wand of Power, translucently glittering and ominously pointed at them, while his other grasped the leash of a snarling creature that strained against it, as though it was mad to leap upon them.

This strange beast was long of body and the size of a coursing hound. It was covered, as with armor, by a tightly joined integument of shining ebony scales, edged with brilliant poisonous viridescent rims, which, as it writhed serpent-like, appeared and disappeared, causing it to constantly take on new configurations in design.

Its razor-sharp claws dug deep into the carpet as it fought the restraining fingers of the master who held it in, and its long tail lashed to and fro, slapping viciously against the throne.

It faced them and hissed like an escaping jet of steam. Its breath came to them as a putrid gust and although it could not see the intruders, for its snaky head was covered by a leather hood, it knew well their position. The blinded eyes were obviously following their movements, for the head swung from one to another of the group.

Among all the transformations of the mountain meadow, one thing only remained the same. Everything else, to Gwalchmai's eyes, was surrounded with the same hazy outline that had clothed Mairtre with unreality until touched by the moly powder.

The unchanged article was the treasure chest. Its edges

were clear and sharp and it was still filled with precious objects.

The wizard chuckled, as his eyes followed Gwalchmai's glance.

"Aintzina, robbers!" he said, with a sardonic smile. "I have been warned against your coming and now you are here. Shall you go away again, I wonder? I believe you are the one, ruddy man, who was told to beware of falling into sin, lest you fall also into a greater danger? What would you call theft? Is that sin or no?"

Gwalchmai started at that sinister mirth. The voice held the same glutinous tone he had heard coming up from below when the elves were menaced by the Worm. For an instant, a cold evil greater than the wizard's looked out of the wizard's eyes and it made his former mocking gaze appear like the frank open stare of a baby.

Gwalchmai realized that the trick of possession was not practiced by Corenice alone. Was this the Lord of the Dark Face in person, or did Oduarpa inhabit this evil being briefly for his own ends?

The wizard spoke again. "The wealth is not hers to give, but mine. I give nothing that belongs to me. Back upon your pedestal, nymph, and guard it again!"

Mairtre was moving forward and Arngrim, despite his fear, tried to stop her, but Gwalchmai had already placed himself before the creature upon the throne, just out of reach of the snarling beast.

He raised Roland's sword and held it out. "By the crosses upon the blade and by the relics in its hilt, I command you to depart!"

The wizard laughed and let slip a few inches of the leash. Gwalchmai held his ground.

"Now shall I loose my pet upon you? Perhaps I should watch you run a little while. Come back to me, Barbo, my sweet basilisk, you King of Serpents, and allow me to unhood your eyes that you may gaze lovingly upon these trespassers!"

He drew the creature back and Gwalchmai took another step toward it, this time with hilt in hand. He swung up Durandal.

The movement caught the wizard's eye and he lifted the Wand. A fury of sparks darted against Gwalchmai, but at that instant a streaming curtain of light, as impenetrable as

diamond and as transparent, surrounded the whole group. It
touched the floor tightly, circling their feet, and rose to an
apex at the ring on Gwalchmai's upraised hand.

The light surged along Durandal in cold waving ripples.
The sword gleamed a noble and menacing blue.

The wizard eyed it closely and the hand that bore it. He
seemed to shrink slightly into his seat. The basilisk crouched
as though to spring. He drew it gently back.

The appearance of a double identity passed from his face.
Whatever had dwelt there briefly now deserted him and departed to its own place, leaving him to face the Paladin's
blade alone. He was not daunted.

"I have been entrusted to give you a further warning.
Enrage my master no longer, lest your soul perish. Be
warned that he who lives longer than other men must also
rest longer than others do. Remember also that while one
sleeps one is helpless and it is well that a sleeping man has
no enemies.

"I am not otherwise advised of your attainments or qualities, nor do I wish to learn more, but I bow to the power
of your ring. The emblem it bears is well known to me. I
pray you, approach in peace and tell me something of it and
the Mage who bore it."

As he spoke, his eyes never leaving Gwalchmai's, his fingers were fumbling with the fastening of the basilisk hood.

Corenice whispered, but Gwalchmai had already seen. Before those deadly eyes could be unveiled, Durandal flashed
down.

The reptilian head leapt from the wildly flailing neck,
from which blood spouted as from a hose.

The wizard's face contorted with hate. Again the Wand
swung up, but as his eyes narrowed with the intent, the
sword of Roland was midway in its sweep.

Durandal passed through the body of the dark man like a
wisp of vapor and clanged upon the throne. As it made contact, everything changed. Like a bursting bubble, the surrounding phantasms passed away.

The pillars of the hall were once more broad-branched
trees. Mist hung again above them and the furnishings were
gone. All this in the time in which the sword continued on
and struck sparks once more from the boulder upon which
dying Roland had sought to shatter it.

The steel rang like a bell, but did not break. Its edge was keen and unharmed.

The five looked around as though waking from a dream. The treasure chest was still full, the meadow was empty and safe. There was only one difference that could be noted from before, to prove to them that what they had seen had been no illusion and that they had stood in a very real danger.

Wherever the blood of the basilisk had fallen, the grass beneath those flying drops lay dead and withered.

"Jesu maitia!" exclaimed Jaun. "I shall go no farther. You people doubtless have busy angels to protect you, but I am not so sure that mine are as hard-working as yours. Gaichoa, friends! This is where we part."

"You were to guide us through the mountains, comrade," remonstrated Arngrim. "We are still among them."

"If you get lost here, you will have to climb the peaks to do it. Keep on down the pass. It leads into France, but I think if I take that road my wife will be a lonely widow."

"Then, not so hastily. Let us first share out the wizard's gold. Perhaps, when she sees what you have brought, you may get a better welcome."

"Xana's gold!" corrected the Basque. "Xanas always reward their friends with gifts."

There was still a hanging back among them. No one seemed to want to be first to approach the opened chest again, possibly feeling that the action might call the enchanter back.

Finally Mairtre, for she had been its guardian, set her little hands to the task of overturning the heavy box; Arngrim hurriedly moved to help her and all gathered around the tumbled riches lying upon the greensward.

No enchanter appeared. It was not long before a rough division of the treasure had been made. With the remainder of the wine they drank a kantu to each other and to their lucky future, as they hoped it would prove to be. After this sincere toast, they sorrowfully parted, heavily laden and looking back over their shoulders—waving and calling goodbyes until they could no longer see Jaun.

They went on a little faster then, as the pass widened and their way dropped down into Gascony. They did not speak very much, for they had grown to like the Basque and all partings bring home a sense of melancholy and man's mortality.

Often, in later years, Arngrim wondered about his oar companion. He never heard what the future brought him, but Gwalchmai, by accident, did.

Much time had passed by. He was looking over a book of maps, in a library in Byzantium, compiled by Idrisi, the Arab cartographer, when his eyes fell upon a familiar name. He read eagerly on. It was the tale of the brothers Magrurin, who had sailed from Lisbon to find out "what it is that encloses the ocean, and what its limits are."

They had assembled a group of eight, all kinfolk, and set out. After eleven days' journeying westward, with a fast wind, they entered a sea choked by weed—"the waves were thick," said the chronicle of Idrisi. They found no land and were obliged to turn back, making landfall in Africa.

By this Gwalchmai knew at last to what use Jaun had put his share of the hidden treasure and suspected how it had come about.

Curious to learn whatever she might, of anything that might be remembered of her ancient homeland, Corenice constantly chatted with Jaun in her own language. In doing so, she disregarded one important fact: Sometimes when people speak of things that interest them, they may learn from each other. Jaun had become filled with a mighty desire to see the fabled land of which she spoke so fondly.

So it was that the Basque expedition did find the fabled site of Cíbola, the Golden City, and came to the continent of Atlantis, but in the end could only sail above it without knowing, becalmed in the Sargasso Sea, beneath which it lies.

As the group went on, Mairtre and Arngrim became very close. How long she had existed as a statue in the wizard's fountain, invisible to human eyes except on Saint John's day, when wicked enchantments fail, she never knew. The only thing she was certain about was that she had not perceptibly aged. It may have been long, but the years had not touched her and she had no doubts about accepting Arngrim's affection.

She cast loving eyes upon him also and it was laughable to the others to see how the ways of the ugly giant had softened, although Gwalchmai and Corenice did not make fun of him. They had not been together so long that they could not realize fully how he and Mairtre saw each other.

They came down out of the mists, just as the sun was

setting. They looked out over the fair lowlands of France and it was a pleasure to them to see that the mountains lay behind. There was little difference yet between the two countries, so close to the slopes.

They soon found that Basque was spoken here also, the Pyrenees being no bar to language, for a group of chattering children came by as they entered a little village and Corenice understood most of what they said.

An ox team plodded toward them hauling a farm wagon, gay fringes hanging from their yoke, bells clanking softly. The farmer greeted the children and looked at the strangers without much surprise.

"Gaihun," he said, and would have passed, but Corenice gave him good evening also.

"Gaihun, grandsire. We seek shelter for the night and food. We hunger and are weary with travel. Is there an inn hereabouts?"

The French Basque looked at them shrewdly and liked what he saw. Here, quite obviously, were two pleasant couples. The men appeared open-faced and, though armed and strongly built, were not brigands, for they had their ladies with them.

Judging by the rich clothes Mairtre wore, even though these were the worse for travel, the Basque felt they must have money to pay for lodging. He wondered how they might have lost their horses, but he did not overlook the fact that they carried heavy pouches and there were lumpy bundles under the jackets of both men.

He knew an opportunity when he saw one. "Soup is hot and waiting in my house for me. There is always enough for visitors. Today was baking day and we can make you pallets, but they will be on the floor. Will such beds do for you, nobles?"

They looked at one another. There was no argument.

"I could sleep on a doorstep if I had something to eat," said Arngrim when Corenice had translated for them.

She nodded to the farmer. "Lead on. You have guests."

They followed him homeward, down the single street of the village, to a small house with thick stone walls and a thatched roof. It had a well-tended kitchen garden and a small plot of flowers. The house was well kept and neat inside and redolent of new bread.

A word from the farmer to his wife was enough to bring
out her smile and a hearty welcome. After a substantial
supper and evening prayers, they made ready for sleep.

Corenice and Mairtre retired to their host's own room,
the farmer and his wife giving it up to take over their children's cots.

The children slept, in their turn for this one night, before
the fireplace, as did Gwalchmai and Arngrim. It was a
crowded house.

They rose early and broke their fast on new black bread,
sopped in wine, and were given two loaves to take with
them.

When they were about to leave, Corenice staggered and
turned pale. A dizziness came over her and she almost fell,
but she thrust away Gwalchmai's anxious hand and caught
herself. The feeling soon passed and she felt able to travel.

Gwalchmai gave the farmer one of the smaller gold coins
he had already separated from the others in his pouch, at
which windfall the Basque couple felt overpaid. Arngrim
did the same, and Mairtre traded her fine dress for a homespun gown more suitable for travel and less conspicuous.
Then they were ready for the road.

When they had gone a little way, the farmer came running after them waving a stout walking stick.

"My own makila. For the sick lady."

Corenice thanked him and they went on. She alternately
supported herself by it and leaned upon Gwalchmai when
the road was rough. After a little while she stepped out
strongly and their pace increased.

As they went on, traffic on the road thickened. There
were few wagons, but many people were walking. Some of
these were carrying sticks or staffs over their shoulders,
with bundles tied upon them, and had evidently come a long
way. There were knights on horseback, who bore themselves
proudly and wore crosses upon their arms.

There were women and children on foot, tired and dusty,
although it was still early in the day. They pushed on slowly,
as though they had walked throughout most of the night and
slept in the fields to hasten their reaching of the destination
toward which all journeyed.

Sick and crippled were moving upon the road in company
with the able, being carried in litters or riding on two-
wheeled carts and barrows drawn by donkeys, mules, or even

being pushed or pulled by the relatives of those who were unable to walk. It looked as though the whole of southern France was being depopulated and was moving north.

Yet obviously this crowd was not a mass of refugees fleeing before an invader. One and all—whether priest, friar, or peasant; lord, knight, or ribald; cutpurse or dewy-eyed innocent—shared a common look. It was a rapt, dedicated expression, as though their gaze was fixed upon something unearthly—something beyond the horizon, something toward which they yearned.

As it became apparent to the newcomers from Spain that they were becoming motes in a tremendous migrating stream of movement and that they rarely met anyone coming toward them, their curiosity grew.

Finally they arrived at a crossroad where one highway continued north and another ran eastward. In this latter direction they had originally meant to travel, for that way lay Rome, where Gwalchmai had long planned to go, and afterward Byzantium with Arngrim, in case his mission failed there.

Both of these great cities were centrally located in Christian kingdoms and both had control of shipping. Therefore, neither could be ignored if Gwalchmai was to complete his mission—to deliver his message and place Alata within the empire of a Christian ruler, although he knew now there no longer existed any Emperor of Rome.

They stopped at this crossroad and consulted on their course of action. Other tired wayfarers had fallen out for a brief rest before going on. All sat together companionably, whatever their wealth or degree, and lunched upon what they had brought.

Nearby Gwalchmai, an old man sat with a crutch across his lap. He carried with him a bag of onions and Arngrim traded a half of his loaf for four of them.

Gwalchmai gestured at the passersby. "Where is everyone going?"

The old man stopped munching and stared at him. His mouth hung open in the middle of a bite. He choked and swallowed. "Where have you been that you have not heard the wonderful news?"

"Across the mountains. What is happening?"

The cripple nodded as though that explained everything. "Of course. They are very ignorant in the hills. There are

people up there that don't know that there is another side
to every mountain! But you look intelligent. Haven't you
heard of the great Crusade Pope Urban is going to tell us
about? The one that Peter, the Hermit, has been preaching?"

They could only shake their heads. He looked amazed.

"I thought all the world knew about it. You do know that
the Pope gives orders to all Christendom, which Kings and
Emperors obey?"

Gwalchmai did not know it, but he nodded sagely.

"There was a terrible battle, called Manzikert, and the
paynim Turks won the day over the armies of Byzantium.
Then the Emperor Alexius appealed to the Kings of Europe
for help. Peter has roused the Teutonic lands to march,
preaching, they say, as though his heart was on fire. He has
seen with his own eyes how the heathen abuse our pilgrims.

"Pope Urban has come into France, from his palace in
Rome, and called a mighty council at Clermont to tell us all
what to do. He will surely urge us to take up the Cross and
march with the Teutons in the following of our Lord, who
will deliver Jerusalem. Then the end of the world will come
and we will all be ready for it—those who have worn the
Cross!"

"Then we shall surely do this!" heartily agreed Gwalchmai
and the other three nodded. Secretly Gwalchmai thought that
he must see this Pope who commanded Kings like servants.
Surely, with such tremendous power and influence, he might
be the man to inform of the existence of Alata and so be
discharged of his mission at last.

However, this news meant to Arngrim only that if Byzantium was in such danger, he as a Varangian, the most trusted
of all Byzantium's soldiers, was far from where he should
be, and the sooner he returned to take up his duties the
better.

So the crossroads became a place of parting. The two
women tearfully embraced and the men gripped forearms in
the old Roman manner, for that much had persisted in both
their pasts, even if they shared little else but comradeship.

Then each man kissed the other's lady farewell and were
soon lost forever in the press of nobles, clergy, and the
ever-present poor.

It was many weary miles to Clermont, but in less than a
week of travel Gwalchmai and Corenice were there, and
none too soon.

There were no accommodations for late footweary travelers, and Gwalchmai wished bitterly that he were able to find some spot under a roof for Corenice to sleep. She looked tired and her face was drawn as though she was in pain, but this she denied and had marched with the best of the pilgrims. Sometimes she forced him to hurry to keep pace with her, as strong and enduring as though she still dwelt in that tireless body of metal he had first known.

It seemed to him as though she too was caught up in this enthusiastic fever of movement that had swept up all the floating population of Europe to see and hear the Pope. For verily it did appear that all Europe must be crowding into Clermont.

He bought a tarred piece of canvas at an exorbitant price, and with three poles, which should have been gold-plated so much they cost, he erected a little tent. For a few days they called it home. Many fared less well, but they did not seem to care.

When at last Pope Urban was to speak, he mounted a high scaffold where all the thousands present could see him. He stood there, a small lonely figure, and raised his arms for quiet.

At each corner of the platform, facing the cardinal points of the compass, a man stood with a leather speaking trumpet. Others were scattered in lines spaced through the crowd, to catch what was said by the Pope, to repeat it in stentorian voices where other listeners could hear and pass along the speech in the same way, until all the vast host was fully informed.

Urban spoke slowly, with a long pause after each sentence, until he was sure he was heard and that his words had carried out to the far fringes.

He began by condemning the cowardice of the Turks and the brutalities they had inflicted upon helpless pilgrims. He continued by praising the courage and strength of Christendom's armies, and their invincibility were they to unite in a common cause. To fight under the banner of their Lord who had died for them was the least they could do.

Then he went on to chide them for their own evil. He brought home to them in scorching phrases the danger they faced in the loss of Heaven, until everywhere the folk went sinking to their knees and beat their breasts in remorse.

"But," he thundered, "no sins are too heinous to be

washed away by one drop of the waters of the Jordan! No evil is too deadly to go unforgiven to those who take the Cross and smite the infidel! You are sure of success! Suffering may await you, but your reward is greater far. By the torments of your bodies, you shall redeem your souls!

"Go then, on your errand of love, which will put out of sight all the ties that bind you to the spots you have called your homes.

"Your homes, in truth, they are not. For the Christian all the world is exile, and all the world is at the same time his country. If you leave a rich patrimony here, a better patrimony awaits you in the Holy Land. They who die will enter the mansions of Heaven, while the living shall pay their vows before the sepulchre of their Lord.

"Blessed are they who, taking this vow upon them, shall obtain such a recompense; happy are they who are led to such a conflict, that they may share in such rewards."

A mighty roar arose, drowning out him and the trumpeters.

"God wills it! Deus Vult! Deus Vult! Deus Vult!"

When the uproar had diminished, the Pontiff went on. "It is certainly God's will. Let these words be your war-cry when you find yourself in the presence of the enemy. You are soldiers of the Cross; wear those crosses on your breasts or carry on your shoulders the blood-red sign of Him who died for the salvation of your souls."

When the milling crowd had dissipated, it had become a sober determined host. Before the day was over, arrangements were being made to march upon Jerusalem. Among the most sober was Gwalchmai.

Nothing could have been plainer from both Pope Urban's words and the people's reaction to them that there was slight chance of obtaining his sponsorship and a grant of shipping to go on a voyage of discovery to a new land.

Even had the Pope been so inclined, and it was obvious that his interests lay elsewhere, he was now committed to support this Crusade he had called. There would be little or nothing available for any other venture.

He was not the ruler whom Gwalchmai had hoped to find. The continent that was in Gwalchmai's power to give away must go to someone else, unless he could convince the Pope by means of a personal interview that such an expedition was feasible and of prime importance.

But how to obtain such an interview? Directly after the exhortation, Pope Urban had left Clermont for Rome.

That night, Gwalchmai and Corenice lay together in their tent. She shivered in the night chill and would not admit to him that she was unwell.

He slept fitfully, distressed by doubt over his impossible mission and torn between his vow and his worry over her. Just before false dawn, he thought he opened his eyes to see a man standing in the entrance.

The light was indistinct and the man's back was to it, but Gwalchmai knew the voice.

"Apprentice! Have you yet learned aught of the meaning of life and the mystery of death?"

"Only a little, Master, but I think I am learning."

"Then I can praise you, for to know that you know little is in truth to know much. Now listen well.

"This sword you carry and which you were given by Thor is, as you suspected, not a brand to be used lightly, to be handled carelessly or lost. It has a destiny and one day it will be called for.

"I know your pledge concerning it, although I do not know what inspired you to make such a vow. I am proud that you realize it is intended for another hand than yours. A Champion of France shall yet wield it.

"Now, I have one more commission for you as I had for your delivery of Excalibur, but this one will not be as difficult or take as long. It is no less important and it must be accomplished.

"Go, therefore, with all haste on the north road until you reach the shrine of Saint Catherine of Fierbois and there make a votive offering of Durandal to that saint. She will keep it until it is called for, and there it will be safe.

"Then you may take your lady, of whom you may well be glad, and go to Rome, where you should have a better chance of furthering your mission than you may believe. Good fortune pursue you, Apprentice. Good night."

"Stay, Godfather Merlin," cried Gwalchmai, leaping up, catching his head in the joined poles, bringing down the canvas upon himself and Corenice in a stiff tangle. When they had extricated themselves, he found it was bright morning—Merlin was gone, if he had ever been there—and a little knot of people were gathered about, pointing and laughing.

Not much later, it was a disappointed and weary pair that

set their feet toward the north, having obtained directions
to the shrine Merlin had mentioned.

That there was such a shrine was proof enough that the
vision had been no dream, but it seemed that the journey
he had begun so lightly was becoming endless and that one
mission accomplished led only to another.

Still, he was convinced that this one was important, and
he meant to do as he was bid—out of respect for his godfather's wishes, who had surely inspired him in the original
thought, and also for the honor of Roland.

He wondered why Merlin had said "good night" when he
had made his farewell in broad day. It was to be months
before he knew.

13

Rome at $\mathcal{L}$ *ast*

As they took the road toward the village of Fierbois, it
became more apparent that Corenice was very ill. It was
evident both to her and Gwalchmai that the body of the
Welsh girl she had inhabited was flawed physically as well
as having had a vacancy as to mind or soul.

In all her long existence, Corenice had never known
feebleness and lassitude such as she now experienced. The
hardships of travel had taken bitter toll.

For some days, as they progressed onward, she successfully hid her illness from Gwalchmai. In the beginning they
had walked, meeting many latecomers to Clermont still on the
road, although there were larger groups wending their way
homeward to settle their affairs before taking up the cross.

The time came when she had to admit that she could
walk no farther. Fortunately it was not long before Gwalchmai was able to hire a wagoner to go out of his way home

to Chinon, in order to pass by the shrine of Saint Catherine. By that time they were only a few miles from it.

Fierbois was a little place, lying halfway between Loches and Chinon. Farms dotted the way and it looked like a prosperous locality and a pleasant place to live. The large city of Tours was not far away, providing a good market for produce and the people appeared to be content with their lot.

The chapel was a popular retreat for both the local visitors and more distant pilgrims. There were a few persons at their devotions when they arrived and after these had finished their prayers, Gwalchmai and Corenice entered.

No priest was in attendance and it was quiet and restful within. Candles burned before the altar and there was a fragrance of spicy incense.

It was easy to see why Merlin had commanded that Roland's sword should be left here in trust rather than a more convenient hiding place, for the walls were hung thickly with weapons.

Bill-hooks stood in sheaves, Morning Stars dangled their spiky balls on short chains among maces, long knives, and daggers that poor peasants had carried in battle. All these had been placed there in gratitude by soldiers who felt that the gracious Saint had in some manner saved their lives and in return for her good offices had from that moment forsworn war. That the feeling was not confined to the hearts of the simple poor was evidenced by racks of swords, in many styles and qualities.

Some were of fine Toledo and Damascus make; a few had high-sounding names engraved upon the blades of this queen of weapons; others were splendid because of their jewel-encrusted hilts.

It was an excellent spot to leave Durandal, Gwalchmai thought, but he did not like to risk such a unique treasure, whose future value to France Merlin had confirmed.

He looked about for a safer nook than on the open wall. The wagoner and Corenice were both on their knees, with heads bowed before the altar. Saint Catherine looked benignly down upon them all.

Gwalchmai wondered to whom Corenice was praying in this holy place and if she prayed for health or something less personal. She had seldom asked her goddess for anything for herself.

Neither was looking at him. He heard voices outside, but

before anyone could enter, he went forward quickly. There was a narrow space between the altar and the wall, sufficient to accept the sword.

He slipped it into the gap as though into a sheath. When he released the hilt, Durandal slid out of sight and he heard it gratingly fall even farther as though there was a deeper hole, perhaps a crypt or compartment behind the altar.

He felt satisfied. Unless the altar was removed or the shrine deserted and torn down, neither of which contingencies seemed likely in view of its popularity, Roland's sword was safe. Now his errand was completed and he could devote his attention to other important matters.

He touched Corenice on the shoulder. Her eyes were closed and her body swayed against him. Her face was pale. With a cry, he caught her tight against him. Her hands were burning hot.

At that moment a middle-aged couple entered, smiling at first to see them thus, though a little surprised at their choice of place.

However, the wise, knowing eyes of the woman saw at once that this was not an act of courtship and she came up to see if she could be of some help. An instant's examination told her all she needed to know. She turned to Gwalchmai.

"When is she expecting?" she asked.

"What do you mean?" Gwalchmai was taken aback.

"How long before the child will be born? Surely you know you are going to be a father?"

He mutely shook his head.

The woman sniffed. "You men are all fools. If she was a mare or a cow, I'll wager you'd know to the minute when one would foal or the other calve. That would be money in your purse, wouldn't it? You'd be interested in that, ey? This might cost you something, so you hope it won't happen or pretend it isn't so. Just like my old man!"

Her words were harsh, but she regarded the couple fondly.

"Sometimes I wonder why God made men and what women see in them! Great hairy, dirty, stupid things—always cursing and killing each other! Get her out in the air. This smoke is enough to choke a mule!"

They quickly carried Corenice out and laid her on the grass. It was not long before she opened her eyes and tried to sit up. The woman gently pressed her back.

"Give me your bottle, old man," she commanded. Her husband rather reluctantly passed it over, as it was nearly empty. She brought out a little cup from somewhere in her capacious skirts, filled it and crumbled in a few dried leaves from her purse, stirring it well with her finger, cooing over Corenice meanwhile.

"There precious, drink it down. Hearty now, drink it all. It will do thee much good. 'Tis naught but a mite of foxglove for thy heart's sake. Dried silkworms would be better for the dizziness, but who can afford them, these days? I would I had a scrap of mummy for thee. That is the best of all."

Thus she rattled on, while Gwalchmai hung over them like a hovering shadow.

It was not long before some color came back into Corenice's wan cheeks and she was able to stand.

"Where are you going?" said the woman. Gwalchmai and Corenice looked at each other. Here was a severe setback to their plans.

Both realized it was most urgent that they be on their way to Rome as soon as possible if Gwalchmai were to secure an audience with the Pope before all forces and shipping were committed to the Holy Land.

There was no way of estimating the delay in accomplishing his mission if this slight opportunity were to be overlooked. Yet it was as plain to each that it was quite impossible for Corenice to travel much farther at the present time.

"We came here as pilgrims from Clermont, to fulfill a vow," said Gwalchmai, quite honestly. "Now, we know not when, but as soon as may be we must take the road for Rome."

The woman regarded them narrowly. She looked at Corenice with pursed lips and shook her head.

"It will be a long time before this wife of yours will be going on pilgrimage again, lad. I think when she does there will be three of you traveling. I asked you how long, precious, but I think I know. About three months gone, are you?"

Corenice would not meet her eyes, but nodded.

The woman harrumphed. "I thought so. And this great lout that thinks of naught but his own will and pleasure, like all men, didn't want to be burdened by a babe, did he?

Poor lass! I'll wager you didn't tell him for fear he would
beat you! Men! They are all the same—every one!"

She glared impartially upon her husband, Gwalchmai, and
the wagoner, all of whom quailed at her sharp tongue.

Corenice's shoulders shook, but not with sobs. Gwalchmai
waited anxiously for her to say something in his defense,
but she only kept her head down so the woman could not
see her face.

He lifted her chin, but she instantly put on a most woebe-
gone expression that made him want to hit her in very
truth, and she shrank away from him as though in deadly
fear.

The woman gave him a shove, with an arm fit for a
fighter, and gathered her against her own ample bosom,
whence Corenice peeked out demurely at Gwalchmai.

"There! There! He'll not lay one finger on you, if I know
it," she crooned. "You are coming home with me to a nice
bed of goose feathers and he can sleep tonight in the barn.
If I had my way, I'd see him in the midden rather!"

So saying, she led the way out to their cart, forgetting
to make the prayers she had come to say. All this time, her
husband had said nothing, seemingly a matter of old custom,
but now he looked from her to the shrine in dismay.

The woman wasted no time or words. She helped Corenice into the cart, gathered up the reins, and clucked to the
old sway-backed horse. Her husband would have been left
behind if he had not hurried. As it was, he climbed in over
the back of the moving cart, which Gwalchmai was not able
to do, as he was delayed by finding a small coin to pay the
wagoner for his trouble.

By the time he had done this the cart was far down the
road, the stiff backs of the three occupants well expressing,
without words, their poor opinion of him. None of them
looked back.

He looked thoughtfully at a clump of slender willows
alongside a brook. He drew his knife and took a step or two
in that direction, then gave up the idea. There was no time
to cut one. He would have to hurry to keep the cart in
sight.

Two weeks later he was on the road again, this time
moving south—and alone.

During those few days, the health of Corenice had mark-edly improved, although she was far from being in any condition to journey farther. The virulent fever, picked up in the crowded assembly at Clermont, soon ran its course, but her weakened condition only emphasized the natural disabili-ty of her body.

The most she felt able to do was to sit in the sun on fine days and watch the passersby. It tore Gwalchmai to see her so, remembering how in Thyra's body she had enjoyed life, being so vibrant and healthy; how they had played together and courted in the deeps; how they had sworn their troth and soared to the heights on broad white pinions that thrummed and sang in the winds above the clouds.

He recalled how she had waited through the long years; how she had saved his life by bringing him out of the ice; he thought about the times she had teased him and the anger he had felt—and he buried his face in his hands as he sat beside her, so that she might not see the tears in his eyes.

Then he would feel her loving palm against his cheek and he would turn and take her in his arms, oblivious of those who marched upon the road, southward, ever southward, toward Marseilles, where the ships were gathering for those who were going to the Holy Land by sea.

She knew how much he desired to leave for Rome. As the days passed and still she was not strong enough to travel, she began to urge him, ever more strongly as time went on, to go.

"Go now. Wait no longer," she insisted, while he still had time to journey to Rome and return before his son would be born—for that it would be a son neither of them doubted.

Surprisingly, their benefactors agreed. Gwalchmai had learned early that the elderly farmwife had a soft, warm heart, although she treated everyone indiscriminately to the rough side of her tongue.

Even Corenice came in for her share of scoldings, when she wished to take some part in the work of the household, for in the Welsh family life, as Nikky, she had picked up all the homely arts and could now churn and weave and sew with the best.

They were honest folk, too, and when he was finally con-vinced by all of their arguments, he knew that the major part of the treasure, which he left, in addition to Corenice's share, would be kept untouched unless she needed it before he came back.

Her time had yet five months to run—plenty enough to journey to Rome and back, he thought. He would have his interview with Pope Urban, convince him of the importance of what he had to impart, and be back again, long before he would be needed by her bedside.

In the meantime, she would rest and grow well and be his own strong girl again.

So, one fair morning, he waved them goodbye and also took the road to Marseilles.

Rome, the Imperial City, Mother of Nations, was no longer the Rome of which his father had spoken so long ago. The Goths, the Cimbrians, the Vandals, and the Huns had each taken their turn in humbling that mighty metropolis. Its armies were long gone, its people scattered. Even the refugees from it had centuries earlier forgotten their heritage.

Its buildings were crumbled and in ruin; its treasures ravaged; its arenas silent to the winds and drifting leaves. Aqueducts still delivered water to its many fountains; its roads of stone sprang from it to all parts of the world, as the spokes of a wheel lead outward to the rim, but no legions tramped them now with iron-studded boots.

Only eleven years before, the Normans had sacked and burned when they came to rescue Pope Gregory, besieged in Hadrian's tomb by the armies of Emperor Henry the Fourth. They had left the city a smoking ruin from which it had not yet recovered.

Fierce, bloody battles had been fought there—from temple, to tomb, to forum—and others were to be fought, but when Gwalchmai arrived from the west and looked down upon it from the Janiculum hill, Rome still appeared to be a quiet stately, impressive city.

It was evening and the unhealed scars of war and time were softened by distance. A light haze of smoke lay over it like a veil, for it was time for the evening meal and although the city population was few in comparison with its former multitudes, there were still many people dwelling within its boundaries.

It had become the center of all Christendom's hope, for it was the focus of Christian thought. Here, of all places, had been thrown down the gage to the men who carried the Crescent on their flag and laughed when they were told that the iron men from the west, who bore the Cross, would eventually demand a reckoning for the cruel deeds done to their brothers on the road to Jerusalem.

Now that day had come, the armies were gathering, and Gwalchmai looked upon the city—to his eyes it was the marvel he had longed to see.

It was the Year of our Lord, One Thousand and Ninety-Five, and he had been four hundred and sixty-three of his years on the road!

Owing to the effect of the Elixir of Life which he had unwittingly drunk and which still coursed through his veins, he still looked to be a comparatively young man. There was a little gray along his temples, a few wrinkles etched in at the corners of his lips and eyes, but that was all to indicate that he was no longer a youth. He felt strong and young— he had lost no teeth, at which he wondered, although actually his years of conscious life were few.

He was yet to experience the penalties that mystic draught was to bring, although the wizard had reminded him that such there would be. He had all but forgotten the warning.

He slept and ate at an inn. He waited a fortnight for an audience and when it was finally granted, he never reached the Pope and never told his story.

Instead, when the doors were opened and his turn came to advance and his name was announced by the Chamberlain, he took three steps only into the reception hall. He saw the slight figure seated at the far end, robed and mitred and waiting; he saw the princes of the church on either side; he heard the grandly dressed man at the door commence a query:

"What is the—?"

Then a mist came between him and all else. He heard an evil, glutinous chuckle in his ear that he had heard before and even then he knew that it was heard by him alone.

A profound weariness came upon him—his tongue was thick with the sleep that was rushing upon him. He thought he cried out, "Corenice! Wait! Oh, wait, wait for me!" but he made no sound. His ears seemed full of cotton wool and he drifted away to slumber.

"He who lives longer than others, must also sleep longer than other men."

As he fell to the long, red carpet at his feet, he thought
he heard an agonized cry in reply—"Oh, no, my darling!
No! No! No!"—but it was only in his mind.

He never felt the shock when his body struck the floor.

PART II

The Sword of
The Paladins

14

The Catacombs

He knew his name. He had been christened Gwalchmai by his godfather, Merlin, the Enchanter, which means Eagle in a most ancient tongue.

He knew where he had been, where he had gone, and why he had come there. He knew that he had a mission to fulfill and that there were obstacles in the way.

He did not know where he was.

He wandered in bliss, in a place of tranquil splendor and beauty. Here were gently rounded hills clothed in asphodel and lilies, and beyond their rondures one perfect snow-capped peak that drew his eyes toward its perfection, its purity of line.

Here were fountains that made music, and when the soft, perfumed winds that breathed across that land touched the leaves of the broad forests, sweet sounds chimed from them. He breathed a fragrance of spices and he saw only loveliness everywhere.

The people of that land were delicately beautiful and their voices were like songs of which he never tired, although what they said in harmony passed through his understanding like mist and left no memory there.

He was not alone, for he held a soft hand in his and beside him walked his beloved Corenice. Here they moved seeing the wonders of that fair place, never tiring, for there was no end to its marvels and no satiation to their happiness.

Here time passed idly over them in this delightful country, for there was no sun or moon to mark its passage and no

hunger or thirst or weariness to divide time into hours as
in the lands of men.

They dwelt there in contentment and peace. Sometimes he
thought giant faces hovered over them, but they were never
dreadful; they were benign, they were always kind and loving.

He did not mind being watched by them—he felt that he
and Corenice were being protected and cared for.

He had thought Elveron was a country whose enchantment could not be surpassed, but this magic and exquisite
region was far beyond the fancies of the elves.

Nothing more could be wished for. Here was desire and
hope fulfilled. This was Tir-nan-og—this was the future toward which all men yearn; the Fortunate Isles; Hy-Breasail;
Paradise!

But Eden can only be visited now; it has long been
marked "Out of Bounds"—no one can really live there any
more.

There came a moment when he knew he walked alone.
Shadows dimmed the lustre of all that wondrous land and
descended upon it rapidly. Quietness stilled the fountains,
the fragile and exotic buildings crumbled, the people disappeared and he felt that he was being hurried away.

He reached out, trying to grasp those fingers again in
desperation. There was nothing else to which he desired to
cling.

His hand struck harsh cold stone. He cried out and
opened his eyes—to blackness!

This was more than night, it was the eternal dark of the
Pit. He stretched his arms, feeling his muscles crack and
strain as from long disuse. He felt rock upon one side and
emptiness on the other. Above him, a few inches over his
head, was a smooth stone surface and beneath him another,
softened only by a thin pad. It was obvious that he lay in a
niche cut into the living rock, but where?

His breath rasped over a dry tongue; his lungs expanded
and ached; he began to live again and his thoughts returned from the vanished realm of delight. He heard the
blood surging in the little channels of his ears—there was no
other sound.

He raised his weak hand to his face. His beard, always
scanty because of his Aztec blood, was thin, but long. Dust
lay thick upon it and upon his skin. His hair was long and

matted with dust. How much time had passed since he had been laid here? How many years since he had been—forgotten?

No! Not forgotten, for he felt that he had been watched and tended. Those faces he had seen! Surely, they were real, if all else was fancy!

In the past, he had met and mastered other illusions, but none like these last. He had spent much time in a place that must have been real. He could map and chart it. He could still smell its sweet scents. He would never be able to rest until he visited that mystic bourn again.

He turned upon his side and groaned with the electric tingling of renewed circulation. He struck his palms against his thigh and the pain seemed more than he could bear. He massaged his legs, kneading out his iron cramps, and rubbed his hands together.

His fingers felt like brittle sticks and were covered with oddly shaped lumps. Then it came to him with his increasingly returning awareness of the present, that these were rings that covered almost solidly his fingers and his thumbs.

Memory came back. Was Merlin's Ring among them? His finger tips searched among the other jewels. Yes!

He searched his remembrance for the proper spell. His slow thoughts stumbled. He concentrated with a terrible effort of will and the words came haltingly out. He rubbed the engraved opal that was the bezel of the ring and it began to glow like a brightening ember, smoky crimson shot with livid green at first, then kindling to a vivid scarlet.

Now the cavity in which he lay could be dimly seen, and as the ring stone ran through the intermediate shades of orange, yellow, and brilliant argent light, the circle of his vision widened.

Across a narrow corridor were other recesses in the stone. He looked up and counted five tiers of them in the opposite wall, some empty, others cemented shut as though other bodies than his lay within. Names, crosses, pictures, and murals were painted on the slabs that concealed those entombed.

How was it that his lay open to the air? Was it known to someone that he was not truly dead, although he lay in what he could only consider as being a vast underground cemetery?

He directed the beam from the ring upward. The ceiling

of the corridor was also stone, rough and gashed by chisel
and pick. He was only inches from the floor. Now he had
the strength to roll out of his cavity. He did so, fell heavily
and lay there panting, but he felt that his strength was fast
returning.

Something had fallen crisply with him. He clutched it and
found it to be a tightly rolled parchment scroll upon a
knobbed spindle.

He breathed deeply, feeling his lungs creakingly expand
within their pleural chamber. It was painful, but he raised
first to his knees and then his feet. He ran his hands about
the confines of the niche and then over his body.

Now he remembered the appointment he had sought with
the Pope. It all flooded back. How he had hoped to divert
the Pope's interest from the dubious venture in the East,
called a Crusade, to the certain benefits available in the
West, which knowledge about the twin continents of Alata
and Atala only he could impart to the man who gave
imperious orders to Kings and Emperors.

How, at the very moment of the approaching interview,
he felt the curse of his long sleep come upon him, the main
drawback to the long existence his draft of Merlin's Elixir
of Life had conferred upon him.

How long this time? A day? Centuries? Where was his
lost love? His Corenice?

He had not worn his sword when he went to his appointment with Pope Urban, but he had tucked his little flint
hatchet in his belt, under his outer clothing, for he had
noticed that others wore ceremonial daggers. As a prince of
Alata, lacking a dagger, the tomahawk had to do.

During his incarceration, and it was coming home to him
that it had been very long, his clothing had been changed.
He was now dressed in loose, flowing robes of coarse brown
linen and shod in sandals. Beneath it he felt himself cinctured by his old leather belt, studded with Roman coins,
which his mother had given him when he left Aztlan.

Nothing else. He had been disarmed but not robbed, for,
running his hands around his pallet, he found that the little
ax lay in the niche. He jammed the scroll in the rough cord
that bound his robes and slipped the ax into it also. Now he
had a more secure feeling than before.

Something dangled around his neck and struck against his

chest. He felt that it was a crucifix. He tucked it into the bosom of his robe, thus doubly guarded.

As he faced the wall he saw an inscription over his resting place. *"Arcanum Sacrum"* he spelled out—Sacred Mystery.

He wondered painfully who had painted it while he lay there lost in dream, but there was nothing to tell him.

Now that he was erect, he felt an infinitely faint waft of air against his face. Probability to the contrary, for it would seem that his body should be completely desiccated if his fears were to be found correct, his efforts had caused him to slightly perspire.

Thus more easily sensing the direction from which the draft was coming, he followed it down the long corridor he was in, passing row upon row of sealed tombs. How many miles if one traced all of the intersecting passages to their ends? How many dead lay here in their thousands upon thousands, awaiting the Resurrection that he had alone so strangely experienced?

He went on, trusting his ephemeral guide. Occasionally he flashed the beam from his ring upon some of the inscriptions that he passed, mentally translating the faded phrases;

"Vivas in Deo. In pace Christi." occurred frequently, but someone, wife or husband, had also written "Here lies my beloved in the Lord." A little farther on, he saw the picture of a young girl, pretty and pensive, limned in vanishing colors upon the slab behind which she slept. Beneath it was inscribed in straggling letters, as though the writer's hand had trembled, "She was as sweet as honey." No name and nothing more.

Here and there lay husband and wife together and above them, once, the words: "They dwelt always in sweetest wedlock. Pass on, holding them in good memory."

Pass on he did, nor could look again at any of them, for now his heart was full of Corenice and the memories were of her and he felt more lorn than he thought anyone who had left a loved one here could have ever felt.

Then there were no more crypts in the wall and the passageway slanted more steeply upward. There were no crosses painted or cut into the rock as there had been and no more sacred inscriptions. He noticed also, now that he was beyond those deeper regions long sanctified by worship, tears, and prayer, that the air was no longer against his face, even though he should be nearing the spot from which it had originated.

Instead, the current had reversed itself and was now an almost tangible pressure against his back! It was almost as though some vast body, or piston-like mass, was pushing upward through the black corridor behind him, filling it from wall to wall, from floor to ceiling, driving the air against him, first as a breeze and then more rapidly blowing as a wind.

He cast the light beam backward. There was nothing, but the gust that struck him was fetid and repulsive and distantly a sound became apparent. A swishing, flowing gurgle that came up and up.

He turned and ran up the slope, but when he came to the place where the faint draft had entered, he found it to be a rough hole barred across by a grating of heavy iron.

He seized and shook it. It was firm and held by a strong lock. The thought came to him that he was trapped, for the sound of a crepitant rushing was very close. He remembered then the wizard at Roncesvalles, who had warned him against his Master, the Lord of the Dark Face, and had advised him against going underground, where that Lord held great power.

He shook the grille in desperation. A little rust dribbled out of the lock. Suddenly the tumblers clicked and it flew apart. He had not realized that he had touched it with the hand that bore the ring.

He scrambled out and stared through a clump of bushes into a little cemetery, studded with crosses, sleeping placidly under aloof and brilliant stars.

He slammed the grille shut behind him and snapped the lock upon it. The crucifix slipped out of his robe and swung against his breast. At that moment, whatever had followed him up the passage came into view. He saw it as a mass of incredible blackness that surged toward him in a rolling motion, crowded with little sparks of brilliance like a myriad gleaming eyes, which tumbled over and over as the thing came on and yet somehow kept him in their glare.

No grille could hold that oozing danger back. He ran to the nearest cross and pulled it from the ground. He leaned it against the iron lattice and closed his eyes, praying.

He heard nothing, but he sensed a withdrawal, a shrinking

back, and as fear came upon the monstrous terror in the passage, courage came to Gwalchmai.

He opened his eyes. The corridor was empty. There was a rosy flush in the sky and a gentle freshness in the air. A little west wind was blowing and he fancied he could smell the sea.

His knees trembled and he sat down upon a stone in the hallowed plot to wait for the dawn. His hands pained and although his fingers had shrunken during his long incarceration, the rings clustered there so thickly began to feel tight.

He stripped them off, leaving only Merlin's ring, whose stone was now darkly no more than any other precious opal. In the strengthening light he could already see that some of the rings were of great value, set with rubies, emeralds, and sapphires, with here and there a diamond of price—the hoops invariably of pure, massy gold and the workmanship most elegant.

He searched his robe, but he had no pockets. Around his sleeves were broad cuffs. Using the sharp edge of his hatchet, he detached one and unfolded it. This gave him a small pouch, large enough to hold the rings. He ripped off a strip from the hem of the robe, tied the little bag tight and hung it around his neck, alongside the crucifix, which in daylight he made out to be silver.

In addition, what he had taken to be rosary beads were, instead, small golden coins. Someone had provided for him well while he slept and he began to have an inkling of that person's identity.

By the time he had finished it was quite light. Now he could look around. The cemetery was situated in the bottom of a long deserted quarry. The stratas of building stone had been removed most anciently and Nature had labored at healing the wound in the earth. Sandpits had been filled by water, leaves, loam from above, and other detritus. New soil had been created and there was a sparse growth of bushes and occasionally an ilex tree of an umbrella pine. Nearby were a few puddles of water from a recent rain, standing in some of the hollows where discarded slabs of limestone still lay exposed.

He stumbled over and drank deeply, emptying several. He soaked up water as a sponge might. Now his thickened blood coursed more quickly through his veins. His temples throbbed and he sluiced the liquid over his face and hands.

There was no one about and no sounds nearby. Distantly there was a murmur of life as though the city was awakening, but he could not determine if he was within its confines.

He stripped and bathed, using the remainder of the water as well as he could. When he had dressed again, he felt refreshed, but weak.

The sun had risen above the edge of the quarry, and as he sat down to rest for a few moments in its warmth before essaying the climb along the ramp the wagons had used, he unrolled the scroll and began to read.

It began: "My beloved and most indolent husband"

He started violently. How could Corenice have found him here?

He unrolled the scroll to its full length and scanned it carefully. The language, in its entirety, was Latin, but it was written in several shades of ink, with different pens. In some entries, he noticed that paint and a tiny brush had been used.

Once a few lines had been added without stain or pigment, as though these had been scratched into the parchment with a sharp point, by someone lacking anything else to write with. It was apparent that the long letter had been inscribed by several hands and at different times, yet the handwriting was always the same—precise, clear, and feminine.

It continued:

"I sometimes think that we must be the playthings of the gods and that they move us about for their pleasures as they obey other forces, perhaps beyond their comprehension.

"It is true—as Ahuni-i told Thor—his days were numbered.

"No one really believes in him any more. When the thunder peals, people no longer look up to catch a glimpse of his chariot, for he has lost his power and none fear his hammer.

"Instead, they kneel everywhere to the Cross upon which your Lord suffered and so address their prayers.

"What a strange thing! I am told that He preached only love and mercy and forgiveness—yet I have seen cities drowned in blood to do Him honor!

"No one ever hurt another person to please my sweet Goddess—my Spirit-of-the-Wave. Can you wonder that I give her my worship?

"She watched over you for my sake in your travels and brought my spirit over those weary miles of yours, when that curse of sleep fell upon you that has parted us.

"How long will it be, my darling, before we can hold each other as we did?"

The next entry was in another color of ink:

"The body I was using became restless and afraid to be underground and I had to leave it. I do not seem to have the power to assume control here for the time I can possess a body on the surface.

"Something fights against my possession of it. I have not often known fear, but I feel a dread of this place. I do not think you are in danger. I felt of your ring and it was not hot.

"Be careful when you leave this sacred place. It will be then that Oduarpa will strike, if it is he and if he can.

"I think that when his body was killed at Gebira in that war of the magicians of Atlantis against his dark hordes, his spirit was released to do more terrible things. Please be careful—for me!

"They were going to bury you in the ground, where there would have been an end to our love forever, but I would not let them.

"I saw you fall and I knew that what your godfather warned you against had come to pass. I entered the body of the doctor who examined you and how I convinced them that you must not be buried!

"You would have marveled to hear me. I was eloquent!

"Finally, they came to believe that you were a saint, for you went on sleeping. For a long time, people came to look at you.

"Can you credit that they actually prayed to you and some went away healed? You have powers I would not have imagined, knowing you as I do.

"I know where you are, because I can see your eyes move under their closed lids. You are always watching something. You smile, so I know you are happy.

"Do you remember how our friend, Flann, thought that when a person's eyes moved like that, he was wandering in the Land of Dream and looking upon the beauties of it? How I wish I could be with you!

"I cannot stay with you very long. I have to hasten back to my body in France, for fear something might happen to it, but I can came again, in the night, when our friends think I am sleeping.

"They took such good care of me when I was sick and could not go to Rome with you. I think they almost thought I was the daughter they wanted and never had.

"I came so many times, to see you. Did you know when I wept over you, so lonely I was for you then? Other eyes, but my tears!

"So lonely I am for you now, my very dear! My only love!

"In the end, such crowds came to see you that you were taken away secretly and placed in this sanctuary underground and after a long while you were forgotten, because no one remembered you but me, who cannot forget you and who will wait for you till you wake.

"Others do not remember the things they do not see, but I shall see you often.

"He was such a beautiful little boy. I wish you could have seen him, my darling who sleeps and sleeps and never answers me. He was strong like you and his hair was brown like yours. He had blue eyes. There were never any tears in them—not even when he fell and hurt himself. He was always brave.

"I wanted so much to hold him at those times and comfort him, but I could only watch over him as I watch over you.

"I died when he was born.

"My body is gone now. I waited so many years to have one with which to love you and now again I must be only a transient upon the earth, but you will wake and I shall have another—Ahuni-i has promised me. So sleep and rest and I will care for you and keep you well and unharmed, but now I am torn between two who are part of me and you are so far apart.

"Would you believe that he is a grandfather now and I sometimes hover as a hummingbird over the playing babies of his son?

"How long the years are, but how fast they sweep over us! Down here, nothing ever changes, but much has happened in the world above. It seems there is no end to war and trouble, yet somehow people managed to live and work and marry.

"I watched the eons pass, when I stood as an orichalcum statue in the swan-ship that floated above my drowned Atlantis, but those years were not like these. I watched nations born, and thrive, and die. I did not care then. It was all like a play, an entertainment arranged for me to watch! Ah! I was not waiting for someone then—there was no one whom I loved.

"So much has happened in these seventy years.

"You would never have been given those ships. The Pope we heard speak at Clermont died and there have been nine others since.

"None of them, I think, would have cared about Alata or wanted it. They have been so concerned with events in the East.

"The Crusade Pope Urban preached went out in its iron strength and conquered Jerusalem, but it was a dreadful thing to watch. Your Lord could not have been pleased by it.

"Since then there has been another one, but it failed and there has been fighting ever since: little wars that may not stop for a long time.

"I went to Byzantium, long ago—do you remember the storks? They fly so strangely. It was fun to ride in one of them—some happy day we must do it together when you wake. Oh, please, please do it soon!

"I tried to find Arngrim and Mairtre. I did not like her very much, but I would have liked to see her again, now that you were not there to see how pretty she was, but I could not find them. There was some talk that they had gone back to live in Spain. I hope they did not fall into the hands of the old wizard again.

"I did find out a strange thing, though, that might interest you if you wake soon.

"Of late years, everyone has been talking about letters that have been sent to the Pope, to Kings of all the countries, and to the Emperor of Byzantium—although they call that city Constantinople now.

"It is said that there is a mighty Christian King somewhere deep in Asia who is interested in the West. He has powerful armies, tremendous wealth, and so many marvelous things in this country that it is hard to believe what we hear. Perhaps he would be glad to help you with ships. Perhaps he would like to be sovereign over Alata if the Christians of Europe do not want it.

"His name is Prester John—John, the Priest, so he must be a good man.

"Some people say he is Saint Thomas. Did you ever hear of him? Others think he is the John whom your Lord loved. All agree that he has lived a very long time, as we have, and he may live a long time more.

"Wake and we will go to find him. Oh, wake! How can I wait for you like this?"

"At last I have walked and talked with you! I wanted it so much that it has happened! Such a beautiful land it is you dwell in!

"I do not wonder now that you stay there and no not want to leave.

"Did you know I was with you? Of course you did. We talked of so many things and now I cannot remember what any of them were.

"I wish I had a map of the Dream Land we were in. Surely Prester John's kingdom could not be more lovely.

"People still talk about him, hoping that his armies will march against the Turks, but Jerusalem was lost long ago. He did not come then and I think he will not come now, if in truth he is so long lived as the reports make him to be.

"There have been seven more crusades since and still men fight and still you sleep. How can you sleep so long?

"If I ever see Merlin—!

"You would be surprised to see how your family has grown. You are a great-great grandfather many times over! All the boys have been handsome—all the girls so pretty! You would be proud of them, I know. Do you like farmers? I asked you in Dream Land, but I could not remember what you told me when I awoke.

"They have all been farmers or farmers' wives. They have not been rich, but they have not been poor or hungry either. The money you and I left with the old people gave our line a good start in life. How lucky that we found the wizard's treasure!

"About money. What you had with you a woman took

when I possessed her mind and brought her down here to tend you. I suggested that she do it and give you her little crucifix on a golden chain. So it has been bought and paid for and it will remind you that you will know me by gold when we meet again.

"Every time I came to see you and take care of you in someone else's body, I had that person leave you his rings. You have many of them now. I was always careful to select wealthy people.

"Do not be sorry for them. They could afford it and it was all I could do for you. How I wish you could speak to me today!

"You are beside me—and I look at you—and I miss you so!

"I have become extremely curious about this Prester John and I am going to seek him. Perhaps, if he is such an enchanter and if he has lived so long, I may find out how to wake you.

"So now I say—stay here until I come back for you. Do *not* wake. I want you here when I return, but if you should wake and I am not near you—I think you will know—then seek me in his kingdom, if I have not written you again.

"If I am not in that realm, search for me in your Land of Dream. It surely cannot be far away.

"Sleep, my dear one. Never did I think before that I should pen those words!

"Oh, yes—the year, as you would number it, is now called 12 hundreds and another 77. How strange! As though the world began then, such a few years ago!"

15

In Search of Prester John

Into Europe, that thin crescent rim upon the vast expanse of mysterious Asia, many strange and wonderful reports had come that could not be disproved, for few travelers had been deep into Asia and returned.

Out of that breeding place of races, perhaps of humanity itself, all the peoples of Europe had been thrust. There their migratory wagons had rolled to the sea until they could go no farther and must learn the ways of Ocean. Behind and following had come other successive waves of landless folk against that watery bastion and in turn had been either thrust back, destroyed, or assimilated.

Hence came the Dorians and the Achaians to people Greece; to teach and to contend with mighty Rome. From them, to the Eternal City, the torch of civilization was nursed to brightness and passed on to Byzantium, which stood for a thousand years as a fortress against other invading Asiatic hordes.

There that light still gleamed, but it was fading and the lamps were a little tarnished.

When Gwalchmai outfitted himself in Byzantium, which he could not bring himself to call Constantinople, he negotiated a passage with a caravan bound for Central Asia. Stories still issued from that section of the world concerning the glittering empire of John, the Priest, and others had gone seeking before him.

Only twenty years previously, William of Rubruk had been sent as envoy to the Great Khan of Tartary by Saint Louis, of blessed memory, in hopes that the French and the drum-led *tumans* of Mongol horse might unite in crushing their mutal foe, the Turk.

The venture came to nothing. The Khan was not Prester John.

Across those lands, so empty of castles and gleaming spires and golden domes, moved the Polo brothers, but they saw no shining capitol, for they did not see with eyes that had been touched by magic.

Following, came Gwalchmai, a more tenacious and far-reaching wanderer than the Venetians.

Gwalchmai had learned that the Crusades were over—the cause abandoned. Except for Acre, the Turks held the land and Constantinople awaited conquest. A new age was beginning—the age of discovery.

Perhaps the end of his long journey might be nearing soon, now that new trade routes must be found to avoid the Turkish lands. Ships must again crowd the seas in search of new sources of wealth.

As the weary miles lengthened so slowly into thousands beneath his feet, he thought of this and the mission laid upon him by his father.

Like many in Europe, he knew the world to be round. If he could not convince an European ruler of the importance of what he knew, surely an Asiatic one would appreciate more room for the immense multitudes of people he ruled. However, it must be a Christian potentate. Obeying Merlin's order, he would give the land to no other. On then, to find if Prester John still lived, or failing him, to speak with whatever son or grandson ruled in his stead.

Bokhara, Samarkand, Kashgar—all these had seen Gwalchmai on his road. Through cities whose names are fabled, through mountain passes that themselves are higher than many other mountains much feared and famed in lesser countries, Gwalchmai traveled, always seeking, never finding.

He had ridden donkeys, mules, and camels. He had ridden in solid-wheeled wagons, greased with butter, stinking with unwashed bodies. He had been sheltered in palaces and honored there. He had begged for a bed in dirty hovels and caravanserais, and drunk sour milk in felt yurts. He had panted in jungle humidity and gasped in the thin mountain

air of the Pamirs; banqueted and starved; formed a part
of miles' long caravans and sometimes moved on to the East
with only a single companion. No one could direct him to the
Land of Dream.

Everywhere there had been rumors of the Empire of
John, the Priest, but its boundaries, indicated by a vague
sweep of the informant's arm, were always farther to the
east.

Toward the east he staggered now, as he had for three
days—and alone. Since his Bactrian camel had died, he had
been on foot. His guide had gone in search of water and not
returned. Gwalchmai was certain that he never would.

The nights were bitter cold. He dug holes in the banks of
dry streams, just large enough for his body, lit small fires of
dead willow roots before them and slept warm at nights, an
old trick he had learned in Alata. He was comfortable,
where another might have frozen, but the days were misery.
There was nothing to eat or drink and he traveled under a
blinding sun that pounded him almost senseless out of a
cloudless sky.

He stood now upon an ancient shoreline and looked out
over a shimmering depression that had once held a primeval,
ageless sea. Upward, out of its wind-worn salt-covered pebbles, thrust mountain peaks bare of verdure, but which had
once been green and fertile islands. Among them whirled
the dust-devils, dangerous to a dying man as the touch of
Djinn or Marid, and as they spun they skirled their wind-song
of menace.

It was the desert of Hang-Hai and beyond its edge lay the
even more dreadful Gobi. Gwalchmai had been warned of
the larger waste, but he smiled cynically at the thought of
any greater danger than the one he faced. It seemed that
he had reached his end upon this prehistoric beach.

He sank down and buried his face in his hands, crouching
low to protect himself against another spinning tower of
sand, which could either burst and bury him or, whirling on,
suck the remaining moisture from his almost dehydrated
body.

As it towered and threatened, it wailed, "Gwalchmai-i-i!
Gwalchmai-i-i!" Every syllable was clear and distinct as its
dark shadow fell across him, but this was nothing new.

While traveling through the many shifting hills and valleys of sand, he had heard such voices before. In the night

he had listened to the passing of long cavalcades; the tinkling bells of the baggage animals and the hum of many people; the tramp of soldiers marching in cadence to the beat of kettledrums and the braying of horns.

There were never marks of their passage through the sands and he had known that he listened to a mirage of sound, preserved forever in this timeless land, where lost armies had trudged the world across a dead sea bottom on forgotten conquests for unremembered Kings.

This shadow was no mirage. Its menace was real. He did not look up, but upon the sand he saw a hideously horned profile of a head, black and monstrous, its jaws open in a sardonic laugh. He knew that what hung over him was more than the shadow of whirling, whistling sand.

"Ah! Spirit of the Wave!" he muttered. "Goddess of the Waters! You have been my friend, without demanding my worship. You, who love the one I love, be my benefactor once more, I pray you. Let me see my Corenice once more, before I die."

The dust-devil must have been very near, for its rushing sound was close. He waited, eyes closed, but it did not break upon him and the burning wind seemed cool upon his uncovered skin.

The sound went on and on without ceasing, but now it was rhythmic and held a pattern and the wind had sunk to a breeze that felt moist. He raised his head and looked out across no dry waste, but a blue and dancing white-capped sea, whose surges broke almost at his feet.

Was he mad? Was this only a mirage of sight and sound combined?

He leapt to his feet and plunged forward—not upon harsh pebbles. But into cold, stinging brine. He laughed and splashed and flung the glittering streams of water into the air. They broke and fell upon him, limpid drops like tears of joy.

Then he crawled dripping up the beach, ten, twenty, thirty feet and began to dig. Seepage came into the hole. He did not wait for the silt to settle, but tasted it cautiously. It was brackish, but drinkable. He drank.

This was not delirium. It was wonderful, heartening, glorious fact—hard, indisputable truth.

Somehow—someone or some being had heard his prayer and had answered in this strange way, but not as he had asked. His life had been preserved, but Corenice was not near for him to see.

Yet a part of what he had asked had been granted. This could be no other than the Sea of Sand, which was part of the dominions of Prester John and where were found the fish of wondrous savor that produced the dye of royal purple and whose scales were flakes of diamond.

He searched the shore for anything that could be eaten. There was nothing. At a distance, he thought he saw the white colonnades of a temple or mansion, among the trees that crowned the nearest island, but there were no boats upon the water and no smokes in the air to prove inhabitance.

He turned his back upon the sea and climbed a little green hill near it, looking backward upon the way he had come to reach this shore.

There were mounds to be seen that he had not noticed before. They were not dunes, but looked like artificial constructions. In their grouping he was sure he saw a village of conical huts, and in the streets of the village, movement.

He walked in that direction. As he neared it, it became evident that what he saw were not people, but animals of an unknown variety. He dropped to the ground and peered through a clump of tamarisks, parting the pink blossoms to give himself a better view.

They appeared to be purposeful creatures. They were burden bearers, constantly lifting, hurrying, carrying; they hustled through the streets, climbed the mounds, disappeared and came back again, tugging, dropping their loads, choosing better spots for placing them and dashing back for another parcel or weight. It was hard to determine their size or identity, with no known size of any near landmark. He did not have long to wait.

He heard no step behind him. In his interested spying, he had failed to notice a dry rustling in the bushes at his rear, until he felt a pressure upon his shoulder like exploring fingers.

He whirled. There stood an ant, the size of a wolf, mandibles parted ready to seize him, should the inquisitive antennae prove him a desirable prey.

He rolled to one side. The chitinous pincers clashed only inches from his arm. Before he could get to his feet, the monster was upon him, snapping and striking out with its jointed forelegs. He had barely time to thrust a wad of his thick cloak in front of him.

He swung around and freed himself from the clinging garment. The giant ant tore and mauled the cloth and finding no blood in it turned upon the man in nervous fury.

By this time, Gwalchmai had his flint hatchet in hand and chopped at the viciously swinging head. The keen edge found its mark and one sickle-like blade hung disabled and dangling.

The monster set up a high stridulation and, oblivious to pain or fear, rushed in, battering at its attacker. It was not until Gwalchmai had hacked the head from the body that the thin shrieking ceased, although the creature did not know it was dead.

The head still tried convulsively to open and close its damaged jaws and the mutilated body curled up, straightened out, and scuttled blindly down the bank, through tamarisk and reeds and did not stop until it ran aimlessly into the sea.

The cry it had set up had not gone unnoticed. Out of the village—which Gwalchmai now realized held no humanity, but was instead a crowded colony of the huge insects— a horde now came pouring in his direction.

He turned toward the water and ran along the beach. For a few hundred feet he thought he had eluded his pursuers. Then in front of him a clacking wave of the creatures streamed over the knolls in that direction and blocked the way.

Behind him, where he had fought, a second glistening expanse of hurrying backs covered the ground, moving rapidly toward him, holding their heads high as though they were smelling him out with their waving antennae, constantly in rapid motion like the leafless twigs of the black birch in a high winter wind. As they dashed upon him they set up a shrill whistling.

There was no refuge except the water. He plunged into it and swam for his life.

The insect masses met and lined the beach, paralleling his course, marching along with him. The only small crumb of comfort available to him in his predicament was the information Corenice had once given him about the Gobi Sea.

The advent of the Lord of the Dark Face from Venus had,

by the fiery blasts from his space-ship, set off an atomic reaction in the minerals held in that body of water in solution, which completely evaporated the sea and left only the desert Gwalchmai had been traversing.

Therefore it followed naturally that if the water was still present, he must have been sent back to a time before Oduarpa had arrived and need not have a present fear of that evil genius, either in the spirit or the flesh.

The giant ants were not kin to the dwergar with which Oduarpa had once menaced him, and the fay, in Elveron. They were not driven by hate and the love of cruelty, but only by hunger. Still, that was enough.

He began to tire as the chill water sapped his strength. It had been a long time since he had eaten and his vitality was low. Several times his mouth opened involuntarily, gasping for air, and he took in choking gulps of water. Then, just as he felt that he must either founder or struggle in to take his chances upon shore, a besom of flame struck down from the sky and swept the beach clean before him, leaving only a burst of seared, exploded bodies and clouds of greasy smoke.

Gwalchmai looked up, with dimmed and smarting eyes, at a vast shadow that swept overhead. A smooth, rushing sound took the place of the alarming stridulations. The clacking horde fled back from the beach, over the dunes, and disappeared.

A hovering Vimana, one of the shining, golden swan-ships of drowned Atlantis, was circling to descend beside him upon the waters of this impossibly existing sea! As it furled its glittering metal wings, extended its webbed feet and landed as lightly as a gull, he realized the fantastic truth.

Small wonder that the Kingdom of Prester John had never been found. It had never existed! Thousands of years previously, when Atlantis ruled supreme and the Gobi was an inland sea, of which this body of water formed only a connecting lake, Atlantis had planted a colony here.

These were the ants that brought up gold in the dirt thrown out from their tunnels and chambers, as legend had told in Merlin's books. Yonder, upon the verdant islands, shone the fanes and temples of a mighty nation's worship. Somewhere, perhaps near by, was the summer palace of the Atlantidean Emperor, constructed of white, translucent alabaster. Above all, in these very skies, flew their lovely ships of air and water.

Marveling, shivering barbarians had watched them in dread, not understanding what they saw. From their tales, the stories had originated to explain the existence of flying monsters. Thus—the legendary griffin, that weird creature with legs, wings, and beak of steel, which stood guard over golden treasures and was consecrated to the sun!

This was why they were said to inhabit Asiatic Scythia; this was why they were reported to be eight times larger than the largest lion!

Somehow, through the ages, the memory of those vanished glories had come down, repeated and garbled in the remembrance. Somehow, back through those ages—by the good offices of the Spirit-of-the-Wave?—Gwalchmai had been spirited, to save his life from the dangers of the desert and his immortal soul from the malice of the Lord of the Dark Face. Now he could see for himself the wonders of which Corenice had told him.

Even the hugest griffin would be small in comparison to the magnificent ship that now, proudly breasting the waves, moved with care into the shallows where he stood waiting, watching through the clear water the slow strokes of its paddling feet.

The swan-ship came to rest. It lay there, rocking. A line splashed into the ripples beside him, from the narrow deck between the wings. Gwalchmai was drawn aboard to receive excited congratulations.

His rescuers spoke the version of the ancient language he had learned from Corenice and Jaun, the Basque, although so much purer that they smiled politely at his barbarous accent.

He followed them down a companionway, into the depths of the body. The Vimana was obviously a work vessel, armed with the dyro-blast for protection.

It was this lethal gush of flame that had spouted from the swan-ship's beak to deliver him from the menace of the ants. He could understand why the griffin was reputed to be death to horses and brave knights, incinerating whole armies that came against it.

Thinking upon this, Gwalchmai murmured, under his breath, lines he had heard sung by a minstrel in the court of King Brons:

> There was a dragon great and grymme,
> Full of fire and eke venymme;
> And as a lion were his fete,
> His tayle was long and full unmete;
> Between his head and his tayle,
> Was twenty-two foote withouten fayle; .
> His body was like a round wine tun,
> He shone full bright against the sun;
> His eyes were bright as any glass,
> His scales were hard as any brass.

Not too bad a description for a creature not actually seen for over ten thousand years, he thought.

There was little time for musing. Already the Vimana had taken to the air, after running awkwardly along the surface of the sea to gain speed, in the manner of the bird it appeared to be.

There was nothing ungainly about it as it flew, and it needed little attention from the crewman. Four of them, captain, engineer, and two deck hands, sat without regard for rank.

In the center of this little group, which included Gwalchmai not as a prisoner but as a guest, was an observation well in the bird's belly. This was floored with transparent plates.

Occasionally they looked down upon the flashing sea, in which the golden ship was reflected in beauty, while they listened to a brief recounting of Gwalchmai's adventures. He edited them to reconcile his period of existence with that of his rescuers. He did not wish to task their credulity too much by telling them that he was a son of their far future. As it was, the Atlantideans often smiled politely and without belief at what he told them, but seemed to ignore discrepancies in any other way, not remarking in asides among themselves, perhaps setting down whatever they did not understand to an imperfect rendering of their language.

The pilot was the only one absent from this colloquy. He guided the craft from his seat in the bird's head, but listened through a communicator, occasionally breaking in with a question.

So they talked while they flew on eastward over many islands. There were small and large ones, mostly uninhabited. A few bore what seemed to be factories—for smelting gold, or processing ore?—but most of the others with any sort of buildings upon them, Gwalchmai noticed, were crowned with pillared mansions with breezeways. Pathways led to the sea or landing ovals surrounded by greensward, and these were paved with colored stones set in geometrical patterns meant to be admired from the air. The land was smoothed and terraced, the trees pruned into patterns and carefully spaced.

Gwalchmai was amazed. This hideous desert, death trap for caravans, this frightful waste toward which for over a year he had looked forward with dread, had once been a pleasure archipelago for the citizens of Atlantis.

Hang-Hai Lake, for now he must so call it, was far behind and they were soaring over the Gobi Sea. Was it possible that this scintillating expanse, surrounded by impressive snow-capped peaks crowned by twinkling beacons and guarding watchtowers, could so vanish with the elevating movements of the land, the cataclysmic destroying atom, and the passage of time?

Ah, yes! Vanish it would. After its vanishing, Atlantis would likewise disappear, sinking slowly as other lands rose. The semi-continents of Ruta and Daitya first drowned, to leave Poseidonis Island for a little while; then this, too, would follow the remainder of the proud country beneath the ocean, leaving nothing but names, legends, and memories behind.

Not even that would survive, within the Gobi, where only the dust-devils and the mourning winds peopled a scorching, freezing haunt. All gone, in a minuscule moment of geological time.

While Gwalchmai meditated, the ship flew on toward the nearing shore of the vast sea. Upon it, backed by a high mountain pass, stood a magnificent city. Its impressive walls were pierced with arched gates, through which moved caravans of ponderously huge beasts, with long, reddish hair and curling tusks. They bore howdahs or immense burdens, or hauled heavy wains with ten-foot wheels. Mammoths, tamed to the use of man!

The Vimana swooped low. He watched the beasts plodding along boulevards, through the marketplaces, as it circled in a descending spiral toward the receiving quays in the harbor, where other boats with furled wings lay rocking. Over the golden domes and towering spires, the swan-ship slid down its airy slope.

It swung around the high walls and crowded streets. Gwalchmai saw upturned faces of guards, ready at their posts, although no danger threatened.

Down and down, closer to the water and the dock-men waiting to catch flung ropes and make hawsers fast to the bollards; down where boys pointed upward and girls waved fluttering ribbons to welcome the bird-men home; down to splash lightly in the harbor and for just one second—for Gwalchmai to find himself struggling in it!

The ship had disappeared! In an infinitesimal part of a second, the water vanished. The captain and crewmen, the docks, people, and animals, the city with its protecting walls and palaces, long to be remembered as the fabled home of Prester John, and the Gobi Sea itself—all disappeared into Gwalchmai's past as he was rushed forward into his present—their distant future.

All that remained were the mighty peaks, down which it seemed the snowline had instantaneously lowered itself for thousands of feet; the high pass between them, choked with snow and ice; and Gwalchmai, flat upon his face, making swimming motions upon another ancient beach, his mouth and nose filled with salty sand.

He had crossed the greatest dangers by the favor of Ahunii, kind of goddess of the waters, and returned to his own time safely, but there were tears in his eyes.

There was no city of John, the Priest; no Christian Emperor to help him to return to Alata and to accept the country as a part of a holy realm. He must wait longer to be discharged of his weary mission, which was sad enough, but, worst of all, he must seek farther still for the one he valued most—there was no Corenice.

16

Through the Magic Door

It was then that Gwalchmai felt a despondency deeper than any before in all of his long wanderings. In the vast expanse of desert that lay behind him nothing moved. Even the wind had stopped.

No mirages cast their deceptive visions to trick him into their pursuit; no delirium of thirst or hunger was enough to create an illusion of life in that deadly waste through the medium of inflamed sight or straining ears.

The futility of this endless striving came upon him as it had not at any other time. To what end his searching? Toward what doom or joy was his mission leading him forever on, without hope or reward? Was there a purpose in existence in which his stubbornness played a part?

His head sank down into the sand and he groaned. He was very near severing the tenuous thread that unites the soul to its body. As he prepared to recite the words that would bring about this irrevocable deed, he thought he heard a tiny voice—in his mind? In his heart? In his memory?

Yes! It was echoing lines he had heard Flann read to Thyra from the tattered book of the Culdees, when he was instructing her in his faith. In Flann's very tones, he heard the voice repeat:

"I will lift up mine eyes unto the hills, from whence cometh my help; My help cometh from the Lord, which made heaven and earth."

He raised his head and stared wildly at the mountains. They were a blinding blur, bright with sunlight and snow. He blinked and wiped away the sand from his face and streaming eyes.

Against the brilliance, he saw a circling black speck, which soared and spiraled outward in an ever-widening sweep. It rapidly came nearer and as though it had been seeking it now broke its circular swing and flew directly toward him. He saw that it was a raven.

Thor's messenger? Corenice, in one of her favorite guises? He probed its mind as it swooped close, peering keenly at him. He lay as if dead. There was no feeling within its red thoughts, except that of a savage appetite. No essence of another entity, no sense of anything merciful or helpful in it. It dropped to the ground and hopped avidly to peck at his eyes.

This was a carrion bird and a starving one at that.

He allowed it to come close and then, as Corenice had taught him, he seized upon its consciousness and made its body his.

Living the raven's life, now Gwalchmai was borne into the air. Higher, higher, viewing the desert lands beneath him—farther into the steely, menacing hard blue of the cloudless sky. He looked down at his body as the raven had seen it, spread flatly, supine, helpless, thousands of feet below. He felt the thin wind through his feathers as he topped the mighty peaks. He was tortured by the raven's hunger; he shared its weariness; and he looked beyond those jagged mountain barriers and saw green valleys where a road ran as a brown cord through emeralds, paralleling that forbidding range, and upon that highway moved people!

A caravan trail! Here passed upon it swaying cameleers. Here traveled the sweating wheelbarrow men with the little sails that aided the wind in pushing their heavy loads. Here he could see beneath him the patient, laden donkeys trotting with their bales of silk along the ancient route toward Persia and the markets of the west. With them moved the convoys.

Soldiers, drovers, pack-bearers, wanderers, priests, storytellers, Mandarins in their palanquins, favored concubines in curtained chairs and litters—here was the life of the eastern world passing beneath his eyes and here was life for himself, if he could cross the mountains and reach that road.

Swiftly the controlled raven returned to the uninhabited body below. Before it could blink or hop away or realize what had happened to it, Gwalchmai had returned to him-

self. His strong hands shot out and grasped the dazed bird.
Quickly, he wrung its neck.

Not bothering to pluck the fowl, he split it from windpipe
to tail with a single slash of his flint hatchet, tore skin and
feathers away and made a meal of the rank, raw flesh. He
gagged and retched, but managed to keep down the life giving food. Somewhat revived, he staggered toward the foot-
hills and the pass he had seen.

There were little streams formed from the melting snows
and there were green shoots growing along their edges, suc-
culent and nourishing. There was a burgeoning hope in his
heart to carry him on and there was the courage he had
always had. It had not died as he had thought, but only
slept for a little while.

So he crossed the pass. No avalanche came near him, no
other misfortune befell, and gaunt, weary, a ghost of himself, he stumbled at last upon that road. After only a half a
day of waiting, he was found by a caravan bound eastward,
with raw jade and raisins, fine horses and slaves.

The children he passed pointed at the stumbling man who
supported himself by clinging to the side of a baggage wagon,
red-eyed with dust. They looked at his ruddy skin, his worn-
out felt boots, his ragged sheepskins and said to themselves; "T'a! T'a!"—for they took him to be one of the no-
mads from the north, against whom the Great Wall had been
built.

Thus he came to Cathay and by the Jade Gate entered the
fabled Empire of Kublai, the Mongol conqueror, whom men
called the Great Khan.

Now began for Gwalchmai a new phase of existence. Had
it not been for a feeling of expectation that might at any
time be realized in some unusual way, he could have been
happy in Cathay.

He fitted well into the scheme of living in which he found
himself.

The returning merchants who had found him had given
him succor only out of mercy at first. When they were sure
that he was not a robber or in some manner attempting to
lead them into a trap, they made him more welcome.

Because Merlin had once known a Chinese wanderer from
Scythia, who had given him a fish compass, he had made a

study of this acquaintance's language. Gwalchmai, while he wore Merlin's ring, found himself in possession of enough words to make himself understood by the traders, although their dialect as a whole was quite different. Still, with such a beginning, communication became increasingly easier as time went on, especially since he had a working knowledge of Persian and some Turkish and Arabic, picked up on his three years of traveling from Rome.

When it became known that he was not a Tartar, but had journeyed from Europe, the merchants encouraged him to remain with them.

He made himself useful in several ways as they journeyed into the Lower Kingdom, but their chief interest in him was what he could tell them of those far lands through which he had passed, for they had a childlike curiosity in the strange and bizarre.

Moving slowly as they did, word of him went ahead and eventually reports sifted as far as the City of the Khan, Khan-baliq as the Mongols had named the new metropolis, recently built in place of the one Genghis, Kublai's grandfather, had destroyed a lifetime earlier.

In this magnificent city, which had awed Marco Polo and who called it Cambaluc, Gwalchmai came to earn an honored place, purely by chance.

The Emperor had called Gwalchmai before him, upon arrival, for much the same reasons that the merchants had listened to those tales he had to offer of the western world.

His meeting with Kublai might have been no more than perfunctory had not the Mongols been arming at the time for an invasion of Japan, which they knew as Nihon. The Khan held great delight in learning of strange countries, their manners and oddities, but he was a busy and energetic ruler, with many interests.

However, Gwalchmai had kept his eyes open during his passage through the Khanate and was able to suggest some improvements in the catapults being constructed to arm the fleet, for he had seen the improved designs being then used throughout Europe and knew something of the intricate engines developed to reduce strong fortifications.

He was offered the post of second-class commissioner, or agent in charge of ordnance, attached to the imperial council, and he accepted with alacrity.

There were two reasons for this. Wherever a man dwells,

if he would eat he must either work at something or steal. Furthermore, Gwalchmai felt that if he were to attain a position of even minor importance it might be easier for Corenice to find him, if she were reborn anywhere in this part of the world.

He had no compunctions against casting his lot with the Cathayans and their war to come against the inhabitants of Nihon, whom they referred to disparagingly as dog-devils. He had never seen one, nor did he ever expect to do so.

He lost no opportunity to make himself known, by name and by his rising reputation, and as both became bruited about with increasing frequency, his hope grew that it would not be long before he met his love again.

As it turned out, word of the tall ruddy man—who looked so dignified with his short brown hair, now slightly sprinkled with gray, his splendid robes, and square cap with vermilion buttons, who disdained a palanquin, but walked like common men—did spread amazingly fast, but purely by accident.

Many had sought his advice, for although his face appeared so young, all knew him to be wise and they were surprised at his quick grasp of their involved and honorific manner of speech.

One of these, a head-bobbing underling, approached Gwalchmai upon his regular tour of inspection of the ordnance depot.

"All-knowing one, Most Beneficent Magnificence, may there never lie stones in your path," he remarked in sincere tones, bowing almost to the ground.

"An extremely pleasant thought and one that does credit to the assiduous labors of the aged parent who doubtless has pride in the superior qualities of his noble son. I trust he is in good health and enjoys his rice?"

"Alas! This lowly person's degraded father mounted the Dragon in great haste these many years past and was carried to his ancestors."

"Such an event, though inevitable to all, saddens us both with regret," Gwalchmai commiserated, preparing to depart. "Still, unless the lamentable fact, which will doubtless cast an aura of melancholy upon the remainder of our day, has some bearing upon the present hours of labor that concern us, I must confess that pressing matters await my immediate attention."

"It has indeed, High Excellence, for the manner of his rejoining his welcoming forefathers was most unusual and this insignificant and stunted individual has made the subject of his unfortunate studies a long and fruitful endeavor.

"It was the hope of this unworthy person that through your beneficence, Oh, Exalted One, that His Imperishable Majesty, upon whom may praise be scattered, might be informed of these weary struggles in the pursuit of knowledge —and thereby some crumbs of affluence be sprinkled upon us both from the overflowing coffers contained in the Royal Treasury."

"Pray continue!" exclaimed the astonished Gwalchmai. "Surely, any plan which will contribute to an addition of even a single string of cash to a chronically limp purse is worth a moment's consideration. Yet, I must warn you, that should this information prove of no value, you will find that this one's anger is not a thing to be lightly ignored."

"Then if the Estimable Councilman will but step this way, this ignorant and unpleasantly appearing mechanic, whose unimportant name is Wu, will instantly impart all desirable elucidation without further unnecessary verbiage."

So saying, he drew Gwalchmai, by hooking a dirty finger into his prospective patron's long silken sleeve, into a noisy godown that had been fitted out as a foundry.

Here in thick and choking smoke, men toiled at furnaces and molds that were being filled with gushing liquid bronze. At the far end of the godown, bronze cylinders were stacked in tiers of different sizes. They ranged in size and dimensions from the simulacra of sections of large bamboo tubes no longer than a man's arm to that of huge objects, beautifully embellished with gods, demons, and mythological animals, mostly longer than the height of a tall man and capable of considerable content.

Gwalchmai turned to Wu, to whom he noticed the others deferred with the instant reaction of applying themselves to their labors with immediate impatience. It was obvious that however deprecating Wu might be of himself, his workmen were under no such illusions as to his temper and capabilities.

Gwalchmai looked about with ill-concealed interest.

"May this obtuse visitor, admittedly slow in understanding, be apprised as to the purpose of these excellent objects of art, constructed with such diligence by the skilled workmen of the all-wise foundry-master Wu, upon whom the gods have obviously smiled?"

"Possibly the gods may have smiled at first, considering the futility of all human effort, but of late their notice has been directed exclusively toward the frustrating of this unworthy person's insignificant plans," ruefully commented Wu, wearing upon his brow a restrained look of care. "It would seem that they now laugh heartily.

"Unless this illiterate individual can speedily obtain an audience with the Imperial Presence, all labor must cease, as he now lacks both material with which to maintain further production and taels with which to purchase more.

"Should this lamentable event occur, it will be accompanied by weeping and it may chance that the Illimitable One will be deprived of a potent weapon against the insulting dog-dwarfs of Nihon, in punishment of whom the avenging fleet is now being prepared." The foundry-master here referred to the planned attack upon Japan, soon to be launched.

While Gwalchmai had lain asleep in the Catacombs, twenty-five thousand Mongols had made a previous landing upon Tsushima, overrun the small garrison there, and fanned out into the interior of the island, until pushed back into their ships by the enraged samurai of the local Barons. Such a setback could not be brooked by the arrogant Kublai, who had lately assumed the title of "The Son of Heaven."

The Khan decreed that so many ships should be built for another assault that the hills would be in mourning for their stricken forests.

This fleet lay now, in near completion, in all the northern harbors, receiving the final touches and awaiting the assembly of the army it was to carry. There were giant junks capable of accommodating two thousand men. These possessed high fighting towers amidships, armed with catapults that fired explosive bombs.

There were fleet scout vessels of all descriptions, swifter than anything they might be expected to encounter, meant to be used in sweeping the seas clean in advance of the news of the invasion. Supply ships were in great numbers, also slow tubby craft, so huge that the cavalry—the supreme Mongol weapon—could exercise their horses upon the decks.

All thirty-five hundred ships were staring with their painted eyes in one direction only—the spot beyond the horizon where lay the shores of Japan.

To imagine that such an armada, planned for seven years, lacked anything necessary to accomplish its conquest, seemed incredible to Gwalchmai. Yet Wu seemed to think so.

He could foresee no benefit to himself in continuing the conversation. He bowed politely and shook hands with himself.

"I fear I must beg you to restrain the flow of your most elegant eloquence. It has been an extreme pleasure to view your industrious establishment, and to inspect the exquisite workmanship of these splendidly manufactured bronze bases, doubtless inspired by the interest of single-minded gods in your behalf.

"However, as I mentioned before, important matters await my undivided attention and as I fail to conceive what value the Supreme Omnipotence could place upon such creations, I must respectfully bid you farewell."

Wu hastily prostrated himself before the door of the go-down.

"Stay, but for a dozen drops of water in the clock, Esteemed Councilor, and thy well-arranged words shall be revised toward the certain profit of us both, if such be directed into the ears of ineffable perfection that ornament the head of the Divine Offspring of the Seventh Circle!"

As Gwalchmai made no tentative movement to step over him and leave, Wu quickly motioned to the nearest workman in a peremptory manner. This laborer nervously shoveled out, with a wooden scoop, a sooty compound from a small bamboo keg and, without lingering, poured it at once into the open end of one of the aforesaid vases.

He laid it on its side into a wooden frame that fitted its rondures. He then packed a quantity of soft paper into it, dumped in a double handful of stones, and tamped more paper in upon that.

Another workman set a large gong against a backing of sandbags laid against the far wall and hastily left its vicinity.

"Observe carefully, Discerning Lord, to whom all things are already known and your intuition as to this invention of little account shall be confirmed."

Wu motioned to the first worker, who now applied a glowing coal to the base of the bronze container. Unfortunately it had not been fastened to its frame, in the haste of preparation, and to the accompaniment of a thunderous bellow and a vast amount of smoke, it straightway leaped into the air as it vomited forth the stones in an improper direction, narrowly missing one of the furnaces with its alarmed attendants.

The stones continued on, tearing a large ragged hole in the wall of the godown and had not friendly demons been in charge of the proceedings, Wu would have exchanged condolences upon the events of the day with his revered ancestors—for the primitive cannon shot over his head while he still lay prostrate.

"Oh, inept and mentally deficient one!" Wu howled, falling upon his clumsy helper with cruel blows of a hurriedly grasped bamboo.

"Oh, witless clown, tarry no longer within the bounds of this establishment! Assuredly, you are as stupid as the cat who thought to grow fat by the eating of oranges. Begone! Should you return there will be the matter of a burning sulphur plaster applied with skill to soothe those wounds of which you now complain so bitterly!"

"Desist, I pray you, estimable foundry-master!" exclaimed Gwalchmai, in a two-edged voice, seizing his arm. "Surely, this buffoon so lacking in judgment has been punished enough by Heaven simply by being an encumbrance to the earth. It is unnecessary to call yourself to the attention of the gods by slaying him and sending him where he will doubtless be unwelcome. It is most probable that the ghost of one of your concerned ancestors will guide his footsteps into a deep well."

Wu considered the happy thought and reluctantly lowered the bamboo. The workman went out of the godown as though fired out of his own tube, neglecting in his haste to request a settlement of the account due him, and they saw him no more.

Wu squatted upon his heels and rocked to and fro, wailing and scattering cinders from the floor upon his head and shoulders.

"This is unquestionably the ultimate misfortune to fall upon this ignoble person whose worthless life has been filled with catastrophe. It is past belief, Imperishable Nobility, that I am not already Passing Beyond before the awesome sight of your well-justified wrath."

"Nay, worthy purveyor of devouring fire. I beseech you arise and let us seek a more private place where we can discuss over a bowl of noodles the practicalities of this startlingly novel use of the earth thunder powder. Possibly we may be able to come to some efficient conclusion of your problem. It might even be that this admitted clumsily handled affair can be turned to advantage by arranging a more carefully managed demonstration to attract the interest of the All-Wisest."

"Such a desirable event would assuredly lift a most ponderous tombstone from the back of this deservedly crushed individual," declared Wu, leaping up with alacrity. "Follow me, Most Incomparable, to the establishment of The Seven Virtuous Maidens, where entertainment and the richest of viands shall be provided for you, entirely at this unworthy mendicant's expense."

It has been justly observed by sages of all lands that although a man may be most happily married and continue in that state with the utmost contentment, it does not necessarily follow that he has therefore been struck stone-blind. Consequently, it was with some curiosity and anticipation that Gwalchmai approached, in the wake of the relieved foundry-master, the inn that bore such a fascinating name.

In the expectation that it would not only be thronged with admiring customers, but also in all likelihood long lines of ne'er-do-wells would be queued in the street waiting impatiently for entrance, not so much as to purchase noodles as to test the alleged high qualities so blatantly announced upon the scarlet lacquered sign without, he assumed that it might be some while before they could be seated.

He was pleasantly surprised that there existed no such obstruction in their way. In fact, those who passed upon that side of the street usually did so looking upward and noticeably quickened their pace when under the overhanging windows of the establishment. When a slop bucket was emptied into the street without warning, Gwalchmai realized the reason for their concern.

The pair had no difficulty in entering or in finding a convenient table. It seemed that all the corners were quiet and most of the booths vacant.

The cause of this peacefulness was made evident when their order was taken by a simpering gap-toothed harridan, whose mother had apparently been frightened by an exceedingly ill-favored dragon at least a hundred years previously. She made suggestions as to the delicacies available.

Gwalchmai hesitated. Wu said, "If you do not care for the mice preserved in honey, or the century-old eggs, let me recommend the pressed duck. It is the specialty of the house and a most excellent dish." Gwalchmai pleaded a slight appetite.

Soon their tea, noodles, and salted pickles, which they had finally chosen, were brought to them by a second antiquated damsel, whose family resemblance to the first was unmistakable. When she left, Gwalchmai noticed two others, certainly no younger, who were serving the few occupied booths on the other side of the room and assumed the remainder of the sisters to be engaged in kitchen duties or attending to necessary labors in the rooms above.

He could only guess at the dubious attractions of those who were farther away, for the semi-darkness of the Inn of the Seven Virtuous Maidens not only insured privacy for its patrons, but also protected them against violent shock and loss of appetite should one look up suddenly in an absent moment and thus come unexpectedly face to face with one of the servitors.

Gwalchmai courteously forbore to express an opinion indicating disappointment while these ladies were creaking by within earshot, but to Wu's ears alone he conveyed a delicate intimation that if the inn should meet with financial reverses or if the fire-god should avidly seize upon its worm-eaten timbers, they need never fear for lack of employment.

"How so, Worthy Councilman?" queried Wu, somewhat thickly through a tangle of noodles.

"Why, surely, it should be evident that Cambaluc, even though it be a new city, must be surrounded by a large expanse of arable country in which are doubtless abandoned farms?"

"That is indisputably so," Wu agreed, listening attentively and for the moment halting the steady plying of his chopsticks.

"Then must it not necessarily follow that some of these farms have vacant buildings that are in sadly dilapidated condition?"

"That is likewise true."

"Considering this lamentable fact, it would seem a most noble act of kindness that someone should suggest to these superannuated sisters that should some worse misfortune fall upon them than the years have already brought—though I truthfully cannot imagine what that might be—they might constantly be in demand for the haunting of the wrecked dwellings, which no doubt are younger than they are."

Wu stared for a moment, pondering the thought, but he was not slow of wit and soon began to laugh.

"Ah, you are thinking of the sign! Your suggestion was at first opaque as a moonless night. You perhaps expected loveliness equivalent to that of swaying plum blossoms in the perfumed wind of spring!

"Let me assure you, Gracious Lord, the sign does not lie. The virtuousness of these seven maidens has never been held in question, for it has never been put to the test. As you can see, by its weather-beaten aspect, the sign has swung over this entrance for a very long time."

"I do not doubt either statement for the briefest of instants," said Gwalchmai, in a somewhat distant voice, his disposition being overspread by a certain flatness and not improved by the belated discovery that the pickle he had just swallowed was spoiled.

The foundry-master was about to turn the conversation in the direction of business, but the opportunity had already passed, for it was at this moment that the promised entertainment began.

A small boy entered, leaping, bounding, and turning cartwheels to the accompaniment of a long string of exploding firecrackers. He was followed by a blandly smiling man in long silken robes, embroidered with dragons, Fong-Onhangs or phoenixs, and the signs of the zodiac. From a capacious sleeve he produced yards upon yards of vari-colored silk, which as it issued he flung over and concealed the panting child. He plunged a knife into its midst.

The heap writhed, seemed to enlarge, and became quiet. From the other sleeve, the magician brought forth a Wand of Power and gently tapped the mound of silk. It was immediately flung aside and a beautiful girl stepped out, clad in the briefest of costumes.

She began to dance about the room, as lightly as a drifting feather. All eyes were upon her as she circled it thrice,, but her glances were only for Gwalchmai, wanton and inviting. She returned to her master, tossed a fold of silk over herself and gracefully sank to the floor.

He tapped again with the wand. The concealing cloth fell away and in place of the dancer, the boy sat cross-legged, holding a large bowl in his lap, filled to the brim with water in which goldfish swam.

The magician took the bowl and placed it carefully upon the nearest table, but as it touched the wooden surface, it became, between his hands, a bamboo cage of singing crickets.

The magician paused for applause. A few clapped, fewer still flung a brass cash; a drunken customer tried to seize the boy, who ran about picking up the rolling coins, possibly thinking that he might again change into the more desirable dancer—and as the trickster bowed, Gwalchmai laughed.

The magician straightened up. His face was calm, but his stiff stride indicated his anger. He came over to the booth where Gwalchmai and Wu were dining and bowed again.

"It is a source of ineffable gratification that the humble efforts of the clumsy and inept Shan Cho have provided joy for the noble lords," he remarked affably. "Doubtless, judging by their apparel, they are in disguise. Possibly the disguise might be improved to the greater satisfaction of all and create even more merriment for the many were they to leave this place upon four feet instead of two—perchance in the form of a mangy alleycat and that of a flea-bitten Wonk, in which to howl a mirthful duet to the uncaring moon?"

As the Wand of Power twitched slightly, Wu blanched to a sickly ochre and would have fled, but he could not leave without pushing the magician aside, so he sat there shivering, looking beseechingly from one to the other.

Gwalchmai placed both hands flat upon the table, to indicate that he bore neither ill will nor weapon.

"All-powerful and inestimably skilled Shan Cho, whose

slightest movement attests to long years of arduous study in
his art, this stupid apprentice and humble follower of the
ancient wisdoms of Loegres, Khemi, and the Danaan was
not by unseemly noises criticizing thy undoubtedly supreme
talents. Rather, these admittedly ill-timed sounds burst forth
without considered forethought at the practice of such unusual and praiseworthy dexterity before such an uncouth
group of insensitive feasters. Can it be that a mage of such
evident accomplishments and infinite capacities is reduced by
malevolent demons to this melancholy means of acquiring
nourishment?"

"Alas, it is indeed as you say," bitterly acknowledged the
mollified magician, who had been furtively appraising
Gwalchmai's ring. "It would appear that nowhere in this
triply condemned city of teeming population and boundless
wealth is there any place for a follower of the mystic
arts—as this person feels confident the noble lords must
agree. It was unfortunate of this purblind one that their
qualities were so well hidden that they were at first not
apparent.

"As it is evident that, judging by the ring which you wear,
this blunt-witted practitioner is hindering affairs of great moment, he will respectfully withdraw, leaving the noble lords
to their subtle and edifying discussions."

He had already slipped the threatening wand back into
its place of concealment and was backing away, attempting
to avoid any appearance of haste, never removing his gaze
from Gwalchmai's quiet hand, upon which the opal engraved
with Merlin's monogram smokily flared like a bloodshot eye.
He stopped nervously when Gwalchmai lifted that hand and
beckoned to him.

"May we suggest that it would be a most desirable termina-
tion of an unfortunate misunderstanding if all of you would
partake of some refreshment with us and indulge in in-
structive discourse to our possibly mutual advantage?"

Wu winced, considering the probable expense, and put
on an expression of horror, in which there was no welcome.
He glowered, but said nothing.

The boy had been rejoined by the dancing girl, who had
slipped in unobtrusively by the back door, and both nodded
violently at their master to accept the offer before it could
be withdrawn.

Shan Cho demurred. "To our abiding distress, we have

not as yet been fortunate enough to have gathered a complete string of cash between us and it is without question that no form of dignified credit is observed in this antique establishment."

Gwalchmai gestured largely at the foundry-master.

"Have absolutely no thought for the trifling amount concerned in establishing a comfortable feeling of repletion. Be assured that my friend is well equipped and anxious to bear the insignificant diminution of his overflowing purse. He is an individual of such ample means and extrordinary benevolence that his ancestors would be grieved for seven preceding generations should you refuse to partake of his notable generosity. He is already the sole support, by the burning of funeral money, of a large aggregation of hungry and homeless ghosts. Is it not so, charitable Wu?"

"Anything that is phrased in such shining words of pearl should be beyond any form of dispute," agreed Wu, without manifest enthusiasm.

His sober and considering looks grew momentarily more severe as the guests avidly absorbed a double order of noodles apiece. When the gallon of tea vanished, he considered the empty bowls with sadness, but it was not until a large pitcher of rice wine was found insufficient and a second was brought that remorse for the events of the day so obviously overwhelmed him.

He arose hastily. "Worthy Councilor, it is necessary that our further discussion must be carried forward until a more opportune occasion. This person has been so consistently cursed by the employment of incompetent thumb-fingered dolts that he must instantly return to their encouragement in their duties. If the godown has not yet been destroyed by their misguided efforts, doubtless sloth has overcome them and only the application of something weighty to their insensitive heads will convince them that they should strive to be worthy, in some part, of their lavish remuneration."

So saying, he was leaving in such haste that he would have completely forgotten to settle the score had not three of the virtuous maidens, who it appeared were not unfamiliar with such sudden fits of absentmindedness upon the part of their customers, casually intercepted him in such a manner that he could not leave until he had disgorged the proper number of coins.

Heaving a deep sigh, he departed, leaving the others to finish the remainder of the rice wine at their leisure.

As the dancing girl continued to direct even more swooning and personal glances at Gwalchmai, the more often she emptied her cup, he could not fail to notice that her beauty was becoming more evident each time his own elbow bent. He shrewdly decided that this remarkable coincidence could lead to nothing but future regret and weak and unconvincing explanations when he should finally meet Corenice again.

Therefore, he confined his remarks strictly to the magician and was much relieved when she flounced out in a pet, followed soon afterward by the well-rounded boy, who belched happily as he walked.

Left thus to their own devices, Gwalchmai and Shan Cho came obliquely and by devious routes to a thorough and complete respect for each other's capabilities and in the course of the conversation the subject of the Wands of Yai Ching was accidently brought up.

Gwalchmai had never heard of either the Book of Rites, or the mystical Changes of Wen Wang, but he did know that there were magics, and a wizardry of Oriental derivation, not akin to either European or Aztlanian lore. He asked for an explanation.

Shan Cho brought out a bamboo cylinder from the bosom of his robes. He uncapped it and shook out six black painted bamboo strips. Each was marked on one side with a band of white, but the markings were in different places on each little wand. He stood them on end and opened his hand. The cluster opened out and fell upon the table, some with the round side up, which had no white band. He pushed them together and the lines formed a pattern —one of the sixty-four hexagrams listed in the Book of Changes.

"This is the Li Chi, an unfortunate sign," he said. "It might bring the seeker unwanted knowledge, but if it should be used by this person, he would not look at the symbol you see, excluding all other distracting sounds or thoughts.

"When the hexagram was firmly engraved upon his mind, he would close his eyes and picture a door before them, upon which he would plainly see the symbol clearly imprinted. This door has never a knob or latch, nor any lock.

"It cannot be opened, but if a person concentrates upon his desire strongly and wishes hard enough, the door will swing widely toward him. Then he must believe that he arises without hesitation and walks straight through the doorway. Upon the other side one receives the answer to his questions and a resolving of his problems.

"However, I must tell you honestly that this seeker would never use this sign of the Li Chi. It has been known to occur that the door does not open, or that the wanderer does not always return.

"Some questions are best not answered and some problems can be solved only by death."

"I have a problem," said Gwalchmai, excitedly, omitting the customary amenities of polite speech. "Let me try the wands."

Shan Cho hesitated. "Be advised of the danger, Pure-Minded Adviser to the Mighty, upon whom be praise. This action may be a matter for regret."

Gwalchmai held out his hand. Seeing his unshakable determination, the magician reluctantly gave him the painted strips. He bunched them together and let them fall. Four dropped face down; the other two showed markings, but were separated by the blank strips that lay between when the six were pushed together in parallel formation.

Shan Cho's face showed his relief. "Ah! This is much better. The third of the Five Changes. A most fortunate sign. It should bring good fortune, a sight of a distant friend, or an answer to an important question."

Gwalchmai shielded his eyes with his hands, and fixed his mind upon the hexagram. The sounds of the room fell away, the face of the man opposite him disappeared; the hard bench beneath him could not be felt.

The symbol became more vivid as he stared at it without blinking. The lines wavered with his breathing, then steadied, growing brighter—they flamed as though white-hot. He closed his burning eyes against their brilliance, then saw the door take shape before him, as with an inner sight.

He stared at it. It was a heavy door, wide enough for only a single person, but it was set within a monstrous gate meant for mounted men or wagons. The whole was framed by a high stone wall on either side, extending far into misty distance beyond his vision.

He did not dare look at the walls, except out of the

corners of his eyes, lest he break the spell. He looked
straight ahead as he had been told.

The outlines of the door hardened. He could see the adze
marks that had shaped its planks. Against its gray plainness
flamed the sign. Without warning, the door swung toward
him, wide and wider, disclosing across a few feet another
door already open, through which a cloud of rolling mist
could be seen eddying in his direction.

He thought that he got up without hesitation and passed
through the door of the hexagram. He could see no more
than if he were in dense fog, but it was warm and flower-
fragrant, and it lay about him like a blessing. He felt happy
without reasoning why.

People seemed very close in the obscurity. He fumbled
on a few steps more, feeling for something solid with his
hands.

Suddenly out of the mist a bearded face came against
his cheek, long robes rustled against his own and strong
arms clasped him.

He knew who it was at once. Merlin! Was he then admitted to the Land of the Dead?

No word was spoken. Gwalchmai felt that the tenuous
connection with his own world might part like a cobweb.
The arms released him. His godfather was gone.

Now there came another clasping—more tender, though
tighter, as though from this affectionate hug he would not
be freed. He tried to place his own arms around that well-
known and beloved form. He knew instantly who it must
be.

"Corenice!" he whispered.

In that instant of knowing, everything passed. The doors
vanished, the gate and wall were gone, the mists rolled
away. Only the evanescent loving touch of a precious kiss
upon his cheek remained—that and a memory.

In that tiny fraction of a second when the mist had dissipated, he had seen a vision, distinct, clear, not to be forgotten.

A delicately featured girl, dressed like a princess, in silks
and jewels, with tiny slippered feet, a child-like form, and
slim pearl-adorned fingers. It was she who had caressed him.

Only once had he seen her like. She was golden in skin
and golden embroidery was heavy upon her silken robe. She
was the most beautiful girl he had ever stood before.

The flush upon her cheeks was like the soft dust upon a just-opened peach blossom. Her hair was black and glossy. She wore the same smiling expectant and inviting expression that Thyra had shown him and which he had seen upon the face of the dark Welsh girl who had named herself Nikky to him before they were truly wedded in the enclosure of the vitrified fort in Britain.

He knew beyond doubt that she could be no other than his lost love and that somehow they would soon meet, for in that flick of time in which he opened his eyes and saw opposite him the grinning features of Shan Cho, he saw superimposed upon the magician's face the scene still visible to his mind's eye that he had seen over the girl's shoulder.

Through the second door, a courtyard, another wall, and beyond it the distant but familiar outlines of the rolling hills and perfect snowy peaks among which he and Corenice had strolled so pleasantly together—in the Land of Dream!

17

The Firedrakes

Gwalchmai had been amused by the abrupt departure of the foundry-master. However, he did not overlook the possibilities in the demonstration he had just seen. He considered them soberly during the afternoon and lost some sleep that night while pondering uses of Wu's invention.

Merlin's books had mentioned such an explosive powder. He was aware that his godfather used such compounds in his magic. Other readings had informed him since that fireworks had been displayed for Roman Emperors, and that Anthemius of Tralles, the architect who had drawn the plans for Saint Sophia's church in Byzantium, had demonstrated likewise before Emperor Justinian.

Here in Cathay, he saw, almost daily, the little paper
noisemakers snapping viciously in the streets of Cambaluc,
to drive away devils or to amuse the children. He knew that
Kublai had massive stone mortars set at strategic points
about the city. These commanded the highways, because
they could hurl weighty stone balls a far distance, with an
alarming noise.

Gwalchmai felt certain that mortars were much too heavy
to be useful aboard junks and too ponderous to be trans-
ported ashore readily in any rapid land assault of the planned
invasion of Nihon.

Whether this earth thunder powder had been invented in-
dependently by Anthemius of Tralles, or if some wandering
Cathayan had brought knowledge of it westward, Gwalchmai had no way of knowing. He did not feel much curiosity
about it—but these bronze tubes of Wu! Here was a marvelous thing!

If these tubes, in assorted sizes, were to be mounted upon
the bulwarks, rails, and decks of the Khan's fleet, no
force the dog-devils might bring against them could stand
for a moment against such fire-power. If a little one could
tear a large hole in the wall of a godown, what might not
its large brother or cousin do to the wooden sides of a
ship?

If small ones were mounted upon wheels of a cart and
made thus in fit numbers to accompany the Khan's horde of
a hundred thousand warriors, land resistance also might easily
be brushed aside.

The man who could bring such a treasure to the Khan as
an easy victory might surely ask any wish and have it
granted.

He pushed far back in his mind the nagging fact that
Kublai, the Magnificent—scholar, patron of the arts, warrior,
and enlightened monarch that he was—was still far from
being the Prester John whom Gwalchmai had come so far
to seek. Although all religions and faiths flourished un-
hampered in his realm, even Christianity as the Nestorians
practiced it, Kublai Khan was not a Christian monarch nor
ever apt to be.

Merlin had specified that, failing a Roman emperor, only a
Christian monarch should ever be advised of the existence
of the new continents.

This adjuration Gwalchmai, for the moment, now ignored.

The Khan had a fleet capable of a long sea voyage. If, after this conquest, he could ask what he wished, it would be for a few of those ships, with men and supplies, to first find Corenice again and then, with her, to sail back to his old home.

He sent word to Shan Cho to attend him at the foundry, for he planned to use the knowledge stored in the devious mind of the magician. When he sought out Wu, he found that both were waiting.

Shan Cho was listening attentively to the foundry-master recounting his woes. Their faces lit up and became animated at the sight of Gwalchmai, who that day had arrived by palanquin and was splendidly attired in his official robes. They were obviously impressed.

Gwalchmai noticed that one of the larger cannon had been set up on end in a small alcove and joss sticks were burning before it. He was interested and inquired the reason.

Wu bowed. "This day, Worthy Councilman, whose calm brow brings peace to troubled hearts, is the anniversary of the absentmindedness of this person's estimable, but careless, paternal ancestor Feng, but one generation removed. While musing upon lofty thoughts beyond the reach of common mortals, he failed to notice the direction in which his independent feet were carrying his aged body and nodding head. He unfortunately tripped and fell into a cauldron of molten bronze at the very moment of pouring.

"Although what remained of his body was placed in our family tomb, his essence is here perpetuated in the shape of yonder thunder-tube. Therefore we do him honor in this manner!"

Gwalchmai made a respectful bow in the direction of the bronze-embalmed Feng and lit three sticks to his imperishable fame. Then, after tea had been brought and the amenities observed, he advanced the thoughts pressing upon his mind.

"It is the belief of this unimportant adviser to his Sublime Excellence—may he know ten thousand years—that should the worthy Feng request a public audience with the Serenest One, speaking of course through the well-shaped lips of his talented son, who will set forth his elucidations concerning his unparalleled inventions through the rough-edged but gilded words of a moderately placed intermediary, an interesting demonstration of yonder thunder-tubes might take place."

"These elegant phrases are arranged with superior conciseness," Wu acknowledged. "However, the interior meaning of them flutters only faintly at the mere border of the consciousness of this narrow-witted individual. Many taels have already been deposited in the grasping palms of thieves in high places to attain such a result.

"No more uproar has followed than as though the coins had fallen upon a soft down pillow, when the expected sound should have drowned out the noise of a score of crashing gongs. It is a lamentable fact that no more taels are now available for that purpose—all others having been invested in bronze and the metal molded into thunder-tubes."

Gwalchmai looked wounded. He clutched his heart as though suffering severe pangs.

"It was not the ill-expressed fancy of this clumsy wordsmith that any expense should even slightly drain the treasure chest of the well-established House of Feng. Rather, as was suggested yesterday, it may befall that some flow of gold from the weighty sacks of His Benign Omnipotence might flow in our directions with the mellow sound of a quarreling brook when the snows melt in the mountains.

"If such should be the case, this person would indubitably forego his share of cash in order to enhance his reputation and enjoy the opportunity of beseeching an inexpensive boon from the All-Seeing One. Naturally, an extra portion of plump, newly minted coins would fall thus into the hands of esteemed friends, who are being addressed at this very moment."

Both the foundry-master and Shan Cho gave him their instant and undivided attention.

Seeing this, Gwalchmai went on: "It is a custom of merit, even between people in high places and such as we who grovel beneath their unsullied slippers, that if we should do them a favor they will not withhold their patronage from us. The only regrettable fact is that the ragged mendicant must first render himself indispensable to the well-equipped noble.

"We all have certain needs that may possibly be joined together to create a complete and satisfactory whole, inside of which circle of perfection may be found the happy answer to several problems.

"The Ineffable Luminescence—may he soon shed his light upon the ignoble dog-devils!—has need of mighty weapons. You, worthy Wu, have them to the power of ten thousand chariots, but cannot approach His Supreme Brilliance.

"He has many taels and you have few, while Shan Cho finds that the brilliance of his many-faceted mind is stultified by the stunted intelligence of those coarse individuals with which, for lack of a discerning patron, he is forced to consort.

"There are ships in the harbors, which this person could use to reach a new continent to the East, but alas!—not even a small, leaky sampan is under his control, although the ear of His Permanent Benignance is well bent in this direction.

"Now, it is no secret that however refined an invention may be, improvements are always possible. With your experienced aid in searching out the various salts of the earth that shall be needed, your knowledge of books of your country's physicks, and your procurement of such rare ingredients for us, accomplished and cunning trickster Shan Cho, our task should be made easy.

"I have a certain knowledge of spells that I shall add to the composition of such an earthshaking devouring fire that will issue from the quiet bronze throat of Feng to startle his own ancestors, enrich his son, and astonish the Exalted Presence into granting all wishes of we three."

"This mention of wealth that is to shower indiscriminately upon all concerned is a most fascinating balm for aching ears," cautiously remarked the magician. "If such a delightful phenomenon is contingent on the aforementioned discovery of a new continent, it should be dismissed from the Councillor's thoughtful consideration.

"Such a land is well known to all scholars of Ch'in. Over seven centuries ago, the Buddhist monk, Hoei-Shin, sailed in search of new lands to the east and found them. The Painted People live there and the name of that country is Fusang, although some call it 'Tahan,' or 'Great China.'

"The Son of Heaven will not be interested. All is lucidly set forth in the Ten Books of Profitable Travels. He can read there as much as you can tell him. His Ineffable Eminence would not allow so much as a handful of wheat flour for your 'news.' "

"There was no intention of opening negotiations with any

individual whose concern is that of the making of bread.
Our discussion should confine itself to the composition of the
earth-thunder powder and its possible improvement. What
are the excellent elements and in what abstruse proportions
are they assembled, high-minded and sagacious Wu?"

"Two portions of the best willow charcoal, two of the
flowers of brimstone, and six parts of nitre—as is used in
rockets."

Gwalchmai possessed an excellent memory. Although he
did not have total recall, he sometimes found himself able
to visualize whole pages out of Merlin's arcane library, now
forever lost.

He closed his eyes and concentrated. He vaguely remembered seeing a formula, in which "Chinese Snow" was
mentioned. Merlin's informant had been a sailor. Merlin,
curious about all strange lands, noted the odd fact that
those who crossed desert and mountain to reach the land
behind the Great Wall spoke of it as Cathay. However, the
sea people who visited the harbors of that country knew it
by the name of China. Europeans called the same realm by
two different names and the alchemists referred to Chinese
Snow. Could this element be nitre?

He struck his brow. He frowned. Formulae came slowly
to his mind, only to be discarded. He had the feeling of a
busy little searcher opening closed compartments in his brain,
only to angrily slam them shut. What was it, this elusive
information?

Charcoal—sulphur—that was another name for brimstone; these other ingredients of the explosive; both Wu and
Gwalchmai's godfather had used them, but with such vary-
ing results. Could the secret be in the proportions?"

Suddenly the words leaped before him as upon an unfolded screen: "Take of Chinese Snow, five measures, com-
pacted; Rhamnus Frangula, trimmed one inch in diameter
and overheated well in a closed iron retort, ground fine—
three measures, packed tightly; Aureate Pollen of Aetna,
alembic distilled and crystallized—two full measures. Sift,
mix, wet, dry in cakes, crumble, sift, and use as desired."

That was it! Nitre, charcoal—but of dogwood, not willow
—and brimstone. The same simple ingredients, obscured to
the uninitiate by the flowery, symbolic language of the alchemist, of which Merlin had no peer—but—"Use as desired"?

Why could he not have been more explicit? Use—how? In bombs? Rockets? Thunder-tubes?

Did Merlin ever imagine such a horror as a thunder-tube? What would happen if this more explosive dust, which Gwalchmai hoped to re-create, were confined, as he had seen Wu's workman use the weaker variety? Perhaps the tube would burst.

Mentally, he turned a page. Ah, yes! Rockets! Fantastically colored balls of whistling fire, ejected from tubes! Here was the remembered list of added ingredients with which to manufacture such marvels:

"A moiety of Friable Acrusite (Good Heavens! How much was a moiety?). A portion of Sublimated Argent Sperm of Yaotzin (also known as *hydragyrum*)—interesting; Yaotzin was an Aztlanian demon! Well—the Azteca called gold "The offal of the Gods." Demon's sperm might be mercury, for he knew from his studies that an explosive fulminate could be derived from cinnabar, the mother of mercury.

Was there more? Yes! "A driblet of distilled essence of Naphtha." That should be easy to procure. "Tears of Resin; Triturated Dragon's Blood—a quantity." A quantity indeed! Gwalchmai cursed in five languages. All that for rockets? The proportions? Nothing came to mind.

Wait—a footnote! The secret was fading, but helpfully a little more remained. "Compounded under the auspices of Venus and Jupiter, under the dominance of Mars—see Celestial Heat Spell in the Book of the Red Dragon."

There, at last, Gwalchmai was on firm ground. Proportions were exasperatingly vague, but the spell was available. It had been carved in Ogham letters, tiny, worn, but readable, upon the outer edge of the Ring's hoop. The spell was constantly in use among alchemists, in the compounding of formulae concerning the four elements—earth, air, fire, and water—that comprise almost everything.

Naturally, Merlin would have kept it handy to aid his memory. Gwalchmai pondered further upon the subject. The thunder-tubes were made of bronze, which is a composition of copper (whose sign is Venus) and tin (Jupiter!) and they were to be used, obviously, in war! Certainly Mars was dominant there! All three of the necessary astrological signs were favorable—and he had the spell!

How could he fail? In the powder, he recognized its essentially earthy nature, its fugacious atoms, and its connection through smoke with the spirits of the air. Of the four elements, he thus had control of three, and, as water was unnecessary, its lack should be no detriment to the efficiency of the compound.

Nor was he disappointed in his choice of the magician as his aid. He cautiously sounded out Shan Cho's knowledge of magical lore, finding, as he had suspected, that much of it was mere sleight-of-hand, or pure trickery. He was pleased to learn that Shan Cho was familiar with the more obscure items listed in Chinese pharmacopoeias.

In addition, he had influential friends in the Worshipful and Honorable Guild of Resplendent Sky-Fire Hurlers and through them he procured for Gwalchmai books on the mystery and the art of making fireworks. The symbols in these books supplemented Gwalchmai's own sketchy knowledge and gave him the clues he needed to assemble the materials necessary.

With the facilities available in the foundry, purification and assembly of the essentials was no great problem, and after many trials the three finally managed to create a most satisfying composition, far superior to Wu's own blend.

It exploded with a fine, shattering report, hurling stones much farther from the thunder-tubes than ever before. It was obvious from the cloud of black smoke emitted that this should prove to all dog-devils that Kublai, the Invincible, was not only Son of Heaven, but also Nephew to Dragons and that resistance to him would be quite useless.

The only drawback to this close communion of minds among the three partners, from Gwalchmai's point of view, was the fact that Mei-mei, the Magician's dancing girl and aid, was continually underfoot. Her name meant Little Sister, but her attentions were far from being sisterly. Mei-mei's eyes were big and her voice encouraging whenever she was near Gwalchmai. He found considerable difficulty in keeping his mind strictly upon his other problems.

Remembering well the nixie in Elveron, he sometimes wondered if Corenice was again teasing him, or once more testing his fidelity. In the effort to give her no excuse for later chiding, he succeeded so well in assuming an attitude of refined no-encouragement to Mei-mei that the dancing girl transferred her ignored charms to the foundry-man. Wu accepted them with enthusiasm and no complaints.

Had Gwalchmai studied Flann's holy books, or even the

Analects of K'ung Fu-tse, he might have been forewarned that a woman scorned would bear watching. Possibly, he might have caught her, late one night, in the act of adding an entirely superfluous quantity of sublimated essence of nitre to the completed store of the mixture.

This might not have mattered a great deal, had not both Wu and Shan Cho, anxious that all should go supremely well, mixed in, unbeknownst to each other, increased amounts of whatever ingredients they separately considered the most potent.

With this original and untried, not to say unusual, compound, the empty bombs were charged. Following this delicate work, the expulsive charges were measured out into bags for the loading of the thunder-tubes.

Gwalchmai had been so pleased with the final trials of the powder that he forbore reciting the spell over it until the actual time of the demonstration, feeling that the Khan should be among the first to witness the new weapon in its mightiest aspect.

At this period in time there was, between the Purple Forbidden City and the Temple of Heaven, a large open parade ground. Here troops were reviewed, public festivals were observed, kite competitions were held, and crowds could be addressed with facility.

Having obtained permission for a demonstration of the improved missile throwers, the three partners issued a challenge to the manufacturers of the old. It was accepted with scorn and a date agreed upon without much difficulty.

Immediately following, stands were erected for the nobility, graded downward in size and comfort from the Peacock Throne of the Great Khan to vermilion-lacquered chairs of Mandarins, upholstered stools for Confucian scholars, teachers, and civil servants, and simple wooden benches for bonzes and other priests.

Artisans, engineers, and workmen hovered around the implements of war, where the standard army-issue catapults and stone mortars were set up at one end of the field.

Ranged alongside these bomb-hurlers, Gwalchmai, Wu, and Shan Cho had already directed the foundry crew in the mounting of the battery of thunder-tubes. They were loaded and ready to fire. Near them were stacked the iron bombs that would be used in the next salvos, now filled with the improved powder, and little carts which held the measured

charges for the tubes, in various sizes for the different cali-
bers.

In front of this array of artillery was a clear field of fire,
stretching the entire length of the parade ground. Behind
the machines there milled a tremendous crowd, munching
melon and sunflower seeds, drinking sweet liquids and hot
tea. They were courting, squabbling, hunting for lost children
or lost parents.

All were having a grand time and most of them were
giving free advice to the distracted workmen who were
nervously adjusting tube elevations for the fortieth time,
driving in more stakes to prevent recoil from the thunder-
tubes or cranking down the long catapult arms in readiness
to place and light the fused bombs that would be thrown
first, before the partners could compete with the new weapons.

When the Khan arrived and took his seat, surrounded
by a group of high officials, each with attendant wives,
concubines, and slaves, everyone else had been waiting for
at least six hours and many since before dawn. They were
hot, sweaty, dusty, and tired; they were ill-humored, anxious,
and out of patience; there was a buzz of voices.

Kublai clapped his hands and those who were able to sat
down and fanned themselves. The noise of the crowd hushed.

The Exalted Chief of Catapult-Engineers, The Elevated
Controller of Invincible Mortar-Men, and Wu, of the House
of Feng, came forward together and kowtowed with the
three kneelings and the nine knockings of the head.

Gwalchmai, standing in a pentagram he had drawn in the
dust, now pronounced the celestial heat spell over the thunder-tubes and the wagonloads of munitions, turning the ring
on his finger as he followed the interlaced words around the
hoop.

He was horrified to find that one letter in one word of the
final phrase was almost worn away. He looked closely, but
could not make it out. Was it a C or a Q? He could not be
sure.

He raised it closer to his eyes and squinted. It seemed to
be the four parallel, transverse lines of an Ogham C, instead
of the five of a Q. He so pronounced it and finished the
phrase.

As he did so, two things happened. A soft, crepitant

rustling or whispering came from the battery of tubes and the stacked bombs near them. One pyramidal pile shook itself apart and the globes rolled and scattered in as many directions, but were speedily restacked.

The other event concerned Shan-Cho. He had been apprehensively performing scapulomancy upon a tortoise shell by piercing it with a red-hot needle and now came up with it in his hand. He surreptitiously nudged Gwalchmai and showed him the cracks the heat had made in the shell.

"Definitely an unpropititious day!" he yammered. "Worthy Councilman, no more unfortunate sign exists in the long history of the art! We must withdraw at once!"

Gwalchmai had time only to give him an indignant look when a catapult arm jerked up, thudded against its padded stop and cast its ignited bomb into the air. A thin trail of smoke marked its passage toward the targets at the far end of the field. The fuse, fanned to light by the wind of its passage, burned too quickly and the bomb exploded short and in mid-air.

The engineers looked chagrined and made more fine adjustments to the mechanism. Using a longer fuse, they prepared another shot.

Now came the turn of the mortars. These fired, at choice, either large stone balls for battering the walls of a city or could lob inflammable packages of tow- and oil-soaked resin into enemy forts and camps.

They were far from being mobile and were so ponderous that they were considered strictly a siege weapon. It was these that Gwalchmai hoped to supersede with the lighter and more versatile tubes, yet the mortars were formidable competitors. They had the advantage of being operated by gunners of long experience and of being watched by generals with conservative minds.

The largest piece was discharged first. Even with the reduced charge of powder necessary under the circumstances of the competition, it let go with a stunning crash. A long streak of flame jetted from the monstrous maw and the shock could be felt in the soles of the feet as the ground absorbed the jar.

The stone ball went high, became a little black speck and then came rushing back, enlarging itself, whistling down until every individual felt himself its target. Yet so accurately aimed was the mortar that the ball thudded to earth almost in the center of the fifty-foot circle which had been drawn to receive it.

There was a storm of clapping, fan waving, and applause. The Khan beamed and sent down a purse of gold to be divided among the mortar crew, who sneered with scorn at Wu and his men, who now came forward with lighted brands to take their stand.

As the bronze tubes were so much smaller, Gwalchmai had determined to make a more impressive display by firing a massed salvo, not exactly in concordance with the previous demonstrations, but within the rules of the competition.

It had seemed fitting to the partners that since the largest of all the tubes was the one holding the essence of Wu's paternal ancestor, the uneasy ghost of Feng might be pleased if it were privileged to make the first announcement of the day that an old order was passing and a new method of war was about to begin.

As highest in rank, Gwalchmai lit the end of the long train of bunched fuses that fanned out to each piece of ordnance in the battery they had assembled. As the little coals raced along the ground, he wheeled and slapped his firebrand to the primed touch-hole that waited beside him.

He was amazed to find that there was no explosion. Instead, a prolonged hissing came from the cannon that was Feng. It increased in strength, the sound like steam under high pressure whistling out on a rising scale until it was almost a high, thin shriek.

Those who could see the muzzle saw also a sharp projection pushing out of it. It moved from side to side, twisting and straining violently as it slowly emerged. Soon all could see clearly that it was a beak, partly opened to reveal a forked darting tongue that flicked hotly over savage fangs. The remainder of the head followed the beak—a domed brow, puffy wattles, and saucer-like, lidless eyes that glared smokily with scarlet pupils at the crowd.

A crest arose and expanded, sharply serrated like the comb of a fighting cock. The creature stared about, resting for the moment.

Heat waves eddied and shimmered around the unbelievable thing. People tried to fight their way out of the front lines, which were in panic, into the rear of the multitude, while others were pressing forward to get a better view. The whole assemblage was in turmoil.

The unspeakable head raised and came farther out. A long scaly neck followed it and short thin arms appeared, ending in viciously taloned digits. The claws gripped the lip of the cannon and the bronze reddened with heat under their clutch.

Muscles in the shoulders and arms tensed and bunched as the creature drew itself out with difficulty. It hissed again as though in pain and anger. A long stream of fire licked out from the now widely opened beak. It strained dreadfully—pulled its elongated body still farther out of the cannon mouth and drooped toward the ground like an exhausted boneless moth emerging from its chrysalis.

But it was not wet like that moth! No! Its form was hardening; its shape was now determined; its scales rang crisply as it dragged itself along the ground!

Soon the crumpled wings spread out like unfurled sails as life, or flaming ichor from its burning veins, poured into them to cause expansion. Its long knotted tail lashed out, the pinions beat wildly, steadied, and the creature took the air in all its flaming, terrible glory and soared, radiating heat like a living sun upon the shuddering people below.

"Fong-Onhang!" moaned Shan Cho and Wu together. "The fiery dragon!"

Gwalchmai knew then that the oldest legend to frighten man had somehow come to life. Naming it would not make this great wonder seem but a little thing, for here before his eyes—because of a faulty compound? too much dragon's blood in the formula? a mistake in the pentagram?—here flew the fabled Firedrake, whose distant cousin valiant Beowulf had slain to his own doom.

And now, as the entire battery of the foundry-master's thunder-tubes was fired, for the action once begun could not be stopped, out of them a hundred more were ejected. They were in various sizes and stages of development. Some were as tiny as sparrows, many as large as ducks. A few could swallow eagles. As all flapped, sqawking and hissing, across the parade ground and roundabout the aghast city of Cambaluc, Gwalchmai saw that the events of the day were not over.

The stacked bombs began to split. They burst like piles of

hatching eggs. Red-hot fragments flew far and wide. Soon another twenty score devil-chicks took to the air to wheel above in scanning circles. They preened themselves. They dropped sparks. They dipped low to scorch the affrighted, scattering people. Beating upward in streaming comet trails of heat, the flying dragons lividly paled the sun with their shimmering radiance.

Gwalchmai saw Wu and Mei-mei running, hand in hand, among the shrieking, fleeing multitude. He saw Shan Cho strip off his robe, so that no one would recognize him as a magician, and disappear, wearing only a coolie's loincloth.

Gwalchmai's faith in sorcery was bitterly shaken. He wished he could do the same, but he stood his ground. How could such a fiasco have taken place? His plans were ruined. His disappointment was bitter. He hoped that in whatever state of Elysium Merlin and Corenice might be, they could know nothing of this day of shame.

Then his face cleared. In a better light than before, he could now see that the four little marks on the outer edge of the ring hoop were in conjunction with a fifth tiny scratch, almost worn away. The letter was not a C, as he had read it! Sorcery was still a valid science!

He walked away with almost a jaunty step, seeking shelter from the heat. "Yes!" he muttered to himself. "Definitely! The letter in that word I mispronounced was Q!"

A tiny mistake, in truth, but enough to set the art of Chinese gunnery back by four hundred years.

Gwalchmai did not return to his well-furnished home. He never saw his office again, nor claimed any sort of reward from his no doubt anxiously awaiting monarch. It would have been difficult to locate Kublai Khan, who had abruptly left the city for his distant summer palace deep in the Outer Lands, outdistanced by most of his faithful but disturbed retinue, who had hurried on ahead at their best speed to make ready for his coming.

Neither did Gwalchmai waste time seeking Wu, son of Feng or Shan Cho, for in his self-abasement he reckoned them scarcely less inept than himself.

It was definitely no place for a man who could not make up his mind in a hurry. Fortunately, he was under no such handicap. He rapidly meditated upon the relative merits of a sea voyage and an extended tour by land, deciding promptly upon the former.

Among his less praiseworthy acquaintances was a junk captain who always maintained a constant readiness for sea, since his conscience plagued him into a chronic restlessness. As this person, being a somewhat impecunious fellow, was engaged in eking out a bare existence by carrying on a smuggling trade between both sides of the Narrow Sea, he was open to reasonably discreet offers.

Shortly after negotiations began, Gwalchmai, considerably poorer, was hidden away from the combined detrimental dangers of sunlight and curious eyes in one of the darker unsanitary corners of the junk's hold.

A few days later he was deposited, at night, upon a secluded beach in one of the less frequented spots upon the coast of Nihon, and was left there, without lengthy farewells, to henceforth shift for himself.

As the small boat departed from the shore, the junk captain gave him, in leavetaking, a friendly word of advice.

"It may be the thought of the Worthy but Canceled-Out Councilor that a time will come when it will be safe for him to return. He should realize that it would not be well for him to keep his head under water until that moment arrives.

"Half the city was burned by his dragons that night and was this person not a man of high-minded integrity and overwhelming virtue, riches would assuredly come to him in heaped wheelbarrows if the Councilor were brought to the Emperor in bonds."

At first, Gwalchmai did not understand. At night? But the firedrakes had been flying everywhere when he left and there had been no fires.

Then it came to him. Of course! The culminating evil of that miserable day should have been evident to him from the very beginning!

Like any other winged creatures, when night came the firedrakes dropped down out of the sky to roost—red-hot and breathing sparks—upon the roofs of Cambaluc!

18

The Land of Dream

Unbeknownst to Gwalchmai, it had been no accident that he was landed upon this particular section of coast. All people are directed by events and causes beyond their control, regardless of how strictly they fancy that they direct their own destiny, and throughout his long life he had been thus influenced more than most.

He had known this through much of his wanderings, but he did not realize how strongly he had been affected on this occasion, nor by whom, as he stood gazing at the boat returning to the junk, which at once raised anchor and sail and soon was lost to sight.

Other eyes had also been watching, and now he saw advancing toward him, across the beach, a strange and menacing individual.

He was short, no more than shoulder high to Gwalchmai, but he looked immensely powerful. His bare arms bunched with lumps of knotted muscle as he walked with an easy swing. His hands were empty, but in his belt were two swords, one long, one short, and both sheathed, although his fingers were very close to the hilts.

Other than this, his body was completely covered with black plates of armor, which looked as though they were created as much to frighten an antagonist as to protect the wearer. The suit was shaped weirdly of heavy leather, some bronze, and a little steel, laced together by heavy rawhide thongs, scarlet silk cords, and thick copper-wire stitching. To Gwalchmai, the outfit resembled nothing so much as the sable chitinous armor that the elves made from the wing cases of giant beetles.

The man's head was crowned by a four-pointed, crested bronze helmet with turned-up peaks. This was held by a leather strap, tight beneath his chin, and his face was covered with a bronze hinged mask pierced with eye slits and small holes for ventilation.

Gwalchmai was unarmed, except for a small dagger and the flint hatchet he always carried. He slipped it out of his sash and weighed it carelessly in his hand, ready to throw.

The armored man stopped about twenty feet away and lifted his visor. He had a pleasant, strong face, although he was obviously trying to look fierce by drawing down the corners of his mouth in a semi-scowl. Beneath it, a natural friendliness showed through.

Gwalchmai was pleased to find that he could understand his visitor, since he spoke in a dialect not much different from that of the sailors on the junk, although some words had a different inflection.

"I am Chikara, Samurai of Daimyo Hidayama, sent to guide you to Shori Castle, where you will be made welcome, Noble Messenger," he said, and bowed with an insucking hiss of breath.

"You knew that I would be here?" Gwalchmai asked, puzzled. "You expected me?"

"Indeed, as you have said. We have patrols out these three days and nights for eight *ri** up and down the coast, but it is I who was secretly informed by my Lady where to look for you and it is I who shall have the reward. Be pleased to accompany me."

Gwalchmai relaxed his grip and placed the hatchet back in his sash. "I do not understand."

His guide smiled. "All will be made clear by the Baron. This way, please." Without waiting to see if he was followed, he set off at a fast pace and Gwalchmai was hard put to keep up with him in the soft white sand.

After about a mile of such walking they rounded a point, where boats were drawn up and a little fishing village of straw-thatched houses crescented the far end of a small bay. Overlooking it and dominating the village, Shori Castle, with its feet in the water and its crest in the low clouds, lay back against a rugged cliff as though it had grown out of the rock.

*twenty miles.

Chikara made a funnel of his hands. "Oh-ei! Oh-ei!" he trumpeted, and one of the fishermen came swinging in to ferry them across the bay. The boat bumped lightly against a small stone quay, where willing hands gripped the side and laughing faces greeted them.

Gwalchmai was more puzzled than ever.

Chikara was surrounded by a group of soldiers dressed as he, who clapped him on the shoulders and congratulated him upon his good fortune. Gwalchmai was gently urged within by a bowing silk-clad, shaven-pated underling who respectfully inquired his honorable name and pattered ahead on straw sandals while the others followed behind and the gate barring the entrance closed behind them.

Upward through winding corridors, with gates and guards at each angle; up stairways commanded by arrow slits in the walls; up ramps that slanted beneath ceilings pierced with holes, from which could pour a deadly flood of boiling water or flaming oil.

Thus they came at last to a large audience chamber, ten tatami mats in size, where the people, who so carefully left nothing to chance, waited there to receive him.

The Baron Hidayama sat cross-legged upon a low dais, gently fanning himself. The front of the room was open to the sea. He wore a black kimono, drawn in by a crimson sash in which was thrust diagonally a curved dagger, half hidden by the coat designating his rank—a stiff haori of heavy silk, embroidered with a single neat white peony.

His face was that of an aristocrat, delicately boned, thin-lipped. His mustache was long, but narrow, and his hair was rolled up in a tight topknot.

All this Gwalchmai took in with a single sweeping glance and then forgot him. He heard the Baron say something, in courteous words of greeting, but a roaring like that of the sea was in his ears and his heart was pounding to shake his entire body. He felt that he was suffocating. He pulled his loose collar still farther from his throbbing throat.

Seated beside the Baron, upon a silken cushion of down, was someone he knew! Here, kitten-curled, was the little golden-skinned princess he had seen and caressed so briefly —who had clasped him with affection and held him to her heart—on *this* side of Shan Cho's magic door!

"Know me by gold!" Those had been Corenice's last words to him. There had been golden hair; a gold-embroidered gown that the nixie had worn to catch his admiring eye; a golden torque cinctured tight around a slim, bare waist. By these hints he had known her various embodiments. There had been nothing like this before.

Here Gwalchmai saw reborn, as though formed in the same mold, the Corenice he had first known and loved, for the expression that had transformed Thyra and Nikky temporarily to the semblance of the soul within was impressed upon this lovely daughter of Nihon as though her features had been recast.

She *was* Corenice!

He had little time to consider this miracle. Already his guide had sunk to his knees and bowed low.

The Honorable Ambassador, Gorome-San from the Emperor of Great Mongolia," he announced.

The Baron inclined his head in courteous greeting. Then, as Gwalchmai remained standing, he also arose.

"I give you greetings and welcome, honored Sir, and offer you the hospitality of my house. I am the Baron Kuroki Hidayama and this is my daughter, the Lady Mitami Uyume. It is she who advised me of your coming. After you have bathed, we shall dine. Doubtless you are hungry and weary. Kindly consider all that you see at your disposal. This is your home." He clapped his hands twice.

Gwalchmai could only stare as though tongue-tied. Gone were all the flowery words, the ornate salutations, the involved phrases, the intricately framed speech that had smoothed his way in Cambaluc and that had been so painfully learned. Gone were his courtly manners, vanished and forgotten as though they had never been.

The Lady Mitami Uyume! Daughter to a Daimyo! Were these typical of the people whom the courtiers of the Khan called dog-devils?

Were such as these the folk against which a mighty nation was arming an invasion and outfitting a fleet? These small, delicate people?

He, Gwalchmai, had been directing all his efforts toward their destruction to suit his own selfish purpose. To obtain the grant of a few ships, he had been willing to bring down consuming fire, terrible death, and slavery upon his Corenice —their Land of Dream!

He had passed through the door in the massive gate of Shan Cho's vision when he had entered Shori Castle. He

remembered the very adze marks in the wood. It was wonderful! It was true! It would go down like paper before the
strength of Kublai Khan!

He would die now before that should ever be.

He followed a maid to the bath, hardly knowing how he
arrived there. He knew he must have said something ap-
propriate to his hosts, but he could not remember what it
was.

While he was soaking in a scalding tub and being scrubbed
almost skinless, while he was gasping under a bucket of
cold water direct from a deep well, and while he was being
pummeled until he expected to be black and blue, although
his pretty torturer called it a gentle massage, he was trying
to recall that lovely face he had seen.

In vain his masseuse used her most subtle arts—he
scarcely heard her sighs and compliments upon his young
face and strong body, despite his graying hair. In vain her
caressing fingers discreetly sought to arouse him for his
pleasure, in vain her eyes said things her lips dared not;
he hardly saw her.

There was only one smile he wished to see, only one hand
he wanted to touch—and only one love he hoped to enjoy.

When he had been dressed in silks and shod in thick white
split stockings and soft slippers, he was escorted to the dining hall where his host and his beloved were seated. His
tensions had been softened away and he found the surroundings relaxing.

The meal was simple. It began with fish from the sea,
with tiny mushrooms flavored with mustard. A clear turtle
soup, with turtle eggs and a dash of ginger juice, was followed by a main dish of thinly sliced chicken, sautéed with
finely chopped green tops of white radish in soy sauce.

After a serving of lobster tails, sectioned and arranged in
the form of peonies, nested in boiled white rice, a rare sake
was brought. A tray of fruit was placed upon the low table.

To the unobtrusively low tinkle of samisens, behind a
painted translucent screen now drawn across the far end of
the hall to provide the diners with a more intimate room,
the discussion began.

Gwalchmai had no way of knowing that the presence of
the Baron's daughter was, here, most unusual. In other cul-
tures with which he was familiar, from those of Aztlan

and the Hodenosaunee, in Alata, to the systems of Britain, Europe, and continental Asia, woman's voice carried equal weight with those of men, although sometimes more shrill.

Nor did it surprise him in his ignorance to find that Baron Hidayama seemed dominated by this young woman. If what he suspected was true, it would have been stranger if his host was not.

He did find it odd that she began the conversation.

"As you have been informed," she began, in a pleasantly low voice, "we have anxiously awaited your coming. Is the message you bring one of war or peace?"

Gwalchmai was puzzled. Either this marvelous resemblance was no more than a heartbreaking coincidence or she was dissembling because she could not admit before her father that they had mystically shared a common past.

"I fear there has been an error. Perhaps I have accepted a hospitality meant for another. I bear no message, no letter of any kind, nor am I an ambassador of high rank or low. It may be best that I offer my apologies and leave."

The Baron lifted a restraining hand. "Pray do not concern yourself. If there has been a mistake, it is surely not of your making, but ours. We knew that you were coming, because you were seen upon your way. Surely there cannot be two such men as yourself in Nihon, with skin as red as yours? If there were it would be even more remarkable that both should wear similar rings I assumed that you were the bearer of a message to the Regent Hojo Tokimune, as there have been five others before you, each carrying words more insulting than the last.

"We despise the Khan, but not the bearers of his letters. All have traveled to Kamakura without harm and have been treated with courtesy.

"Still, you were seen and I know who you are, if not what you may be."

"And I also know who you are," murmured the Lady Mitami, but so low that Gwalchmai saw the words on her lips more clearly than he heard them.

The Baron permitted himself a faint smile. "My daughter has been allowed the privileges of the son I never had and she is worthy of them. Some women have powers and insights above those of men and it is well that when the gods grant such talents they be encouraged, not suppressed. When Mitami became a woman she was to have wed a son of

the Akagawa, to whom she had been promised, but she
would have none of him. She wept and languished and
said that she had seen in a dream the only man she would
marry.

"She refused to eat and pined away in longing for this
man, who she said would come from the sea. Her favorite
treasure was a mirror in which she said she sometimes saw
him when she was not sleeping and so followed him across
the world on his way to her. She said that she had a friend
who looked back at her, out of her own eyes, when she
looked into this mirror. I insisted that she must go to the
man to whom I had promised her.

"We are a feeble clan and I feared to make the Akagawa
our enemy, but it seemed that she would die so strong was
her will to combat my determination that she should obey.

"Then, as she lay so pale and weak, it came to me that
I loved her more than my promise or my pride. At that moment, I prayed to the Fox Goddess, Inari, who has a fond-
ness for our house, that Mitami should live again, for we
thought she had died—there was no mist on the mirror
when we raised it to her lips.

"I bent and whispered into her ear that she should wed
whom she chose and at her own time. She opened her
eyes and smiled and asked for food and slept. I knew that
Inari had sent her back and my heart was full. It cost me
much to buy back my promise from the Akagawa and they
are now my enemies, but I have had my treasure in her and
we have both been waiting for the red stranger from the
sea that she predicted would come in a time of great need.
I am glad that you are he and not the ambassador I expected. Can you tell us aught of Kublai and his plans?"

Gwalchmai hesitated. If it were true that Cambaluc
had been partly burned, the invasion, set for midsummer
might have suffered a temporary setback. He did not wish
to rouse false hopes or to pretend knowledge he did not have
or to disclose his own share in upsetting the schedule of the
Khan.

It seemed that, even across the Narrow Sea, he could feel
the powerful stare of seven thousand painted eyes, fixed
malevolently upon Nihon and upon himself.

To claim that he had interfered against such power, in
such an odd way, might seem that he spoke in vanity or

self-aggrandizement. If he told the embarrassing truth it might prove himself a clumsy ally. He had already decided he must be an ally to these people.

The Baron, seeing his indecision, misunderstood. "If it is a matter of honor, you shall not be pressed for information that you cannot give."

He rose with a stern countenance and was about to clap his hands together, signifying the talk was at an end, when the Lady Mitami delicately touched the sleeve of his kimono.

"Honored Father, I am sure that our guest pauses only to choose his words with care. Sir, are you for us or against us?"

Gwalchmai folded his hands and bowed. He looked steadily into her eyes. "For you, now and always. Never let it be doubted."

She bowed in return and as she raised her head their eyes met again and clung. Her lips curved sweetly and he knew that the slight emphasis he had employed had not gone unnoticed.

"Be seated, Father, and ask what you would know. I am sure honor is not a factor in this matter."

Skillful questions brought forth the information the Daimyo desired. Gwalchmai held back nothing, and as he spoke on and on, the pertinent information was taken down upon rice paper with brush and ink block, in exquisite calligraphy. The ships were numbered in their thousands, their probable armament and materiel were recorded; the tumans of cavalry were set down by name and emblem, the hordes of foot soldiers, the engineers were described along with their resources and equipment. Everything he told was mentioned in this report, even such intangibles as audacity, obedience, and élan.

When it was considered complete, a thick pad of paper sheets lay before the Baron's scribe. Gwalchmai felt exhausted, his mind plucked clean.

Kuroki rose and this time did clap his hands. He gave the account to the retainer who answered the summons.

"Have twenty copies made at once. One shall be sent to the Mikado at Kyoto in all haste. One goes to the Shogun at Kamakura, and the others to the heads of all clans, far and near. Specify that this is of the utmost urgency and urge that all personal animosities should be set aside and that the seacoast is to be guarded so tightly that not a crab will cross a beach unseen or a bird nest upon a cliff be visited by the bird unwatched.

"When the copies are ready, bring them to me, no matter how late, and I will sign them. At that time, have twenty couriers ready to start."

By the hour of the Horse, which is midnight by Western clocks, the scrolls were signed and sealed. Long before another bell had marked the hour of the Sheep, the lighted torches that the couriers carried were far out of sight in twenty different directions. Fortunate indeed were those runners whose destinations were those of the nearer great houses.

Kyoto was six days from Shori Castle; Kamakura, another three hundred miles, four days' journey for couriers who ran in relays at speeds fit to burst the heart of a strong, dedicated man; they often fainted when they felt their message seized and knew they need run no farther.

While the messages went on their way, the people on this little section of coast made ready. In one of the loveliest lands on earth, man must gear for war that it remain so. There were beacons on headlands, armed men on guard, and fishing boats swept the seas on patrol, doing double duty as they brought in their nets.

Food was brought in to the castle, walls were strengthened while the merlons upon them were raised higher and the crenels were widened to give the archers better aim. The armorers worked in shifts through the day and night, repairing armor, sharpening swords, making the turnip-shaped arrowheads that screamed so dreadfully to affright an enemy.

Every householder knew that when the time came all must enter the castle; everyone had laid a train to fire his home when he left; everyone had sworn a renewed allegiance to the lord, which would hold till death.

The Itari River runs turbulently over sharp rocks into Haga Bay. It is no considerable waterway at the present time, but then it was deeper and lapped the cliff, forming a natural moat. Here the water was swift and was crossed by two bridges of wood and turf, supported by pilings. Above lay a small lake, artificially impounded by a dam of logs and earth, its spillway faced with stone. This body of water served as an attraction for wild fowl and a source of fresh-water fish. The bridges and the dam lay well within the range of longbows from the castle battlements, which also supported catapults that commanded most of the harbor.

Long ago Shori Castle had exacted tribute from all who passed by land or sea. It was a strong hold. Its keep, five stories high, lay flat against a backing cliff, which was fortified and crowned by a beacon. It looked down upon the whole of the fortifications below, which were high earthen ramparts, three in number, ten feet thick, lined on both sides with stone and pierced by passageways that were like tunnels with heavy gates at each end.

On the sea side these triple walls were protected by the aforementioned moat, which had been made wide and also sheathed in smooth stone, moss-grown and slippery. If these walls and moat should be passed, attackers still had to cross a wide courtyard under arrow fire from the castle or the fort on the cliff, which could be entered only through the castle, since the cliff itself had been made smooth by chipping away the original paths that had once given access to its pinnacle. It was a monolith and its landward side was as smooth as the others. The tunnels inside it represented the last redoubt of the defenders.

Above the ramparts was a superstructure of fascines, wattled stakes, sharpened and burned hard, in double rows of bundles, with an inner core of earth and pebbles, whitewashed on the outside and loopholed for the archers. Above those, in stepped-back series, rose the heights of the castle, its walls, its embrasures, and its battlements.

Higher yet, its steep roofs caught the setting sun. As they were covered with red tiles, they were visible far out to sea—a landmark for sailors. Because this was such a conspicuous sight, the advance elements of Kublai Khan's mighty fleet set in toward it to accomplish a landing when the coast of Nihon was sighted.

Upon the flagship, the Admiral Chepe Ketoyan Be studied this natural pass into fertile hinterland beyond. Through a tube of leather his keen sight made out the column of rising smoke from a beacon and the burning thatch of the fishing village and he knew that the fleet had been seen and the countryside was being warned.

His lips writhed in a sneer. Fluttering signal flags went up and the following squadrons of junks spread out, up and

down the coast, seeking other harbors and beach heads.
The Admiral's unit drove straight ahead for Haga Bay.

Shori Castle was as ready as it would ever be. No answer
had as yet come back from Baron Kuroki's runners, but he
knew the clans must be gathering. He thanked Inari that
there had been time to prepare.

It had been fortunate that this stranger Gorome had arrived. He seemed a man of many talents. To his superior
plans, stone throwers had been constructed and their raised
arms pointed heavenwards along the battlements. The Baron
had never seen such increased strength before, but he ap-
preciated their worth.

Gorome stood now by his side, gazing out to sea. It was
late in the evening, but it was still summer—August of 1281
by Western reckoning, 1941 by the Baron's. The stars were
huge and bright and by the aid of a fingernail paring of new
moon it was still light enough for them to see the wide
spread of the dark massed fleet lying at anchor off the harbor mouth. They could also discern the small boats issuing
from it, rowing out on either wing to secure the two headlands.

The Baron knew that although the outworks had been
cleared of visible observers, a select few remained below
ground in well-covered pits, awaiting complete darkness.

The Mongols, with their auxiliary Chinese and Korean
forces, met with no resistance in occupying these strategic
points. To all purposes, the harbor now belonged to the
invaders.

The Baron turned to Gwalchmai. "It is the hour of the
Tiger and the Tiger is the symbol of our power as the
Dragon is theirs. If we strike now we will gain face and they
will lose it. Yet I should prefer complete darkness."

Gwalchmai smiled. "If I may make a suggestion, Noble
Sir, the Mogu have a contempt for face. Whatever small
advantage this sally may accomplish will mean nothing to
them. They are a fierce people and respect only strength, of
which we have little.

"However, it is undoubtedly true that anything we do
tonight will give our people heart. If we can hold out until
the Shogun's army arrives, we can ask for no more. We
should leave no expedient untried and the correct hour is of

the utmost importance. If we can gain a little time while we still live, it is possible that they may not get farther than this pass for a few days. If the army can meet their array on the plain beyond the pass, it may be in more even battle.

"Wait a little longer. Strike at the hour of the Chicken (three A.M.) when they will be at their coldest hour and heavy with sleep. They may be expecting nothing. Perhaps they will be at their weakest. A chicken is not noted for bravery."

The night wore on and the campfires of the Mongols on the two points sank low. The riding lanterns of the motionless fleet cast long streaks across the calm bay. There were no sounds of labor upon either ships or shore. All but the sentinels on each side were apparently sleeping. It was the hour of the Chicken.

Then an eye of light winked thrice upon the battlements of Shori Castle; an instant and it winked again thrice more, but the angle had been changed. It had beamed first at the left headland. Now it was directed toward the right.

Silently, on oiled hinges, trap doors covered with cemented gravel were raised, disclosing deep pits. Out of them came naked men who ran, bearing sword and dagger, into the Mongol camps.

Sentries choked on their blood and died without a cry. The attackers shouldered the sentries' spears and walked the posts of the slain. Others slipped into the water and swam out toward the fleet, leaving no more ripples than the fish. It was all very quiet and quickly accomplished.

Time passed. Gongs marked the hour of the night, but before the watch was changed strange things began to happen out on the placid sea.

Some of the farther junks swung erratically upon the rising tide; they drifted in toward shore, deeper into the close-packed gathering of stationary ships. They collided. Startled sailors woke and rushed toward the companionways to find the hatches battened down, smoke everywhere and dead sentries underfoot.

The holds might still be Mongol, but the decks belonged to Nihon!

Next, the furled sails caught flame as the captured vessels still came drifting in, but now as fire-ships. With their hawsers cut, they smashed into the anchored vessels, tangling their rigging inextricably. The fire spread.

The naked men of Shori, distinguished only by a white fillet binding their hair, signifying their willingness to die fighting, leapt from the burning junks into the excited mass of bewildered enemies. They slashed in all directions with knife and sword and the Mongols likewise struck out blindly, not knowing friend from foe in the dark. A score of bloody battles raged before all were cut down who had come up out of the sea.

On shore, the tents burned, set alight by those who had played sentinel. These hurled their brands at random and then plunged into the water. Of these, half a score reached the castle to receive the plaudits of their companions. None came back from the fleet.

Less than forty minutes had passed. It was not yet the hour of the Dog. The beleagured defenders now took what rest they could, but there was no sleep for the invaders the remainder of that night.

In the smoke of morning, it could be seen that much damage had been done. Smoldering hulks were canted over the rocks where the falling tide had left them. The fleet, widely scattered during the night, was now beating back against an off-shore wind. There were dead horses on the beach and gashed bodies of men floating half submerged in the water, but too distant to identify from the castle. Still, to the Mongols, all of this was no more than a minor irritation. As far as the eye could see, smokes were rising up and down the coast, signifying where landings had been successfully made and villages or fortifications were burning. There was no need for beacons now.

Against these overwhelming numbers disembarking upon the shores of Nihon from the Mongol armada, such an affair as Haga Bay was no more than a flea bite to an elephant. Now it was the elephant's turn to retaliate.

Already many tumans of soldiers were in formation. Scaling ladders were being prepared. There was a great bustle of carpenters and engineers, bringing up and assembling missile throwers, constructing hoardings to protect them, stacking stone balls, fire bombs, and explosive petards for their use.

By ten in the morning, Chepe Ketoyan Be gave the signal for the first assault, feeling that the time was auspicious. It was the hour of the Dragon. The scaled, many-legged monster went against the ramparts, roaring in angry fury. It went back moaning and limping—upon fewer legs.

Two columns of armored attackers ran across the two bridges, holding their shields high against a dropping fire of arrows that slithered through the interstices and took a bitter toll. As they came into the range of fire from the loopholes between the fascines on the first rampart, many fell. Perforce they must lower their shields for protection. A dropping fire continued from the castle heights, gravity lending impetus to the drive of shafts.

Sheer force of numbers carried the host on and up the earthen rampart. Digging their toes into the cracks between the stone blocks, forming human pyramids or swarming up the ladders to be hurled down by the falling dead, they finally gained the top of the wall and leapt—upon sharp stakes set to greet them. Those who survived found themselves penned in a narrow corridor, between the first and second walls, with barred gates on either side and no enemy to meet.

The indomitable men of Shori had fallen back into the second line.

Now the attackers were in a precarious position. Those in the corridor, being without ladders, were helpless to get out. The gates were jammed with bodies. More dead fell upon this heap, out of the ranks of those who still flooded the rampart. Into both masses, Shori archers shot with deadly speed and precision, from the second and third walls. From the battlements, skilled marksmen placed their arrows more slowly, picking off officers.

Some Mongols never went farther than the stakes of the fascines. Impaled, unable to move, they screamed, struggled, or limply hung.

Eventually, the hampering bodies against the first double gates were hauled away. When the gates were unbarred from the inside by what few survivors still remained between the walls, the corridor was clogged with dead. The toll had been severe and the gains questionable.

The reinforcing columns clattered across the bridges. When the narrow strip of landing between the moat and bridges was full of men, the first corridor jammed and heads rising upon the fiercely contested wall, a buzzing shriek wailed overhead. All eyes followed its course through the air, as a massive boulder tumbled jaggedly into the center of the first bridge, splintering, tearing it away, smashing down through the thickly packed men, and driving its stout fabric in ruin into the swift current.

An instant later came the thump of the released arm of the catapult that had flung it, but no one below heard the sound. The screaming of the crushed and drowning men was too loud. Almost instantly the second bridge collapsed under a similar blow from another catapult on the cliff. The Mongols at the ramparts were separated from the main camp by the rushing Itari, which for a little while ran vividly pink.

By midday there were no Mongols left in the corridor. A few clustered in the shelter of the river side of the first rampart, not daring to raise their heads, waiting for others to come so that they might advance again in strength.

This the attackers were preparing to do. Movable bridges were being constructed and missile throwers being brought up just outside of archery range. These movements were covered by a wasteful outpouring of arrows from Mongol bowmen, well shielded by plank hoardings that inched their way up almost to the edge of the moat.

In the meantime, companies of pioneers were pecking holes and driving pins in order to scale the cliffs and come above the defenders. They hoped to seize the cliff top by sheer force of numbers, but were hampered and harassed as they climbed by stones rolled down upon them by the fishermen, supplied by their women and children. Yet, because of the seemingly endless crowds of men who climbed, the lines of warriors steadily neared the top, although many fell.

An artillery duel now began. Soon the catapults upon the battlements came under fire by the more powerful Mongol engines set up on the beach. Many were struck and disabled by the exploding bombs, which were strong enough to do terrible damage, though not filled with the mighty powder which Gwalchmai had first developed. Now he thanked God that it had not been a success.

Under the protection of this bombardment, the troops brought up the bridges they had constructed and began pouring across the moat in their disciplined order. Clouds of smoke from the black powder and burning fascines now darkened the sun and cast a murky red glow over the distorted faces of the howling besiegers.

Looking down, the defenders could see only eyes and open mouths. It was a day of horror.

Then, as the climbers finally gained the top of the cliffs in spite of the heroic opposition, the people of Shori were forced back. The men fought desperately, contesting every inch of the cliff top, while their supporting families turned and ran for the openings that led down into the tunnels and rooms in the rock against which the castle was built.

As a last gesture, the catapult still in the hands of the folk cast its final immense boulder. In preparation for this last blow it had been aimed with the minutest care not at either of the bridges, but at the dam built across the pass.

The rock lifted ponderously in the spoon that held it. It whirled out and down. It fell like a thunder-stone, smashed away the masonry facing, and plunged far into the earthen ramp.

Cracks spidered out around the deep hole and water welled up to fill it, gushing out, crumbling the dam like wet sugar, widening the gap. The Itari sprang over its banks; it leapt and roared and rushed upon the missile throwers and hoardings.

The whole body of the lake flung itself upon the beach in one great tumbling wave, hurling men, matériel, and smashed artillery into the sea.

As a last act, the rearguard on the upper cliff fired the second beacon before they followed the women into the tunnels. The smoke spiraled high, a final appeal for help, which was not yet in sight anywhere, either by land or sea.

Then, as the Mongols followed down, oil-soaked fires were lit below, driving them out again with heat and fumes of sulphur and cannonade of cracked and crumbling stone. With that fury of flame, which stormed against the tunnel sides, the tortured stratas of rock collapsed and filled the upper shafts with red-hot fragments.

By nightfall, although the slaughter had continued and the attacks gone on unabated until then, a temporary truce was mutually concluded.

The Mongols now held the heights unopposed and the pass was open, but it could not be used without severe casualties while the castle still commanded its entrance; the beach was torn and guttered, though still occupied by the enemy, whose strength, constantly replenished from the ships, appeared undiminished and formidable.

From the defenders viewpoint, the situation appeared bleak but not hopeless. The first rampart had been once lost, but after the flood it was reoccupied and the damage repaired. The moat was gone, but the river had not been rebridged and its new channel formed another barrier to the encamped host.

From time to time, the stone-throwers lobbed a missile among the tents on the beach, but there was no answering fire from the few catapults still standing there. It was more to prove that Castle Shori was still on guard and undaunted that this activity went on, than in the hope of accidentally hitting something important in the dark.

As the night wore on, the sounds of hammering rose to the listeners. By daylight, they faced again a battery of catapults and found that an additional menace was in sight. In the dark hours, a broad, tubby, strongly built mortar boat had been towed in as far as its draft permitted. The black muzzle of the mortar was trained upon the battlements and a smoking linstock betrayed that it was ready for firing.

The engineers were standing at their triggers, the tumans were drawn up behind their officers in precisely aligned ranks, filling the beach with their thousands, and horses were splashing ashore from barges in preparation for the cavalry to ride out into the interior when the way was made clear.

Against this host the garrison of Shori Castle, counting men, women, children, and babes in arms, numbered less than four hundred; the trained soldiers, both archers and samurai, only five score! But all posts were manned and ready, and above them the peony flag of the Hidayamas still proudly flew. Spirits had not yet quailed and the issue was still in doubt.

It was at that moment, while everything seemed to be holding its breath, that a tall richly dressed man strolled out from the throng of Mongols and hailed the castle.

"I speak for the puissant Huang Ti Kublai. Cease this futile resistance! Everywhere our victorious troops are marching upon the Wang of Nihon. Your situation is hopeless. You are surrounded. No help is coming to your aid. Only here do men fight and you will be dead within hours if you do not surrender. I am the Admiral of the Fleet and I can grant you safety. Submit to the Khan and save your lives. You may consider for a quarter of one hour—no more. The attack will be to the death!"

He swung upon his heel, preparing to return, but Baron Kuroki's response was instant.

"I challenge you, Admiral, to personal combat. If I win, your army shall withdraw and your fleet seek another shore. If I lose, the castle will surrender under the condition that all lives will be spared except mine. Myself I place in your hands."

Gwalchmai was aghast. "Daimyo, this is a mad thought! No Mongol is to be trusted to that extent. If you step out from behind these walls you are a dead man!"

Mitami, at his side, clasped her father in her arms. He gently thrust her aside, but stood with his arm around her waist.

The Admiral considered briefly. "To save unnecessary bloodshed, I agree. Let us meet upon your side of the moat."

He turned to his nearest aide, said a few words, and took the man's sword.

In the center of a group of personal guards, he walked to the edge of the moat. A single plank for bridge was hastily thrust across. They stood outside the gate in the rampart and waited.

The gate opened and Baron Kuroki came out, in a similar group of samurai. Admiral Chepe met him with a disarming smile. His sword was sheathed and he held a scroll in his hand.

"It may be that there is no need to fight, brave Lord. The terms of Khan of Khans are most merciful to his allies. I beseech you to read them and risk the lives of your people no further. Your personal valor is not in question. Should one man's pride bring woe to so many? Your honor has been well upheld in yesterday's battle. Now is the time to take thought and profit by your own wisdom and the Khan's charity."

As he spoke, in a mild musical voice that would have charmed a bird out of a tree, he held out the scroll. Baron Kuroki reached for it. His sword was also sheathed. As he extended his hand, the Admiral winced as though in pain and glanced down. He was wearing soft thin slippers.

Apparently he was also standing upon sharp pebbles. He took a step back and then another, still looking down to place his feet upon a smoother spot.

The Baron followed him those two steps, still holding out his hand for the scroll. Instantly, the group of Mongol guards, who had not moved, closed around him, snatching out their blades, thrusting aside the startled samurai. While some of them engaged the castle men, the others slashed the Baron to pieces.

"O-a-oo-ong!"

From a dying samurai's throat rang out the bell-like cry of danger. "Treachery! Treachery! Strike, Brothers! Kill! Kill!"

The Admiral flung himself headlong into the moat. A Mongul arrow flight sped across the space where he had stood. It feathered indiscriminately all who still stood and fought before the half-open gate, but without success. Before the charging company of waiting Mongols that followed it could plunge into the moat and scramble up that slippery moss-grown side, the gate was closed again. Into them then tore the answering volley.

Down slammed the stones from the battlements; up rose the exploding bombs, tearing now into and through the red-tiled roofs, bringing flame, dust, and coiling smoke.

The serried companies advanced with their portable bridges and ladders; the arrows whistled and wailed and the battle was on.

Look for the last time on Shori Castle! Its outlines remain as though etched against the cliff. The roofs are gone, the crenels and merlons of the battlements are blown away; the walls themselves are crumbled into shapeless heaps. Still the mortar boat, lying out of range in Haga Bay, continues its slow bombardment, pounding the stout masonry into ruin.

There are no more missile throwers to answer it from those battlements, but now and again a helmeted head bobs up from the piles of rubble and an arrow arches down toward the beach.

It is still unsafe to risk the pass, although three days have passed since the murder of Baron Kuroki.

Inspect those ramparts held so well by men of honor! The double gates are gone from the outer two—the first one in the third wall was torn away by a powder charge early upon this final day; the last one hangs by a single hinge at the end of its ten-foot tunnel, yet beyond it the defenders are waiting.

Here sit or stand the remaining war-brothers, oiling their hair, bathing, sharpening their five-foot swords. They are not now a hundred—they are not fifty. Eighteen in all—no samurai without his wound; behind them a few supporting fishermen with axes and the spears they will first throw before closing; and six archers, who have so far kept the gate and perhaps can do it once more.

If, after that grim meeting, any survive, they will die in the winding corridors of the building's interior, for above it the peony flag still flies and there is no one there but feels himself a Hidayama now.

All wear the white fillet bound about their brows. Even the women and the children have sworn to wear it to the death. When the last stairway falls and the ladders of the hated Mogu are raised to the last high chamber in the cliff, they will wait until those ladders are crowded. Then those women who still live will hurl the children to clear those rungs of warriors and leap upon the others, using their own bodies in death as one last weapon.

Even now, there is little else. The arrows are almost gone, the pikes are broken, the swords are notched—yet, deep in the heart of Shori Castle there is one beautiful quiet room, untouched by fire or smoke, and here, as though all eternity stretched before them, an elegantly dressed couple are being wed.

They are robed all in white, for this is a day of parting. It is a day of happiness also, for this pair are no more than renewing vows made long ago and neither of them believes in the permanence of death.

Gwalchmai sipped the last of the nine cups of sake and passed it to the Lady Mitami Uyume. She touched it to her lips and set it down. Their eyes met. He smiled, seeing only Corenice as he had seen her first—seeing her now in her loveliest of guises.

"Ahuni-i promised me that she would be here at the end, but she has not come." There was a note of regret in her golden tones.

He heard, as so many times before, the reminiscent chiming of the tiny bells always most evident when she felt deep emotion.

"Perhaps she feels that you no longer need her, now that I am your lord and master," he whispered, so none of the few others present could hear.

"Daimyo of Shori Castle, Hidayama by marriage, but always my lord—always my love."

Their lips met for the first time, in this so brief reunion, and only briefly for this moment.

Chikara staggered in, his broken left arm bound tightly to his side, his bare sword held in his right hand.

"Arm, my Lord Gorome! The last assault is upon us!" He whirled and went clattering down the stair to take his place at the gate.

Under their streaming yak-tailed tougs, the Mongols no longer rushed headlong upon those long two-handed swords. They had learned a great deal in four days. They did not advance in gaiety and disdain, for they had learned respect.

Because of this, there was a little time for Gwalchmai to don his armor. He was glad that the Baron had been a man of his own build, for it fitted him perfectly. He had not been told that only five important families in the land were permitted to wear such metal, but he did know that it suited him and he meant to do it honor and not disgrace the man who had formerly possessed it.

He stood among the group at the gate and waited; sword in hand. The ring upon his finger was scorching with heat, tokening the desperation of the hour. Mitami had kissed him in farewell, dry-eyed, and taken her place among the other women inside the ruins. The Mongols came on slowly.

The archers drew back their bows. No arrow-point trembled. The eighteen samurai thrust back the sleeves of their sword arms.

A sudden thought came to Gwalchmai and he thanked God he had not been able to send the Mongols against Alata. Was this why, he wondered, Merlin had specified a Christian ruler whom he might notify of that new world and none other?

Around him, the men were praying, but not in fear. He heard Chikara quote a little poem:

> Pray for Ise's Wind Divine,
> Let it destroy the Mogu fleet
> Then the Rising Sun shall shine
> And Peonies laugh at their defeat.

Gwalchmai struck his brow in despair at his thoughtlessness. Merlin! The Divine Wind! Merlin's Ring! Perhaps all was not yet lost.

He hastily removed the ring, read the spell, and pointed the long end of the constellation directly at the offshore fleet. A little breeze began to blow. A brassy tinge came over the sky. Clouds gathered. Then he had no time to see more—the Mongols were charging for the gate.

Twice the archers shot into the thick of them as they came. After that, the besiegers and besieged were too closely intermingled, for the gate offered almost no resistance to the force that struck it. Down it went and the infuriated horde thrust into the courtyard and the weary defenders. The clashing of the fine steel was like the shrieking sleet that fills the icy wind that howls eternally across the razor bridge that leads to the Seven Hells.

They were outflanked, but retired swiftly in good order. The ponderous castle door was still undamaged and open, for there women stood with drawn daggers to hold that opening until their men should come.

They came, step by bloody step, knowing that it was open, never looking behind them, backing across the courtyard, contesting the way and leaving a carpet of Mongol dead to hide the gray flagstones and pollute the goldfish pool.

With ax and sword play they hurled the enemy from them in one last savage forlorn attack. Then they ran in, those that were left, and the bronze barrier clanged shut.

Counting all—archers, samurai, and ax-men—there were only ten beside Gwalchmai. One of them was Chikara, who had never left his side.

Stately, dainty, and proud, the Lady Mitami came to greet her husband. She saw him spattered with blood, but with no grievous wound. Others were not so fortunate, and around them the other women gathered, tending them, binding their gashes, giving them heart.

Now began the booming of the great castle bell, but not to call to prayer. The children above, grasping long ropes, were swinging the suspended beam against it, neither as alrum or as dirge.

Bar-room! Bar-room! Bar-room! The measured cadence went on, so that those who listened to the one hundred and eight strokes might be purged from the one hundred and eight sins.

Bar-room! Bar-room! Mingled with the sound, and in itself shaking the weakened fabric of the remaining castle walls, there rumbled the clanging thunder of a log beating

at the bronze portal, and over all a sound so distant yet
that they were unaware of it—the mutterings of the gathering storm.

He heard a child cry out from high above: "Tsunami!
Tsunami!" but he did not know what the word meant. The
weakened door bulged in. The men gripped their slippery
weapons, the women drew their jeweled daggers once more
from their obis and made ready.

Again came that high joyous cry, for that child had seen a
great dome of water well up like a sleek green hill growing
in the center of Haga Bay. It mounted toward the sky and
with it went junks and little boats and streamers of weed
and drowning men. It sank and raced out in a wide circle,
high upon the shore, where within rolled helplessly, with
flailing arms and legs, Chepe Ketoyan Be and all his arrogant entourage.

It struck against the two headlands and upon those tearing
fangs the ships anchored close went into sad wrack and were
crumbled, with all their crews. The floating timbers were
hurled on the outgoing waves into the far mass of the fleet,
striking like lances into storerooms and holds, or battering
broadside like jagged rafts, ripping tremendous rents into
which rushed the sea.

The sound of the cataclysm came distantly to those deep
in the recesses of the castle. Only a little water came in, almost unnoticed.

The defenders stood shoulder to shoulder, almost at the
top of the first ramp, behind them the tunnels running deep
into the cliff.

When the Mongols poured in, only to find no one close,
they paused briefly, then began to surge up the slope. Above
them all, smoke that was thick, choking, and heavy seeped
down from holes in the ceiling. When those who remained
had retreated to the top, the ramp would become a river
of flaming oil.

Suddenly a terrible war-cry arose outside. The Mongols
stopped and turned back, scattering wildly, only to meet an
inrush of their fighting companions. Following these instantly, there waved the paper banners of the Akagawa, the
Taira, and the Matsuyamas. The assembled clans had come!

In retreat, the Mongols charged the ramp. Trapped between the forces, they struck out in these last few moments
most savagely of all. Chikara was beaten to his knees.

Gwalchmai bestrode him and struck out over his follower's head in a mad whirl of steel.

His sword broke. He whipped out his flint hatchet, split a skull and flung the weapon at another attacker who turned to run. It missed.

The Mongol saw it clatter at his feet and Gwalchmai without a weapon. He swept up the hatchet and flung it clumsily back.

Gwalchmai saw it coming directly at his head, but he was penned in by those about him and could not dodge. His senses seemed preternaturally sharpened. The tomahawk floated at him, spinning lazily through the air. It moved so slowly, yet his reflexes were not rapid enough to avoid it.

Against his temple it struck like a heavy hammer, but not with its keen edge. He felt bone give under its blow, but it did not seem to him that he became unconscious. There were flashing lights, but no pain. There was a subtle change in all he saw as he walked unhindered, out of the building.

The grass blades became edged in light. The cherry petals tinkled as they fell from the nimbus-crowned trees that had suddenly sprouted up from the courtyard, from which all signs of battle had vanished. The very pebbles on the shining paths were jewels.

He did not see the hideous face of Oduarpa show briefly and disappear in the writhing clouds of the typhoon he himself had called up. He did not hear the shrieking winds that struck down on the western coast, driving the assembled armada of Kublai Khan, with all their drifting swarms of ferocious soldiery, into drifting, smashing flotsam upon those rocky shores.

He did not know that even then, between the Islands of the Five Dragons, the bodies of the drowned were already washing ashore in such masses that they would form bridges for the clans to march over, seeking out the living. He could not realize that those who survived would henceforth be slaves and few would ever get back to carry the news of the fearful catastrophe to their humbled Master.

For, to him, there were no clouds in the sky. There were no destroying waves, no litter on the marvelous beach he strolled. He did not recognize it as Haga Bay. He sat alone and gazed out over the water, and there, where the water dome had risen, he now saw rise the faintly scaled, exquisitely shaped form of Ahuni-i.

She raised her webbed hand to him in greeting and sank again below the surface—Corenice's affectionate goddess, the Spirit of the Wave, speeding back to her deep and distant home.

In the sky was not the sun he knew, but a thing of supernal glory. It was no longer round and yellow, but framed in twisting fountains of flame that spouted and flung themselves out into space in joyous splendor. All the air was filled with harmony and he recognized it as the music the spheres of Heaven make as they roll upon their appointed way.

Here was beauty, here was magic; here was no enemy, no worry, no carking care. Here was the Land of Dream—the rolling hills, the perfumed zephyrs, the place of seeking where wishes are always granted—the home of angels, where lost loves are always to be found.

He picked himself up from the soft ground and went in languid reverie to seek Corenice.

As though his wish had called her, she was there. They were not again to be soon parted, he knew, for this was not a place of partings, but a country of enchantment wherein they could live enchanted lives.

Somehow, in this one spot on earth, perfection from another dimension impinged upon the soil and the seas we know; somehow they had passed through to where it lay in all its unmarred loveliness—the Terrestrial Paradise, lost Eden, the Blessed Isles, the Delectable Country where were all the denied delights to which the finite perceptions of man have wistfully aspired to attain.

They subsisted on nectar and ambrosia and the fragrance of flowers. They slept when they were weary and weariness was bliss and waking together was happiness. They wandered up and down the foam-edged coasts, where seagulls do not cry but sweetly sing, and where little boats with rainbow sails dot the water like floating blossoms.

Across and back and roundabout the Land of Dream they roved in delight with the restless winds.

19

Soldier of Fortune

Gwalchmai awoke.

He found himself standing upon the beach, looking up at the undamaged outlines of Shori Castle, clean-etched against the cliff. There were no signs here of war, or that there had ever been such.

The fisher village stood unmarred by fire. The Itari flowed smoothly in its accustomed course, crossed by its two bridges, and once more the moat was fed by it, protecting the gateways where the gates stood strong and undamaged, as he had seen them first.

He looked quickly toward the sea. Behind him a little boat was drawn up on the sand. Evidently he had just disembarked from it, for he held a fishing spear in his hand and a net was draped wetly over its shaft.

He suddenly felt dizzy. A scintillating wheel of light spun before his eyes and he swayed unsteadily. A gong beat in his ears.

A strong hand grasped his arm, and he saw for the first time that two people were near him. One was a sobbing woman, upon her knees before him. She lifted a tear-wet face.

"Come, my Lord Gorome! Oh, come quickly! She is asking for you. There is not much time!"

Gwalchmai did not at first understand. He shook off the strong hand of the man who supported him. "Thank you, Chikara. I am myself now."

Concern deepened upon the man's countenance. He peered closely at Gwalchmai.

"Are you sure, Lord? Do you not know me? I am Han-shiro. My father was Chikara. He died thirty years ago."

Gwalchmai's blurred vision cleared. Split memories joined. The past came rushing back and he realized the truth. While he and Corenice had remained young and live and loving, their eyes touched with magic, their souls in union as never before, denizens of that perfect country—cruel Time had lain his withering hand upon the bodies in which those souls were housed.

He remembered, in one crowded awakening instant, the rebuilding of the castle, the honors that came to him and the other survivors of the dreadful siege, the confirming of his status as Daimyo by the Emperor, his long and happy life with the Lady Mitami, last of the Hidayama, as his wife.

As he hurried through the gates, he recalled that she had expressed a desire for a slice of turbot and that he had gone out to find and spear a fish, thinking that her sickness was on the upturn.

She had refused all food the previous day.

Had she sent him away that he might not see her die? He ran up the ramp. As he did so the great bell, which he had thought to be a gong, tolled out another slow and muted stroke.

Was it over, then? All that they had shared? Their double life of the body and the soul? For the better part of a century he had lived two lives in one. With her passing, one of them was ending, but which was reality and which illusion he did not know.

When he entered her chamber, gasping for breath, he could not see her because of his misted eyes and the weeping women gathered around her sleeping mats.

He pushed them aside and sank to his knees beside her.

Was this aged woman, with hair of silver, his sweet young playmate? Oh, God! Was this what time could do?

Then she smiled, that smile which alone in all her changes had always remained the same. It seemed only a moment ago that they had walked together upon a whispering strand and he had kissed her when she smiled that way. He knew now that it had been in the Land of Dream.

(Ah, Corenice, ever ageless, ever young, ever loving, are we to part once more? When, if ever, shall we meet again and in what distant place?

Oh, cruel Fate, which toys so harshly with us—make an

end! Release me from my vow! It has cost us far too much and there is no purpose in it!)

Thinking thus, he felt her gaze upon him. She saw his grief and feebly raised her hand to his face, gently cupping it against his cheek. Her fingers were soft and wrinkled, but he saw nothing now but the delicate beauty he wanted to see.

Time does not destroy such memories. It only fixes them more permanently—with brighter colors drawn from the heart.

Looking upon her whom he loved, he saw the two in one. The Lady Mitami Uyume, daughter of the Hidayamas, fragile, doll-like, patient and devoted, and Corenice, warrior-maid, ever-changing faithful comrade and sweetheart—equally patient, gallant, and brave, making his destiny hers and waiting on its accomplishment. So closely intertwined were these two lives he had lived, that he did not know which of the twain he loved was speaking.

"Do not despair, my darling, we part but for a little while, though it comes to me that we shall not meet another time in this manner.

"Do you remember the swans? What a day that was for us! We agreed that if we became as they, then we should never really be separated and it has been so.

"I think it may be now that we have had as much as we deserve. Our lives have been like no others since the beginning of the world. Perhaps we have been allowed more than our share of love, if it so be that affection can be apportioned.

"I know what you have been thinking. Release your dagger. When were our thoughts ever secret from each other? This is not the place for an ending. Look into your ring and you will see that you must complete that destiny which is also mine.

"Farewell, for a little while."

Her hand fell away from his cheek and he knew that those last moments of waiting had been possible only because her iron will had made them so. Her fingers were cold and her eyes had closed. He placed her hands together across her breast and laid his own upon her brow.

For a brief glance his eyes fell upon the ring as she had bid. In the depths of the opal he saw a swift blur of motion. Armored men, in fire and smoke, rushing headlong at a

mighty fortress. He saw himself in that frantic crowd, crying on those behind to the assault, but among them no face
that he had ever seen before. Where or when this battle was
to be fought he could not tell, but he knew that he must be
there.

In the van, he saw the standard bearer, enshrouded in
smoke, pointing the way with a gleaming sword, standing in
a hail of missiles. He could not see the device upon the
banner, nor the face of the bearer, but he knew that the
days of his years were not yet counted and that this battle
was a part of his destiny yet to be.

He turned his back upon the wailing attendants and did
not glance at them again. Nothing he had loved remained
in that deserted room. He was certain that if this long existence be spun out, through the curse of Merlin's elixir, till
the end of time, another moment so terrible as this must
never recur again.

He went directly to his room and began to pack. Once
more, Corenice had given him courage to go on to an appointed time, although the thought of long, bleak, lonely
years appalled him.

Midway in his sad labor he heard a scratching on the
door and slid it back. Hanshiro stood there, his face twisted
by grief. He could hardly speak, but his swift glance took in
what was going on. The samurai dropped to his knees upon
the matting and touched his forehead to the floor. Gwalchmai bade him rise.

"My Lord, where is your desire? What would you?"

"I would seek the wars of the world and die in battle!"

"Then, not alone, my Daimyo. Not alone."

When the mourning was over and the bell had stopped
ringing and that which must be done had taken place and
the lights of Shori Castle had been extinguished, Gwalchmai
and Hanshiro slipped away under cloud of night.

A long wandering began. As two masterless men they
fought as ronin, for whatever feudal lord would hire them.
They gained scars and honor and some wealth. They were
widely known as grim fighters.

They roamed the island chain of Nihon from one end to
the other. Never did Gwalchmai see the scene he had beheld in the magic ring, and finally he came to realize that it
was in another country and perhaps another time.

He scarcely realized where he was or what he was doing. He had no plans, except to die. Once he came to himself, sitting upon a rock, gazing eastward upon the sea. Beyond that tossing waste of water he knew Alata lay and although he realized that the centuries of his life had brought inevitable change, he was filled with such a longing for the land of his birth that it seemed his heart would burst.

He muttered to himself, "What curse is there that lies upon me or Alata, that never may I cross the ocean to my beloved home?"

It has been said that wherever Adam was outcast that place was Eden, if only Eve was there. So Gwalchmai had thought of Corenice, but now that she was gone, Nihon was no more than a wilderness to him and he desired to leave. His opportunity came soon.

A sickness of land came upon him. They sought a harbor and took passage upon a coaster that had many ports of call —southward along the islands, westward across the Yellow Sea, south again to Taprobane.

The inseparables met pirates and fought them, saw elephants and rode them, starved together or banqueted side by side. In India they sold their swords to the highest bidder, went singing into battle and came out alive—to be paid in diamonds and rubies, which they scattered like wheat and went on as wanderers.

It was a new and dreadful period of Gwalchmai's life. As time went on, he forgot how to laugh. He strode through the world with a bloody sword, hardly conscious of where he went or how the years passed. One day he saw that his hair was entirely gray.

Where war was, there they went. He was wounded often; he suffered fell blows that would have killed another man and he recovered from them more slowly than in the past; he was many times in deadly peril, but he could not die.

Many countries knew him as a leader of forlorn hopes, a roisterer without joy. Then he became aware that he was alone. Either age or warfare had taken Hanshiro from him, but he felt no older unless a cold weariness was age. He had no desire to mark the passage of time.

It was enough that somewhere he would see that fortress wall and stand behind that waving banner. That day might mark the end he yearned for. He came out of Asia into

Europe by way of countless wars, still a terror to his enemies. He made no effort to make friends.

Finally his loneliness and desperation subsided.

There is a perversity in existence. Ah-Puch, the Black
Captain, does not always take those who wish to die. In
time grief passes, for it is no more permanent than other
emotions; dynasties perish; Kings know despair; swords can
break in battle or they can rust away from lack of use; men
return to recapture a lost moment in the haunts where they
dimly remember they once were happy.

A sorcerer was busily engaged in a fair little meadow in
France. It was the first week in April, and although the rain
had fallen, the sun had come out warmly and dried the
ground, so that he was comfortable and whistled as he
worked.

He was a brilliant man for his age and time; an amateur
physician, a theologian, philosopher, astronomer, and chemist—all of which talents were useful to him in his profession.

At the moment, he was crucifying a pale-green butterfly.

Being thoroughly absorbed in building a tiny pyre of
twigs, he did not hear a man approaching him from behind
in the deep soft grass. He placed the last twig, refastened a
tiny thorn into a wing that the suffering insect had torn loose
in its struggles, and was about to set the little crucifix into the
pyre when a scornful voice said, "It would seem that wanton
pain amuses you, my Lord. Kill the helpless thing mercifully
and at once, or release it."

The sorcerer slid his hand under his cloak, slowly and
with care. He prepared to turn, but a sharp point pricked
into his neck above the spinal cord and just below the hair-
line. The hand came back into sight, open and empty. He did
not turn or try to rise, but knelt without moving, his eyes
fixed upon the butterfly.

"Are you Armagnac or Burgundian? Do you declare for
England or for France?"

The point sank a hairsbreadth deeper and the sorcerer
felt a warm trickle run down his neck, as his captor answered
casually;

"My political affiliations need not concern you, for I have
none. However, what you are doing concerns me much. I
heard a prayer for help from one who was being tortured.

I answered that call and have found you. Say now, to whom should I grant mercy—the criminal or the victim?"

Despite his predicament, the necromancer began to laugh.

"I cannot imagine who you may be, but surely you are mad! What is the life of an insect against that of a human being?"

"The Earth belongs to all things that live upon it and not to man alone. It may well be that in God's sight we three are equal here and one to be regarded no more than another."

"Ah, God indeed!" The sorcerer spat in disgust. "There have been many gods. Some I have served and some serve me, as you may soon learn, rash fellow! You hold me at your pleasure now, but you little realize in what danger you lie. Still, because of your ignorance, I will be merciful and explain the importance of this work, which you so stupidly believe to be wantonness.

"Know then, rash fool, that I have accepted English gold from Duke Philip of Burgandy, to slay a witch and lay France at his feet.

"When this butterfly burns, so then will Charles, the false Dauphin, be bedded with a wasting fever; the fleur-de-lis, of which the butterfly stands symbol, shall vanish from his banner and the witch who influences him shall meet her doom and his gathering army be destroyed to a man."

"Then it is hardly meet that such calamities shall occur, if the scattering of one life can save so many. Say, sorcerer, are you familiar through your grimoires, or even by hearsay, of this Ring?"

The point did not stir from the kneeling man's neck, but a hand came within his vision. His eyes opened wide and rolled upward in a vain effort to see the face of the man behind him.

"Not you? Not Merlin! Hecate! Oduarpa! Belphegor! To me, I command you! This man is dead!"

"So are you!" Gwalchmai said grimly and thrust the dagger home.

Gently and tenderly he drew out the tiny thorns. The butterfly fluttered weakly, then took the air, circling, dipping erratically around its savior's head.

"Flit home, little fay," he murmured. "I have thought about you. I have missed you, as you said. I am happy that not all of you are gone. Do not judge all men by such as these. We need you more than you will ever know."

He drew out the poniard and looked at it with disgust. It was dark with blood. He dropped it and rubbed his dry hands together.

"It would poison me to handle it again!"

He watched the butterfly staggering in zigzag flight across the meadow. When it was out of sight, he muttered to himself: "I told that monster I had no interest in his politics, but I have in those of whoever is against him and those he served. If I am to fight them I must reclaim my sword once more. Perhaps here in this struggle I may find that fortress and that banner."

He stood there thinking, remembering. A long time ago, he had passed this way.

"Yes. The shrine of Saint Catherine de Fierbois should lie a day's journey to the west."

A moment later the little meadow was empty, except for the body of a man who had been slain to save the life of a butterfly.

No longer were the islands of Britain harassed by the Danes, no longer were they ravaged by internecine war; Norman and Saxon had melded by time into one nation— young, arrogant, venturesome—and now there were other wars.

Many changes had also taken place in France since Gwalchmai had been away. Torn between England and the expanding rival power of Burgundy, true France lay as a corridor that had been trampled, marched over and ravaged by organized armies and warring groups of outlaws, thieves, and bandits. Yet, somehow, cities still existed as such after a hundred years of war.

Somehow, the baking of bread continued as it always had, fields were tilled, cows freshened, and life went precariously on. New thatch replaced the burned, babies were born although fathers might be slain and never see them. Youths looked into the eyes of maidens and each saw there what they wished to see and dared to dream.

One spring followed another.

In that April of 1429, a banner took the wind such as had never been seen before, or since. Looking upon it, a despairing man who had a longing to become a king felt within him a hope he had not thought to know during his lifetime.

In that month of April also, Gwalchmai came to the shrine where he had left the sword of Roland in safekeeping and, asking for it, he learned that it was gone.

It was in a savage mood that he faced the lay-brother who acted as custodian of the chapel. It seemed to Gwalchmai that this one disappointment was the culmination of many unhappy days and that trouble rode his back like the Burr-Woman. He seized upon the altar in his wrath and shook it with his strong hands.

"You say it was sent for? No one knew it was there but me! I placed it in the trust of Saint Catherine—long, long ago!"

"Then surely Saint Catherine knew it lay behind the altar. Does it mean nothing to you, fair sir, that it has been kept safe, however long since you left it, until last week, when it was asked for, searched for, and found to be where it was said to be hidden?

"None of us knew it was there. We took the finding of it to be a miracle. Perhaps—of course it must be so—Saint Catherine told the Dauphin's Commander-in-Chief that the sword was here.

"It was the only one in the shrine that bore five little crosses. There was a powdering of rust on it. As we lifted it, the rust fell away like magic. We polished it reverently and gave it into the hands of the messenger who had come asking for it."

"Where was it taken? I would have words with this commander. Where can he be found?"

"The Dauphin holds his ragged court in Chinon. It is about all the grandeur left to him and when Orléans falls he will not have that much, for the fall of that city will open all the Loire valley to the English.

"His tiny army is gathering for the relief of Orléans, but there is small hope for its success. Until the army marches, you might find your sword there."

Gwalchmai turned on his heel and stamped out. A few feet away, he bethought himself and turned back.

"His name? How is this thief called?"

"You will have no trouble in finding the Commander-in-Chief! Anyone will direct you. Ask for Jean Dark."

"Sounds like a renegade Englishman. No wonder you have little faith in your cause!"

Gwalchmai spat on the ground, glared at the intimidated lay-brother, and left the shrine in a fury.

He had not gone far when his temper cooled. Harking back, his memory brought up a fact he had forgotten. There *had* been one other in the shrine when he had slipped the sword behind the altar, away back—when was it? Could it be possible? A little over three centuries ago?

Yes, one other was watching. One other knew—and only one other in all the world could know now!

Corenice had returned! She was somewhere near him! This was her way of leading him to her!

On then to Chinon—on the wings of the wind!

20

Forward—The Banner

She was a little strange, but dear.
Voices she heard, we could not hear.
The Saints she saw, we could not see.
We did not mock her piety,
When Voices told her what to do,
We knew that what they said was true.
We loved but a single mother.
She had two. France was the other!

Songs of Huon

It was late in the day when Gwalchmai left Fierbois and, hurry as he might, early evening had approached when he reached Chinon.

The town was crowded and in some fields tents were up and a smell of cooking was in the air. Gwalchmai stopped at one of these campfires and made himself known as a new recruit for the Dauphin's army. He jingled his few coins in his pouch while he talked.

As he had hoped, he was invited to eat, on condition that he contribute to the general fund. He went into the town and bought bread and a bottle of wine. When he came back, the kettle of soup was ready and he sat down upon the grass with the four men who shared the tent and they ate together.

They looked no better than bandits, but were respectful at Gwalchmai's bearing and careful in their speech. At times he caught their quick glances at his face, but when they saw he noticed, their attention was at once directed elsewhere.

He did not realize how the recent savage years had taken their toll. His face was deeply lined, though as impassive as his mingled Aztec and Roman blood had always made it. His ruddy complexion was now more coppery than ever, burned so by hot southern suns and almost constant outdoor living. Because of the rejuvenating qualities of Merlin's elixir he still possessed a full set of teeth, although he could not have told how many times some of them had been replaced. His eyesight was not dimmed and his glance was as feral as the eagle for which he had been named.

Scars streaked jaggedly and pale along his right cheek and neck, where a spear point had ripped him when Delhi fell to Tamerlane. He limped slightly from an older wound got at Acre, when it was captured by Sultan Malek of Egypt and the Holy Land was lost. His left arm swung a little crookedly. His horse had fallen upon him, hiding his body and enabling him to become the sole survivor of the massacre of the Catalan Company's cavalry at Adrianople.

Yet, although his hair was gray and tending toward white, his arms were knotted with muscle and he knew himself to be still virile and strong. The fires of youth, still fed by the Elixir, burned brightly within him. With the thought of Corenice to encourage his seeking, it was with the heart and mind of a young man going to his first rendezvous that he rose from his meal. He shouldered his little pack of necessaries, although the others urged him to return there and sleep, and went into the town, to learn what he could of the mystery that plagued him.

He inquired where the Commander-in-Chief might be found and thought that folk looked at him strangely, but did not understand why. Behind the Dauphin's headquarters,

which was by courtesy' called the castle, although it was
nothing impressive, there was a long tilting ground. Here
some gentlemen and knights were jousting and a few onlookers were leaning upon the surrounding rails, happily
pleased to see the nobility take a fall.

As Gwalchmai came up, a shout of laughter rose and a
crash of armor sounded as horse and man went down.

"Mon Dieu! Unhorsed again! I swear D'Aulon is too old
to hold a lance! Hoi, back to the quintain and the popinjay,
Intendant!"

The fallen man smiled ruefully as he struggled to his feet
in his weight of armor, aided by a younger man who turned
indignantly upon the jeering crowd.

"Nay, it is no shame to fall before that lance! Which
among you will ride against it? My feet went out of stirrups
and I clutched pommel or I would have been flattened too."

"Peace, Duke Alençon," D'Aulon said. "I think no shame
to myself. I did not expect to avoid a point steadied by
angels. After all, it is not in tournament, but only in play. It
was a shrewd blow that felled me. God grant many a
Godam will feel as shrewd a one at Orléans!"

By this time, his contestant had turned and come canter-
ing back, to leap lightly down, patting the black charger on
the neck and then raising visor to disclose a laughing face,
framed by the steel helmet that bore no plume or device.

"By my baton! This is a fine horse, mon beau Duc!" The
sweet, womanly voice rang out clearly as a bell across the
tilting ground.

Hearing it, Gwalchmai's heart gave a great leap within
him. Without thinking that he was interrupting, he clambered over the rail and walked toward the little group.

He heard the young man say, "He is yours now. No one
but you shall ever ride him again." Then they all fell silent
watching the grim-visaged stranger who strode in their direction.

Gwalchmai stopped a few paces away, his eyes fixed upon
the girl in the plain armor. Her black hair was cut like that
of a page and she looked like a slight beardless boy. Her
metal had obviously not been made over to suit a feminine
figure, so he estimated that she was very young and as yet
unformed. From whence then, her skill and strength?

He could see that her eyes were gray and although she
was smiling in a puzzled way, as though she was trying to

identify him, he had the feeling that those eyes could take on a hint of blue that would cause them to glint like fine steel. He thought he would not want to be the one to cross her will.

She was not beautiful, scarcely more than pretty. Her frank, open countenance was that of a clear-minded, honest country girl. As Gwalchmai looked upon her face, which seemed strangely familiar, a word came unbidden to his mind and it was—winsome.

Then, in that strange quiet instant, before anyone broke the silence, he knew that the features were indeed familiar, though not those he had hoped to see.

As though she had been born again to haunt him with sad, dead memories—out of that steel casque there looked curiously upon him the face of the Welsh girl, Nikky, with whom as Corenice enlivened, he had adventured, loved, and spent a twelvemonth of days so bittersweet that he could scarcely abide to remember them!

It seemed that she too was striving to recall something lost, or was it only because he looked at her so intently that she took a half step toward him, her right hand slightly raised in greeting?

"Gaihun." He gave her the Basque greeting deliberately, wondering if the old Atlantidean word would bring out a flash of knowledge.

"Bon soir," she said, looking directly into his eyes, and it was with grief that he saw no further sign of recognition, or any intimation that except through intuition she understood the meaning of the word.

"Good evening, Sir Knight," and he realized that she gave him the title only because, in one sweeping glance, she had shrewdly estimated his qualities as a fighting man and not through any other knowledge of him. "Have you come to join the army of my gentle Dauphin and strike a blow for France?"

"Are you the one called Jean Dark? Can it be that you are War-Chief of an army?"

She laughed. Again his heartstrings thrummed at the sound, so like—so often heard—so long ago—and not quite the same.

"Here they term me chef-de-guerre. In my town they called me Jeannette, but my birth name is Jeanne. Since I have come to France I have sometimes been known as Joan.

I have many names—the Godams call me witch, but my Saints, when they speak to me, say 'Thou Child of God.' I think I like that best.

"You are very dark, Sir Knight, and of a strange hue. Are you a Morisco?"

Duke d'Alençon spoke up before he could answer.

"By his greeting, he is Basque, my General. There are others such in the army. Recruits are flocking to your banner from everywhere."

"What arms do you carry, Basque? What lineage have you?"

Gwalchmai thought quickly. Upon his answer depended his status in this mad hodgepodge of soldiery that was being assembled to meet English and Burgundian power. Should he be man-at-arms only, or give himself qualities that would bring him in closer contact with this strange girl to whom he was so strangely drawn?

"I have come from very far away to be with you. My name is Gwalchmai." Recognition? In her face, only polite interest and curiosity. Oh, God! Could he be wrong?

No! At her side there hung the sword Durandal. It was she who had sent for it. It was she alone who had known where to send and where it could be found in the shrine.

"I have fought in many armies. I am skilled in war. My name means Hawk or Eagle, take your choice. My father was a King."

D'Alençon grunted, deprecating the last statement. "Every Basque who has a stone house and ten sheep thinks he is of the nobility!"

But Jeanne's face lightened and she gave him her hands warmly.

"Then I give you good welcome, Sir Basque, and I say to you as I did to my pretty Duke, when he entered my service against his wife's will: 'The more of royal blood are gathered together for this venture the better.' Let us march with courage and in brave company, for if men will fight, God will surely give us victory."

Now that he was accepted, he placed his hands between hers, thus in courtoisie recognizing her as his liege, as she considered the Dauphin hers, but not King until he would receive his dominion through her from her real Lord—the King of Heaven.

She gravely acknowledged Gwalchmai's homage, coloring

prettily at his evident admiration, and released his hands. The others gathered around, introducing themselves.

Besides D'Aulon, Jeanne's squire, who watched over her like a hen with one chick, and the young Duke of Alençon, only recently released from an English prison upon the payment of an immense ransom that had impoverished himself and his wife, there were several notables who had gathered to see the fun.

The Dauphin stood nearby, his weak chin trembling with the late excitement of the joust. He was ill-favored in face and bodily appearance, and his hose had been padded to hide his knock knees.

He seemed all the more unprepossessing, for beside him stood in ironic contrast one of the handsomest and the wealthiest man in the country.

Gilles de Rais held for ancestor Bertrand du Guesclin, in his time the most popular hero of France, and bade fair to equal his exploits. At twenty-five, he had proven himself a brilliant and dashing soldier and had become the dread of the English. He had been first in at the taking of the fortress of Lude and slain the English commander, Blackburn, in hand-to-hand combat.

He was the darling of the people, who ignored his darker side—his antipathy to women, his not well-concealed orgies, his merciless slaughter of prisoners taken in battle, and his setting aside of his sixteen-year-old bride shortly after their unsatisfactory honeymoon. Through her, his already enormous wealth had been increased and other ladies sought to console him, but his interest was confined to one only.

From the moment the Dauphin had attempted to deceive Jeanne as to his identity, by hiding among the incredulous and hostile court until recognized at once by her, the Seigneur de Rais had made himself her friend and champion.

Against all skepticism and even active enmity of the Dauphin's self-interested counselors, he insisted in his belief in her divine mission. De Rais changed his mode of living and interested his cousins, Guy and André de Laval, the Duke D'Alençon and Dunois, known as the Bastard, Commander at Orleans, in her cause.

He advanced the Dauphin vast sums of money, to be used in the assembling of the army, and in gratitude, Charles, always deep in debt, made him protector of the Maid on the field, at her own request.

When Gwalchmai was introduced to him, he saw a man as
strong as himself, a little pouched under the eyes from
excesses, and attractively sinister in aspect. His face was almost hidden by a carefully tended growth of glossy black
hair that in bright sunlight gleamed so vitally he had been
given the sobriquet of "Bluebeard."

His grip of welcome almost crushed Gwalchmai's hand.

"Ride beside me, L'Aiglon, when we travel to Tours. I will
be glad to have your strong arm near me. Seek me out tomorrow and I will see you outfitted properly."

"I thank you graciously, my Lord Baron." Gwalchmai
bowed to all the assembly and took his departure, thinking
that the offer, however kindly meant, sounded more like a
command than he liked to hear.

Certainly this new acquaintance was a man accustomed
to being obeyed without question.

Somewhat pensively, he returned to the tent where he had
supped. He did not know if these men would relish seeing
him again, so he thoughtfully provided himself with more
wine, as there seemed no other accommodation in the
crowded town.

Both he and the wine were greeted with enthusiasm.
Gear was tossed aside to make room. By morning they were
firm friends, and Robert, the Archer, one of those who had
brought Jeanne from Vaucouleurs, guided Gwalchmai to be
outfitted as a knight.

He chose black armor, such as his patron wore. He wore
no favor on his helmet, nor did he seek one—although De
Rais directed him to a limner to have arms emblazoned on
his shield.

When he was mounted he too presented an impressive figure. A swan—Or—with wings closed, floated on a rippled
sea—Azure. Its beak was open, breathing flame—Sanguine
—the whole against a glittering field—Sable.

Jeanne admired it. He had hoped that, if the Maid were
truly an avatar of Corenice, or under his lost love's influence, the design might stir her memory. She gave no sign
that she knew it to be one of the Ships of Atlantis.

Some days later, Gwalchmai, with immediate friends of
the Maid's, which she laughingly called her Battle, though it
nowhere nearly approached the strength of that military
unit, rode to Blois, where many had gathered to await her
coming.

Her presence acted as a catalyst upon the rag-tag band of hellions who had come together thinking of loot and rapine, and suddenly found themselves receiving communion, hearing Mass, and becoming assoiled. Every man in the army, for once, was purified—from the highest noble to the meanest forager—stupefied by the fact, surprised at themselves.

They awaited the word of command, feeling a unity in motive and a common incentive for action. Many had complained that there could be no victory because they did not march under the oriflamme—the great war standard that had floated over all armies in the campaigns of the past wars of the French. As this was held fast in Paris, an English city for the last ten years, the effort was bound to fail.

Among the assembled captains, Jeanne sat her horse that bright morning beside De Rais, waiting for the banner to be brought that she had commanded to be made to her design.

James Powers, the artist, an aged Scot from Tours, unfurled his creation. He handed her the staff. All gazed reverently upon the beautiful flag.

It depicted our Lord, crucified. The background was a brilliant blue, studded with golden fleur-de-lis. High above the cross, a white dove rose to Heaven on widespread wings. Below, were the words Jeanne set at the head of her written pronouncements: "JHESUS-MARIA" in the purest of gleaming gold.

Her eyes shone. She raised a corner to her lips. She said to the Scot, "I love my sword, but I love this banner best. I shall carry it into battle, so that I may never kill anyone."

The wind swept into its folds. It flared wide for all to see. Gwalchmai felt a surge of exultation. It was the banner he had seen in the opal, being carried toward a mighty bastion, half-hidden in rolling smoke and cannon flame. He had hunted it down across a world. He knew now that destiny was coming to a fulfillment. The banner was in the hand of its bearer!

Impulsively he raised a shout. It was seized upon. It roared through the ranks. "Hail, Jeanne! Jeanne, of Domremy! Our oriflamme!"

She colored prettily. D'Alençon cried, "It is because of you, Maid, that we are gathered here. It is for you to give the order to march!"

Jeanne shook her head, smiling. Then she stiffened, accepting the honor. The banner snapped in the wind. Her clear, girlish voice rang out, strong and true, "To Orléans! For our God and our King! Sound trumpets and to horse!"

For one breathless instant everything was very still. An ascending lark carried its notes of happy courage high into the blue. A trumpet sang and men swung into the saddles.

Bustle began throughout the field. Whips cracked, commands rang out—the priests, marching at the head of the moving column, swung their incense, chanting *Veni Creator Spiritus*—and the convoy fell into line behind the moving banner.

Food for the hungry! Powder for the guns! Men for the walls! Forward now! No turning back! Three thousand men on the road to the beleaguered city of Orléans, bent upon as mad a venture as history records.

The last army of France was taking the field, the sweepings of the kingdom, most of whom had not thought to ever bear arms again. It marched to battle as a forlorn hope, to recapture disaffected cities in an occupied country. It meant to crown a king who doubted not only his own courage—for he had none—but also his legitimate title to the throne.

It was led by a seventeen-year-old maiden who had said to her Saints in dismay, "I am but a poor girl who knows nothing of riding or of war."

But she had said, in her secret heart, "We will take the king with us and fight our way through!"

The Dauphin and his retinue watched them all march away—priests chanting, drums beating, pennons flying; then he returned to Chinon, to the relaxing pleasures of the court.

If this enterprise failed, there would not be another.

The success or failure of the desperate mission concerned Gwalchmai as little as it did Charles. He sought every opportunity to exchange a few words with the Maid, hoping to find some common meeting point. Finally, in despair, he bluntly brought up the subject of Alata, Merlin, and his own mission. She listened attentively.

"Did you ever hear of the prophecy of Merlin, that France should be ruined by a woman and restored by a Maid who would come from an oak wood, on the Marches of Lorraine?

"I often played with other girls near the Fairy Tree, which stands near a stream in an oak wood, and France has surely been ruined by the Queen of Charles the Seventh. So much of the prophecy is true, at least. It is said that Philip of Burgundy would not have allied himself with the English and split the country if it had not been for hating her.

"What a wonderful thing, if out of all this bloodshed and despair some common interest might reunite the Duke with my King and bring back his great dominions. Together, they could hurl the English into the sea."

"Is the Dauphin truly a Christian monarch?" Gwalchmai was mindful of Merlin's adjuration.

She straightened indignantly in the saddle, weariness and armor bruises forgotten. "My King is the noblest of all Christians!"

"Then, perhaps, if this war is won and he regains his kingdom, through your good graces he might grant you the favor of some ships? He could send colonists to this land of Alata, to take and hold it for the glory of Our Lord.

"Do you think that Duke Philip would forget his quarrel and unite with the King in such a venture?"

Her shoulders sagged. Sometimes dreamer, always the realist, she frankly admitted, "I fear me that Burgandy will never make peace, except at the point of a lance, but I will surely send word when we arrive at Orléans and ask that the letter be sent on to him, when I summon the English forts to surrender."

"What shall you ask for reward, Maid, at the coronation?"

"Only that the people of Domremy and Greux need never pay taxes again. They are so poor. They work so hard."

"Nothing for yourself?"

"I have never asked anything for myself, except from my Saints. I asked them, when everything was over, that they would take me with them to Paradise. This they have promised to do.

"They say that I must be a good girl and God will help me. They say it will not be very long and my Dauphin must use me quickly. But he is surrounded by false councilors. It is so hard for me to convince him!" Her voice broke in a little sob, and Gwalchmai asked, quickly, "Is it because you know your Saints will protect you, Jeanne, that you are not afraid to ride thus into battle?"

She had gained control and answered with spirit. "I am in as much danger as any other soldier. They will protect the men as much as me. As for fear, I am afraid of nothing but treachery!"

But, as Gwalchmai turned his horse's head away, thinking: "There, if ever, spoke my own warrior maid!" his side glance read Jeanne's lips, which moved in the very faintest of private whispers: "And the fire!"

He was not meant to hear it. He gave no sign that he had.

In later years, that tiny instant of self-revelation meant more to Gwalchmai than any of the other incidents he was to live through within the city of Orléans.

Once arrived, Jeanne began promptly to make her power evident to her captains, who would have used her as a tool for their own plans. Knowing that the English momentarily expected reinforcements, she was roused to fury when the herald she sent out to summon surrender was held prisoner.

The only time Gwalchmai saw her smile in the early days of intrigue was when Louis de Coutes, her page, called them both to the arrow slit from which he had been watching. They saw a Frenchman stick his head up from behind a merlon and take careful aim with his culverin at the nearest fort.

This hand cannon, with a heavy rest, took some time to adjust. Before he could fire the monstrous musket, a shot came from the enemy. He leapt up with a loud cry, flinging his arms wide. Flat on his back, his legs kicked out dramatically. Only his lower limbs and feet were in plain view of the English, who craned their necks to watch the twitching, which went on, Gwalchmai thought, unreasonably long.

Jeanne was appalled at his suffering. She turned to the page. "Find someone to bring him to safety. This is shameful!"

"Wait, Mistress!" Louis hastily seized her sleeve. "I have been hearing about him. He doesn't need any help. Just watch. That's Master Jean, the Lorrainer!"

The feet were imperceptibly being drawn in. On the opposing parapet, the English were standing, clearly exposed, the sniper modestly taking his plaudits—a group of his friends surrounding him and clapping his back.

Suddenly the culverin bellowed. The spreading charge of small shot knocked down three of the group. Others staggered away, holding on to themselves. The sniper lay still.

"See! That's Master Jean. He does it somewhere every day. Sometimes more than once. Ma Foi! Those Godams never learn. He has died like that more than forty times."

Gwalchmai went over to admire the redoubtable weapon. It was a deadly instrument of great beauty. It was also capable of exquisite precision, as the Lorrainer demonstrated by firing single aimed slugs. He took considerable pains in measuring the powder and choosing the proper bullet.

Gwalchmai smiled to himself, remembering the unfortunate Wu. Ambitions come to naught through carelessness. He made a quick friend of Jean by deliberately acting as decoy. Many an unsuspecting Englishman exposed himself —never more than once.

When reinforcements finally came in, through the one free gate left to Orléans, the city went wild. None had arrived for the English. Jeanne rode out with her Household—crack troops she had personally selected—and convoyed in the provision wagons.

She retired in the heat of the afternoon. D'Aulon lay down in the anteroom and both were soon asleep. Excited people milled about the streets, bragging, shouting, drinking, telling each other what they would do to the English the next day.

Gwalchmai walked around for a while. He breathed in the excitement, before retiring to his own quarters, almost upon the other side of the city. He awoke to the sound of cannon.

His upstairs lodging fronted on a wide boulevard, emptier than he had yet seen it. He hastily slipped on his boots and ran downstairs, not stopping for helmet or body armor, buckling on his sword as he reached the street.

The intermittent thudding beyond the city wall was not coming closer, but a growing uproar drew him in that direction. Soon he met a crowd of wild-eyed frantic people rushing down the boulevard. Many were wounded, some staggering about as though blinded, with their hands to their eyes.

Great blisters covered the faces and exposed skin of those who stumbled and screamed. Gwalchmai knew from long experience that unslaked lime, scalding water, or boiling oil was the cause.

As he met and entered the retreating mob, he heard a galloping horse overtaking him at full speed. He cast a glance backward as he ran on toward the fighting.

It was Jeanne. Never had she looked more like his own warrior maid. She was leaning forward like a racer, her standard butt thrust deep into the saddle boot and the shaft firmly held in her small hand. The long war cloth streamed out behind, cracking like a whip in the wind.

She recognized Gwalchmai as she shot past without pausing, calling back, "Quickly! Quickly! Frenchmen are dying!"

They had almost reached the city gate. A tougher knot of people held this position, milling there uncertainly, looking over their shoulders as though the enemy was close.

As Jeanne came up, they raised a cheer. Gwalchmai was proud to see that they threw themselves in her way. From a retreating rabble, they took up an almost shapeless formation, but it was a fighting one.

"The English have come out of the fort! They are right behind us! Go back, Daughter of God!"

The great horse slowed to a heaving stop. Gwalchmai reached its side, just as a man fell against him, soaked with red from shoulder to waist. His face was a mask.

"Is that a Frenchman?" Someone cried, "Yes, Maid!"

"Ha! Never did I see French blood spilled, but my hair stood on end! Forward, men of Orléans! Follow me!"

She did not look to see if anyone came. Would they? Did any have the courage? She sank in the spurs. The charge rushed toward the sound of cannon fire. The irresolute group, Gwalchmai at its head, followed in a cheering surge.

High the banner! Fast and free in the wind! Horsemen pounded in its wake. Here rode D'Aulon, savage to protect his small charge. Close by came D'Alençon, affection and anger in his face, and beside him Jeanne's brother, Pierre, jostling little fourteen-year-old Louis de Coutes, who had somewhere found a horse,

They followed the banner, over the dead, striking hard into the thick of the aghast English, who were drawn up before the open gate of their fort.

Gwalchmai passed a body. It was covered with tar and still burning. It might have been man—it might have been woman. It did not move.

"Forward, men of Orléans!" The crowd roared. It went forward, behind the banner. It crashed into and over the English ranks. It swarmed through the gates of the fort.

When Gwalchmai came out of the fort, with De Rais beside him, both with dripping swords, they saw Jeanne sitting on the ground, holding the head of a wounded English soldier in her lap, cradling him in her arms. She was crying.

"Oh, Basque! He had no time to be shriven! He is only a boy! He was asking for his mother. In God's name, why do not these people go back to their own country?"

Gwalchmai had no answer. He heard De Rais mutter," By the raddled honor of an immoral blue mouse! There has never been anyone like her before! I will prove me on the body of whoever says that there has."

Gwalchmai did not reply, but in his heart, he thought, "Only one other. My fair lost love would have wept thus. Shall we ever meet again?"

And aloud, as he felt of the youth's forehead and found it cold, "Come, Maid of Orléans. Let us return to the city. It is all over now." He took her gently by the arm.

It was the first time that anyone had called her by that name. By morning the army had decided from whom it would take its future orders.

21

Corenice—At Last

As we passed beneath Rheims' trees,
There like living fleur-de-lis
Butterflies in merry dance,
Clustered round the flag of France!

Songs of Huon

Jeanne paced the floor, impatiently striking her thigh with a gloved hand, framing the challenge to the English King and his Regent. Gwalchmai's heart swelled with pride for this little cow-girl, who could rise so to every occasion. His admiration grew with every word, and he was especially delighted to see that, even in this critical hour, she remembered the promise to him.

"Duke of Bedford, the Maid prays you not to bring about your own destruction. If you do her right, you may go in her company where the French shall do the finest deed that has yet been done for Christendom.

"If you will not believe this news from God and the Maid, wherever we find you, there we shall strike. We shall raise such a Ha-hey! as has not been heard in a thousand years."

"There," she clapped Gwalchmai heartily on the back, "that is the best I can do for you now, without giving away your secret to the English." She beamed upon him. "We may find ships for you yet. Rest assured, Duke Philip will be informed later. If he shows any interest, we will tell him more after the English are thrust out. Now, find me an archer, Basque."

Robert, Gwalchmai's earliest acquaintance, was delighted to be chosen. He pushed a tavern wench off his lap, hastily finished his mug, and as they quit the Inn of the Green Tabard and walked toward headquarters, he sheepishly admitted: "When my master and I escorted her here from Vaucouleurs, we planned to do away with her. She represented a terrible danger. The enemy had been warned to look out for her. Three hundred miles of enemy country to cross and armed bands out everywhere! We never thought we could do it.

"Then—she grew on us. So patient, never complaining—always so sure of herself. All of a sudden, she was our beloved little sister."

Jeanne, Robert, and Gwalchmai went to the mantelets that had been raised to protect the Orléans side of the broken bridge. They raised a white flag and stood out in the open to parley. Jeanne rolled the script tightly around an arrow shaft and tied it with a thread. Robert arched the arrow high, and as it fell within the wall of the Augustinian monastery the English had fortified, Jeanne cried, "Behold, here is news!"

"Hearken, all of ye! Beware!" mocked a jeering soldier. "Here is news from the Armagnac whore!"

Jeanne paled, then grew red. She cried out, indignantly, "You lie! I pity the souls of all of you!" The soldier spat on the message and threw it into the river.

Robert saw the tears in her eyes as she turned away in

shame. He had not caught the words. His grip on Gwalchmai's arm was iron. "What did he say to her? What did he say?"

Gwalchmai repeated the slander. "I know just which one it was," gritted the archer. Heedless of the arrows that buzzed around him, Robert stepped out from the protection of the mantelet. He took careful aim. A scream attested to his accuracy.

"That one won't laugh again!" said the man who had himself once plotted her death. They moved back to safety, knowing that reason and diplomacy had failed and that force of arms was now to be the only deciding issue.

Next morning the banner went forward to battle, through the Burgundy Gate. Gwalchmai felt himself fey, looking upon it, as it advanced upon the Augustinian monastery, which, outlined in the fire from spouting cannon, must be taken before the Tourelles—the main objective—could be attacked.

Jeanne raised the banner high, trusting it to no one else, her face alight with confidence of victory to come. It seemed to Gwalchmai that something of this glow was reflected upon the silk itself. It shimmered like a living thing—this banner —as it moved across the water, on a hastily arranged bridge of boats, fastened together under fire.

It gleamed and rippled. De Rais and the grizzled old guerrilla captain La Hire lowered their lances for Jeanne's protection as they clattered off the bridge. She spurred her horse and all three advanced upon the English drawn up in serried ranks before the walls.

Gwalchmai, close behind, under the leadership of De Rais, saw her turn in the saddle, waving them all to come on, crying, "In God's name, forward! Forward boldly!"

Bullets and bolts tore through the cloth and rattled against armor. A few townsmen fell. The untrained militia faltered in its onrush.

Gwalchmai could not hold back while she was in danger and almost unsupported. He surged out of line.

"Keep your place, Basque!" shouted D'Aulon.

"You love her as a daughter, Intendant? Come then. She needs help!"

A Spaniard, also a man of De Rais' company, sneered, "You are brave, Basque, but braver than you are obeying orders!"

"Then do you come with me! We will see who is bravest today!" Thus taunted, the Spaniard seized Gwalchmai's hand. They rushed forward, where a giant Englishman stood in the entrance with a two-handed broadsword, covering the retreat inward of the garrison.

By this time, Jeanne and De Rais had come under a merciless fire. De Rais thrust her behind him, taking the brunt of the missiles upon his excellent armor. In the vanguard, neither Gwalchmai nor the Spaniard could effect an entry. Suddenly, their adversary tottered and fell. Master Jean had come up with his culverin.

In rushed Gwalchmai, followed by his companion, cutting down those who struggled to close the gate. In rode Jeanne, striking hard with the flat of her sword, De Rais at her side slashing brutally, offering no quarter to those who flung down their arms. In swarmed the townsfolk and regulars, with ax, halberd, and knives. The monastery was soon French.

Next morning, the assault was cried upon the Tourelles— the towers at the bridgehead—which faltered about noonday. Ripped, tattered, and pierced, the banner floated close by the wall. Jeanne raised it high, laughed, and waved the soldiers on.

She sprang to a scaling ladder and mounted a few steps. The banner rose with her into the smoke, and the English hand guns swung to meet it; an iron curse was bellowed forth from every mouth of fire.

The banner swung and waved and fell. Jeanne fell with it, covered by its folds like a shroud. A clothyard arrow, driven by the full strength of an archer's arm, pierced her shoulder plate, passing completely through armor and body.

Gwalchmai and D'Aulon were closest. They lifted her tenderly under a hail of arrows and arblast bolts. Out of range of the guns, they found the point stood out her back a full hand's breadth.

She was conscious. While D'Aulon was cutting off the arrowhead, to draw out the shaft, Gwalchmai said, "Maid, let me cure your wound. I have a sovran remedy at hand."

He showed her Merlin's ring and would have touched her shoulder. She looked at its odd carvings and shrank away.

"It looks like sorcery. I will have no sorcery."

"Then let me sing over it," he gently insisted. "I know a song of healing. I will get a drum and cure your ill for you, as the medicine men of my country do."

"No charms. No sorcery. No magic." She accepted an anointing of olive oil and lay back to rest till evening. By that time the battle had lost its vigor. Jeanne took her place again, weak and worn, supporting herself with a staff.

Four great assaults had been made. Now the lights of Orléans were coming on. Dunois, Captain-General of the town, came up.

"Maid, there is no hope of victory this day. In a month this fort could scarce be taken."

"Wait just a little more! Doubt not! The place is ours. Let me pray for but a moment. Basque, guard my banner well."

She sank upon her knees and buried her face in her hands, as more than once he had seen Corenice do. He wondered to whom she prayed.

Without waiting, Dunois' trumpeter sounded the recall. She looked up, but continued with her prayer. Some stood, others came back; the English raised a glad "Hurrah" at the retreat.

D'Aulon seized Gwalchmai by the shoulder. "The courage of our men is still high, but if the English sally out, the standard might be taken. That would be a death blow to us. If I go forward to the foot of the wall and cry our troops on once more, will you follow with the standard?"

Gwalchmai said, "I will!"

The two leaped down into the dry fosse. As they clambered, with difficulty, up the other side, Jeanne saw the banner waving wildly. She ran and seized its end, not understanding.

"Ha! My standard! Basque! Is this what you promised me?"

Leaping into the ditch, she took the standard herself. A crowd of rallying French and Scots poured in and up, behind her.

"Watch! Watch till the tail of my standard touches the wall!"

"Maid! It touches now!"

"Then enter, in the name of the King of Heaven! The town is yours! The Tourelles will fall!"

Gwalchmai, left behind in the rush, saw her standing in glory. The banner was aflame with mystic light. Here in all its exactness, was the scene he had beheld in the opal of Merlin's Ring.

There was the crumbling fortress wall. There, the blazing cannon, fire, and smoke and death; there, just ahead, the slender, straight back of the standard bearer, but he knew no more about her identity than he had so long ago at the death-bed of his love.

"Glasdale! Brave Captain! Yield thee to the King of Heaven! You called me harlot, but I grant pity upon your soul!"

By dark, all was over. Glasdale was dead, the Tourelles had fallen, Orléans was safe and every bell in the city ringing.

As, years later, Gwalchmai let his mind's eye rove, it was not the short campaign that lingered most. Victory hurried on the heels of victory, in a grand sweep of successes. What impressed him chiefly was the mystical thing that he, and he alone, perceived in connection with the banner. City after city fell, by siege or capitulation. The English stood to open combat at Beaugency and again at Patay, and then no more —both times to be crushed in open battle. At each triumph, Gwalchmai saw a single new fleur-de-lys flash into added brilliance, and when proud Rheims opened its gates for Charles, the Dauphin, to enter for his coronation, the flag shone in its entirety as he had seen it first—but, he knew with surety, not for Charles.

Once thus lit for Gwalchmai, it so remained. He regarded this wonder as some new and unsuspected virtue of insight, granted him by the ring. No one mentioned it to him. He forebore speaking of it, even to Jeanne.

Joy! Success! The wonderful apogee of the coronation, where Jeanne stood, in white armor, holding the standard in one hand, her bared sword in the other—defiant, proud, ready still to defend to the death the stained honor of her sawdust king.

Under the shimmering folds, ragged and battleworn, she knelt to embrace the knees of Charles.

"My gentle Dauphin! At last you are my King!"

And in the end, Gwalchmai knew, with tears of pride in his eyes, it was Jeanne to whom the crowd roared, "Hail!"— although she would not have believed it had she so been told.

On, at last, to Paris! But too late. Still believing the lies of his councilors, the King procrastinated. Finally he granted permission for the army to move. Then it was found that the truce between himself, England's Regent, Lord Bedford, and Duke Philip, whose lands were greater than both the others and whose hatred of Charles was greater too, had been used to make Paris the most impregnable city in Europe.

Marching behind that proud banner, which as yet had never known defeat, the army moved out from Rheims. At its head rode the faithful captains—La Hire, D'Alençon, Dunois, De Rais. Behind them were the ever-watchful guardians, D'Aulon and Gwalchmai, who were never far away from the little bright figure holding the standard.

The Archbishop of Rheims rode along with them for a space. Gwalchmai heard him say, "Jeanne, where do you expect to die?"

She was in an unusually somber mood. The army felt its spirits lagging. They were poorly armed, their pay in arrears, and they were often hungry. These facts were reflected in the thoughts of the leaders.

"Wherever God pleases. I know not the hour or the place. Would it were His pleasure that I might now lay down my arms and go back to my father and mother, who would be right glad to see me."

Gwalchmai, his ears attuned to every nuance of her sweet, disconcertingly familiar voice, could tell that for once an infrequent melancholy had seized upon her.

At that moment they were passing along a road lined upon both sides with Lombardy poplars, and as though her words were a signal a fluttering host of butterflies came down about the heads of the marching soldiers like falling leaves. They spun and circled and lifted lightly, following the pennons and guidons, a drifting mass of living beauty, darting in rippling sweeps through the sunlight slanting through the branches of the trees.

Gwalchmai started. Crystal clear, hauntingly nostalgic, far away in time if not in distance, came to him the winding of a silver hunting horn he had once heard in Elveron. He looked covertly around, a quick glance that swept those near him. Apparently no one else had heard the descending notes.

So brave, so happy, they rose again challenging the Fates, and he knew this was the Assembly call of the fay—the great gathering, the final flitting from Earth to Astophar—and he knew also that this was farewell.

Had anyone else heard? The butterflies soared and came together and dropped around the standard like a benediction. Thick, so thickly swarming, yet never touching one another or Jeanne, who bore the flag, for she rode in steel and the touch of iron is fearful death. They gathered there briefly

like winging fleur-de-lys and in their whirling center, Jeanne
watched them and leaned back in the saddle, laughing with
head thrown back as Gwalchmai had so often seen his
lost love do, no soldier for this brief time, only a young girl,
happy in the summer sun.

Once more the clear notes rose and with them rose the
host. Into the trees and higher. An eddying cloud, rising,
dwindling—a ball of silver midges, a gleaming point still
caught by the straining eye—until it was gone forever on
the long sky road to a friendlier star.

But not all! One pale-green butterfly lingered on the safe
cloth of Gwalchmai's surcoat, opening and closing its maimed
and ragged wings, gazing at him with its jeweled eyes.

There was a jaunty devil-may-care attitude about this strag-
gler, from its scarlet antennae to its slender legs. There was
no doubt in Gwalchmai's mind.

"Always faithful, gay minstrel, brave friend! Help me guard
my dear courageous leader, whoever she may be."

The butterfly bent its legs and sprang into the air. It swept
before Gwalchmai's eyes and sped to the standard. It came
down upon the gilded wood of the shaft's point and there it
rode.

There was a new spring in the gait of the marchers. They
had seen what they thought was a sign of victory. On to
Paris!

There is a nadir for every zenith. From the top of a hill,
the only way off is—down. The long delayed advance on
Paris was the beginning of the lowering slope, the end fore-
doomed.

"I fear nothing but treachery!" Gwalchmai felt those
words strike home before the walls of Paris. The dreary
siege dragged on: no supplies, no reinforcements, the army
dwindling in the long nights, grumbling deserters knowing
well that the lick-spittles of the court fawned upon the
King to their own advantage and the death of hope. Finally,
Jeanne dared wait no longer for an assault. Finding that no
one had taken the trouble to sound the moat at the St.
Denys gate, like a good commander, she herself went forward.

Accompanied only by Robert, as standard bearer, the two
crossed the outer dry fosse. Immediately they came under

fire. She cried, "Surrender to Jesus!" and plumbed the moat water with her lance.

At that moment, as cool and deliberate as she, an English archer drew his bow. The first arrow nailed Robert's foot to the ground. In agony, he raised his visor to assess his injury and died, struck through the eyes. The standard fell.

The third arrow, aimed with precision, went completely through Jeanne's upper thigh. She threw herself backward, into the dubious shelter of the fosse, and rolled to its bottom.

Gwalchmai heard an agonized, strangled cry by his side. "My angel!" Rushing past him through the battle, Gilles de Rais thrust him heavily aside, ran through the firing line, and flung himself down beside Jeanne, covering his girl comrade and leader, and protecting her with his own body.

A heavy fire was instantly concentrated upon them. Gwalchmai could hear bullets strike De Rais' fine armor and ricochet whining away. Neither moved. The battle went on with savagery, but now such a downpour of missiles filled the air that no one could reach the pair and live.

They burrowed into the ditch bank, inch by tortured inch. Into the afternoon and the evening the despairing friends of Jeanne could hear her gallant pain-filled voice still raised to encourage them, calling on the charge: "Forward! Be of good faith! The town will be yours!"

As the day wore on, the clear voice grew weaker, but the words remained the same. After dark, Gwalchmai, D'Aulon, and de Gaucourt, almost blind with tears, fumbled their way out through the dead and helped De Rais, who had only minor wounds, bring her in.

De Rais went away, leaning on de Gaucourt's shoulder, to have his wounds tended. D'Aulon hurried off in search of a leech. Gwalchmai took out the arrow as he had done before at Jargeau, for De Rais had not dared to do so lest she bleed to death. He glanced around. No one was near. She showed no sign of pain.

It was evident that she was deeply unconscious, from loss of blood and shock. He touched the wound with Merlin's Ring. The welling forth dwindled to a few slow drops. He bound up the injury. Even in the uncertain light of a single flickering torch he could see her waxen pallor.

He brushed her thick dark hair away from her cold, moist

brow. His heart was very full. That haunting resemblance!

He lifted a heavy wave of her hair in his hand. It flowed over his trembling fingers, as he brought it to his lips, remembering the delight it had given him to see that hair flying defiantly free in the wind.

Torchlight gleamed on her little golden rings. They were her only ornaments. Her chiefest treasures. How often he had seen her look at them, kiss them before going into danger! Gwalchmai was once told that they were gift rings from her mother and brother, and engraved with sacred names.

He thought how Corenice had bid him to know her through the ages, by gold.

He sighed. "My precious, lovely, lost one! I look upon this strange, brave girl and I see you!"

At his gentle touch, Jeanne moaned a little. Her eyes remained closed, but she turned her face toward him and her lips moved.

"Ah, my darling! Was it for this we spoke of love at the Lake of Swans?"

Gwalchmai could not believe his ears. "Corenice! Can it be you?"

"Only for a little moment, my dear one. Only while she sleeps. Our grand-daughter's will is so strong! I have never been able to control her—only to give her a little comfort and advice. There are others who give her more and better guidance than any she could receive from me.

"Do you still love me? I thought love was dead in you. Had you not forgotten me for a while?"

"How I watched you through the eyes of your comrade, Hanshiro, the samurai! Did you not think it strange that he would follow you across half a world, guarding your back in all your madness of killing in so many wars?

"It was that which has kept us apart. You would not have known me while you were trying to die. Did you suspect nothing, my only lord?

"You must not despair. The end of your journey is so close. Mine will end with yours and we will be together. Did you not know that I led you here?"

"Oh, Corenice! I was so sure that you were she at first. Since then there have been so many little things about her that I remembered in you. How can she look so like you, when you were Nikky, and not be you again? I cannot bear it unless you two are and will remain the same."

Jeanne's eyes were still shut, but her lips smiled. That long-remembered, long-awaited smile.

"Can you not guess, my own one husband? Count back the years through the many generations. Her mother's mother's mother, and other mothers before that one, and there was still another who was the daughter of your son!

"I never told you what I saw in the spae-wife's crystal. She knew what had come of our meeting and she showed me what was yet to come. At the end of the vision she gave me, I saw a girl riding, clothed all in clean bright steel, without decoration or emblem. Her face was like mine, but I knew it was not me.

"I saw her ride on to her destiny and everlasting fame— and in her face I saw a consciousness of that and more. I saw something in it of you and something of myself. I knew then that it was no accident that we two met.

"Oh, Gwalchmai, you have seen my goddess and you love her. I have never seen your God, but I know now that He lives and I love Him too.

"It cannot be that the world spins aimlessly on with no directing plan. It has been worth all our separations, and pains, and our long waiting, to be the ancestors of such a girl!"

"Yes! Oh, yes, Corenice! With such admiration—such pride! And so much like you. No wonder I thought you had come again!"

"I have been told that we shall soon be together and then we shall never part. We have been but small pieces in an immensely intricate plan. I know that now and so must you.

"I saw a little part of it in the crystal. So far-reaching and divine it was that it awed me until I could not speak of it to you, lest the knowledge of it in some way bring about its failure.

"I learned then why we two had been born to love and I knew joy and pride that we had been chosen. I have also lived with grief, for I was shown what that destiny of hers, because of us, must be.

"They are coming, my darling. I must say farewell. Ahuni-i has told me we must return where our long journey began, to that place of ice and fire. We shall go there together, I promise you, when all is finished here. It will not be long. Be patient and hold me—hold me ever in your heart."

Jeanne—Corenice—stopped speaking. D'Aulon and de

Gaucourt came up with anxiety plain upon their faces. The leech panted up with his bag and looked questioningly at Gwalchmai at the sight of the bandaged wound.

Gwalchmai placed his finger on his lips. He spoke with a smile.

"Quietly. Bear her easily away. She has been tended and is sleeping."

His words were easy and without care, but in his heart he mourned, for now he knew that Corenice was gone.

Peremptory orders from the King, safe in his court at Senlis, broke off the siege. The hungry army was only too glad to return and be disbanded, caring nothing for the months of uselessness that followed.

De Rais, promoted to the rank of Marshal of France, quit the stifling atmosphere of the court in high dudgeon. Dismissing Gwalchmai from his entourage, he asked, "Will you now accept a permanent place in the Maid's Household, until I recall you?"

"That I will, and gladly!" So D'Aulon and he became close companions in Jeanne's care, while she followed the King's company from castle to castle, like a pet dog, in idleness and despair.

And the banner lay idle, gathering dust.

From Guy de Laval—these, to his revered grandmother, Relict of Du Guesclin:

"My Dearest Grandmother:

"I kiss your hand. Much has happened since we returned to Senlis. The Maid was pleased that you liked the small golden ring she sent. She bids me say that she would be happier were it a better one.

"Would you appreciate the jewel more if you knew it was given her by her brother? It came from her own hand. She still has another, but these were her only precious things.

"When I told her how you had written that, before her, France had nine champions, but now there were ten, she was greatly touched. She pulled off the ring, having nothing else valuable of her own and said, "Send this." She is so impulsive.

"You remember I wrote you how Compiegne was recovered for the King and how, ever since, it has lain under the

cannon of the Burgundians? Duke Philip is greatly wroth
at his lost city's resistance. It is said here he has sworn that
unless the city surrenders immediately, no one in it over
seven years of age shall remain alive when it is taken.

"The maid has been deeply concerned. The King has refused to grant her money and soldiers for relief. He hopes
for a bloodless peace with Burgundy. Alas, it would be the
peace the mouse enjoys, after the cat has dined.

"At any rate, without the King's sanction or support, the
Maid has left the court, for whence we can only suspect.
She took with her no more than her own Household. Old
faithful D'Aulon, of course, her confessor, Pasquerel, her
two brothers, and that odd white-haired man I told you about,
whose face looks so young and grim.

"That last, I might have guessed. He follows her wherever
she goes. Most of us are afraid of him. Some say that he
must be in love with her.

"When she left, she said that she meant to go out riding at
her pleasure. I know not if that were true—but she has not
returned.

"Written at Senlis, this third day of April, in the Year of
Our Lord, 1430."

"By my baton! We are enough! I will go to my good
friends of Compiegne! Let those who love me, follow!"

So the banner took the wind for the last time. It flew
above her tent at Lagny, where many who loved her rallied
to it. Scots, Catalans, Italians, and French came riding in,
asking for nothing except that they be led, in good faith, by
one they could trust.

The banner rippled out above the moving column, marching on Compiegne, and, in good omen, Gwalchmai saw
what he had seen when a larger army left Rheims for Paris
—a green butterfly that came down upon the peak of the
standard, to ride there for some while, to circle about his
own head, and then to flutter onward and disappear.

"You are still with me, little fay? Bring good fortune to
the one I love and you will bring happiness to me."

He fondled the hilt of his sword. On the morn, Jeanne
had called him—as Captain of her Battle—to receive his orders of the day. She looked pensive and sober. She picked
up her beloved blade from the camp table and said, "Basque,
take this sword of Fierbois and carry it in the campaign.

I will exchange for yours. It will be safer with you, when I fall into the hands of the English."

Gwalchmai was aghast. "God forbid, Maid, that such should be."

"It is beyond doubt. My Voices have announced that I shall be taken before St. John's Day. They have never lied."

"Then give up the campaign, I pray you, until after that time."

Her smile was wan. "It would avail nothing. To do my devoir is my destiny. They say—although they do not explain —that it is necessary, so that a great victory shall later be won. What befalls me is of little import. It is for this that I was born."

"Did you ask your Saints to intercede for you, that you might be spared?"

Jeanne hesitated, then answered slowly, "I asked only that I die quickly and not suffer long. They told me that it should be as I asked. Afterward I should be with them in Paradise."

When the column moved out the sword Durandal hung at his side. Legend held that Charles Martel used it against the Saracens at Poitiers, long before it fell into the possession of Roland. Gwalchmai did not know if that was true. He was certain that two Paladins had warmed its hilt, and one rode before him on the road to Compiegne.

He raised the blade reverently and kissed the cross of the hilt. His eyes fell upon Merlin's ring. It was cool upon his finger. He found it hard to believe that he was riding into personal danger. He formed a sudden resolution.

Urging his horse forward, he pushed between Jeanne's two brothers. He held out the ring to Pierre.

"I have noticed that your sister now wears only one ring. If I offered her another, even for remembrance and the affection you know I hold for her, she would not accept it. She fears sorcery and—I must be honest with you—this ring does have certain properties that could be most useful to her were she in danger.

"It will become warm on her finger and warn her of peril. It will unlock doors and loosen chains. If this gift comes through you, she may accept it and be protected."

"Why not keep it for yourself?"

Gwalchmai searched his soul for the answer and then he

too heard a Voice. It sounded like little golden bells. A great peace came over him.

"I do not need it any longer. I shall never need it again."

On the morning of the twenty-second of May, when the Maid brought her small force into Compiegne, by breaking through the thinnest gap in the Burgundian line, Gwalchmai, riding close in her protection, saw that she wore a ring on each hand.

Destiny came, as predicted, on St. John's Day. After a sally out of the city, to destroy the enemy's supply dump, the five hundred men that Jeanne had led out out to war turned to fight their way back, through an immensely augmented intercepting force.

Harried on all sides and intermixed thoroughly with the enemy, her force struggled almost to the open city gates. Gwalchmai struck aside many lances aimed at Jeanne, acting as rearguard.

"Do but play your part and they will be beaten! Turn! Strike back and we shall have them!"

Her surcoat of scarlet and gold and her waving banner made her the object of the main attack. Up went the drawbridge of Compiegne. The fall of the portcullis saved the city, but left the rearguard to be captured.

The Maid was fighting for her life. The flashing sword rose and fell, crashing upon helmets, necks, and upraised arms.

"I will never kill anyone!" she had sworn. Gwalchmai saw that even in this extremity she used, not the edge, but the flat of the blade. Even so, her strong young arm still had the power to empty saddles. He saw horses running free and senseless soldiers lying in the road.

He fought to reach her side. D'Aulon was down and captured, faithful to the last. Her brother Jean unconscious, Pierre snared in a twisting knot of men. Gwalchmai slashed his way almost through to her. Too late, he saw a horseman upon him, swinging one of those heavy lead mallets used mainly by the warrior-priests, because their orders forbade them to shed blood.

Durandal went up to fend the blow. It was struck away like a feather and the massive weight crashed against his right side. He felt his ribs collapse and splinter and he fell.

With his last failing eyesight he saw a Picard bowman
seize her surcoat and unhorse the Maid. The banner filled
the sky above him. For one instant the whole fabric of it
flashed into glory—its fleur-de-lis a constellation of racing
meteors dazzling his vision. Its edge touched the ground—
the silken wonder dulled. It was no longer an oriflamme; it
was ordinary cloth. It swept across his face.

With his last moment of strength, he tried to grasp and
hold the fringe. He could only press it to his lips, as the
blackness of night descended upon him and the banner and
the one who had so nobly borne it were snatched from out
his ken.

22

For the Maid!

> The Dauphin is crowned. The battles are won.
> All The Voices said she would do, is done.
> Never a trumpet—never a drum—
> The rescuing army—when will it come?
> Before this country can be truly free,
> Must there be another Gethsemane?

Songs of Huon

In August of that same dark year, Gilles de Rais, Marshal
of France, visited Gwalchmai, an invalid now, in the laxly
besieged town of Compiegne. Some were able so to enter,
under cover of darkness.

He sat in Gwalchmai's chamber and bent a saturnine gaze
upon his former follower.

"I came here to kill that scoundrel Flavy, for the closing
of the gate, but I wanted to see you first. When the Garrison

Commander gave the order, what words did he use? Did it sound like treachery to you?"

Gwalchmai's ribs were knitting well, but it was still painful for him to breathe and talk. He wondered if he would ever again be the man he once had been. He spoke slowly and carefully.

"I did not hear the order, my Lord Marshal. I was without the wall, in the Maid's company, when the gate was shut."

"You saw her taken? You were there? You were with her and you are still alive?"

De Rais' face became suffused with dark blood. His voice throbbed with rage. He towered over Gwalchmai, helpless in a reclining chair. The Marshal's fists clenched, as he shook in impotent passion. Gradually he forced himself to calmness and sat down, clenching his jaws and breathing in deep gusts.

Gwalchmai waited. "My Lord, I love her too." Under the laws of chivalry, now that the Maid was prisoner, the Baron was again his liege lord. Over him, De Rais possessed the rights of High and Low justice and, even in Compiegne, might have him slain. Feudalism, though dying, was not yet dead.

He was surprised to learn that this man of somber reputation could, if he wished, control his temper.

"I am sorry, L'Aiglon. I know you do. I spoke in haste and anger. If you could have done aught, surely it would have been done well. By the way, looking at you now, with your cheeks sunken in like that, your eyes so large, and yon thin beak of nose you have—stap me, if you do not look more like an eagle than ever! Whoever named you chose the right word."

"It is a Roman nose, my Lord, and it can sniff out treachery. There was none here. If Flavy had not ordered the gate closed, the town would have been taken and all the Maid's devotion gone for naught. She would never have had it so. She loves the town. She freed it once. Compiegne will not surrender now—because of her."

"Have you heard that the Maid has twice tried to come to the rescue?"

Gwalchmai shook his head. He stared dumbly. "But she was a prisoner. Has she escaped?" His face lit up with hope.

De Rais shook his head also. "She was taken to the castle

of Beaulieu, where she made the first attempt. My spies
have learned that she somehow managed to unlock her door,
or perhaps it was not locked."

Gwalchmai started. He became all attention.

"She slipped out and managed to shut up all the sentries
in their own guardroom, but was captured by the porter.
Afterward, she was held in a more secure place, until she
was removed to Beaurevoir castle. It was there she heard of
Philip's threat.

"I understand that she said afterward that to prevent him
from carrying it out she would die there or die on the road
to Compiegne if it must be so. She was taken to the parapet
for the air. She broke away, stood between the merlons,
squeezed through, and jumped. My God, L'Aiglon, it was
seventy feet!"

"Then she *is* dead. I knew when I saw you, Baron, that
you bore evil tidings."

"No, not dead, but she was grievously hurt, poòr dear.
You can imagine the guards could not believe their own
eyes. They raced down and found her alive, with no bones
broken. She could not stand, but she was crawling—dragging
herself along—just a few pitiful feet, in the direction of
Compiegne. They picked her up and carried her back captive. She has been prisoned ever since. It was three days
before she took food."

A thought nagged at Gwalchmai. "My Lord Marshal, do
you know if the Maid still has her rings?"

"I heard they have been taken from her by the Burgundians, who kept one as a memento. They sent the other one
on to the Bishop of Beauvais, who is negotiating to buy her
for the English. The King must be waiting to see how
much will be bid, so he can go higher. As yet he has made
no offer for her recovery."

His smile was fleeting and sardonic. "Well, I must be off,
L'Aiglon, it will soon be daylight. I shall pray for your health
and I will not harm Captain Flavy. It was a sound military
measure, but—that girl is worth many towns."

Abruptly he was gone, to make his way to safety in the
dark. Gwalchmai sank back on his pillows. Superseding all
other news, one grim thought went round and round in his
mind. Jeanne no longer possessed Merlin's Ring. He had no
doubt she had benefitted by it. It had unlocked doors; it had
probably saved her from death in her desperate bid for

freedom. With its loss, her only hope of escape from prison, short of ransom or relief by a French army, was likewise gone.

The investment of Compiegne was lifted at the end of October. De Rais, acting as guerrilla leader, along with the forces of the old wolf, La Hire, attacked in force. The Burgundians fled in bloody defeat, pursued by La Hire's redoubtable band. It was a running slaughter, ending in massacre.

De Rais and Gwalchmai took the air on the promenade wall, looking out upon the river Oise. It was apparent to Gwalchmai that the months had made the somber man more morose than before.

It was a slate-gray day and a chill rain was falling. De Rais apostrophized it. "Weep, Sky! Wail, Wind! I have bitter news for you, L'Aiglon, well suited to the weather."

"Greater ill has befallen the Maid?"

"The worst." He nodded heavily. "You knew she has been prisoned in Rouen? Sold for a price to the English, like a doe to the fleshers? Yes, of course you would have heard.

"The trial has begun. What a mockery! She has no counsel and she is doomed. They mean to discredit the King by proclaiming her a witch. If they can prove his throne gained by witchcraft, that will render him no King at all—but she will die."

"I thank you, my Lord Baron, for lingering here. You must not wait longer on my account. You will miss the battle."

"What battle?"

"The attack, my Lord. Would God I could ride with it! Surely every man and boy in France must be marching on Rouen! Even the King cannot lag behind now."

De Rais laughed, but it sounded more like a snarl. "There will be no attack on Rouen. The King has disbanded the army. The expense of its upkeep was too great. He could not afford to keep both his Queen and mistresses in their pretty furbelows."

"My Lord!" Gwalchmai's heart choked him. "You are wealthy. Cannot you pay her ransom? I will give you the rest of my life."

"The time has passed. They would not trade her for all of France. If they can prove her sorceress—and they will; they

have sixty judges against her—she will burn. It is as simple
as that, L'Aiglon. I know one thing and I tell it you now.
If that girl burns, there is no God!"

Gwalchmai looked at his liege in horror. There was no
doubt that De Rais was sincere. He had the face of a man
in torture so great that he could no longer scream.

"Then there is only one thing to do. We must plan a
rescue."

"That is why I have spent this time with you. I would
storm the walls of Hell for her! I have another horse, with
an empty saddle. Will you come?"

"If I do not, then may I never ride or walk again!"

No armies moved against Rouen. No word of sympathy,
no offer of ransom, not even a threat of vengeance from
her "finest Prince in Christendom."

De Rais and Gwalchmai, holed up in disguise some miles
from Rouen as a matter of precaution, found the countryside quiet.

They were able to pass through the gates of the city along
with its normal traffic, while the slow trial ground on.

Manchon, Scribe to the Judges, and secretly in sympathy
with Jeanne's travail, willingly allowed himself to be bribed.
He furnished the Marshal with daily reports. So, when she
flung down her final ringing ultimatum to her persecutors, it
was soon in the hands of her two friends.

"Think well, you who set yourselves up to be my judges. I
tell you truly I was sent from God. You are putting yourselves in great danger. I know these English will do me to
death, thinking when I am dead to gain the Kingdom of
France.

"If they were a hundred thousand Godams more than they
are now, they shall not have the Kingdom. I know for a
certainty that the English will all be driven out of France,
all, that is, except those who die here.

"I come, sent by God. I have no business here. I pray
you send me back to God from whom I am come."

De Rais dashed his sleeve across his eyes. He strove to
control himself, as he laid down the parchment. After a
moment:

"It is all over, L'Aiglon. She has fought her last battle.
She is asking for death.

"That lice-breeder Cauchon! That miserable persecutor

who calls himself a Bishop! Cochon—swine—it should be. I swear the dogs shall drink his blood like Jezebel's!"

"Is she so mistreated?"

"Manchon says she cannot hear Mass, cannot have communion. The door of the chapel she passes to go to the courtroom from her prison cell has been permanently closed so she cannot see the altar as they hurry her by. Do you know what she does? She looks at the door, she bends her knee, and whispers, 'I know my Lord is still within!'"

"I wish I knew it. L'Aiglon, does God care? Is there a Heaven to receive this noble soul?" His voice raised to a howl.

He stalked up and down the chamber. "Is there a God?" His face was purple and bloated with fury. His hands, balled into fists, struck bleeding against the walls. He whirled.

"Basque, go to Orléans as swiftly as if you were in truth an eagle. Fetch me Master Jean, the gunner. If it must be that she die—then by Hell's fiery pavement, she shall not burn! There are others who shall die with her, but she shall not die like that!"

Easter passed while Gwalchmai was on the road. D'Alençon gladly permitted the loan of the gunner, who had taken service with his Duchy, but only as a courtesy between nobles. He had no faith in the possibility of a rescue.

By the time Gwalchmai and the Lorrainer arrived, to find De Rais moodily staring at the latest scroll, it was the evening of the twenty-fourth of May. The long ordeal was almost over.

Gwalchmai was shocked at the change in his friend's appearance. He sat in front of the fireplace, seemingly unconscious that the soles of his long boots were smoking. Not long after Gwalchmai had left, he had shaved off his famous blue beard. The exposed skin was deeply tanned, his cheeks sunken, and his eyes pouched, as though he had spent many sleepless nights. He looked much older than his twenty-seven years.

"What has happened?" Gwalchmai anxiously dreaded the answer.

"What? You may well ask. I can answer in three words. Misery—tragedy—death. She has recanted. There is no faith in anyone in the world, L'Aiglon. Not that I blame her, poor weary love." He hastily added, "Woe to her tormentors!

Agony to her King—her do-nothing King! I swear Charles shall pay dearly for this. I will have him off his throne!

"Yet, who would burn if a cross marked on a scrap of parchment could prevent it? But to finally surrender! It is unbelievable."

"A cross? Let me see the message." Gwalchmai hastily scanned Manchon's report. "Why, this is three days old. And look—." He smiled and handed it back. "Examine the cross closely. See where it was placed. Manchon must have made an exact copy of the transcript.

"She has not surrendered. She has won one more battle. Her Saints promised her deliverance through a great victory. She is still waiting for that promise to come true. She has gained a little more time for us to help her.

"The cross! You have forgotten. The cross was our sign that any missive so marked should be known as false, if she was ever captured."

De Rais brightened. An almost holy expression swept across his face. "I *knew* she was unswerving. When the time comes, she will repudiate her confession. They will take her out to burn her then—but we will be there. If there is no other way, there is always the mercy of the knife."

He turned the page. His hand shook uncontrollably. He stared and let it fall. Gwalchmai snatched up the sheet and read aloud the last few lines. Manchon had added:

"What they mean to do, I know not, but if you mean to help her in any way, my Lord Baron, it should be done quickly. Faggots are being brought into the Old Marketplace and there is no other burning toward that I know on."

De Rais ripped the letter into shreds. "It seems the time is now. Come. We too, shall take faggots into Rouen."

23

The Marketplace of Rouen

There need not have been this misery
Had a certain man had more pride.
The only King in Christendie
Who dares not with his army ride!
                    So
Iron bells, brazen bells, bells bright as gold—
Swing where you are hanging
Sob, as you are clanging,
Never forget how our darling was sold!

Songs of Huon

During Gwalchmai's absence, De Rais had made some preparations. He laid by the outfit and arms of an English pikeman for himself. For the other two, he now procured the simple clothing of woodcutters, bought a donkey and a small cart and enough wood to fill it.

Master Jean took his culverin apart, wrapping the barrel tightly inside one bundle of faggots and hiding the long stock and rest for it in another. Powder, slugs, and cleaning tools were bundled and concealed in a third.

Thus equipped and disguised, the three men entered Rouen without difficulty, just before the gates closed on the eve of the twenty-fifth of May.

They found the city in a state of excitement. It was not until they had found a stable for the donkey, attached to the inn where they obtained quarters looking out from an upper window on the Old Marketplace, that their worst fears were confirmed.

The hostler looked at them in surprise. "Where have you been that you have not heard? Your forest must be far away. The witch has relapsed. You will be able to sell your wood tomorrow."

When he left, they quickly tore apart the bundles, wrapped sections of the musket-cannon in some old sacks, and smuggled everything up to their room. De Rais paid the innkeeper in advance for a week's lodging for the woodcutters, saying that he owed them a debt and would pay it in that way. He haggled over the cost, got a reduction, and stipulated that he should have a refund if the burning took place earlier— insisting, in that case, that the two should leave before the week was up.

De Rais hoped all this would disabuse the host of any suspicions he might have had at seeing an English pikeman in such company. Later, after ostensibly reporting to an imaginary unit, De Rais returned, bought a bottle of wine in the common room, and went upstairs to his friends. He thought no one noticed that he did not leave.

His hope was vain. With the intention of making no mistake and attracting no attention, the three plotters did both, simply by remaining in their room most of the day.

Time did not hang heavy on their hands. There was much bustle in the square, where seats were being erected directly across from the inn. Knowing this to be the customary spot for those who came to enjoy executions, De Rais had insisted upon a room with as good a view of the stands as of the stake.

They studied the situation from behind drawn shutters. Master Jean set his support firmly into the rough plank floor of the chamber and fastened the culverin into it. Directing it toward the platform, which held the stake with chains dangling from its top and sides, he pulled a nail at the bottom of one of the narrow boards in a shutter. Allowing the board to swing aside, suspended thus, he obtained a perfect sighting and was well hidden.

It was now that the secret of Master Jean's phenomenal accuracy was revealed. Other handgunners placed the butts of their portable cannons between arm and body, or against the breastbone. They pointed in the general direction of the enemy, closed their eyes against the flash in the pan, when the fuse came down, and prayed for good luck.

Master Jean had a small point sticking up on the end of

the six-foot barrel. There was no rear sight, but as the barrel was not bellmouthed, he could squint along it as he held the stock against his shoulder, protected by a heavy woolen pad against the recoil.

He swung the little point along the row of seats, until it centered chest high on anyone who would be standing on the platform. He moved it along the row of seats and pondered.

He laid out a measured charge of powder and six small slugs. He arranged his rammer, his screw for withdrawing the charge, the touch-powder for the firing pan, and his fuse for lighting it.

He weighed a much heavier single slug in his hand, tossing it absently and catching it, and as he did so, he looked ever and anon across the square. He estimated the distance and he frowned.

De Rais watched him impatiently. The gunner shook his head and muttered under his breath.

"What is the matter? Is it too far for your engine?"

The Lorrainer grunted. "I fear me so, Lord Baron. Too great for accuracy. 'Tis a good fifty feet beyond my usual range."

"Then put in more powder!"

"That is not the answer. The lead will reach, but the charge may spread into the crowd."

De Rais snorted with contempt. "So be it that we blow the foul lives out of my Lord Bedford and Bishop, the swine, who will be as loving as two snakes in the winter. I care not who else is struck. We have no friends in the stands."

"You perceive not the problem. If the charge spreads, those two will be unharmed. The slugs will go by them, left and right. With a single ball I can slay either one you will and create consternation, for you to attempt the rescue. You cannot have both and there will be no time to reload. We must flee the inn at the instant the shot is fired."

De Rais was at a loss. He absently stroked his naked chin. Gwalchmai said, "Master Jean, do you mix your own powder?"

"That I do, Sir! Whom else would I trust? The best corned powder in France, mixed of the finest ingredients, wetted with the purest water, caked, rolled, and sifted with my own hands and measured out to my own scrupulous exactness. There is no other gunner as precise as I am."

"I know. I believe you well. And I know there is no

gunner so accurate. Tell me, is it not true that with greater
strength of powder, your bullets would fly forth with increased force and speed and mayhap have no time to
spread?"

"That is a fact well known to all of us." Master Jean hung
his head. "Even though I have charcoal of limewood, the
purest of sulphur, and thrice-crystallized saltpetre, I gain no
greater strength."

De Rais had been following the discourse with interest.
Now he interrupted. "Gunner, you spoke of saltpetre. Is it
true that this is refined from human urine? No wonder they
call it villainous!"

The Lorrainer nodded. "Nitre is found in caves, or under
piles of manure as yellow crystals, but by far the best is
distilled from the wastes you speak of. A beer drinker's urine
is good, a wine drinker's is better, according to his appetites.
The urine of a cardinal or a bishop is best of all, because they
drink the best of wines."

De Rais was aghast. "By the slavering fangs of Cerberus!
Do you mean that Bishop Cauchon is good for something
after all? I would never have believed it!"

Gwalchmai found this conversation reminiscent of that he
had held with the hapless Wu, of Cathay. He had no intention of personally meddling again, either with ingredients or
composition, but only asked, "If your finest of all powders is
the touch-powder and if you have sufficient, you might try a
blend of half of each to gain both the strength and range
you desire."

Master Jean's dour expression cleared. He beamed. "It
may work. It is worth trying." He set about the blending
and made two charges.

"If there is time, I will use both. The first as you say, and
the second through that door, because the hall will be full of
English soldiers."

"Just get the Bishop and Lord Bedford," snarled De Rais.
"I will save the Maid from the fire, in one way or another."

The day wore on. When it was dark, after eating in the
common room, they paced off the distance as though they
were ordinary strollers. It proved to be, as Master Jean
had feared, a good two hundred and fifty feet—bad for his
problem.

Absorbed in dismal thoughts, they returned to the inn,

not noticing that the innkeeper followed at a discreet distance. He observed them with curiosity.

These woodcutters and their English soldier friend were odd people, he thought, to have so little interest in city life. He knew they had not visited a church. He was aware that they had remained in their hot room all day. He followed them out and he trailed them back, suspicious and watchful.

That night, the three heard creakings of floorboards in the hall outside, but as they did not speak to one another, whoever was listening soon went away. After a while, they slept.

They dressed hastily to an uproar. Already a crowd, held back by pikemen, was overflowing the square, although it was not yet seven o'clock. Through their spy-hole they could see every window filled, the roofs clustered with people hanging to the gutters, the ridges, and the gables.

De Rais cursed at the sight, but did not give up hope. He took command and snapped out crisp orders.

"It may be impossible," he finished, "but I shall try for the rescue. If I can reach her at the moment she is taken down from the cart, I will pretend to hold her fast for the executioner to bind on the chains.

When I stab him—when you see him fall—shoot into the judges, if you cannot fix directly on Lord Bedford and his jackal. Kill as many as you can. In the excitement, I will run with her into the church of Saint-Sauveur, crying, 'Sanctuary! Sanctuary!"

"They will not dare refuse me entry. Before England can get her out again legally, her Saints may bring about a miracle. If those devils try to get her out without law, the people of Rouen will tear them apart, in fury at the sacrilege. They are still French!"

Gwalchmai realized that De Rais was snatching at the faintest gleam of hope in formulating this mad plan.

"You will only go to your death, my Lord Baron, if you expect the English to honor the laws of sanctuary. Those were outmoded two hundred years ago. Did not assassins slaughter Thomas à Becket in his own cathedral?"

"He was English. The murderers were English. This is France and I know my French."

A great shouting brought them again to the window. The sad procession was entering the marketplace. The cart could hardly be seen, so closely were the soldiers of Jeanne's guard ranked about it, striking right and left with their pike butts, as they had cleared passage all the way from her prison.

A deep growl came up from the mass of the people, but it was not directed at the small girl in the long gown. Hearing it, Gwalchmai felt his heart leap. It would not take much to tip the emotions of a mob, in any direction. Perhaps, it *might*, just barely might, go the way that De Rais envisioned.

She was praying, as the cart moved toward the platform. Those who could hear her words fell silent as it passed. Some sank to their knees and began to pray also.

It was the moment De Rais awaited. He cast a terrible look upon the other two, sprang to the door, and in an instant they saw him fighting his way into the crowd, driving into a place among the marching men. They opened for him in his uniform, as though he was a latecomer to their ranks. The first step had been achieved.

Master Jean was calmly making ready, talking to himself as he sighted the culverin at the platform. "Ah, my beauty—patience, my pretty one! Soon you shall preach to these proud churchmen out of your mouth of fire! So, a little powder in the pan—up goes the cover and it is waiting. A slow-match, comrade!"

Gwalchmai handed him a smoking fuse and the gunner fixed it into the tube of the drawn-back serpentine-shaped trigger.

"That is it—thus into the sear and soon into the pan and quickly go some souls flying fast into Hell! Do such as these have souls, I wonder? How black they must be!"

The pyre was now ready. They could see that it was composed entirely of dry wood. It would be the torment of a bright fire, instead of the mercy of green wood and suffocating smoke.

De Rais was nowhere to be seen. Gwalchmai wondered what had gone wrong. Jeanne, who had been continuing to pray, as the cart moved up to the stake, was now relieved of her hat, which had before hidden her face. He saw that her head had been shaven. Upon it, one of the Bishop's serving men placed the paper mitre of shame and derision. HERETIC. RELAPSED SINNER. APOSTATE. IDOLATOR.

She could not read the slander, but she knew what the words meant. She wept then—and with her wept many in the crowd.

Some of the judges covered their faces, clambered down

from their platform and fled, pursued by curses. Even Bishop Cauchon squeezed out a tear. Jeanne gazed at him steadily and said, "Bishop, I die through you." He could not meet her reproach and looked at the ground. It was her only word of blame.

The executioner touched her shoulder gently. Two Dominican friars stood by him to escort her to the stake.

"Is it time? I ask your pardon, reverend fathers, and you also, sir. I did not mean to keep you waiting."

She stood up. Supported by the executioner, she stepped down from the cart, but before mounting the stairs, she stopped and cried out, "A cross! Am I not to be given a cross?"

There was a swirl in the array of pikemen and a man broke free. An officer struck out, but he came on. It was De Rais.

He swept up a couple of fallen twigs from the cobble stones, drew his knife, and went up to the group, binding the crossed twigs together—the knife still bare in his hand, as he held out the little cross with the other.

Jeanne recognized him, for even at that distance, Gwalchmai saw her eyes widen. She smiled and took the cross and kissed it.

He took a quick step closer toward her, swinging upon the executioner as he did so. The knife glittered. He reached— and the officer, with two burly sergeants close behind, had him in an iron grip, to hale him, struggling, fighting, cursing, back into the ranks.

Jeanne, placing inside her gown the last gift that any friend could give her, mounted the stairs without looking back and was fastened to the stake.

The second friar, who had run into the church, came back bearing the crucifix from the altar. He held it up so she could embrace it. She kissed it ardently.

"Keep it, I pray you, in my sight until the end." He could not speak, but with face twisted in grief and pity, merely nodded.

While this was going on, Gwalchmai had come to a decision. He was far from being a fatalist, but he remembered that Corenice had said that a plan, of which they were but an infinitesimal part, was being followed. Was it possible that this part of the plan?

Jeanne had said, "I must do my devoir. It is for this that I was born."

Was it more than accident that De Rais had failed; that he himself now found it impossible to aid Jeanne, either by force of arms or magic?

Without Merlin's Ring, he was bereft of any aid that might be derived from sorcery. Had it been intended that he should be so disarmed? But it could not be necessary that she should suffer!

He knew himself faced with the same dreadful choice Huon had once been forced to make.

"Master Jean, the only thing that girl ever feared was the fire! Can you reach the stake with your culverin?"

"Not with the six slugs. Perhaps with a single one. But I could never do it—I could not pull the trigger!"

"Then in God's name, make ready! Pull your charge! Aim your cannon at her heart and I will fire the shot. She must not burn!"

The gunner quickly dismounted the culverin. With a twist of his screw, he pulled the patch that held the loose shot and tipped them out. His fingers trembled as he dropped in one large slug to fill the barrel and drove it well home.

Gwalchmai looked out upon the scene below. As though to confirm his thoughts concerning mystical interventions in the plans of man, he now saw an individual he recognized. It was the landlord of the inn where they were staying.

He stepped out of the crowd and peered into the face of De Rais standing in the ranks, still held there under restraint. He said something to the officer and pointed up at the window where Gwalchmai was watching. Other faces lifted. Gwalchmai knew that they had come under suspicion.

He turned on the gunner. "Hurry. We have been found out."

"Almost ready," Jean panted. He pounded in another greased patch of linen with his ramrod, slammed the culverin back into its fork, and sighted upon the straight small figure leaning against the stake. The executioner was whirling his torch to fan it into flame.

The Lorrainer stepped back. He motioned Gwalchmai to take the gun. Already the hall echoed with running feet. A heavy body crashed against the chamber door. Jean hurled himself against it.

"Shoot! Shoot!" he cried. Gwalchmai hesitated. "It is all

you can do for her now!" The thought of Huon's courage
steeled his heart.

He pulled the trigger and the sear dipped down into the
firing pan. There was no explosion. In his haste, Master Jean
had not reprimed, for when he stood the hand-cannon on
end to pull the charge, the touch-powder had fallen out.

In the next instant, the room was filled with shouting men
and they were prisoners. He could see nothing from the window as they hustled him away. It was well, for he could
not have borne the sight of what he knew was taking place.
The sound was terrible enough.

Yet the single long cry that went up was not a wail of
fear, not a scream of agony. It was a jubilant voice holding
praise and trust. It was a prayer from one attesting to a
great truth—who had been granted a vision in itself a confirmation of a lifetime of belief—an utmost proof of a sublime faith.

One word was enough, a word that held in it the essence
of all man's hope. "Jesus!" Only that and then the rush and
crackle of the rising flames.

But following it—in the ghastly silence that had fallen
over the immense crowd—was another cry receding from
the square as though the man who uttered it was running
for his life, in blind madness.

As with the first voice, this too was one Gwalchmai knew.
Gilles of the Blue Beard, Lord of Mâchecoul, Baron of
Rais, Marshal of France, master of many manors and
castles—today, at this tragic moment, a man stricken to the
heart, who felt his soul was dying, who saw the end of faith
and hope and dreams. It was a scream to chill the blood:

"Ye are all damned! Ye have burned a saint!"

24

The Play's The Thing

People in high places, we common folk despise,
And they believe that what we think is nothing much to
    prize,
But I know what I saw and I saw it with these eyes—
A Princess of God's Kingdom, going home to Paradise!
Now the man who rests on velvet can bleed like other
    folk
And peasants are not oxen, though they wear an unseen
    yoke,
And I for one, do think it time an angry voice be heard
To find out why our Saint did die—without a saving word!

Songs of Huon

The dungeons of Rouen were cold and grim. Gwalchmai languished there, without news of Master Jean, for many months. The gunner had in fact been slaughtered out of hand, having long been a marked man to the English. Sometimes food was thrown in; sometimes Gwalchmai was neglected for what he was certain was more than a full day. He was left in silence and in ignorance of events.

He surmised that he was spared torture only because of his white hair. His limp, also, gave him a decrepit appearance he did not feel. The marvelous elixir still held some potency, but it did not cure the cough he contracted, where water was puddled on the stone floor and nitre lay white against the walls. It did not ease the pain of his crushed ribs.

Upon a day in spring, when his mood was somber in the extreme, his cell door was flung open. His surly guard motioned him out. He blinked in the courtyard sun, with rheumy eyes.

His back was stooped and his bones ached from the damp. He was dirty, gaunt, and unable to recognize the splendid figure before him.

"Who are you?" he croaked, in a voice rusty with disuse.

"Ah, Basque, can this poor wreck be really you? Do you not remember old D'Aulon?"

Gwalchmai reached out and touched his visitor with a grubby hand. More than one phantasm had kept him company in his cell of captivity. There had not even been mouse or rat into which he could insert his spirit as Corenice had taught him. Nor had she communed with him at any time. He could not imagine the reason.

"Intendant? How can you look upon me? We failed your charge. We loved her and we failed her. Do you know that? We tried and we failed.

"She said to them, 'I come, sent by God. I pray you, send me back to God from whom I am come,' and they did, didn't they, D'Aulon? They sent her back—by the fire! Oh, Intendant, what a poor, gray world it is now without her!"

Weak tears streamed down his cheeks. D'Aulon put his arm around Gwalchmai. "Come, brother, it is all over. You are free. Your ransom has been paid. We are going to do something about it.

"The English think the war is over and France is theirs again. They shall see that the Maid still has friends. A Phoenix will rise from those ashes. Come now, where brave knights are gathering. Come home with me."

"Where is home, D'Aulon? What home is there for a transient in this world like me?"

"Where the man lives who bought your freedom. To the Baron De Rais and the castle of Mâchecoul."

D'Aulon supported him to the guardroom. The warder flung down Gwalchmai's little pile of possessions. His shirt of mail, still bloodstained from the struggle at the inn, which he had worn under his woodcutter's clothing, Roland's sword and Jeanne's, which he had never thought to see again. Often he had regretted carrying it to Rouen, but at the time he could not bear to be parted with it.

These things held precious memories, but there was one other more ancient than they by far—the leather belt, studded with Roman coins, which his mother had given him when he started on his long futile journey still stretching so endlessly before him.

He buckled it around him snugly. It felt like her loving clasp. A little of his old confidence and courage came back, but he felt that the arrogance he had once possessed would never return. It had been purged from him by the death of the Maid and the long, dark, sleepless days and nights in the dungeon.

It had been a little more than a year since Gwalchmai had seen De Rais. Though still a young man, the Baron seemed to have aged a score of years. His remarkable beard had returned in its vital, electric glory—for hair grows at the rate of half an inch a month—and was as blue-black as ever, but Gwalchmai was shocked to see that the thick locks, cut shoulder-length, were shot with gray.

His lips were thin, compressed and cruel. His eyes looked haunted, as though dark thoughts peopled the brain behind them. Yet, even as Gwalchmai was wondering what dragons were driving him to distraction, De Rais smiled with genuine pleasure to see the two enter his study.

He sprang up from his desk, and threw down his quill. As Gwalchmai limped forward to meet him, his expression changed to one of concern.

"Ah! They have much to answer for, those Godams! They did not overfeed you, I can see that. Our turn will come. We will drink their blood and warm our feet at their burning towns. Rossignol, bring wine!"

A handsome mincing boy came in with a silver ewer and goblets of Bohemian glass. De Rais saw Gwalchmai's glance. He laughed and took the large pitcher.

"Bah! A pox on pottles! We cannot have our sweet choir-boys trotting back and forth every few moments. They will be too exhausted for the other work we expect of them. Eh, my love with the nightingale's throat?"

The boy smiled and flushed delicately. De Rais pressed his arm, fondled him, and watched him out of the room. When he was out of sight, the Baron filled his friends' goblets.

Food was brought to the study. Afterwards there was more wine, dark and rich. Gwalchmai became drowsy with the heat of the fireplace, the heavy meal, and strong drink. It had been long since he had enjoyed any of these luxuries.

He felt himself surrounded by a thick mist. It pressed

like wool against his ears. It impeded his hearing. He was
dimly conscious that the Baron was reading from the papers
on his desk. The voice droned on and on, changing timbre
to indicate various parts in an extremely long play.

Once he heard De Rais declaim, "Fair she was, like the
sweet white rose," and meant to ask if he spoke of Jeanne,
but his tongue had grown too thick. He could not get out
the words.

The next he knew, he was sitting up in a soft bed. He was
alone in a dark room and wide awake. Something had
shocked him out of a deep slumber. There was a dim remembrance of a high-pitched scream, similar to those he
had heard upon battlefields when a horse knew itself to be
wounded to the death.

The hair on his back and arms thrilled to the horripila-
tion of his skin. He listened. If there had been such a sound,
it was not repeated. He lay back in the bed, still listening.
It was not long before he slept again.

When he awoke a second time, bright sunlight was streaming in from a narrow slit in the thick wall. He had been put
to bed, by whom he could only guess, in one of the upper
rooms of the tower. A serving maid, curtesying to see him
awake, brought him an ewer—water this time—and fair
white cloths for his laving and clean garments to wear.

She curtesied again and departed. The bobbing up and
down made his reeling head even more unsteady. He poured
some water over it, drank a little—terrible stuff, no wonder
the Baron drowns his thoughts in wine—and sloshed the rest
over his chest.

It was a long way down five flights of spiral stairs. He
made the trip without falling and came at length to the breakfast room, where De Rais, D'Aulon, and several others were
gorging.

The sight and smell of food gagged Gwalchmai. He made
an immediate decision to drink his breakfast, averting his
eyes from pork crackling and brawn, from dripping pasty
pies and steaming puddings. He helped himself lightly to a
small bunch of grapes and a large goblet of wine.

De Rais said, "Let me introduce you, L'Aiglon, to the
others who are working with us, as I told you last night."

If he had, this was the first that Gwalchmai knew about
it.

"Madame Perrine Martin, our wardrobe mistress, who

loves to have children in her care and goes by the name of
La Meffraye."

The lady in question smiled and bowed, darting the Baron
a peculiar, quick glance, with a slight shake of the head. She
was of middle age and had evidently once been a notable
beauty. There was a stern, tense look about her Gwalchmai found somewhat disturbing.

"Gilles de Sille, an old army companion; Roger de
Bricqueville, my cousin, and Messer Francesco Prelati, an
alchemist of note. These three attend my fortunes and my
ambitions, feeling as I do, that the world is out of joint and
we must labor to set it right."

Gwalchmai acknowledged the introductions cordially, but
the fumes of the wine were drifting away and his politeness
was forced. He saw them clearly, as people with whom
De Rais could easily be congenial. About himself, he was not
quite so certain.

It was not that there was anything about them that he
could identify and say, "This is repellant to me." Rather, he
saw in them a tight little group who shared some complicity
that shut him out.

Also, now that it was day and his weariness had somewhat passed, he noticed a bitterness graven deep in De Rais'
expression and a slyness about the others at table that he did
not like. They seemed about to snigger at him directly and at
De Rais when the Baron's back was turned. There was a
secret here.

Yet, even in his depressed mood he knew Mâchecoul was
where he must stay. This was part of his destiny. As D'Aulon
had said, "Home, now, was where the Baron dwelt."

So, in this bleak castle, the web of intrigue was woven
that woud capture the hearts and minds of slothful men until
they could be inspired to risk their lives once more for an
ideal.

Plays—crass propaganda, it is true—were written and
lavishly financed by the Baron's seemingly inexhaustible
wealth; the burden of the theme in each presentation was the
message the Maid had so proudly and so humbly borne, the
cravenness of her king, and the perfidy of the English.
Groups of traveling actors performed pantomimes and mo-
rality plays all over the country, and as each free entertainment followed in quick succession, their popularity grew.

The citizens began to wonder what could follow to surmount in opulence and interest the magnificent productions to which they flocked in ever-increasing numbers. The traveling troupe of players was anxiously awaited, fervently applauded, and their most quotable lines long remembered.

The climax came with "The Mystery of the Siege of Orléans," a vast pageant with hundreds of actors and literally thousands of others attending the long strings of extra horses and mules that carried an immense baggage train of provision wagons bearing the costumes, wines, and the tremendous portable stage with its impressive sets and scenery. Again, there was no charge for all this magnificence. Indeed, feasts and fine wines were provided for the audiences, free clothes given away to those who had need. Largesse streamed from the coffers of the Baron.

Starting in Nantes, "The Siege" traveled on to Bourges, Angers, Montluçon—a pageant of twelve thousand. Everywhere people came to be amused and went away with full hearts, enthralled with the drama, infuriated by the injustice so newly brought home to them, inspired anew with patriotism. "The Siege" played in Orléans for ten months and the expenditures went on as before. Fresh costumes were worn at every performance. The people arrived as guests, eating and drinking without cost, and they came from all over France. Day after day the performances continued while De Rais's wealth diminished like snow in the sun.

Was all her divine and superbly courageous effort to go for nothing? People rose in fury, flocking after every performance to take service where recruiting stations where handily set up for Bands of Free Companions to carry on the dragging stalemate of the war to a definite conclusion.

The small Bands cohered into small armies, which marched against the hated English wherever they still maintained a foothold in the sacred lands of France. The French moved and fought, with or without the sanction of the King —who increasingly began to feel that he wore a shaky crown. Thus, in actuality, the Phoenix arose from the ashes of Rouen, even as D'Aulon had predicted, conceived, financed, and executed by the will and fortune of Gilles de Rais.

Eventually, feeling dangerous pressure upon him, Charles the Seventh, King of France, and Philip, Duke of Burgundy, formed an alliance. Together, they hurled their combined forces against Paris.

"Before seven years are out, the English will lose a greater prize than Orléans," Gwalchmai's beloved had prophesied from her dungeon. So it came to pass.

By that time, De Rais' immense fortune had been spent. There was no more intrigue. There were no more plays. Neither was needed. The troupes of actors, the knights and men-at-arms of his personal forces—even the cortège of servants—all were disbanded and discharged.

When the Baron and his friends left the hotel where he had been staying until accounts were settled, there was not enough money remaining to pay his bill.

Gwalchmai, who had long foreseen this event, attempted to express his sympathy. De Rais only laughed.

"Truly a small matter. Hardly worth our consideration, friend Basque. Be of stout heart. It will all come back tenfold. Messer Prelati will see to the replenishment of my fortunes. If he does not, there is One who will give me all I ask.

We will go and live at Tiffauges. That, at least, still belongs to me."

25

The Fiend of Mâchecoul

> Now, he, a pilgrimage must start
> Seeking peace for an aching heart.
> Nothing like this was in his plan—
> Thank God, that *I* am not a man!
>
> *Songs of Huon*

The stronghold of Tiffauges, with its formidable walls, looked to Gwalchmai what it actually was—an almost impregnable fortress. Situated on granite heights, overlooking the Sèvre valley, it was surrounded by a harsh and sterile landscape.

The poor soil and its sparse verdure afforded little luxury for the people of the valley. Yet, even here, the rust of war had corroded the country and left behind it the burned shells of houses. Here were fields turned sour, dogs gone wild, and wandering orphaned children.

As many times before, in other places, such as Champtocé and Mâchecoul, it became the Baron's pleasure to offer hospitality to these homeless waifs. Some were sent on at once to the sanctuary of the Foundation; others remained in the castle for a while, and the grim walls echoed to their happy voices as their hunger was appeased and they felt at home in the charity of their Seigneur.

Gwalchmai was amazed at their early ingratitude. Here, as at all the other places the Baron had given such children his protection, it seemed that even the youngest soon left him to wander again, leaving sometimes during the night without offering him the courtesy of a farewell or tendering him their thanks.

Many of these children Gwalchmai had himself brought in from their pitiful shelters in the woods or caves, for he and Gilles de Sille, in company with Messer Prelati, often rode abroad on such errands of mercy and it grieved him to see evidence that De Rais' bounty was received without appreciation.

He did not realize for some time that these disappearances might have another explanation.

Not all of the little ones met their would-be rescuers with confidence. Some hid in their holes and had to be dragged out, kicking and screaming. Some ran across the open fallow fields or the wild stony barrens known as "deserts" in the hope of outdistancing the horsemen who hunted them.

At such times, Prelati and De Sille cantered after them, laughing to see their terror. Gwalchmai was indignant at their callousness and often spurred his own horse ahead to pick up the frightened children and breathe comfort into their ears.

One such little boy he found himself drawn to mightily. When Gwalchmai scooped him up to his saddle bow and looked into his face, it seemed that he saw himself as a child. The dark skin and hair held great similarity. He thought he saw in the fear-distorted features a likeness also to Nikky as he remembered her and when the pounding heart calmed under his soothing and the boy smiled, his heart went out to him in love.

This could have been the small son he had never seen.

Gwalchmai kissed and fondled away the boy's fears and soon his pitifully thin arms went about his captor's neck in trust and growing affection, as they rode back to Tiffauges.

"I am Gwalchmai. I am taking you to a place where you will never be hungry any more and there will be other boys to play with. What is your name?"

"Maman called me Jean. I like you."

He nestled confidingly into Gwalchmai's arms and they rode on in silence to the castle.

Because of the personal interest Gwalchmai had suddenly taken in the child, the loss he felt was all the more poignant when he learned the next day that the boy had run away during the night.

He brooded upon the matter to an unusual degree, without understanding how he could be so affected. He was moody and short-spoken with the others for some time.

The night before May Day is Walpurgis Night. During those dark and evil hours of April thirtieth, in the year 1439, Gwalchmai lay sleeping soundly in his room. He woke suddenly.

There had been no sound he had detected, but he felt a presence beside him and a stirring of the air as though something breathed upon him. He had been dreaming of the missing boy and he opened his mouth to call his name.

Before he could speak, fingers fell across his lips and he heard the voice of La Meffraye say, "Quiet, as you love life!"

He could not be mistaken, for there was no other woman in the castle, but there was a sweetness in the voice that was familiar to him and that he had never heard in the tones of the Baron's former wardrobe mistress.

He clasped the fingers in his own and kissed them, whispering, "Oh, my Corenice, have you come back to me again, after so long and in such a guise? It is well that it is dark, for you would not wish to see me as I am!"

Lips came tenderly down upon his. "I was not able to come before, my darling. I am not always permitted to do as I will. It was necessary that we should be apart for a time, for what you have done was a part of your destiny alone, not ours. Now that I have come, I cannot be with you long.

This body has a strong and dangerous will, and there are forces moving it that bring me fear of destruction."

Gwalchmai grunted in disbelief. "Fear? My Corenice? Incredible!"

"It is so. Come. There is only a little time we can be together. We must not waste it. Your soul is in danger and if yours is lost, mine has no destination forever. Come! Do not wait to dress."

He caught up his long shirt, for he slept naked in the fashion of the time, and cinctured it about his waist with his ancient belt of coins. The stone of the stairs was cold beneath his feet.

Corenice drew him quickly down the lower corridor and led him to other stairs, which brought him deeper underground below the level of the moat.

Here the very air was gelid, but there was the smell of burning without any of its heat and the reek of sulphur stung his nostrils.

They went down a long corridor and Gwalchmai saw the light of a torch fixed in a wall bracket. It was short and had obviously been left to burn itself out. The archway beyond was dark.

Corenice motioned toward the opening.

"Look within and farewell! I am losing control. This body must return or it will be missed. Learn why you must leave quickly and flee this place. Vengeance will soon fall upon the Baron and his retinue and I would have you gone."

"When shall we meet and where?"

"As I told you once before, we must go back where we began our journey. When you have done your devoir—you will know when it is completed—we shall be together and go back together, never to be parted again."

Another quick kiss and she was instantly gone. Gwalchmai knew that La Meffraye would remember nothing of this, wherever in the castle she came to herself again.

He peered into the underground chamber. At first he saw nothing, although he guessed from the empty sound of his breathing that he confronted a large open space. Then, high above him, he saw two red sparks like coals.

He looked at them, into them, for he had an eery sensation that they were also looking at him. It was hard to tear his gaze away from their gleaming. The smell of brimstone was overpowering and there was another, heavier smell mingled with it, a reeking odor like that of a slaughter-house.

With a distinct effort he closed his eyes and, breaking the hypnotic effect that the glowing objects had upon him, plucked out the torch stub and went into the room.

By the flickering light, he thought he saw a giant shape move forward at him. He stood still and the shadows quieted. He saw then that the presence was a huge horned statue and the two ruddy lights were its lordly and de-spising eyes.

The glaring orbs looked down upon him and upon the altar between himself and the image.

Some distorted imagination of the carver had created a gloating expression on the face of the creature. The body seemed to be shaggy. The legs ended in fetlocks and hoofs. The arms and talons reached out at the altar as though to snatch at whatever was placed upon it, although at present it was empty.

Gwalchmai reached out and touched the stone surface with a dreadful surmise. The altar was sticky with blood that had not long since congealed.

He stood staring down upon it, comprehension of many things flooding in upon him. Now he thought he understood whence the missing children had disappeared, the cry that had come in the night as he lay sleeping at Mâchecoul; the reason why the country had been scoured for little ones who had no parents and no friends.

In revulsion, he looked at his hands. This blood was no more than the thinnest of stains! The blood he felt responsi-ble for shedding, even though he was an unwitting accom-plice to the act, should have made those hands thicker than themselves!

He stood, chilled to the heart, naked and defenseless, in horror and in shame. Self-revulsion choked him. The smoke from the torch rose into his nostrils and the reek of sulphur was strong. The walls of the chamber seemed to race around him and the statue to lean forward as though it reached in his direction.

It was not all illusion. The eyes were larger now and boring into his. He could not look away. He felt as though he was being pulled toward them and they grew and swelled and swam before him like pools of bubbling lava. Gwalch-mai was helpless to resist. There were spells to meet such evil and he knew them, but his mind was being sucked empty.

He took another step nearer the altar and the grasping hands.

The eyes opened wider yet, smokily scornful. The lips curved in a gloating smile. The carven hair upon the arms seemed to lift and the statue lean forward and reach out for him.

The talons opened, they touched and gripped his waist; then they recoiled as though the creature could also know pain. Gwalchmai had felt no more than a brief tightness upon his belt, but he heard a hissing like flesh seared by hot iron.

He felt that he was surrounded by a sheltering warmth and he knew from whence it came. The belt had been created in love, presented in love, worn in loving remembrance.

. His tongue clove dryly to the roof of his mouth and he could not speak, but he thought, "Ah, Mother! I should have known that if all else failed, your never-forgotten love would surround and protect me."

A little mouse scurried into the room. In the terrible silence of that quiet, but deathly struggle, the pattering of its little feet was distinct, and enough to distract Gwalchmai's attention. He looked at it and took his first deep conscious breath for what seemed many moments.

The piercing eyes lost their power over his muscles and he drew back.

"Let me in!" said a tiny quiet bell chime in his mind. A great peace and strength came upon him. The little mouse, which had just touched his foot, fell over unconscious upon its side.

He knew and sensed a second presence within him—a well-loved personality now a part of himself. His eyes were opened as they had never been before and he saw that he was not alone.

He did not dare look long away from the statue, for he perceived that it was more than stone. Its outlines were obscured by a loathsome jelly with a form that flowed and shifted and was more dreadful than before.

The statue had eyes and they burned. It had a mouth and it spoke:

"This one was warned against going underground! He was

warned against falling into sin! The man is mine! Who dares say me nay?"

A gallant lithe figure, all in green, with a cithern slung upon his back, stepped up from behind to Gwalchmai's side. He doffed his cap with the long red feather, swept the flagstones with a low bow, and laughed in the countenance of the horror. He threw down a little clutch of branches, as one who hurls a gage to an enemy.

"By the leaves of oak, ash, and thorn—by the power of the mistletoe—I, Sir Huon of Elveron, say thee nay and am prepared to maintain my challenge with my life!"

"Knowing that you have no soul—knowing also that death, to you, is extinction, dare you still risk all the little that you have to stand beside this man?"

The words were scornful, but Gwalchmai noticed that the writhing pseudopods avoided the green leaves.

"On my honor as a Knight of Faery, I can do no less!"

"I have no quarrel with the Fay, but this man has plagued me far too long. He destroyed my people at Elveron; he robbed my magician at Roncesvaux; he has confounded my plans; he has murdered my sorcerer for your sake; he has set aside my dooms!"

"You will do well to have no quarrels with either of us, Oduarpa. Our magic is older than yours, and more potent."

The thing, which had been the statue, grinned contemptuously.

"That shall next be tested. You are no more than a fly in my sight. Die then!"

It raised a menacing hand. It pointed a curved claw at Huon. A ravening bolt of curdled crimson fury shot forth at the minstrel.

An immense dripping shield was interposed to meet it. The lightning splashed harmlessly against the protecting barrier, sank into and spread as a broad, swirling blossom of incandescence. White, pure, and smokeless, each petal became a flame of fire.

The transformed levin spun and hummed like a giant bee. It darted upon the statue. The hairy arm drew back.

"I met you once before, Lord of the Dark Face, to your sorrow," sang a liquid, rippling voice. "I can still protect my children. Do you remember?"

"I remember, Spirit of the Wave! Your realm is Ocean. My power is greater upon the land than yours can ever be. You

will do well to protect yourself, square-eyed Ahuni-i, who
have but one worshipper and whose strength is small!"

A dark turbulence of sooty cloud enclosed both statue
and enveloping rose of flame. When it fell away, the flame
was gone. The cloud thickened and writhed along the floor.

It took shape. It was a python, a hydra, a dragon of seven
heads—each shape shifting into another as it hissed, and
rearing, flung itself upon the three. It seized upon the shield
with massive jaws and coiled about it.

"But your power is not greater than this!" A stunning
crash jarred the castle as a giant hammer descended upon
the Protean monster. Its fragments coalesced into a pool of
ebon particles like flowing foulness; they united, became a
hawser, a rope, a tendril that coiled and raised like a threatening cobra, swiftly to be withdrawn into the body of the
thing.

Red-bearded Thor stepped up beside the others and
leaned upon his hammer in careless defiance. A questing,
single uninjured member of the pseudopod struck out at it as
though to test his strength further.

Thor threw down a cluster of Rowan-berries in its path.
The pseudopod avoided them as though they were red-hot. It
twisted and turned and withdrew.

The Lord of the Dark Face scowled. "So there is still life
in the godling! How many of the Aesir stand at your back?
How do men look upon you these last days, Shape-Changer,
Trickster? Whose worship—what horse upon your altar
gives you strength? As you see, I dine upon better fare! My
worshippers and I drink the Red Milk together. Strike again,
if you can! I do not think you are able. I am waiting!"

"Ala-la-la! Ala-la-la!"

A fearsome war-cry sounded, and Gwalchmai thrilled to
hear the eldritch scream of Aztlan's heroes.

"Is it blows that must protect the soul of this man? Then
you must face mine! You boast of your tiny successes, you
puny fool! Your little altars, hidden in dungeons; your offerings that are given you in secret and by night; your sacrificed babies!"

A fearful apparition took its place in line. In the shape of
a man, it towered above them all. Around its neck it wore a
necklace of skulls; upon its head a jaguar's grinning mask
served as helmet; its left arm bore a round shield fringed
with hummingbird's feathers and its right hand carried a

heavy wooden sword, studded with teeth of volcanic glass.

Its armor clanked as it moved forward in menace, for this was the overlapping steel of a Roman centurion.

"I am Huitzilopochtli, God of War of the Aztlan Nation, and because I was once a man, I have not forgotten my son! Twenty thousand hearts have been ripped from human breasts to do me honor in a single day. They were warrior hearts taken from captives my people conquered in battle to make me strong! Rivers of blood have flowed to give me my power! Before my son I too raise my shield and stand beside him with my maccahuitl!"

The form around the statue twisted and eddied in shapelessness. It undulated viscidly. Angry crimson and pitchy blacks waved like ribbons in the reaching, translucent worms shot forth and withdrawn in hideous fury.

"Your strength is greater than all the rest, for your worship is rising instead of falling. Yet mine is rising higher and will remain when yours is forgotten, for my strength comes from the evil in human hearts, not from the reverence you are offered by your sacrifices. I base my strength today on those future sacrifices you will not have! Do you dispute my ascendant might? No? Then this stained soul is mine!"

Gwalchmai spoke for the first time, but the voice was not his. Never before had he heard that lovely golden chiming issue from his own lips. "Then you must take us both, Demon from the Stars, for we are one!"

The reaching hands had almost touched Ahuni-i's shield again, but now they shrank back. Once more there was a lambent light illuminating the dark chamber, but this time it lay like a barrier between the thing and the defiant group. It was a line of brilliant glory that ran along the floor like a living creature; it turned, it angled, it surrounded the group —it was a pentagram.

The rod, which had traced the mystic design upon the stones, was lifted in the hand of the majestically bearded man who had joined them and stood inside of the protecting diagram. It quivered and pointed at the statue.

The man's feathered headdress lifted and swayed with a movement of air the others did not feel. His long robes swung and billowed as though they were being puffed outward from his body. All about him was breezy motion.

"I am Quetzalcoatl, Lord of the Winds! My people call me the Feathered Serpent. You may have heard mention of me as Merlin. I, too, stand beside my godson and will test my strength against yours, Oduarpa! Do you accept *my* challenge?"

Under that threatening Wand of Power, the amorphic semiliquid mass sank reluctantly into the body of the statue.

Its outlines became clear and sharp.

The burning orbs flashed forth with great brilliance. Gwalchmai was caught by them. Once again he could not look away. He heard the hated voice snarl, "You have powerful friends, man. I release you, but trespassers must be punished. Go, then, bearing my mark!"

The light burned into Gwalchmai's brain. He felt a blinding pain in his right eye and clapped his hands over both. It was a torture beyond any pain he had ever felt, yet his suffering seemed in the manner of an atonement and he was almost glad.

He moaned and took his hands away. It was very dark and he knew that he was alone. He was not certain he had ever been otherwise. Had he stood thus before the terrible statue, which now again was stone, and lived this ordeal only in fancy?

No! It could not be, for now vision was coming back to him, but dimly so. The pentagram was gone; those who had rallied in his defense had departed and even the mouse had disappeared.

He still had the memory of them all.

In confirmation of his dire thoughts, he picked up the fallen torch. There was a difference in his perception of its light.

With his left eye, he could see it plainly. His right eye had been blinded.

He glanced again at the statue. It was only a carven image. It did not move, but the eyes of it had become for a second time red sparks of malevolence.

Then, at that moment, the light of another torch fell upon him and a quiet voice spoke from behind.

"Barran Sathanas! My Patron and my Prince!" It was De Rais.

Gwalchmai whirled upon him. "Hell waits for you, Baron!"

"L'Aiglon, I am in Hell! So are you. So are we all. Is it strange that it took me long to realize it? Others have always known it. I learned it at Rouen.

"Look you—if I dwell in a country and make my home in it, then I owe allegiance to its Prince. Therefore, I must needs worship Satan while I bide on Earth.

"I renounced God when that torch fell into the pyre in Rouen's Old Marketplace—and I renounced Him forever. Surely, wherever men burn angels can be nowhere else but Hell!"

"This then is your true Foundation of the Innocents! How many young innocents have you sacrificed to your lump of stone?"

"Is it? Is *He* a lump of stone? Look closely into his eyes and tell him that!"

Gwalchmai gave the eidolon another quick glance and as quickly averted his eyes. He felt the pull of that malignant gaze and could not doubt there was something dangerous there that was no friend to him, however it might regard the Baron.

He flung down the guttering torch and pushed by De Rais into the corridor. De Rais, holding his own torch, caught up with him and lit the way for them both to the upper levels.

"How could you do it? You, who loved her!"

"You know what I think of the sex. I never thought of her as woman. I worshipped her. She was my angel—my saint—all that was good in me. Now I am burned out, L'Aiglon. Hell is in my heart and I live with fiends. You asked how many children, but you did not ask why.

"Messer Prelati is working with me. He knows how to make gold. The prime ingredient is the blood of an innocent child, but it seems impossible to find one who is innocent.

How many? Forty at Champtocé, another forty at Mâchecoul—almost two hundred here. I cannot guess how many as we toured France or lay at Orléans—and not an innocent among them! What use to hire an alchemist if I cannot find what he needs to make the gold I want and must have?"

Gwalchmai retched. Never since he had parted with Merlin's ring had he wished more fervently to possess it than now, that he might bring this demon-haunted tower down upon its inhabitants.

In abysmal self-revelation, he felt that he would not move a muscle to escape the doom of the others, if such a thing were possible.

"I thank the God you have revolted, Baron, that D'Aulon

left you at Orléans. This would have broken his heart. I wish I had gone with him. I am leaving at once. Do not try to stop me!"

"It is your privilege, L'Aiglon. For our old friendship, you shall not be hindered."

Gwalchmai stopped and looked him steadily in the eye.

"Baron, I spit on our old friendship!" And suiting the action to the word, he entered his own room and slammed the door.

He lit a candle and looked at himself in the mirror. He felt he must be changed beyond human recognition. How could a man procure innocent souls for torture, death, and destruction, even though it was unwittingly, without such debasement showing in his face? He looked no different to himself. Was it possible that he looked no differently to others?

He thought: the most terrible thing of all is this. A monster need not be horrible in appearance. It can look just like you!

He made a small pack of his spare clothing and belted on the sword of Roland and of Jeanne.

He went out. All was quiet. It was not yet morning. He passed by De Rais' chamber and paused to listen at the door. Behind it he heard the deep breathing of a peaceful sleeper, untroubled by conscience.

He took out the blade and stood there a moment with his hand upon the latch. Then he sighed and slid it back into its scabbard.

"*You* touched it. *You* carried it in honor. *You* held it with pride. I will not dirty it now."

Softly he passed down the corridor and let himself out at the postern gate.

The country he traversed was level for many miles and by daylight he could see far, but he never looked back once at the accursed castle of Tiffauges.

26

The Traveler

Men are such romantics—
Women know their daughters well.
The things they do, the thoughts they think.
The dreams they never tell.
They say a father loves a daughter most.
A mother loves a son.
We thought of that, at the King's court
Where we saw justice done.
Soldier—Kingmaker—never a wife—
What did she really have from life?

Songs of Huon

From time immemorial, a trail had been worn through the thick forests of Europe by the feet of those who carried the amber south to the Mediterranean and the others who brought the bronze weapons and tools north to the Baltic.

Towns sprang up where such trade routes intersected, only to disappear when the need for them vanished. Houses sank into ruin and were overgrown again by the patient trees.

Bridges fell into the rivers and were not rebuilt. Again men used fords, for they had forgotten how to make such prideful things as the ancients used.

The seas had become tamed and goods moved in ships instead of by packhorse or the backs of men, and the trail grew narrow and winding. It never quite vanished, for there were those who preferred to dwell in solitude and there were always travelers who used it, who for reasons of their own preferred to avoid the well-trodden ways.

One of these pushed north on a gray December day. It was nearly night and snow was falling. He was surrounded by forest and he was hungry, tired, and cold. Somewhere ahead, wolves were calling, but he moved on the Amber Road as though he was contemptuous of them or had little care for his life.

There was nothing to mark the snow-covered trail, but his feet found it surely, although they sometimes stumbled. He supported himself with his long staff and pressed on. As he did so, he limped.

A little after dark, when the wolves seemed very near, he came suddenly upon a woodcutter's hut, set in a little clearing. He stopped and looked at the streaks of light showing through the shutters. He stood there for a long moment, making up his mind to go on. A wolf howled. He sighed wearily, went up to the door, and knocked.

A man called, "Who is there?" He did not answer, but stood patiently waiting. After a moment, he knocked again.

The door was opened a crack and the woodsman peered out, ax in hand. He saw the traveler—a tall man, but bowed, clad in a long gray cloak and wearing a broad-brimmed gray hat, pulled down low upon his forehead.

"What do you want?" The traveler said nothing, but stood there quietly.

The woman of the house stood behind her husband, a brood of toddlers clinging to her skirts and another, whom she had been nursing, held in her arms.

He raised his head and looked at her. At the sight of the patch over his right eye, she gave a little gasp and nudged her husband in the back. He frowned and she whispered urgently in his ear. He opened the door a little wider, though somewhat ungraciously, and said, "Pray enter and honor my humble house."

The traveler inclined his head without speaking and came in with the blowing snow.

There was an inglenook by the big fireplace, and the woman cleared the scurry of children out of it, took the man's staff, and outer garments. He sat down and held out his hands to the warmth. He was very weary and his hands trembled.

Now they could see that he was dressed all in gray, his tunic and breeches, his heavy shoes and cross-gartered leggings.

She knelt before him and unlaced them and brought a sheepskin to wrap around his bare feet. He leaned his head against the warm stones and submitted patiently. His long white hair fell to his shoulders and, being wet, began to steam.

A little cloud of vapor hung about his head and the light striking through it appeared to the others in the room like a glowing aureole. They looked at him in awe.

It was expectantly quiet in the room. The children watched him with big eyes. The woodcutter sat upon a bench, his chin in his hand, and studied his guest. He also seemed impressed.

The woman swung out a kettle on its crane, away from the fireplace, dipped a ladle into it, and filled a bowl with steaming soup. The ladle grated on the bottom of the kettle. She placed the bowl on the table and put in a wooden spoon. She unwrapped the heel of a loaf of black bread and laid the edge of a knife upon it to cut a slice. She paused, reconsidered, moved the knife a little farther down and made the slice thicker.

She held out the bowl to him. "Eat," she said.

He did not offer to take it. His hands lay clasped in his lap, but he raised his head and looked at her and she could see the deep lines of pain and resignation in his face.

"Please eat," she said and held the bowl closer. His lips moved, but no sound came out. He smiled. It was an expression of such sweetness that the breath caught in her throat at the sight of it.

He tried again. The voice was as husky as though it had long lain in disuse. The words were very low.

"Is there enough for the little ones?"

Now it was her turn to find it difficult to answer. She said, "All of us have eaten our fill. Do not be afraid for us. You are most welcome here."

She placed the bowl in his hands. They cupped themselves around it, but when he tried to use the spoon it slipped from his fingers.

The woodcutter said, "Wife, get the children to their beds."

He took the spoon and sat beside the gray traveler and

carefully fed him, with long pauses between each spoonful, breaking the bread into small pieces and soaking it for him, bite after bite.

He had seen starving men before.

A little color came back into the gray cheeks. The traveler's eyes closed in spite of himself. The woodcutter caught him as he was about to fall into the fire, laid him down before it upon the sheepskin and was about to cover the sleeping man as gently as any woman when he noticed the sword he wore.

He unbuckled the belt and was about to stand it up alongside the traveler's staff when he paused. He weighed it in his hand and examined it carefully. It was very heavy.

Molten lead had been poured into the scabbard while the sword was sheathed. Under no conditions could that blade be drawn again unless the lead was melted away.

He whispered this to his wife as they lay together in their closed bed. She nodded in the dark. He felt her warm breath against his ear.

"Of course," she whispered. "He has taken a vow never to kill or hurt anyone again."

"How can you know that?" he asked, amazed, but she would give him no answer and he set down, in his mind, one more mystery of woman.

In the morning, the sun was shining and the snow had stopped.

The traveler was fed and once more made ready to take the road. On the threshold he turned and held up his hand in grave courtesy.

"Bless this house and all in it," he said in his rusty voice, then bent quickly and picked up the littlest boy. The child put his arms around the traveler's neck and the man cuddled him close for an instant, kissed him, and turned away without a backward glance.

The family watched him limp slowly across the clearing, without speaking to one another. This had been a visitation of great wonder, but there was yet something strange to follow.

Before he reached the trees, a raven dropped down, circled him, and came to rest upon his shoulder. He raised his hand and petted it. It leaned its head against his cheek affectionately and so they went on together, into the forest and out of sight.

The man and wife stood there, looking after him for a long moment, then looked at each other with a question in their eyes.

The woman crossed herself, hesitated in doubt, and falteringly made the sign of the Hammer.

Her lips quivered.

"I know it had to be. I know the world has changed. I know it must be better so, or it could not have been—but to *see* him! To see *him* so and in such guise! Why did it have to be us to give Odin One-Eye shelter? What little we could give him! And he asked for nothing!"

She threw her apron up over her head and began to sob. Her husband took her in his arms and held her close.

"Aye, woman, the times be hard—even for the gods."

Not everyone he met took Gwalchmai for a homeless god. Some saw him as he was, a footsore wanderer with a purpose and an objective. He came upon them unheralded, he never begged, he seldom spoke. His muteness was respected, for it was not a rare thing for a pilgrim, or a sinner who was expiating a penance, to take a vow of silence.

He stayed with some for a single night, if shelter was offered; with others he made his home for months or even years as the mood struck him.

All children loved him, for they sensed the love he had for them. He could not take his eyes away from them, especially the very young, and they came to him as though drawn by a lodestone.

He tended sheep; he cut wood; he taught swordmanship in the houses of the great. He was regarded as a lucky guest in some castles—as a worthless tramp in others.

He took his place in the long lines waiting where abbeys fed the poor, or he pulled cresses by the rivers edge and ate fish of his own catch. Somehow, as he moved north, he managed to exist.

He did not hurry, for a man who has an indefinite appointment with destiny is in no need to make haste.

He had no companion but the raven. Those who saw him pass remarked in awe upon the close affection which the twain held for each other.

He had no other friend upon his long journey and with the raven there was no need for speech. Yet he remembered speech. His mind was crowded with memories. They haunted

him; they consoled him; they came to him as pictures in the
night, or as illusions, as he walked or sat quietly resting.

There was the picture in which he saw himself talking
with Gilles de Rais, Lieutenant-General of Brittany, Coun-
selor of the King and Marshal of France, held in chains as
a common criminal and confined in the tower of the Castle
of Nantes.

It was a private conversation, for De Rais, although his
guilt was in no doubt and his end assured, still had the privileges of his rank.

At that moment Gwalchmai held no hot rancor toward his
former friend, for his own guilt, however unwitting, lay dis-
mally upon him and he felt that it was by the merest whim
of fortune that he did not also find himself a prisoner.

"How goes the labor?" asked De Rais. "Do the English
still run?"

"It goes well, my Lord," said Gwalchmai. "Your efforts
have borne much fruit. The Duke of Burgundy has made a
lasting peace with the King and he furnished part of the
ransom money for the Duke of Orléans."

"Orléans has returned to his city? Then the last of the four
things the Maid predicted has come to pass! Ah! That is good
news."

"La Tremouille has fallen out of countenance with the
King and has received a dagger thrust in his fat belly. No,
it unfortunately did not kill him. I trust he has more suffering in store.

"The English are being hunted out. Rouen still holds, but
they have lost much else. They hold Harfleur, Caen, and
Falaise, and are strong only in Guienne.

"The Bastard is Lieutenant-General now and the army is
in high spirits. The King is as indolent as ever, but he is
getting worried.

"There is talk of a new trial for the Maid, but all expect
it to come to naught."

"By the scarlet flowers of Hell, it shall not! She shall have
justice! I swore it and I still do!

L'Aiglon, I ask you to do one thing, not for me but for
her. Not for friendship, for I know that is dead between us,
but if you feel yourself in my debt for your ransoming from
the dungeons of Rouen, discharge that debt now and feel
free. Can you find the Maid's brothers?"

"Strange that you should ask, my Lord. A week gone, the Duke of Orléans gave Pierre the Ile aux Boeufs as his holding, for his able services. He dwells there with his mother, Isabelle."

"So much the better. L'Aiglon, I would require you to take this purse of gold to the Maid's mother. Bid her use it to make a journey to the Pope, in Rome, and beg his intercession in the Maid's behalf, that her character be cleared and she be rehabilitated in the eyes of the people. Will you undertake this commission and remain in France until the deed is accomplished?"

"Right gladly, my—Liege! For this I can forgive you much!"

He took the purse. Then he put his hand through the bars again and took the hand of De Rais. "And yourself? Do you have what you need? Can I do aught else for you?"

De Rais smiled wanly. "Here I do not need money. Soon I shall need nothing but your prayers. I dare not pray for myself. The pleading would fall on deaf ears."

Gwalchmai looked at him without speaking. He pressed De Rais' hand with warmth and sympathy. After all, there was nothing more to say.

There was the terrible scene in the court where Gwalchmai saw De Rais tried and sentenced after hearing his confession of horror piled upon horror. At the first hearings he had met the charges with defiance and bravado, but as the massive evidence built up against him his bluster vanished and he became as resigned as he had been in the dungeon. He kept his eyes downcast.

Suddenly he fell upon his knees, weeping, and entreated the Bishop of Nantes to remove the ban of excommunication under which he had been burdened. The Bishop, convinced of his repentance, did as he wished.

He began his confession, freely and in full;

"What I did, I did driven by my own imagination and my desire for the knowledge of evil. I will tell you the truth and everything as it happened. I will say to you all things as they are and enough to kill ten thousand men."

And so the fearful tale went on. Murder, torture, excesses, blasphemy, demon-worship—he spared himself nothing. His voice trembled, but he continued.

A woman, perhaps the mother of one of the slaughtered

children, gave a piercing scream and fainted. The priests and judges shuddered.

The Bishop of Nantes rose from his seat. He moved toward the crucifix that hung above the judges' tribune and taking his black cowl, he veiled the face of the Saviour.

De Rais fell upon his knees, sobbing. "Oh, God, my Redeemer, I ask pardon and mercy! I renounce the Devil and all his works!"

He turned upon the stunned and horrified spectators.

"Oh! Parents of those innocents I have cruelly murdered, I beg the charity of your prayers. Beseech Heaven, I pray you, that I may still be redeemable. I wish to remain your Christian brother. Forgive me! Forgive the ill I have done you, as you yourself desire pardon and mercy from God."

Sometimes Gwalchmai started awake, with a pounding heart, reliving the scene at the gibbet.

De Rais, the first to die, commended his soul to Saint James and Saint Michael, whose intercession Jeanne, his angel, had asked at her death.

All three of the sentenced were hung, but were cut down while still quick and hurled alive into the waiting flames of their blazing pyres.

From none of those coiling towers of black smoke did any white dove arise.

There were more pleasant pictures to review as time dragged on and Gwalchmai journeyed into the northlands on his way back to where his seemingly fruitless traveling had begun. He seemed no nearer than ever to accomplishing his impossible mission of turning over the continent of Alata to a Christian monarch.

He consoled himself with memories.

There were the lush fields of Domremy, where the young girl, Jeanne, had watched her sheep, had listened in ecstasy to the sweetness of the Angelus, had run and played and dreamed.

He walked and mused where she had first received her commission through her Voices and dedicated herself to duty and virginity, "for as long as God willed."

Here she had given herself little to games and frolics—as little as she could! That revealing phrase!

Here stood the Ladies Tree, where she, with the other

young people of the village, had come to dress its branches
in May to the honor of the Fairies and the joy of being
alive in spring.

And here stood lonely Gwalchmai, in a later May, in the
December of his life, with flowers in his hand, watching butterflies fluttering about the ancient tree.

There was a pale-green one among them! There was a
leaf-hopper with a speck of red upon it at his feet; there was
suddenly beside him a languid, smiling fellow with a cithern
slung across his back. That casual, sardonic bow—that elegant thrusting forward of the leg—that Huon!

"We meet for the last time, Sir Hawk. You need me no
longer and my Queen commands me to her side. I would I
could embrace you, but there is iron in your blood and steel
at your belt. This is goodbye."

"I know you have been near me when I have not seen
you. I know you have aided me in ways I dimly comprehend
and cannot repay. Must you go? There are others who
need you—who will never forget you and your kind."

"Earth is still beautiful to me, but it was once so much more
fair. I am the last to flit. I stayed so long because of you.
Astophar will be a delectable pleasaunce, but this was home!

"Sir Hawk, tell your kin to prize above fine jewels that
which we bequeath to them. It is Man's World now."

Distant, faint, there drifted down from somewhere high a
jubilant but peremptory bugling. The horns of Elveron for
the last time stirring nostalgic echoes in the air of Earth.

"They are calling. I must go. Farewell, comrade. Farewell,
Sir Hawk. Another comes to visit you."

Huon faded like a mist, in the very act of unslinging his
cithern.

In his place the pale-green butterfly spiraled into the sky.
As distant as a voice in dream he heard that elfin chord
accompanying the receding words:

> "Let us make a wreath in memory
> Twine in a sprig of rosemary
> If we hang it on the Fairy Tree
> Who knows what revenant we may see?"

He knew the voice. He twined the wreath. He placed it
high upon a branch and the wind blew through it, scattering
its fragrance.

There was a hush. The sunlight took on a splendor. Everything seemed new and beautiful, as though the world had just been touched with glory.

He felt the lightest touch imaginable upon his cheek. It was like the evanescent wafting of air set in motion by a butterfly's wing, but it felt like a kiss.

He heard a soft whisper—or was it only a wishful fancy?

"Dear Basque!" He smelled the faintest aroma of woodsmoke all around him.

Then there was nothing left of the magic moment but a haunting memory of bright laughter, the clash of steel, and a brave banner floating free in the sunlight of a long summer.

There were dates to remember. 1449. A year of present joy and remembered grief.

Gwalchmai stood beside Lieutenant-General Dunois and watched the English garrison ride out and lay down their arms before the surrendered city of Rouen.

He could not cast away the thought that here at last stood the army that could have saved Jeanne. Why had it come so late?

1450. In that year, the English were defeated at Formigny and ran again before French artillery, as they did on the seventeenth of June, 1452. Their aged general, Talbot, was slain on that date at the battle of Castillon. Guyenne was lost, Bordeaux fell, and the Hundred Years' War came to an end.

The English, as the Maid had warned, had lost all that they had possessed in France. Only the dead now remained there.

1455! The year De Rais had striven for! The year long awaited! The greatest year of all for Gwalchmai.

An immense crowd filled the Cathedral of Notre Dame in Paris.

Through the concourse and into the assembly moved an aged woman, slowly, haltingly—supported on either hand by her two sons to set forth her claim and plea for justice and to hurl defiance at her dilatory King.

Popular opinion is a yeasty thing and it takes long to rise, but there had been time and talk and searching of souls.

De Rais' leaven had worked at last. His millions had not been spent in vain.

Through the long corridor, opened for her through the multitude, the three relatives came. Here walked Jean and Pierre, brothers of the Maid, to give their testimony as to their sister's virtue and integrity; here was their mother and hers, called Isabelle Romée now, because of her pilgrimage to the Pope.

Only the father and husband, Jacques d'Arc, was not with them. He had died of a broken heart.

There were tears of pity among the onlookers, as they saw how feebly Isabelle approached the group of prelates, doctors, and professors who were to pass judgment upon her plea. Their hearts thrilled to hear the strength in her voice as, in sudden anger, she pressed aside the arms of her sons and stood alone before the judges.

It was no little thing to face those who had condemned her daughter, even though she was backed by Papal commissioners, but they quailed before her flashing eyes. She threw back her coif and mourning veil, that they might see her face plainly.

It was the strong, wrinkled visage of a hard-working peasant woman, calm with an inherent majesty and confidence—a true woman of the people, the very face of France. In it, Gwalchmai thought he recognized something of the strength of Nikky, the courage and determination of Corenice.

She began in a low voice, which quickly became animated;

"I had a daughter, born in lawful wedlock"—a little sob, quickly suppressed. She stopped to gather strength, and went on. "—whom I had furnished worthily with the sacraments of baptism and confirmation and had reared in the fear of God and respect for the tradition of the Church. As far as her age and the simplicity of her condition allowed, for she had grown up amid fields and pastures, she was much in the church. She received every month, after due confession, the sacraments of the Eucharist, despite her youth, and gave herself up to fasts and orisons with great devotion and fervor.

"The wants at that time were great that the people suffered and she held great pity for them in her heart. Yet although she did never think, conceive, or do anything whatever that set her out of the path of the faith, or spoke against it, certain enemies . . . had her arraigned in religious trial.

"Despite her disclaimers and appeals, both tacit and expressed, and without any succor given to her innocence, in a trial perfidious, violent, iniquitous, and without shadow of right, they condemned her in a fashion damnable and criminal."

She paused, seeking words, and swayed as she stood. Her sons took her arms, but she shook them aside and went on, proudly meeting the sympathetic gaze of the court.

Her voice rang out like an accusing trumpet. "And then they put her to death very cruelly by fire—for the damnation of their souls and in notorious, infamous damage done to me, Isabelle, and mine!"

The rest was anticlimax.

The crowd went wild. Women wept, men stood and shouted, "Justice! We will have justice!" There was a monstrous uproar and stamping of feet. Order was regained with no little trouble.

Finally the Trial of Rehabilitation continued, unimpeded by interruptions.

Many gave testimony in the Maid's favor. La Hire and De Rais were both dead, but D'Aulon was there and spoke fervently in behalf of his beloved charge. Lieutenant-General Dunois gave evidence as to her military skill and generalship; D'Alençon, her "pretty Duke," spoke warmly on her qualities of honor, courage, and tenderness to the defeated.

Depositions were read, offered by a hundred people who had known her as a child, testifying to her goodness and devoutness and her virtuous life.

Even the judges who had condemned her now spoke in her favor. It seemed that after so long a time they could remember nothing evil against her, for their memories failed them often.

Apparently the flagrant sin of wearing man's clothing was no longer of paramount importance. Now it appeared that it was forbidden to women only so far as it might serve as a temptation to pride and license. Yet it was this very point Bishop Cauchon had so constantly stressed and with such venom that it had finally brought about her death.

Six months later, the verdict of vindication was read pub-

licly in Rouen, at the very spot where the fatal pyre had
stood, and in all the other cities and towns of consequence
in the Kingdom. .

There was one who did not hear it. Bishop Cauchon had
died long since, an embittered and unhappy man. The dogs
could not drink his blood, as De Rais had promised they
should, but the next best thing was done. His bones were
disinterred and flung into a sewer, by an enraged group of
Jeanne's friends.

Gwalchmai wished that Gilles could have been there also.

It was in that good year of 1456 that Gwalchmai set
about his journeying northward. His promise to De Rais had
been accomplished at last. Now he was free to travel where
Corenice had told him they should come together, never to
be separated again—the land of ice and fire.

27

Merlin Explains

—Doubt not through the ages one increasing purpose runs

—Tennyson: *Locksley Hall*, line 2?

A little boat came in on a black lava beach, not far from
the Bay of Reeking Smokes. Gwalchmai stepped ashore and
looked about him. The raven came down from the short
mast and perched upon his shoulder.

He pushed the boat off and watched it float away. Then
he turned his back upon it and went up into the hills. He
walked aimlessly for a long time. Just before dark he found
a cave and set about making it habitable. He was weary of
war and battle-shock and of life itself. He would have welcomed the peace of death.

But while a man lives, he must obey the rules of life. He built a little fire to warm himself; he gathered grass for a bed and spread his blankets there; he cooked some oat porridge and ate his last small piece of dried meat. Then he lay down upon his bed and waited.

If there was to be a fulfillment of the promise that had been made to him, it should be soon. He did not have long to wait.

He became conscious that he was not alone. The entrance to the cave was not much obscured, but someone had entered. He sat up.

"Is it you, Godfather? Have you come to grant me oblivion? I have failed you in all things. I have been a careless apprentice, a poor magician, a sinful man, an emissary who was unable to complete his mission. You would do well to hold me in your contempt."

A phantom became visible. Its appearance solidified and took on a firm and definite shape. Merlin, in his robes of a Mage.

"It has not been failure in your life, but a great success, my godson. Once I told you that if you could instruct me in the meaning of life I would expound to you the mystery of death. Can you do it now? What have you learned from your long life?"

Gwalchmai hung his head. "Godfather, for all my years, I am very young before you. I have learned little and I am certain of nothing. What I have learned may be of no importance.

"I know that the body is only the house for the soul and in itself is of little worth, for I have known many and loved a few and it was not the love of the body that brought gladness to me."

"That is something to know. Go on."

"As to the meaning of life, I know nothing. Mine, it seems, has had neither purpose nor meaning. The good are trodden upon, the evil triumph, virtue goes unrewarded, the innocent suffer. The purpose of all this escapes me. Life seems a random, accidental thing and its events no more than a madman's dream."

"Did you ever use the ring as a speculum and look ahead in time to see what was to come?"

"I only know what I saw on the walls of Arthur's tomb."

"Then let me show you what the world would have been

without you. If you had not come here to be buried in the ice
and resurrected by your sweetheart—Thyra, who was in
habited by her to save you, would have wed Biarki to whom
she had been promised. She would have been treated brutal
ly and died young, without issue.

"Flann would have remained a thrall all his life long and
would not have become a father.

"Mairtre would never have been born. Because of her
nonexistence, Arngrim, the Varangian, could not have mar
ried her and become the ancestor of the man whom you
have been brought here a second time to meet. Thus, the
wheel for you has come full round.

"Had you not wandered as you did and met your love
again in the body of the Welsh girl, whom you knew as
Nikky, you would not have had the child by her who became
the ancestor of the Maid of Orléans, who turned back the
tide of English conquest, made France a nation, and
changed the history of Europe and the world!

"Let me show you what would have befallen, except for
you and your Corenice."

Merlin placed his hand over Gwalchmai's eyes.

He saw in vivid pictures and in rapid succession vignettes
as upon a long scroll that displayed an alternate history in
which, as there had been no son of Gwalchmai's, there had
been no Isabelle to marry Jacques d'Arc and thus no Jeanne
Without her encouragement, the Dauphin's heart failed him
He fled the country and exiled himself as he had planned.

Deserted, Orléans fell. France became an English appen
dage, from which base English armies swept south into
Spain, dislodging the Moors and making Spain an English
colony. They followed the Moors. North Africa became
part of their growing empire, exploited ruthlessly. War fol
lowed war.

Jerusalem fell to an Elizabethan crusade and the riches
of the Middle East, Asia Minor, India, and Persia came pour
ing into the treasure house England became. There were
other wars, which went on without end.

In the north and east, Duke Philip, "the Grand-Duke of
the West," whose possessions extended from the Alps to the
North Sea, used his enormous and growing strength to ex
tend his holdings deeper into Scandinavia, seizing Norway
and Sweden. All his lands were milked of their manpower.

A second uneasy alliance was formed with England to crush Germany.

The combined armies met and destroyed the rising power of Muscovy and later they turned against each other, in civil strife and mutual antagonism that rendered Europe a wasteland, before England emerged predominant and enforced an English peace over a desert inhabited by cannibals.

Gwalchmai thrust aside Merlin's hand. "Such horrors!" he panted. "Such slaughter! So many burning cities! Such ruin! I could not have believed any people to be capable of such cruelties and oppression."

"Great power breeds great arrogance and injustice. It was necessary that English power be humbled at this time and no other. It will never be forgotten that a seventeen-year-old girl threw down the gage to the finest generals in Europe, told them what she would accomplish, and did it!

"Almost all that ninety years of war and conquest won for England the Maid took away in a single week. Since then, as you know, the remainder has been lost to them. The English will be busy at home with their own problems. Philip will be drained of his power. The nations they would have dominated will develop in different ways.

"Now, when England and France go into this New World, which I and your father found, they can go as equals and what they make of it will be up to them. The future still remains mutable, but because of you and your dear one, that which you saw in the mural in Arthur's tomb will surely come to pass."

"Then I have been only a tool?"

"Even as myself. Are we not all God's tools?"

"Why was it necessary that Jeanne die?"

"She, who was called the Daughter of God, was promised that, by her suffering, she would win a great victory. She did not know what that victory was to be; she won it without knowing. How can the world forget her now and the lesson that she taught? Great victories are bought with a great price. She had faith that never wavered. You must have no less."

"If there is indeed a purpose in all this, why must it be accomplished by so much struggle and pain?"

"The Maid answered your question when she said, 'God

will give the victory, if only men will fight.' No part of your long journey has been mere aimless wandering; nothing you have done but has been a tiny section of an intricate plan.

"In the great gamble that is life, we are all no more than pieces of small account. Yet, the game cannot be played without us. Nor is it well that the pieces should understand the meaning of the game or who the contestants may be."

"I am sorry I could not have been a better apprentice to all your teachings."

Merlin laughed. "In my apprenticeship I was a sore trial to my master, Blaise. I was so inept that the children threw stones at me and cried me down! It was a long time before I was eligible to take my examinations and be admitted to the Fraternity of Magicians."

"You are well respected now. Everywhere I showed it, your ring was recognized with deference."

Merlin was pleased. "It, also, has served its purpose. In the main, you used it well, although I think sometimes you could have done without its help. You could become a potent mage in your own right."

Gwalchmai shook his head. "I am done with magic. I have forsworn war. I wish you would take my sword and place it where it may be at hand, if another champion needs it when Arthur draws his."

"I will see that it is placed where it will be available. Now can you tell me more? What do you think you have learned?"

Gwalchmai considered. He said slowly, "I have known four women above all others in my life. From Thyra, I learned the meaning of courage and trust. From Nikky, I was given humor and devotion. From Uyume, delicate affection and undying patience. From Jeanne, I was shown, for the first time, the importance of steadfastness and faith.

"And from them all, through Corenice, the understanding of a love such as no other man has ever had."

"Then you need never fear death, for death is only of the body, and love transcends it all, and the body is nothing, as you already know.

"Now I will leave you, for one is waiting who longs to have me depart. She will wait with you, until the other, for whom you must await, has come. Then you shall be set free of your vow. God bless you both."

He laid his hand upon Gwalchmai's forehead, this time in

benediction. When Gwalchmai opened his eyes, Merlin was gone, but he was not alone.

There was a whisper in his ear, a kiss upon his lips, a warm clasping about him. The arms he could not see did not let him go. It seemed that he sank into their embrace.

The strangeness he had felt so briefly at Tiffauges, before the eidolon of Barran-Sathanas, was repeated. He knew that he was no longer the individual he had been and it was a joy to be so accepted.

This was a symbiosis of two souls that far superseded any possible physical union. He and Corenice understood each other's inmost thoughts, partook of each other's lives. They were truly one.

It was an amazement to both of them to savor the youth of the spirit, to understand the unimportance of the body's aging, its aches and pains, its only function as the house for the soul.

This was a spiritual melding far more wonderful in its completeness than the strange relationship they had known in the Land of Dream. For the first time, both understood that strange blending of two personalities in the mystery of possession, wherein neither owned nor was owned, but became an integral *part* of the beloved.

It was a union for Gwalchmai he had never imagined, a fusion for Corenice such as she had never experienced.

The days of the land-takings, the bitter quarrels, and the bloody feuds had long been over in Iceland. The explorers had made their voyages, planted their colonists in the West, left their sons, their axes, and their carved runes in Alata and retreated from it, leaving only legends in the land that was not for them.

In Iceland the sagas were becoming old and loved and told in Europe, by the skalds, the troubadours, and minnesingers. There was an awakening of curious minds. There were those who wondered about that far land the Greeks called Thule.

It was a safe place to visit. Christianity had followed the Vikings who had gone there to escape it and the thoughts and actions of their descendants had been softened by it.

The next day after Merlin's visit, an aged and mild-mannered man came to the cave. He carried a long staff, but bore no weapon. The two men regarded one another for a long moment. To Gwalchmai, he looked much like Bishop Malachi of the Children of God. He understood that similar thoughts can mold the faces of different individuals to a striking similarity.

"I am Ragnar Ragnarsson. We saw you land last night and I have come to bid you welcome. Will you come down to live among us, or do you mean to dwell apart? Whichever you choose, you shall live as you wish."

"Then, if it is of my own saying, I would prefer to remain here. I have known many countries, have sailed many seas, have committed many sins. I would commune with my soul and be alone with my God, for I have much to answer for."

"It shall be as you say. You shall not be disturbed."

He bowed and went away.

Now Gwalchmai lived the life of an ascetic. He saw no other visitor for many months, nor did he feel the lack of company, for it was impossible that he should ever be alone again.

Food was brought and left outside the cave for his body's sake, as other hermits in the mountains were fed by the people, for in that way all acquired merit.

Shy children laid down the packages their parents sent— and ran. He scarcely noticed them at first. He was never sick, or cold. He lived always in a warm glow of mutual affection with the other half of his dual self. He needed no other.

After a long time of this self-imposed solitude, he began to mingle with the other people of the lower village. He seldom spoke, but often joined them in their fishing. In this way, he and Corenice felt they earned the food that sustained their single body. They were very much content.

He gained the reputation of being expert in the ways of the sea. The villagers knew him for a far traveler and made up stories about him, but they respected his silence and did not ask questions.

Time passed and he was happy. It became a custom for the children who brought gifts to the cave to stop and wait for a story of strange lands, and they were seldom disappointed. He became an institution.

Ragnar Ragarsson died and his son, also called Ragnar, sometimes brought food and stayed to listen. More often, the duty fell to his little daughter, Sigrid, who had no fear of the old hermit on the hill. Both felt a proprietary ownership of family. He belonged to them.

Gwalchmai loved to have her near him. He admired the pale gold of her hair as they sat in the mouth of the cave, looking out to sea. She was a quiet, understanding girl and they knew a strange happiness in their company.

Without expression in words, an entirely new aspect of love was evinced to him from this communion between himself, Corenice, and this small girl-child. It was sympathy.

One day, when she came early, bringing bread and that clabbered milk called *skyr*, he was surprised to find that she was guiding a stranger to him.

He was a sturdily built man, under thirty years of age, beardless, tanned, and with ruddy hair. He had blue eyes with little wrinkles at the corners from long squinting into the sun across endless waves. Gwalchmai liked his looks at once.

He took off his sailor's knit cap and bowed, in a style Gwalchmai thought singularly disarming and polite. It reminded him of Huon, yet there was none of Huon's sardonic and nonchalant air in this visitor.

"I am told that you are a man of the sea and know something of lands to the west of Thule." Gwalchmai started.

"How did you learn that?"

"It is common talk in the village that you have widely voyaged. I came here on yonder English herring boat, out of Bristol, hoping to learn of lands to the west. There has been much comment concerning lands beyond Greenland and speculation that India and Cathay might be reached in that direction. I have made the theory my life's effort and I mean to prove it. Can you tell me aught of those countries? Would you be willing to draw me maps or act as pilot thither?"

"From whence came you? You are not a native of England?"

"Nay. I was born in Genoa, which is in Italy. I can find few there who agree with my ideas. Most laugh at me. If I can prove that I am right, I mean to take the evidence to Portugal or Spain. Perhaps I can interest one or the other. Portugal is much taken with seafarers."

Gwalchmai began to wonder if this could be the man

awaited—the one Merlin had promised would seek him out.

"What are you called?" he asked.

"I was christened Christopher. My surname is Columbus, but some call me Colon. I think I have always had a yearning for the ocean."

"Were your people sailors?"

"There is a tale in my family records that one of my ancestors was a man of the north, in the service of Constantinople. Somewhere he found a treasure and spent it for lands in Italy. Most of our men have had a desire to wander. It is in our blood."

The descendant of Mairtre and Arngrim! The man he was to meet! The wheel had indeed come full round.

"What of Spain? And Portugal? Are they Christian kingdoms?"

"Both of them. Of the two, I would say that Spain is the most Christian kingdom of any upon earth because, except for a few Moors who hold the city of Granada, no others live in Spain but ardent Christians.

"No others can live in that country. Granada is under siege and by the time I get back, the city may well have fallen. Such are the latest reports."

"Then I would by all means seek aid in Spain. I think I can promise you success. My prophetic soul foretells it. Yes, I will draw you maps and act as your pilot, if you will stay here and hire a sailing boat. I believe it will do me good if I take one more sea voyage."

For some weeks, the old hermit disappeared from his cave. His absence coincided with that of the sailor who jumped ship from the English herring boat and who as unaccountably was seen again at the same time that a missing Icelandic sailboat turned up drifting aimlessly off Reykjavik.

There was certainly a connection but it could not be proved, and the English sailor, for so they thought Columbus to be, kept his own counsel and an extremely tight mouth. Later, he found another berth and sailed away again. They never saw him more.

As for asking questions of the old hermit—long ago folk had found that vain.

A few days after the return of the pair, little Sigrid went with her father to bring food to the cave. They found their friend lying with eyes closed and smiling.

She ran to him and touched his hand to awaken him. The flesh was cold. He did not open his eyes.

She turned from him. Her lips quivered.

"Father, is the storyteller dead? What are the bells, father? Can you hear them ringing?"

Ragnar hesitated. He thought his small daughter was far too young to be introduced in this way to such a hard fact as death.

"Let us not call it death, darling. We will say a prayer for him. Let us say—he has gone home!"

They knelt on the bare floor of the hermitage. As he took her hand in his and they bent their heads, at the instant of the touch of fingers he too suddenly heard the heavenly chiming of little golden bells that filled the cave—a melody that faded farther and farther away, into infinity and beyond—as the tenants passed forever out of their ken.

Epilogue

There is a single piece of evidence on record that is hard to dispute.

Were you to take the trouble to closely inspect the original charter given to Christopher Columbus, under the seal of their Most Christian Monarchs, Ferdinand and Isabella, of Aragon and Castile, you might, if you have good eyes or a powerful microscope, find an alteration, an erasure in the first wording, as though the scribe had made a foolish mistake and corrected it.

Under the words giving the Admiral of the Ocean Sea an interest in the lands that he will discover, you may be able to discern the earlier phrasing. It reads "the lands which he has discovered"!

A minor change perhaps—but of what tremendous significance.

And what of Gwalchmai and Corenice?

This tale is not the end, for no story ever really comes to any definite end. There is only a pause in life—a change, a blending, a transmutation into something new, which in itself is impermanent.

It continues changing toward a development known only to God.

If, sometime, you again have that experience common to all of us—an eery sensation of looking upon familiar things and for an instant finding them new and curious, do not be alarmed.

Flann would have thought that both Gwalchmai and Corenice should have been translated to dwell forever young in Tir-Nan-Og, the place of Eternal Spring.

The Vikings would have gladly seen Gwalchmai as a warrior in Valhalla and granted Corenice an honored appointment as Sheild-Maiden.

The Fay would have been happy to receive them as joyous guests in Astophar.

Surely Jeanne would have used her good offices to obtain them a place in Paradise.

But neither would have been content. This wandering pair could never be happy in any one place very long.

Remember, if *you* have this feeling, it may be that one of them is today using you as a medium and gazing out through your eyes—using them as windows which open upon the many wonders of the world.

Do not be afraid. Be kind. Let that one briefly share your life.

It may chance that the other is very near, and in repayment for your kindness, you may also feel, for just a moment, the love they possess for each other—for all eternity.